SEVEN WHO DARED

Other Books by Soul Esprit

The Great Deception

The Coming of Wisdom

Fools Paradise

The Criminal Fraternity

When Will the Illuminati Crash the Stock Market?

Genesis 1:29 Diet

Fractal Trading

Everything is a Test

BOOK ORDERING INFORMATION AT END OF BOOK

All praise, honor, and glory be to God –
the LORD God Almighty, the Lord Jesus Christ

SEVEN WHO DARED

Soul Esprit

Servant of the Lord Jesus Christ

NarrowGate Publishing

Seven Who Dared

All Scripture verses quoted are from the Authorized 1611 King James Bible.

ISBN: 978-0-9841279-8-6

Library of Congress Control Number: 2009906999

For the survivors of Satanic Ritual Abuse,
and the many millions of other children that did not survive.

O LORD God, to whom vengeance belongeth; O God, to whom vengeance belongeth, show thyself. Lift up thyself, thou judge of the earth; render a reward to the proud. LORD, how long shall the wicked triumph? How long shall they utter and speak hard things? and all the workers of iniquity boast themselves? They break in pieces thy people, O LORD, and afflict thine heritage. They slay the widow and the stranger, and murder the fatherless. Yet they say, the LORD shall not see, neither shall the God of Jacob regard it…. For the LORD will not cast off his people, neither will he forsake his inheritance. But judgment shall return unto righteousness: and all the upright in heart shall follow it. Who will rise up for me against the evildoers? or who will stand up for me against the workers of iniquity? Unless the LORD had been my help, my soul had almost dwelt in silence. When I said, my foot slippeth; thy mercy, O LORD, held me up. In the multitude of my thoughts within me thy comforts delight my soul. Shall the throne of iniquity have fellowship with thee, which frameth mischief by a law? They gather themselves together against the soul of the righteous, and condemn the innocent blood. But the LORD is my defense; and my God is the rock of my refuge. And he shall bring upon them their own iniquity, and shall cut them off in their own wickedness; yea, the LORD our God shall cut them off. – Psalm 94:1-7;14-23

If thou forbear to deliver them that are drawn unto death, and those that are ready to be slain; If thou sayest, Behold, we knew it not; doth not he that ponderth the heart consider it? and he that keepeth thy soul, doeth not he know it? and shall not he render to every man according to his works?   — Proverb 24:11,12

I have commanded my sanctified ones, I have also called my mighty ones for mine anger, even them that rejoice in my highness. The noise of a multitude in the mountains, like as of a great people; a tumultuous noise of the kingdoms of nations gathered together: the LORD of hosts mustereth the host of the battle. They come from a far country, from the end of heaven, even the LORD, and the weapons of his indignation, to destroy the whole land.   — Isaiah 13:3-5

... the people that do know their God shall be strong, and do exploits.
                                                                                    — Daniel 11:32

PREFACE

Although the Castle of Darkness is an actual physical entity located in the South of Belgium, the main characters are fictitious. Nevertheless, it is possible they exist somewhere other than within these pages. Rare individuals today, on the entire planet there could very well be only seven righteous men with the Godly conviction and courage to voluntarily do what these seven did. For this reason, in a sense, they are *real people*; and despite the name changes, their spirit lives on.

It is even possible they may someday chance to read this book.

– Soul Esprit
November 4, 1999

ACKNOWLEDGEMENTS

The list of names for the European Black Nobility was provided by an insider source who wishes to remain anonymous. The individuals named as participants in the Mothers of Darkness scene were identified by numerous independent eye witness reports of the actual rituals, and have been confirmed by other researchers. The identities of the four perpetrators in the Most Dangerous Game scene were provided by eyewitnesses who survived the trauma. The author acknowledges the following SRA survivors for the valuable documentation they have contributed: Arizona Wilder, Cisco Wheeler, Cathy O'Brien, Brice Taylor/Susan Ford, "Svali," and many others who wish to remain anonymous.

Fritz Springmeier deserves mention for his scholarship in identifying the upper echelon members of the Illuminati, their goals and objectives. In response to his most recent book edition of *Bloodlines of the Illuminati*, he was falsely accused and sentenced to 10 years in a federal prison.

Johnny Todd is acknowledged before God for his valiant efforts to bring to light the overall design and purpose of the Global Hierarchy. As an Illuminati defector, to silence him from revealing the truth, he was falsely accused and imprisoned, then murdered on the day of his release.

—1—

"Queen's bishop to King's knight four."

While considering his opponent's last move on the chessboard, Eric Rider smoothed his dark mustache with thumb and index finger. After pausing a moment to assess the strategic possibilities, with a quick deft movement of his left hand he repositioned one of the chess pieces. "King's knight to Queen's castle two. Checkmate."

Seated across from him was Jeffrey McGuire, who registered a fleeting look of disappointment. "How do you always *do that?*" he said in a resigned tone, continuing to study the game, even though it was now over. The question must have sounded incongruous to their small group of friends seated at a nearby coffee table, especially since Jeffrey had graduated from an Ivy League University, Magna cum laude.

"You were fortified in all the wrong places," Eric replied, a subtle grin creasing his ruggedly handsome features. "No defense is impenetrable."

Deborah, his fiancé, went over to stand at his side and ask, "When are you two ever going to put your swords back into their scabbards and join the rest of humanity for some civil conversation, coffee and pastry?"

Her soon-to-be husband answered, "Civil conversation is an acceptable diversion, but I'll pass on the other. I have too much respect for my health."

She smiled and said, "That's one of the things I like about you, Eric – you demonstrate character even in small matters."

Affectionately patting her slender hand resting upon his shoulder, he replied, "The great issues of life consist of a series of seemingly *small matters*. Even so, I know that consuming coffee and pastries is not in my best interest. Besides, I have to give my ole' buddy here another chance to win before he goes back to graduate school. What will be your Ph.D. *this* time, Jeff?"

Still perplexed, he tersely replied, "Physics."

"Ah, yes," returned his nemesis. "Maybe you should pursue another field – psychology perhaps. Now *there's* a career where you can at least *bluff* your way with a poker face." He smiled. "Just kidding."

The two of them got up to join the others in the group.

"… I read about it in one of the tabloids," Todd, a store clerk, was overheard saying as they arrived. "It's a total media blackout. No one even knows it exists … at least, not until now."

Marilyn, Deborah's best friend and Maid of Honor, sounded concerned when she said, "But you don't *really* believe it, do you? I mean, nothing that horrible could actually happen … could it?"

"It happens all the time," Todd confidently replied.

"*What* does?" Eric interrupted as he pulled out a chair and took a seat, his alert eyes darting around the table to scan the varied expressions of the others. "What are you guys talking about?"

Jack, Marilyn's husband, casually responded, "Oh, there's supposed to be this musty old castle – a real-life chamber of horrors – over in Europe somewhere. It's rumored that babies and little kids are ritually sacrificed every morning by fiendish ghouls who –"

"– who wear three-piece suits and have titles like, Prince, Prime Minister and President … as in 'President of a Country'," Todd summarily appended.

Sterling Harlet, a third year law student, said, "Typical tabloid trash. You get hype stories like that coming out all the time. It's like the Roswell incident – pure speculation. No one ever proves anything. It's all just a fabricated hoax."

"Oh yeah?" challenged Todd. "I can prove to you there's more truth reported in the supermarket tabloids than in the major newspapers and on the evening news! Anyone with a working brain knows that the media is completely controlled by the powers that be!"

After blowing out a suppressed puff of mocking air, Sterling scorned, "Yeah, right. Ever hear of Freedom of Speech?"

"*Freedom of Speech!*" Todd exclaimed, raising his voice in escalating indignation. "What cave have *you* been living in for the last –"

"Where exactly is this place?" Eric calmly interjected, ignoring Sterling's inflammatory remarks.

"It's somewhere in Belgium," answered the tabloid reader, regaining his composure. "There's been tons of reported UFO sightings in that region for decades."

"Tons. Un-huh," derided Sterling.

"UFO's are blocked out of the news," someone quipped.

"I don't see what that has to do with anything," returned the apprentice barrister. "Belgium is one of the major financial centers of the world, *and* it also happens to be one of the locations for the mainframe computer database of our new international government that's about to emerge. Ergo, your so-called UFO sightings are merely hightech military aircraft on reconnaissance maneuvers. Some of the new aviation technology is declassified and so advanced that it passes for what you call UFO's." He forced a laugh, then muttered in a furtive tone, "Little green men in flying saucers ... Ha!"

Todd was persistent. "They're not green, they're *grey*."

"Ritual murder ... Belgium?" reiterated Eric, introspectively searching his memory for connections.

Todd explained further. "I remember the article said something about the place being located South of Brussels. Yeah, that's it – Brussels. And – get this, you guys – they call it *The Castle - of - Darkness.*" He paused for effect, observing mixed reactions from the audience. "Sounds spooky, doesn't it?"

His wife, Pamela, joined the conversation. "Do you always have to be so melodramatic about everything?"

The harried husband defended himself. "And do you always have to correct me in public? I'm only relating factual information. This isn't my opinion. It's *fact*."

Jack abruptly stated, "Did it ever occur to anyone that the tabloids might *also* be controlled?"

Connie, a Registered Nurse, said, "We sometimes get suspicious Intake Admission Reports on children brought into ER. Their injuries are downplayed by the doctors and some of the other nurses I work with. It's all hush-hush, and, of course nobody's supposed to talk about it … but some of us still do. The courts seal the medical records and keep it out of the papers. Judges rule that all court proceedings occur behind closed doors and that reporters and public advocates must leave the courtroom and not return. It's like it's all some kind of big secret or something … like … like no one's supposed to know anything." She paused to look around at the others, then, confidentially leaning forward, said in a whisper, "Those poor little children are involved in something that's a whole lot more serious than what the doctors and lawyers and judges want us to think. I *know* they're being abused, and I'll bet the hospitals and courts are somehow in on it. You know what? … If such a place does exist, it wouldn't surprise me *one bit*. Nothing surprises me anymore."

Her live-in boyfriend, Glen, said, "I think you're just paranoid. Doctors *help* people, and the courts are there to *protect* kids."

Connie wore an expression of stunned disbelief when she looked at him, then, in an exasperated tone, replied, "Yeah, *right*. Give - me - *a* - break."

Sterling again assumed the initiative. "All you're dealing with here is divorce cases. For example, where one parent takes the kid over State lines and gets slapped with a kidnapping charge by his wife, or visa versa. It's all routine jurisprudence. The missing kids' pictures were put on milk cartons, but that was a long time ago. They're … a, not there anymore." He had to pause briefly to refocus. "Deadbeat Dads, that's all it is."

The hospital caretaker glared at him. "You can give it any name you want, but I *know* what I'm talking about. It's called *Child Abuse*. Plain and simple. *Organized Child Abuse!*"

When Eric spoke once again, his voice sounded distant and detached. "You say they kill little children there – at this ... Castle of Darkness?"

"It's more than that," answered Todd. "First they torture them, and then they *sacrifice* them. At least, that's what the article said."

"Sacrifice?" the chess master echoed. "To whom? Or what?"

Sterling let out a condescending sneer. "You folks are still living in the Dark Ages. This is the twenty-first century. The era of the Witch Hunt *is over.*"

Eric's concentration remained focused, his gaze now upon the table, as if envisioning the logistics of a game of chess. Imperceptibly, he nodded.

"What is it, Honey?" whispered his mate, intuitively.

Suddenly emerging from a reverie, he mumbled, "Uh ... nothing ... it's – it's nothing." There was a brief lull in the conversation, when shortly he raised his head to look forward and said to no one in particular, "I imagine this Castle is heavily guarded."

"Probably," Todd agreed.

"And I don't suppose there's ever been anyone with enough guts and brains to attempt a coup of the place?"

"Are you *crazy!*" Todd adamantly exclaimed. "*That* would be *suicidal!* Certain death. Anybody dumb enough to try that would be fighting against the very gates of hell itself!"

The women looked frightened; the men were amused.

Sterling said with contempt, "You've been reading too many tabloids, my boy."

Jack and Glen joined the junior lawyer in a hearty laugh. Meanwhile, Deborah's eyes were on her fiancé when she asked, "Eric, what are you thinking?"

No response.

"I recognize that look," observed Jeffrey. "You always get it before you're about to make a move." When there was still no reply, he pressed further. "Eric? Hey, a … I know you enjoy a challenge, but … you're not *serious … are you*?"

Eyes downcast, brow furrowed in deep thought, Eric remained silent, while smoothing his mustache.

— 2 —

According to some accounts, Brandon Wells was considered a first-rate scholar. By the time he was forty he had published ten books – all of them full length treatises; the majority, critiques of various aspects of the occult or related matters, such as exposés of government corruption, media disinformation, CIA mind-control programming, and other federal government "black ops" projects. Now, at age fifty-three, among peers he was a recognized authority in his field, having gained worldwide renown for his expertise. Yet, ironically, his work was not well received by the general public, and was rarely given press coverage. Even modest acclaim came with a price, one that could be measured in terms of police surveillance and government harassment. Because of his unpopular stand against organized political tyranny and the emergent global Police State, his fame was short-circuited by the controlled media; and with the publication of each new volume, his reputation further degraded into notoriety. Because of media smear campaigns, in the public eye he was infamous; yet, among a small following and a select few of his colleagues, he was somewhat of an icon. Spurious literary reviews were calculated to discredit him; the media often branding him as a "dangerous terrorist." Because he had devoted his entire adult life to uncovering the misdeeds and hypocrisy of miscreant high-level government officials, there were several attempts made on his life. Death threats over the telephone and delivered in the mail were commonplace and often a normal part of his daily routine. It was the price he paid for the pursuit of truth.

His current book, number fourteen, described a phenomenon popularly known as Remote Viewing – an occult-based program developed by the CIA, NSA, and Russian KGB. This obscure research found practical application in military intelligence operations, government covert citizen surveillance, and political and corporate espionage. Most of the data for his primary research was gleaned from the esoteric literature, or was collected from declassified government documents such as Project Third Eye, Project Garden Plot, Project Blue Beam, and MK-Ultra Project Monarch. Some of the preliminary Top Secret information was gathered from research conducted by WWII Nazi extermination camp scientists, and also from subsequent scientific papers written by government-funded Behavioral Psychologists employed at American Universities during the human potential movement of the 1960's.

He was typing on a keyboard at his desk, comfortably seated in a dark blue leather wing back chair in his spacious wood paneled library, the computer monitor displaying text of his growing manuscript. Pausing when interrupted by the faint sound of the chiming door bell, after glancing at a security camera positioned upon his desk top, the researcher got up and walked over to a nearby window to peer through an opening in the floor-length curtain. Satisfied that the visitor was not hostile, he flipped a toggle switch on the side wall, deactivating an electronic circuit capable of delivering lethal voltage to the metal front door. Returning to his desk, he then pressed a button on the house security console that instantly retracted dead bolt locks on the inside of the door, leaving the locks on all the other doors and windows secure. Speaking into an intercom microphone, he said, "I'm up in the second floor study. Come on in."

Minutes later, a once familiar presence stood at the threshold of the room. "This place is like a fortress!" exclaimed the visitor. "I'm surprised I wasn't attacked by guard dogs."

Brandon walked forward to offer his hand. "A necessary precaution. And my team of Doberman are concealed in the back kennel." He blithely smiled. "Nice to see you again, Eric."

They went over toward a setting of comfortable furniture. Along the way, Brandon reactivated the front door locks, and his guest inquired, "So, tell me, what does it feel like to be famous?"

The author laughed modestly, pushing up wire rimmed glasses with his index finger. "I didn't know that I *was* – at least, not to anyone whose opinion I respect. History proves that those who stand for the truth are usually hated. As someone once said: '*Truth lives a wretched life, but always survives a lie.*'"

Brandon motioned the visitor to take a seat near a wall of towering bookshelves. "Refreshments?" offered the host, standing at a small glass table, and about to pour fruit juice from a crystal decanter. "I seem to recall your habit of preferring organic sustenance."

"Good memory," said Eric. He was soon handed a filled glass.

"Over the phone you sounded like your usual imperturbable self," commented Brandon, easing into a chair across from him. "Reminds me of the good old days back at the University."

Eric took a sip. "That was a long time ago, and even now in retrospect, those days weren't really that good. I wasn't concerned about getting an employable degree. Joining the rat race held no interest for me. And *you* were the avant-garde of the Sociology Department; definitely ahead of your time. Professor Wells was the best darn researcher they ever had. That's why I chose to do my graduate study with you. Since your departure, I doubt if they found anyone to replace someone of your caliber."

Brandon seemed relaxed, yet keenly aware. "That's being liberal. There are those who might disagree. The University Board of Directors, for instance. We had a … slight conflict of interest. You see, I loved the truth. They didn't."

"Is that why you quit?"

"I didn't quit." Brandon took a sip from his glass, then said, "Got fired. But I was glad it happened. I no longer wanted to prostitute my talents." He took another drink before stating, "Colleges don't teach, they brainwash, they indoctrinate with the government agenda. At least, that is, in the social sciences. In today's political climate there is a broader meaning to formal education. The government has always had a hand in deciding what the students are taught. Presently, we're about to enter a worldwide totalitarian Police State that will make Stalinist Russia seem like elementary school."

Eric commented, "Big Red Brother wants everyone to be good little New World Order citizens."

"Exactly," confirmed Brandon. "Their tacit goal is to maintain students in a state of ignorance regarding the important issues of today: globalism, collectivism, mass mind-control, planned moral disintegration of the culture – to name only a few. High School and College students are taught a revisionist version of American and world history; the truth has long since been discarded down an Orwellian memory hole. Graduating students have been pre-conditioned with government propaganda; for the most part, they have lost any ability to think independently. This is even more evident at the lower levels of education – elementary and secondary schools. The agenda of the NEA is the same as that of the NWO globalists: *mind-control of the masses*. Schools control what students think by neurosensory programming, essentially Classical Conditioning techniques Pavlov used on his dogs. Government and Education are part of the same system; they're basically the same entity. Both are corrupt to the core. In today's Brave New World Order of mind manipulation, parents who send their children to a public or private school are very uninformed, or simply don't care." After pausing a moment to redirect, he added, "But, I digress. Back to the matter at hand … how can I be of assistance, young man?"

Eric said, "I know you're busy, so I'll try not to occupy too much of your time."

"No problem," the scholar replied. "That's what friends are for."

His junior by twenty years began by saying, "It was Winston Churchill who once observed: *'Most people, sometime in their lives, stumble across the truth. Most jump up, brush themself off and hurry on about their business, as if nothing had happened.'"* Eric let out a controlled breath, then added, "I've recently stumbled across something that I can't walk away from."

Brandon affirmed, "So you have laudable convictions! That's a rare trait, especially today. Yet, it's one that we both share in common."

His former understudy continued. "I've considered the preliminary implications of a situation that's somewhat intriguing – from a strategic perspective. Also, I find it quite disturbing. I have good reason to believe this issue concerns the occult, an area in which you're well-versed. The matter specifically pertains to an international child abduction ring and the ritual sacrifice of young children."

The author seemed unfazed when tersely replying, "I've written a book dealing with that subject."

"Yes, I know," said Eric. "And that's why I wanted to talk to you first." He leaned slightly forward when confiding, "Have you ever heard of a place called, The Castle of Darkness?"

Brandon gave a significant blink before responding. "I have. And, as a matter of fact, I was fortunate enough to procure relevant documents that leaked out, and were subsequently squelched. Not much is known about the place, or what goes on there."

"Is it true that infants and children are involved?"

The writer rose up to pour himself a drink before replying. "Yes. As far as I was able to develop the research – that is true." The sound of ice cubes tinkled in the pitcher. "It's all true, and a whole lot more." His hand trembled when attempting to fill a glass.

Eric asked, "I know this may sound ingenuous to someone like you, but, why hasn't anyone done anything about it? I mean, what we're talking about here is wholesale mass murder of human beings – innocent little children … *aren't* we?" There was a long interval of silence during the time Brandon was turned away from his guest. The visitor prompted, "Why isn't there a child protection agency or amnesty group somewhere to intervene? It's systematic cold-blooded murder of the worst kind. Don't you agree?"

Again, no answer.

Brandon's gaze was now fixated on the ice cubes, the crystal-clear ice that seemed to him like tiny mirrors, windows into his past. Shattered glass was one of his programmed triggers. In his mind he heard a cruel demanding voice that shouted: *"Either hurt the one you love, or we'll hurt both of you!"* There followed a series of tormented shrieks, then, the pathetic cries of a helpless three year old blond-hair blue-eyed child pleading for his life. When the filled pitcher slipped from his grasp, he thought it was the ceremonial ritual knife, the long curved blade that his mother had secured in his little hands, using her own to tighten his grip – it was the weapon that he was given to kill his childhood friend. A memory trace from the past protested, *"No! I won't do it!"* His adult body was in the present time, but his mind was now that of a child. Brandon remained still as a statue while re-surfacing events rapidly flashed before his glazed eyes, flooding his mind with unforgettable horrifying images from a netherworld of un-speakable torment. Now as he stood there trembling uncontrollably, he relived the childhood trauma: the mental, emotional and physical torture; the sexual perversions, the abject terror. His body quivered from the high voltage electroshocks; he could feel the soles of his feet seared with a hot iron, spiders and snakes crawling over his naked body, razor blades slicing into his flesh. When refusing to kill the sac-rificial little boy, they tortured Brandon until he was unconscious, then left him to die. Upon reviving the next day and realizing they had slit the child's throat, drank his blood, and cannibalized parts of his body, he let out a protracted wailing scream that traversed across space and time, echoing through a long twisted corridor in the cav-ernous recesses of his mind.

"Brandon! *Brandon!*" Eric was now standing before him, grasping his friend's arms and shaking him to snap out of an hypnotic stupor. *"Brandon!* It's *me*, Eric!" When he looked into Brandon's eyes, he could tell that he was somewhere else. Carefully, he led him back to a chair, then offered words of support. "It's okay. You're going to be all right. *You - are - going - to - be - all - right.*" It was several minutes until the accomplished writer began to regain his composure.

Eric handed him a glass of Bourbon. "Medicinal only," he said.

The researcher ran a shaky hand through tousled graying hair, his voice unsteady when he said, "I-I guess I still have difficulty with it … that aspect of my childhood never seems to go away."

Eric sympathetically replied, "I think I understand."

Brandon gulped the whisky. "Just give me a few moments … I'll be fine." Soon, after taking several deep breaths, he feebly said, "I didn't think the memories could still be triggered. But I suppose they can. That sort of thing never completely leaves you." He once again drank from the glass, then slowly exhaled a controlled breath. A few minutes later, he began to explain, "As a child, I was part of a government project involving trauma-based mind-control programming that experimented on children born into generational incest families during the 1950's and 60's. My cult family goes *way* back; most of my ancestors were pedophiles, child pornographers, sorcerers, Satanists, witches – call them what you will. The Old Religion used to be underground then, much more hidden behind closed doors than it is now. Today, it's more out in the open, and Satanic Ritual Abuse is very prevalent, but you would never realize it because the government is the principal abuser, and the media is controlled by the government, so it doesn't get reported." He paused, hand on his forehead, collecting his thoughts before continuing. "As any ritual abuse survivor will tell you, police departments are run by Satanists. Involved judges and attorneys are either part of the cover-up or too intimidated to do anything about it. Some of these legal parasites are indirectly affiliated with international child abduction and CIA mind-control projects like MK-Ultra, or one of its many sub-programs, like Montauk, Monarch, Bluebird, or Naomi. The child abduction network is structured like the military rank and file. Politicians are involved all the way up to the top. But, more precisely, it's the shadow government that controls the lower minions. In America, U.S. Naval Intelligence runs the occult activity.

"Key people in government use their power to cover up the child abduction and white slavery organization that is a global operation. People in authoritarian positions: doctors, police, judges, and those working within the psychiatric and social services, are in collusion to keep the truth hidden from the public. Congressional committees refuse to authorize an investigation because they themselves are involved. Hospitals redact intake reports of child abuse; the cops – Fraternal Order of Police Freemasons – provide legal protection for cult activities." He finished off the bourbon. "And that's only the beginning."

Eric partially refilled the empty glass of his distraught friend. "Just how much government complicity is there?" he asked.

Brandon replied, "To give you some idea, the FBI maintains statistics on stolen vehicles, but not on missing children. There are over one million children missing every year in America, never again seen. Nearly all of them were abducted and sacrificed in satanic rituals. As I said, the perpetrators are given sanction at all levels, all the way up to the White House, and beyond." Eric remained speechless, appalled by the injustice.

The author continued. "The code name for MK-Ultra is Project Artichoke, for, indeed, like pealing away the layers of this vegetable, there are many personality layers created in a totally mind-controlled slave. Satanic Ritual Abuse – also known by the acronym, SRA – and Child Abuse in general, create alternate personalities in the victim resulting from amnesic barriers which develop around traumatic memories. Government operatives use the more systematic MK-Ultra trauma-based or electroshock-based form of torture to program assassins and specialized military operatives. These programs were never terminated, as the government committees claimed, but are still very much in force.

"I had undergone intensive trauma conditioning by government-trained handlers, some of whom were members of my own family and community social network: parents, aunts and uncles, church members that ritually abused my brothers and sisters and myself. They typically start the trauma conditioning before birth, while the victim is still in the womb. At a very young age, as far back as I can remember, I was forced to participate in blood ritual ceremonies where animal and human sacrifices were common. The group practiced satanic rituals involving horrific torture and desecration of the innocent. I was several times tortured to the point of near death. My eyelids were taped open and I was deprived of sleep for three days; I was mind-control programmed by being forced to wear headphones and listen to a single phrase for days at a time; I was put in a sensory depravation chamber; I was forced to participate in some disgusting things that I can't even talk about." He stopped for a moment to validate his surroundings and maintain perspective of the real world from the illusory world of madness that he was describing.

"My handlers were experts in mind-control techniques; they were trained to reprogram the memories of ritual abuse survivors who might reveal guarded secrets that would result in criminal prosecution of those involved in government Black Operations. The entire network is part of the cover-up: psychiatrists, psychologists, social workers, trauma unit hospitals, rehabilitation facilities, recovery programs, government children's services, CPS, and other government social services – *all of them* are infiltrated by the same kind of demented people: fiendish pedophiles, child pornographers, legally protected murderers, sadistic serial killers. The courts are part of the collusion. It's a well run conspiracy. Even the orphanages are infiltrated – Boy's Town and Girl's Town in Nebraska are prime sources for pedophile procurement. The only child abuse cases prosecuted by the courts are the less severe ones, the cases that don't involve government complicity. In those few instances, the meager press coverage is all for show. The majority of ritual abuse cases never make it to trial, but are classified, sealed, not allowed to be released to the public; police records are redacted or destroyed. No one is convicted and no one goes to prison, or even gets indicted. If ever they did, high-level politicians would find themselves behind bars. Essentially, a pervert pedophile guild runs Washington D.C.

"The abusers are protected by the legalized crime network: police and the judicial system. Any cult abuse survivor who goes though the corrupt injustice system is *revictimized*, then *further* revictimized when traumatized by a society that doesn't believe what happened to them is true, and which labels them a danger to themself and to others. If I told anyone what was being done to me – anyone who was not part of the CIA Operation – hardly anyone believed me. Consequently, there was no place for me to run, no place to hide." He gulped another drink from his glass. "And that's what the cult fiends tell you: '*Who you gonna' tell? Nobody will believe you,*' they say.

"The personalities – the multiples, alters – were embedded in my subconscious mind during trauma-based programming sessions. The cognitive-shattering experiences which a ritual abuse victim endures is so intense that the mind, in order to maintain a semblance of sanity in their world gone completely mad, becomes fractured, fragmented, compartmentalized into distinct identities which are uniquely able to cope with incomprehensible horrors that would otherwise over-whelm an intact rational mind." He paused to exhale another un-steady breath of air. "As I said, I was part of a CIA program that uses children from generational incest occult families to produce totally mind-controlled slaves for government research and black operations. They programmed my memories so I had no recollection of my cult personality; no conscious awareness that my own parents and relatives were pedophiles, rapists, pimps, pornographers, murderers, vicious animals dangerous to be around. Outside my cult family I had few friends, and if ever I told anyone what they did to me and my broth-ers and sisters, my *handlers* – the government trained overseers of my trauma conditioning – would punish me with torture. My parents and most of my relatives had all been mind-controlled and actually par-ticipated and contributed to the torture that was forced upon me; they did nothing to stop it. I can recall everything that happened, only, most of it is still filed away in my subconscious. When a young child is subjected to intense physical or psychological torture and abuse, a scarring of their brain stem occurs that results in them acquiring a photographic memory which retains a perfect record of everything seen or heard. Later in life the buried memories of the abuse began to resurface in my conscious mind; I started to remember I had been programmed – the flashbacks stored in compartmentalized areas of my mind ..." He trailed off, then remained silent, lost in a moment of forgotten time. After a long pause, he resumed once again. "But I was one of the fortunate ones who broke the programming. I received help to become deprogrammed. It was no longer able to hold me victim." Thoughtfully, he added, "That's when I started writing books. It was therapeutic, an escape into sanity."

Eric's voice was empathetic when he asked, "But why did they do it, Brandon? *Why?* I don't understand."

The author's expression was contorted in a pained grin when he repeated, "*Why? Why* do they torture and ritually murder innocent little children? *Why* does the federal government spend billions of dollars each year researching ways to kill off or maim a world society of drone-like obedient slaves? I'll tell you why ... They do it for two reasons: power and control.

"They want absolute control over your life; your mind, body, and soul. They systematically torture and traumatize their victims to literally drive them out of their conscious mind so they will exist only through their reprogrammed subconscious. The trauma-based psychological conditioning takes away your free will and ability to reason to such an extent that you no longer question anything that's being done to you. Intense physical or psychological trauma makes the victim compliant and highly susceptible to suggestion. Ultimately, like a mindless soldier or police officer, you automatically do whatever you're told." He repositioned himself in the chair before stating, "Even if you are told to go kill someone."

Eric thoughtfully interjected, "What you're describing sounds like planned government terrorism of the American people."

Brandon managed a brief smile, "Yes, it is. And so-called *terrorism* is sanctioned or carried out by governments. Inducing passivity and compliance in citizens is not an accident, but planned."

Eric agreed. The scholar continued. "They punish their victims with torture in order to fracture their mind, break their will, psychologically induce compliance to control them so the fiends can *do whatever they want* to them. They use carefully crafted propaganda to indoctrinate and brainwash minds. They mutilate and murder the innocent to instill in the other members of the cult society a sense of fear and group loyalty. The abuse is intended to make the children feel helpless and ashamed, because the more helpless and hopeless people feel, the easier they are to control. This, of course, is what exists in today's Police State America – a society that was engineered by many of the same demented psychopaths who organize and run the international child abduction network. Their goal is to cause a total breakdown of the culture, then restructure it to their own perverse liking, creating what they call a New World Order. This is exactly what they do to the individual mind-controlled victim; it's what they attempted to do to me; and it's what they're now doing to an entire world culture. People need to realize that Satanic Ritual Abuse at the individual level is what the world controllers are doing to the general population on a massive scale. It's the same spirit, the same agenda, and oftentimes, it's the same people who are the perpetrators.

"All branches of the U.S. federal government are following the identical Marxist script of past despotic dictatorships: Nazi Germany and Stalinist Russia, for example. Psychiatric clinics, police departments and penal institutions – jails and prisons – are staffed by this same type of psychopathic personality, lacking any moral conscious. Some of the most demented members of any society are in charge of running the government, at all levels: Federal, State, local. Anyone who works within government is mentally ill; their psychological profile mirrors that of a serial killer; they're basically souless beasts. This is so because a psychological urge to control people is *aberrant behavior*, and thus, a psychopathology. The desire to exert control over others is a trait that all those associated with the human control mechanism known as *civil government* share in common. Psychologically healthy people have no such desire.

"Government affiliated institutions are subcategories operating within a larger sphere of influence and control. On both, the level of the individual and in groups, their objective is to completely dominate the lone person and the masses by controlling what *they think*. And that is where the government-controlled media comes in. All major political news reported on the television networks, all politically sensitive information put out by the print media, has been scripted by experts trained in mind-control techniques. Nearly everything you see or hear on the major television networks, the movies, in the controlled press, has been engineered to subvert your ability to think critically, rationally, or to oppose tyranny, or to perceive the Orwellian nightmare that has been created before your very eyes. At the highest levels of government the perpetrators are motivated by spiritual considerations, which you probably won't understand."

Eric looked puzzled when asking, "Why don't you think I'll understand?"

Brandon introspectively replied, "Because I'm not sure if even I understand it, and I have studied and directly experienced it."

The chess master challenged, "Try me. Abstract thinking is my game."

Without further hesitation, his former mentor acquiesced. "Okay. I'll tell you: Those occupying the upper echelon of the Global Hierarchy do it to appease their controlling spirits that promise them material rewards and power to control other people. Only at the highest level of command and control are they fully aware of this hidden agenda. Those at the lower levels are compartmentalized; the tens of millions of operatives: politicians, judges, attorneys, police, social workers, and all other government wards of the state, are entirely unaware of the role they play in the overall large scale plan. They're like worker bees, mere drones in the Masonic beehive assemblage of useful idiots. In much the same manner as the many lone groups of cult misfits throughout the world that are not directly affiliated with the government conspiracy, they want personal power and riches – power to rule over others – to control them. Their minds are so warped and twisted, they lead people to believe they will help them, but only end up using them to satisfy their own perverse needs. They derive a sense of exalted power by dominating, manipulating and destroying people; they want to so totally usurp individual free will volition as to take away one's personhood and identity, absorbing them into themselves. Many of those functioning within government will do anything to get this kind of power and control over others, including selling their soul to the Devil."

Eric responded, "I was always taught that evil spirits and the Devil were from our medieval past; myths born of ignorance and superstition."

The elder laughed unemotionally and said, "*That too* is a masterful piece of propaganda, courtesy of all those who hate the truth. The *Witch Hunt* cliché is a common diversion tactic used by those of like mind to discredit the truth and convince unthinking people that Satanic Ritual Abuse doesn't exist. There's even an organization that was created by the CIA for that very purpose – to discredit the truth about the reality of SRA. It's called the False Memory Syndrome Foundation, and it's run by government-sanctioned Satanists. As expected, they are well-funded by the satanic federal government to spread *False Memory Syndrome* propaganda that protects the abusers and discredits and denies the unspeakable torture experiences of ritual abuse survivors. Satanic Ritual Abuse, on the personal and group level, is the means to an end, and that end is total control of an individual." He laughed once again. "The ongoing discrediting campaign is strictly disinformation; it's all a cover-up deception, and the joke is on the mind-controlled public." There was a stern expression on his face when he said, "People should be outraged, but they don't want to know about it. That's the most pathetic and disgusting aspect of the SRA cover-up."

Eric reflected for a moment, then sounded bewildered when stating, "Why do you suppose they overlook the obvious?"

The former college professor answered, "Reality denial resulting from Cognitive Dissonance. As I said, it's all true, and there's a whole lot more." He finished off his drink.

"I'll get you a refill," his protégé offered, rising up. "And I could use some more cranberry juice myself."

"Thanks," Brandon said, adding, "This time, make mine the same as yours."

While filling the glasses, Eric said, "It sounds like I need an education in this. It's new knowledge for me."

Brandon replied, "Not only *for you*, my friend, but in today's media blacked-out American culture, it's new knowledge for practically everyone. The general public is abysmally ignorant of these matters. Most simply do not want to know the truth, because with knowledge comes responsibility. Since they lack the integrity to live up to that responsibility – and do not want to upset their safe and secure bubble of illusion – they simply ignore it. They don't want to have to think; they want someone to tell them what to think; and agents of government disinformation are always willing to accommodate. The truth causes people to reflect, reevaluate, discover they are living a lie. Rather than confront the lie and deal with it, they disregard it, pretend it's not important, or doesn't exist. Essentially, they're cowards. A coward cannot know the truth because acknowledgment of the truth requires courage, a quality which they do not possess. Most people would rather ignore the truth and go their own self-deluded way. Churchill certainly knew what he was talking about."

Eric returned with the filled glasses. After resuming his seat, he said, "It concerns me that a place like this Castle exists. I want to find out more about it."

His former mentor replied, "I've done the primary research, and I'll tell you what I know, but only if you'll promise not to seriously doubt what I have discovered. The realm of the spiritual seems like a bizarre world to us finite mortals, so don't expect my analysis to conform to any preconceived notions you may have concerning what you think is reality. Once the flimsy veil is removed, the next level is nothing at all like the world of common experience."

"Fair enough," responded his re-enlisted student. "No serious doubting; no preconceptions. I promise."

Brandon took a sip from his drink, then set it on the ivory coffee table. He shifted his weight in the plush cushion, and said, "With that understanding, we will proceed." As if lecturing before a classroom, he announced, "I'll begin by simply stating in general terms that there is a spiritual basis undergirding all human experience. Of course, few are aware of this. Most people will adamantly oppose those who suggest there is indeed a spiritual reality to consider, and they are the very ones most impacted by the consequences of their own ignorance. Those thinking themselves to be rational, or *scientific,* are often the least likely to recognize this seeming paradox. The reason for their limited perception is typically because they are being controlled by a higher dimensional ordering of spirit manifestation, which have been known throughout history by various names. I will leave this point for now and save any philosophical issues for perhaps another time. This discussion will address the matter relevant to your inquiry – that is, government operations for creating an entire world culture of submissive mind-controlled slaves, of which, organized child abduction and SRA are subcategories.

"Most of those involved in this sordid affair are lacking any broader spiritual understanding of their criminality. Their victims may *also* be unaware of the deeper spiritual significance of their SRA cult experiences. Like an alcoholic in denial, they are typically unable to gain insight into their affliction, and hence, remain perceptually oblivious to the spiritual realities adversely affecting their life. There are several critical reasons for this lack of self-awareness. I'll summarize: First of all, *both* the abusers and the child victims have been mind-controlled in order to create a base level of awareness which enables them to function in society without their cult involvement being detected by outsiders. At the same time, they are yet sufficiently conscious to willingly execute the cult's mandates. The cult members, government agents, or other common sociopaths, subject the young child to a rigorously applied system of intense trauma *that controls them with terror,* and which indoctrinates them into the cult programmed belief system. This is intended to destroy the victim's free will, transform them into submissive slaves, and bring them into conformity with the twisted desires of the cult leader, mind programmer – also known as the *handler* – and other members of the group. As you previously observed, this is what the government is doing to the public through staged acts of terrorism. SRA is merely a microcosm of what the New World Order is all about: m*ass mind-control by creating planned acts of terrorism.* In the macrocosmic picture, it is the media that is the mind-control programming *handler.* Throughout the course of this discussion, assume that what I say regarding SRA, and Child Abuse in general, also applies to what the Global Hierarchy supra-government is perpetrating against the world population. Within both frameworks, the same psychological mechanism is being implemented. The world leaders are actively engaged in creating mind-controlled zombies among their own kind, who, in turn, use similar trauma techniques to manipulate, control and neutralize large populations of people.

"As part of the infrastructure for this worldwide human programming network, various methods are being employed to control the victim's behavior, even at the level of personal thoughts. Globally, in addition to staged acts of government saboteured terrorism, further examples of trauma-based conditioning are: directed microwave frequencies from cell phone towers and a powerful transmitter located in Alaska, known by the acronym HAARP; television electromagnetic emissions in the 1-100 Hertz range; and government propaganda seen and heard on the major television news networks. On the individual level, control is affected by intense physical torture, electroshock, starvation, water deprivation, sleep deprivation, hypnosis, use of hallucinogenic drugs, and various psychological manipulation techniques requiring the child to compromise any sense of right and wrong. Often the cult will force the child to witness the torture and murder of a beloved pet or another member of the cult in order to instill in the child's impressionable young mind an overpowering sense of fear and disempowerment. In addition to group conformity, the purpose of this traumatic psychological conditioning is to desensitize the victim to witnessing or experiencing pain; emotionally anesthetize them to create a sense of reality denial by forcing their conscious perceptions to become subconscious. On a larger scale, the government accomplishes this effect with each successive act of terrorism, such as when certain departments within the U.S. government, – under the direction of the Global Hierarchy – planned and allowed airliners to crash into New York City's Trade Towers on September 11, 2001. By the use of repeated intense trauma experiences, abuse victims are psychologically terrorized into denying the harsh reality of their experiences. The general public is too traumatized and frightened to deal with the truth, and the individual abuse victim has been threatened not to report their abuse or otherwise make it known to those outside the cult. If they did they would be further tortured, or killed.

"Cult members abuse their children from birth – emotionally, physically, sexually – so that by the age of six, the child is traumatized to the point that psychological damage is often irreparable. Victims of Satanic Ritual Abuse develop multiple personalities, or what is known as *alters*, in order to cope with the psychological pain and trauma that is part of their daily life. Their fragile mind becomes fractured, compartmentalized, and disassociates from the immediate trauma experience. Victims usually have a separate personality that functions only in the cult context, during the actual ritual abuse and torture sessions. This personality, or personalities, may sometimes have no conscious awareness of a life outside the cult, and may be amnesiac of their everyday persona which appears to be quite normal and well-adjusted. The physical and emotional pain and trauma which a cult member experiences is so intense that it shatters their primary identity such that, when returning to the world of daily experience, they may be amnesiac of everything that transpired during the ritual the night before. This selective recall is a consequence of their brain compartmentalizing the painful SRA abuse in order to function on a rational level, and is also a result of trauma programming instilled in them so they will not be able to remember the abuse. By employing certain key words, phrases, sounds, colors, smells or images programmed into the child's subconscious mind during torture sessions, the abusers can more easily manipulate and control their victim by later *triggering* the child to access personalities on cue. These alter personalities are the multiple identities the victim develops as an adaptation for coping with the moral conflict and physical torture. Typically, most ritual abuse survivors remain unaware of the fact that they live a dual existence; the full impact of the ongoing nightmare may not become fully conscious to them until later on in life, as an adult.

"By implementing intense physical trauma torture techniques, the cult members program a series of subconscious behaviors into a victimized mind-controlled child. Many of these programmed actions are intended to prevent the cult victim from defecting and telling others about the cult and the violent crimes committed by its members; crimes so heinous they would be disbelieved by anyone who is not part of the group, and that would result in criminal prosecution. When a child speaks to a professional outside the cult – a social worker or psychologist, for example – in recounting details of murders, mutilations and gruesome torture, this true account sounds preposterous and absurd, and is therefore not believed. The scientific-sounding term, *False Memory Syndrome* (FMS), was manufactured by the cult network itself, and was created by the CIA for the purpose of discrediting such truthful reports. Twenty-six percent of prosecutors in America have litigated cases involving ritual abuse, with nearly zero convictions, thus proving the effectiveness of the FMS defense. Those collaborating with the cult – such as judges, attorneys, psychologists – use the convenient FMS ploy to nullify the veracity of a child's statements in court. This discrediting ploy renders prosecution of the abusers nearly impossible.

"SRA is without question the most heinous crime against the individual, and on a larger scale, against humanity. It involves torture, mind-control, cult programming, blood rituals, child mutilation, murder, incest, bestiality, and every kind of sexual perversion and debasement practiced by primitive cultures. It even includes cannibalism. It is repeated, systematic, humiliating trauma to the physical, emotional and spiritual health of the victim. Characteristically, the abuse in not a single episode, but occurs over a protracted period of the individual's lifetime. Although small children are the primary target, it may also involve adolescents and adults of both genders. SRA is practiced by hard-line cults and other organized groups, where it constitutes either the sole purpose for the group's existence or is part of a larger ritual agenda. Most victims have detailed foreknowledge of the harm they will suffer – when, where, and how – and are helpless to prevent it from occurring because they feel there is no way to escape it and no one to offer them help and protection. Ritual Abuse can be perpetrated by anyone in a position of power or authority, real or perceived. Governments are the number one ritual abusers of the individual and collective humanity.

"Trauma-based mind-control techniques were first developed by WW II Nazi war criminals who tortured concentration camp prisoners. The cultists plant into the child's subconscious mind psychological programs designed to later elicit a response denying and discrediting the cult's criminal activities. For example, there are *Verbal Response Programs* which are rehearsed answers to questions about the cult's activities; *Flooding Programs* that interfere with attempts at clinical rehabilitation; *Recycle Programs* cover any memories inadvertently revealed; *Silence-Shutdown Programs* make the victim stop talking; *Nightmare Programs* afflict the child with horrible dreams; and, of course, there are *Suicide Programs* in which the victim kills them self prior to exposing the cult. Any of these implanted programs can be *triggered* by the sensory cues already mentioned, or they may automatically be set off as soon as the child seeks help or attains a certain age.

"When applying these mind-control concepts in a larger context, such as an entire nation, it is the government-controlled media that acts as the cult programmer. The massacre of innocent children and adults at the Branch Davidian compound in Waco Texas was only one example of how media propaganda works to program the uninformed public into whatever disinformation mode the government handlers want the people to function. The Davidians, portrayed by the media as "terrorists" – a common disinformation ploy used by the U.S. government – were peaceful individuals murdered in cold blood by government assassins. This situation was similar to Jonestown, Guyana, where the leader was a CIA mind-control operative. Likewise, Timothy McVeigh, a CIA programmed Delta subject, in regard to the bombing of the Merrill Building in Oklahoma City. School shootings, sniper attacks and, as I already mentioned, the destruction of the New York City World Trade Towers – all of these are examples of government orchestrated acts of terrorism that were misreported and covered-up by media disinformation. These mass media *Response Conditioning Programs* were designed by government mind-control experts for bringing about consensus among a traumatized national population, a group *mind think* of invisible control. The covert plan is to manipulate the masses into believing they need to be protected from *the terrorists*, which is actually the *federal government itself,* or, more specifically, the shadow government Global Hierarchy of cult Satanists who run international affairs. The ruse of "terrorism" allows the cult globalists to legislate more oppressive laws, and thereby further erode and eradicate the Constitution and citizen freedoms granted by the Bill of Rights. The individual that is not being mind-controlled will immediately realize that *national governments* are the "terrorist organization" behind all acts of global terrorism. Governments create terror in order to control large masses of people; it's by skillful use of the government-controlled media that they offer to the public a *convenient solution* to the conflict that was caused by the government itself. This is a military strategy that has been employed for centuries: divide and conquer. The people are the enemy to be subjugated; it is *their mind* that is being divided. The end result is a nation of fearful mind-controlled people ruled by a small group of politically influential elitists that use Ritual Abuse techniques to enslave them."

Eric asked, "Is it possible for an individual, or even an entire nation, to be mind-control programmed and not even realize they have been mind-controlled?"

"Absolutely," his teacher affirmed. "And that's precisely what has taken place in America today. The global ritual abusers in the upper echelon of political power have essentially hypnotized an entire culture by the use of television *programming*. America, especially, is a nation of television-watchers; TV is often the exclusive source for obtaining the information which they consider to be the truth. If they hear it on the news or read it in the papers, they will believe it, regardless of how ridiculous it may seem to a rational person that is not mind-control programmed. Because they are being electronically and psychologically controlled, they no longer have any truth discernment. In other words, by the very act of watching television or perusing the daily newspaper – and without realizing it – they have been influenced by subtle mind programming. They become what they see, hear and read.

"Satanic Ritual Abuse is far more widespread than the statistics indicate. There are organized murder cults in every large city in this country. These are directed by a chain of command that can be traced to the national and international level. The grassroots witches and Satanist covens are protected by the police, some of whom are themselves members of a local witch coven or satanic cult. An example of this is the cult Luciferian organization known as Freemasonry, and its subdivision, the Fraternal Order of Police – FOP – of which all police are members. Consequently, satanic ritual homicides and cult child abusers escape criminal prosecution and flourish in Anytown USA because the political infrastructure is in place to allow for it to be covered up. If the clandestine ritual murders should somehow inadvertently leak out to the public, the news report or rumor is quickly squelched or discredited by government-controlled media disinformation. Children horribly abused in a local coven, or by their parents at home, are the microcosmic representation of a global human slavery enterprise that's rapidly growing. The occasional loner prosecuted in the media for child abuse is not part of the organized government network. Typically, an abuser who acted alone was set up by complicit detectives to make it appear as if the police are *doing their job*.

"Most people would be shocked to discover that the friendly neighborhood policeman, judge, attorney, congressman/congresswoman are members of a ritual child abuse cult. Merely being affiliated with government is evidence of this, since government itself is essentially a very large satanic coven. Typically, those associated with government are supporters or participants in Wiccan witchcraft or are Freemasons, which, in principle and practice, is synonymous with Satanism. This high degree of continuity within the so-called Freemasonry Great White Brotherhood enables governments to perpetrate horrendous crimes against the individual and against collective humanity. In America, for example, an international child abduction and Satanic Ritual Abuse network *of massive proportions* exists virtually undetected. Conservative estimates of unrecovered missing children and ritually murdered victims are far in excess of 1 million per year, and that figure only applies to the United States. Globally, it is much higher. The overall operation is covert and well-organized. At the top of the cult hierarchy are the world's wealthiest families consisting of multi-generational satanic bloodlines that have inbred to concentrate their hereditary occult power. At the highest levels, the organization is populated by those few which control the media and are therefore able to suppress the flow of information that would otherwise expose their global SRA operations. Key individuals in all major world governments cooperate in suppressing the truth, yet, media propaganda portrays these individuals as normal fun-loving human beings. In reality, they're some of the most degenerate vile creatures to ever walk the Earth. It is a well-known maxim that the higher one looks in the occult pyramid of government power the more witches and Satanists one finds. Thus, the largest and most wicked cult entity of all is the totality known as *human civil government.*"

Eric interjected, "I take it they're not your favorite people."

Brandon replied, "I sound the alarm on these vermin. That's why they oppose people like me and would much prefer me dead." He smiled briefly. "And that's why I have to use security precautions."

The researcher took a sip from his glass. "Torturing and murdering little children is the most monstrous form of human desecration. The child's innocence is stolen at a very young age. Children and other victims who belong to these cults are surrounded by dangerously demented psychopaths that torture, rape, mutilate and murder people at will. They are immune from prosecution because they're either part of the governmental system or protected by it."

"That sounds like what governments have traditionally done," commented Eric.

"Mass rape of humanity," Brandon acknowledged. "There are official government programs in effect that employ the FBI, CIA and other federal agencies to kidnap children for use in satanic rituals. An international group known as *The Finders* works with U.S. federal agencies and private corporations such as Dyncorp and Halliburton to procure children for cult ritual sacrifices. Former U.S. Vice President, Dick Cheney, is the CEO of Halliburton, so he's implicated in the international child abduction network. The U.S. federal government is one of the world's largest suppliers of ritual abuse victims.

"They abduct children from backyards, school play grounds, or while riding their bicycle along a friendly neighborhood sidewalk. Traumatized cult children are sold by their own parents to CIA and FBI agents who psychologically condition them with trauma-based or electro-shock programming. Some are destined to become mind-controlled assassins, sex slaves for high-level politicians, or ticking time bombs set to go off at a predetermined point in time that fulfills a government agenda. All the media-hyped terrorist attacks, rogue snipers and school shootings are carried out by individuals trauma-conditioned by government mind-control programmers to be killers. In fact, they have a name for such programmed children – they're called *Delta Slaves*.

"As I said before, ritual abuse cults are structured by rank and file, checks and balances, like the military and organized government. In America, all mind-control handlers and programmers eventually link directly to the federal government. From that juncture, international leaders are involved in a worldwide conspiracy to unite the world politically, economically, and religiously. They are working furiously to mass mind-control and brainwash the world population so the people will accept globalization, especially the present generation of children. Ritualized child abuse is a prominent feature of this scenario, so it should come as no surprise that it is routinely practiced among high-level politicians and other key members of the global satanic cult network."

"I'm beginning to see the connections," commented Brandon's understudy. "It's simply a matter of scale."

The former professor nodded to confirm before resuming. "All governments function to psychologically condition the masses of people through media propaganda; they create vast amounts of misinformation and disinformation designed to shape and mold public opinion. Today, almost everyone has been brainwashed and mind-controlled to some degree. This is especially true if they watch television, read the newspapers, or participate in the general culture. Much like trauma-conditioned SRA children, the average citizen is not aware they have been brainwashed through psychological techniques."

Eric asked, "How did *you* manage to escape the brainwashing?"

Pointing at his forehead, the astute researcher replied, "Selective censoring. I don't watch television and I stay away from the movies. I don't read newspapers or magazines, and neither do I listen to news on the radio. I carefully filter the information from alternative media sources such as the Internet and select books. I do not allow my mind to be influenced by Hollywood or the polluted stream of lies and deceit flowing from the highest levels of the supra-government Hierarchy into the raw sewage known as Washington DC, *District of Criminals.*"

Eric said, "You have my vote on that one."

The author now seemed more at ease. "I'm just getting started. As you probably realize, since all those associated with civil government are essentially insane, or at the very least severely psychologically compromised, the participants involved in the government-orchestrated SRA global cult network are therefore likewise deranged. To hold a government position, it helps to have a sociopathic personality, a mind without a conscious. No one advances to higher political office unless they are amoral and destitute of any esteemed virtues. Those occupying positions of power and influence derive a genuine sense of pleasure from inflicting discomfort and pain upon others. True sadists, they revel in witnessing people suffer. For them, a tortured child screaming for his mother is music to their ears; the ritual murder of a newborn infant is a wonderful sight to behold. And needless to say, passing abortion legislation or restrictive childbirth policies seems to them a wonderful idea. They're calculating serial killers, socially acceptable criminals, misfits who profiteer from the child slave trade. The international multi-billion dollar child abduction, pornography and child prostitution industry is operated at the highest levels of government; SRA cult people often occupy significant positions within national governments. A very large majority of leaders at the Supra, Federal, State, and even local levels of government are *pedophile homosexual sadists* that truly enjoy torturing and desecrating little children.

"The international child abduction enterprise traffics in the most extreme perversities: bestiality, snuff films, cannibalism. Positioned at the top of this dung heap of human detritus are the international elite members of what are collectively known as the *Illuminati*, a worldwide group of generational witches who believe themselves to be *the Illuminated ones*. These are the people who rule the world from behind the scenes. They consist of extremely wealthy dynastic families that have been inbred for centuries."

"Is that where the Castle of Darkness comes in?" asked Eric.

"You got it," answered the expert in the occult arcane. "They combine their spiritual agenda with their political agenda. They want to rule the world and its inhabitants, and consider themselves to be gods worthy of rulership. Think of the Castle of Darkness as merely another Camp David, an exclusive meeting place for the world's top people abusers. It's only one among many such locales throughout the world – clandestine headquarters where high-ranking Illuminati witches meet regularly to perform blood rituals to appease their indwelling controlling demons."

Eric inquired, "These rituals at the Castle ... what actually takes place there?"

Brandon's voice fluttered with resurfacing anxiety when he stated, "It's not pretty. Are you sure you want to know?"

Eric took a drink from his glass. "I wouldn't be here if I didn't."

The researcher bluntly responded, "Okay. I'll tell you." He cleared his throat before beginning. "The abducted children – I estimate between 200 to 300 of them at a time – are impounded somewhere in the Castle, probably in the lower level, where they're kept in electrified wire cages, and as part of their trauma conditioning are periodically tortured using high voltage electroshock. During their brief stay before they are ritually sacrificed, they are subjected to physical deprivations of food and water, and, if they somehow manage to survive the pedophile attacks of their rabid keepers, they're murdered in a ritual ceremony. But the horrors go much deeper, because remember, what we're dealing with here is not only the ritual murder of hundreds of thousands of children globally, per year, but also, the motivating spiritual dimension."

"What do you mean?" questioned Eric.

Gazing intently at his former understudy, Brandon pushed up his glasses with his index finger and said, "The murderous fiends who kill for recreation and to appease their demented nature are not fully human."

"They certainly aren't," Eric confirmed.

"I mean that *literally*," Brandon flatly corrected. "They, a ..." he hesitated briefly, then said, "... they're human-demon hybrids."

Eric looked askance. "*What*?"

The scholar replied, "Yes, that's right. Members of the old surviving aristocracies of Europe, key world politicians, and certain elite religious and corporate magnates are of a different spiritual genetic strain than the rest of humanity. Their *true identity* is physically manifested during the child sacrifice blood rituals. In the heat of their lust to destroy life, when they torture and then murder a yet breathing child, is when they transmutate – shape-shift into their reptilian hybrid form complete with iridescent scales, flickering tongue, unblinking lidless eyes. The description of this morphological phenomenon has been corroborated by numerous independent eyewitness accounts. Credible reports have surfaced which document that during their feeding frenzy upon the sacrificed child's still living body, participants in the Castle ritual spontaneously grow two feet taller."

Eric nervously rattled the ice cubes in his glass. "Shape-shifting reptiles," he mumbled. "Two feet taller."

"I warned you."

"I'll have to ponder that one for a while."

They continued the discussion for a short time longer, until finally, when the visitor was escorted to the door, Brandon said, "Eric, you can count me in. If for no other reason than because I want to do for those children what no one was able to do for me."

— 3 —

A roaring crowd of more than twenty thousand Red Chinese Nationalists filled the sports arena to overflowing capacity. Camera crews from all over the world were there to film coverage of the highly publicized World Kickboxing Championship aired live from Hong Kong and broadcast to every continent on the globe. Over the last several months, pre-fight coverage was front page news in major international newspapers; the prized bout was the cover story for the most prestigious magazines. Worldwide, hundreds of millions of people sat transfixed before their television set, anxiously awaiting the premier spectator sporting event of the decade.

Strategically positioned throughout the auditorium were a series of large wide screen video monitors displaying a live image of the international contender as he now made his entrance and began the long walk down a narrow isle toward the illuminated fight ring in the center of the arena. The heavyweight champion of the East was closely guarded by an entourage of managers and trainers that prevented him from being mobbed by a thronging mass of fans pressing in from all sides.

Upon seeing their national hero, the vast assemblage was incited to chant a mantra of praise; and when the indoor stadium monitors registered a close-up view of the confident self-assured oriental, the masses instantly responded with a thunderous response of euphoric approval.

Wu Lin was undefeated throughout his ten year fighting career. Known for his savage barbarism, eighty-six percent of his knockouts occurred in the first round. His attacks were of such extreme brutality that 38 of 63 opponents suffered permanent disabilities; six died in the ring; 11 died soon afterward. This was Blood Sport, an athletic event where it was not uncommon for participants to be killed in the heat of the contest. The fierce unchecked violence was tantamount to ancient gladiators battling to the death in a Roman coliseum.

The tempo of the crowd's rhythmic chanting increased still further as the pugilist approached closer to the spotlight circle of illumination that focused upon the roped off elevated canvas ring. The Asian champion was six feet two inches tall and weighed 240 pounds, of large stature for someone of Eastern descent. He wore a bright yellow silk robe, on the back of which was displayed his identifying moniker – the red dragon. Around his shaven head was a wide headband bearing the black and white Yin-Yang symbol of Eastern occult mysticism. A Shinto high priest, some speculated that it was because of Wu Lin's deeply religious spiritualism that he was empowered to overwhelmingly defeat all those who contended for his title. Even the CBS Sports newscaster had previously commented there was something unusual about his gaze, "an hypnotic effect that was spellbinding." After parting through the ropes to enter the ring, he went over to his corner and sat down upon the canvas, crossing his legs in a passive meditative posture, seemingly oblivious to the raging spectators thirsty for blood.

Moments later, when his opponent appeared at the top of the long descending walkway, the massive audience expressed their condescending ire with tones of disapproval, howling and shouting obscenities, loathing the very presence of the defending World Kickboxing Champion. Dressed in a plain shiny black robe, Tony "Knockout" Nichols, aka TNT, began his walk down through the auditorium. At six feet five inches in height, he was 255 pounds of solid rippling muscle. When just twenty-four years of age, he had already successfully defended his world title twelve times. Subsequently, he acquired the nickname, "Knockout," because in all his 76 professional bouts, he knocked unconscious every rival that was pitted against him. His physical strength was legendary; his bone-crunching punches tested at a force equivalent to that required to break a two-foot section of wood two-by-four; his kicks were more than twice that powerful. The champion's exceptional athletic fighting ability was rated superior to that of the greatest boxers of all time. In fact, professional sports betting handicappers had offered a wagering proposition to the public when simulating the expected outcome of a contest between this World Champion kickboxer and a composite fighter with the skills of Rocky Marciano, Joe Louis, and Mohammed Ali. The odds were calculated at 7 to 1 – *in favor of Tony Nichols.*

Along the way, the champion paused to answer questions from persistent reporters strategically positioned for television cameras to view his response. "Tony, do you have any final words before going into the ring to battle against Wu Lin?"

The fair-haired thirty-two year old appeared calm when replying, "I just want to tell all my little buddies out there that if you want to be a champion when you grow up, believe in Jesus Christ. No matter what anyone says, trust only in the Lord Jesus, and you'll always be a winner ..." As soon as he said, "Jesus Christ," the announcer instantly responded to a cue from Station One Control, moving the microphone away to render his voice barely audible. In the background, he could still be faintly heard: "... and *fight* for the truth, because Jesus Christ *is* the *Truth*, and the *Truth* is the only thing worth fighting for ..."

Upon his entry into the ring, the camera zoomed in to the inscription displayed on the backside of his black warm-up robe – prominent stark white letters piercing through the black darkness:

THE LORD JESUS CHRIST
IS NUMBER ONE

When this was transliterated and viewed on the oversized monitors, the thronging mob objected with a resounding vehemence, demonstrating their disfavor with pained groans and tortured wails.

Tony Nichols went to his corner, took off his robe, then, sitting on the low wooden stool, bowed his head. He could not hear the raging audience when reciting from memory a Scripture from the King James Bible: Psalm 18:36-42;46-49:

"Thou hast enlarged my steps under me, that my feet did not slip. I have pursued mine enemies, and overtaken them: neither did I turn again till they were consumed. I have wounded them that they were not able to rise: they are fallen under my feet. For thou hast girded me with strength unto the battle: thou hast subdued under me those that rose up against me. Thou hast also given me the necks of mine enemies; that I might destroy them that hate me. They cried, but there was none to save them: even unto the LORD, but he answered them not. Then did I beat them small as the dust before the wind: I did cast them out as the dirt in the streets…. The LORD liveth; and blessed be my rock; and let the God of my salvation be exalted. It is God that avengeth me, and subdueth the people under me. He delivereth me from mine enemies: yea, thou liftest me up above those that rise up against me: thou hast delivered me from the violent man. Therefore will I give thanks unto thee, O LORD, among the heathen, and sing praises unto thy name."

When the opening bell rang, East met West in the middle of the roped off ring. Almost immediately, Wu Lin gained the advantage when delivering an explosive side kick that sent his opponent back against the ropes. Then, the ungloved champion was repeatedly battered in a quick flurry of smashing fists and flying feet; the contender's pitiless offensive made it appear that the defending champion would not recover. The NBC fight commentator announced to the world: "It looks like it could be all over for Tony Nichols! Wu Lin has him cornered, and *isn't* letting up! There seems no way he can escape. Oh! A flying back kick! … and yet *another*! Ow, *that one* must have really hurt! Wu Lin's punches are landing every blow! How much more can the champion take?!"

The massive crowd was ecstatic in witnessing their adversary mercilessly pummeled, howling deliriously each time their nemesis was struck with yet another vicious assault. Blood from Tony's face splattered the ring; his legs were unsteady, hands drooping, no longer able to hold up a protective defense to deflect the unrelenting attack. "He's gonna' *kill* 'em!" shouted someone nearby the Press microphone.

The delirious audience was chanting: "Die! Die! Die! Die! Die! Die! …"

Booming excitement in his staccato-like voice, the sports correspondent quickly apprised the situation: "This match is subject to China's Kickboxing Regulations which stipulate that the combatants must fight to a decisive conclusion. If the champion cannot save himself before the bell sounds to end the round, then it is entirely permissible for Wu Lin to deal the final death blow. International Fight Regulators have heretofore suspended the eight count ruling that normally precedes a technical knockout – a ruling that could have very serious consequences for Tony Nichols – and for whom, over the next ninety seconds, could *literally* mean the difference between life and death!"

The immense Asian crowd, 99.8 percent pagan, was now standing in their seats, feverishly chanting encouragement to their favored son as he continued to overwhelm his wounded opponent, now swooning against the ropes, about to fall. *"Kill him! Kill him! Kill him!"* The tempo was increasing with each passing moment; their bloodlust building to a raging crescendo, escalating to a frantic pitch. *"KILL HIM! KILL HIM! KILL HIM! …"*

It was exactly two minutes and fifty-one seconds into the first round – with only nine seconds remaining until the bell would sound – that it happened….

The final blow appeared to come from out of nowhere. It was fast, almost too fast to be seen by the naked eye. It was powerful; so powerful, in fact, that it lifted its recipient completely off his feet – a single punch – that catapulted him across the ring, to land sprawled, face down, upon the mat. The auditorium erupted into a frenzy of mixed emotion, and during the ensuing mayhem, raising his voice above the hysterical mob, an American announcer broadcast the consensus of disbelief to the entire world: "Ladies and gentlemen … *this* is *incredible! Unbelievable!* In my long career as a sportscaster I have *never* before seen an athletic feat like this! It's almost unreal! *What - a - comeback!* Tony Nichols has rallied from certain defeat! It was only moments ago, in the final seconds of the first round – when it seemed a certainty that the Champion was defeated – but then, in the next instant, in the blink of an eye, He returned to wreak utter devastation upon the opposition. *Wu Lin isn't moving, ladies and gentlemen!* Tony Nichols is standing triumphant! This is *absolutely* incredible! *He's not human!* Tony Nichols remains the undefeated champion of the world! I can find no other words at this time to describe what has just taken place, other than to say that it's incredible! … incredible! … *incredible! … incredible! … incredible! … incredible! …*"

———— • ✦ • ————

"… Incredible. You're incredible, you know that, Snooty?" The small black cat meowed, then playfully rolled over to allow his owner the privilege of stroking its sleek glossy fur. "That's why I call you, *Snooty,* because about the only time you're friendly is when it's time to eat." The sun was shining bright, birds were singing; there was the scent of spring blossoms in the fragrant air. The frisky feline, marked with a white star on his chest, rolled onto his side, then quickly turned his head to look back at his master and flash large green eyes. "But that's okay, Snooty. Know why?… Because I like you." The cat meowed once again, then jumped down from the wooden porch, his owner smiling after him, and saying, "See you at dinner."

Gazing out across the mountain meadow, in the distance he noticed an approaching automobile coming up the long winding dirt driveway, a billow of trailing dust in its wake. Simultaneously, his two Golden Retrievers sounded the barking alarm, anxious to ward off the unfamiliar intruder. Now easing back into a creaking rocking chair, he awaited the arrival.

Minutes later, after stopping just short of the porch, and before exiting the car, the driver shouted from an open side window, "What the heck you doing way out here in the middle of nowhere?" He then stepped out and walked over to the large modern A-Frame log cabin nestled on the fringe of a pine forest. "Good to see you again, ole' buddy," he said, the dogs eagerly sniffing at his legs.

Rising from the chair and walking down three wooden steps, the big man acknowledged him, "It's been a while."

They shook hands. "Still as strong as ever, I see," observed the visitor.

The dog's owner said, "This here's Samson, and that one over there's Ulysses."

"Pleased to meet you both," said Eric Rider, addressing the tail-wagging canines. "Any friend of Tony Nichols is a friend of mine." He reached down to give each of them a pat on the head. Then turning to the scenic view that stretched out before him, he said in awe, "It's beautiful." He scanned the blossoming fields painted with splashes of crimson, gold and purple, framed by a tall pine forest. "Wild flowers, trees, animals, birds … and you've even got a lake. This is Paradise."

"Or about as close as any of us get to it here on earth," Tony replied, adding, "Come on, I'll show you around."

They walked over toward the barn, passing along the way a flock of chickens scratching in the dirt. As they stood at the open barn door, from somewhere inside, a cow let out a lowering bellow. "That was Molly," announced Tony. "She produces milk and cheese; I get eggs from the chickens and fish from the lake. Even got a flock of ducks around here somewhere, and migrating geese that stop by occasionally."

Nearby was a plot of freshly tilled ground. He pointed. "Over there's the vegetable garden. I plant corn, beans, potatoes, sunflower, and about twenty other varieties of produce from heirloom seeds; then, God waters it and gives the increase."

They walked through a field of knee-high grass until arriving at a one acre clearing of low-profile cultivated fruit trees. "Here's the orchard: apples, pears, peaches, plums, cherries, and a hedge of grape vines. Hickory and walnut trees are over there. No pesticides, no genetic modification. All organic."

"This place is like the Garden of Eden," commented Eric. "You're completely self-sufficient!"

"God blessed me," was all that Tony replied. They continued on to a stand of towering pine trees encircling the shoreline of a crystal clear 10-acre mountain lake. "There's Rainbow Trout in here from the run-off streams that flow down the mountains. Perch, Bass, and Blue-gill too." Stepping into a small boat, they rowed to the other side, where early blooming wildflowers covered pristine meadows with a kaleidoscope of vibrant colors. "I bought the place and moved up here after my retirement," said Tony. "That was two years ago. It's been the best years of my life."

"Sure is remote," replied Eric, while scanning the panoramic expanse of gently rolling Appalachian foothills. His eyes were drawn to the near horizon that dropped off into a deep glacial valley below. "Do you ever miss civilization?"

Tony laughed. "Civilization?" He shook his head, then said, "What you call civilization, I call a wasteland. This is the only place for me."

The visitor asked, "Why did you pick here? With all that prize money, you could have lived anywhere in the world for the rest of your life."

The fighter answered, "I gave most of it away to widows and orphans. It didn't belong to me, but to God. Besides, money's not the reason why I went into the ring."

Eric had a puzzled look. "Oh? If it wasn't for money, then … why did you do it?"

Tony answered, "To glorify God with my testimony of Jesus Christ. I'm not the Champion of the world – *He* is." They walked on.

Climbing a steep grade, they followed a high ridge that half encircled the small farm seen down below. Tony explained further: "There's people in the public eye that get a lot of Press, fame, big money: athletes, movie stars and other celebrity types. They're in it for themselves, for their own glory. They think they've accomplished something, as if they did it all on their own, through their own self-will, ability, or brilliance." He plucked a weed from the ground, then chewed on the stem and added, "Nobody does anything on their own."

"Interesting," mused his friend. "Sounds like you're still into religion."

Tony quickly responded. "I'm not into religion, as you might think of it. Some of the world's greatest hypocrites are religious. I'm not religious; I'm just into the truth. There's only one place today where the truth can still be found – and that's the 1611 King James Bible. There's a lot of religious phonies out there that give God a bad rap in the name of Christianity. They think they're serving the Lord Jesus Christ, but who they're really serving is them self. They do everything for their own glory, to be admired by other people. I don't want the praise of human beings...." He tossed the wildflower to the ground. "... I want the approval of God Almighty." He motioned his hand in a sweeping arc. "The One Who created all *this!*" They continued walking.

For a long while nothing more was said, until finally, Eric spoke. "Tony, we grew up together. We were best friends in High School. Everybody respected you – not just because you were bigger and tougher than they were – but because you stood for something, something beyond yourself. You ... were different, and we all sensed it."

"It's no great mystery," the prize fighter replied, gazing up at the sky. "What I have is *faith* in God. I know, beyond any doubt at all, that Jesus Christ is the Lord of all creation; He's the Messiah, the Anointed One; He's the Son of God; He's *God Himself.* It was through Him that all things were created. He's the *spoken Word*, and he left us His *written Word:* the 1611 King James Bible. From reading Romans 1:19 and 20, we can also begin to know Him just by looking at His creation."

Eric struggled to relate to the convictions that Tony had long held. He wanted to understand what was of such vital importance to his childhood friend, but was not able to receive it.

Suddenly, overhead, they heard a piercing screech that sounded like steam escaping from a tea pot. When looking skyward, Eric saw a large bird circling high above them. "That's Screal," said Tony. They watched the hawk swoop and glide effortlessly on rising thermals, as if performing acrobatic maneuvers just for the sheer joy of it. When Tony gave a loud whistle, the bird of prey folded back its wings and went into a steep dive, then, in a matter of seconds, alighted on the outstretched forearm of its master.

"Magnificent!" said Eric, simultaneously amazed and struck by the sheer beauty and strength of the soaring hawk. "How did you get it to do that?"

"I raised him from the time he was a baby. We're friends."

The urbane visitor to the country inspected the wild creature more closely, noting the large clear eyes, stern brow ridge, piercing gaze. "He looks ferocious with that curved beak and those long sharp talons."

"He *is* ferocious," Tony affirmed, "but only if he thinks you're food."

Eric laughed and said, "I'm glad I don't resemble his lunch."

— 4 —

Traveling North on the Interstate highway during the four hour drive from the mountains of West Virginia, the two friends relived past memories, then talked of the present, and plans for the future. "Once a month I make it up to Cleveland to help out at the inner city rescue missions. It's volunteer work," said Tony while driving his ten year old pickup truck along Route 77. "On the return trip I stop by Columbus, Dayton, Cincinnati, Frankfort, Louisville, then back to Charleston. That's the loop. Takes me about a week."

In the passenger seat, Eric said, "You must enjoy what you do. No monetary reward, the time expenditure, inconvenience –"

"It's no problem," said the driver. "I wanted to do something to help disadvantaged people, especially little children, the ones with single parents; and orphans, with no parents at all. I do whatever I can to help them. Most of the people there are hurtin' real bad … I only wish I could do more."

Eric looked over at him, observing the profile features of a professional fighter, reminders of days past: the saddle-shaped contour of his nose, the scar above his right eye. "You've always cared about the welfare of kids. Is it because you don't have any of your own?"

"Naw," Tony answered. "Wouldn't matter whether I did or didn't. Children are special. They still retain the image of God. That's what I see when I look into their eyes. That purity and goodness is God looking out at the world."

"Interesting," the visitor said.

It was two hours into the trip before Eric finally revealed the reason for his visit. "I came to see you today – not just to reminisce about old times – but to tell you about a situation that I think you would find to be of some interest … Tony, there's this international child abduction ring that … well, they hurt little kids. In fact, they brutally torture them, and then … they kill them. The people who do this are not arrested and sent to jail. They're accountable to no one and never spend time in prison. They're mostly high level politicians, the rich, the elite, world leaders that are above the law …" As he related further information, he noticed Tony's tightened grip on the steering wheel. "They destroy innocent life. Nobody stops them. They get away with mass murder. For them it's like a form of recreation, but deadly serious. What they do is the worst kind of evil, and that's why it especially disturbs me." The driver remained silent, his gaze focused straight ahead.

"The operation is organized from the top down. It starts in the halls of justice and ends on a bloody sacrificial altar. It's in every neighborhood across America; it's an interlocking network that's all over the world." He paused a moment to gaze out the side window at the scenic byway: the blue sky and gently rolling green-covered hills. "Tony, there's this place over in Europe that's known as the Castle of Darkness, where they ritually mutilate and murder little children in the most gruesome ways imaginable. I don't have all the details yet, but what I know so far makes me want to … " He stopped short.

Tony asked, "What do you want me to do about it?"

Eric tersely replied, "Help them."

Without hesitation, Tony said, "Okay."

His childhood friend beamed with admiration. "I knew you wouldn't back down."

They parked the truck in downtown Cleveland, at the corner of Carnegie and East 55th Street, then went inside to the City Mission, an old five-story brick building that served as the Administrative

Offices and temporary shelter for the inner city homeless and destitute. After introducing Eric to the shelter's volunteer staff, Tony took him on a guided tour of the nearby streets. "This is where I do most of my work," he said. "There's people out here living on the edge, barely surviving day to day. No one cares about them. No one knows who they are, and they don't want to know. Sometimes they die from hunger or exposure to the cold in winter. There's broken men and women lying on the sidewalks in the middle of the day, and no one cares enough to help them. Some have a family with little children, and that's an even greater tragedy. I take them to the Mission, where they get food and shelter, but more importantly, they get pointed in the right direction – the Lord Jesus Christ."

Several blocks later, when approaching Euclid Avenue, up ahead they noticed a crowd of people gathered on the sidewalk near a busy intersection. Approaching closer, they observed a man standing on a footstool, head and shoulders above a sparse audience that consisted mostly of the indigent homeless living on the streets. On the periphery were an assortment of pedestrians – secretaries and office workers on their lunch break, and middle class men and women pausing briefly before moving on. The timbre of the speaker's voice increased in volume as they came near: *"Blessed be ye poor; for yours is the kingdom of God. Blessed are ye that hunger now; for ye shall be filled. Blessed are ye that weep now; for ye shall laugh. Blessed are ye, when men shall hate you, and when they shall separate you from their company, and shall reproach you, and cast out your name as evil, for the Son of man's sake. Rejoice ye in that day, and leap for joy; for, behold, your reward is great in heaven; for in like manner did their fathers unto the prophets.*

"But woe unto you that are rich! for ye have received your consolation. Woe unto you that are full! for ye shall hunger. Woe unto you that laugh now! for ye shall mourn and weep. Woe unto you when all men shall speak well of you! for so did their fathers to the false prophets."

Those passing by, dressed in business suits, and who overheard the Bible reading, had a condescending smug expression on their face as they went about their business. The speaker again quoted Scripture when saying after them: "*Ye serpents, ye generation of vipers, how can ye escape the damnation of hell?*"

Without stopping, one of them shouted back, "You're a terrorist who should be reported to the police!"

The man who stood above the others answered him from the Bible: "*Ye are of your father the devil, and the lusts of your father ye will do. He was a murderer from the beginning, and abode not in the truth, because there is no truth in him. When he speaketh a lie, he speaketh of his own: for he is a liar and the father of it. And because I tell you the truth, ye believe me not.*"

A gruff voice in the crowd bellowed, "Chill, man! You ain't righteous!"

The African American street preacher responded, "That is correct. I'm not righteous … but, Jesus Christ *is*. And it's by His shed blood that I can claim His righteousness. You see, He died to make me righteous in the sight of His Father, the LORD God Almighty. Because there can be no forgiveness of sin without the shedding of innocent blood, when Jesus Christ died on a cross in my place, and also yours – if you turn away from your sins – my sins are forgiven. And you too can have that same forgiveness and enter into fellowship with your Creator. You can have eternal life if you will believe that Jesus Christ is God in the flesh, and that He died and rose from the dead so that you might be saved from this wicked world, and if you will do all that He commands of you in His Word – the 1611 King James Holy Bible – and if you persevere until the end, *then* you shall be Saved and made clean, and He will wash you whiter than snow."

"Whaaat?" scowled a barely literate tattooed youth dressed in trench coat Gothic attire. "I can't hear a word you say, man!" His spiked hair was dyed jet black, a metal stud in his nose and tongue; silver rings pierced his ears, lips, and eyelids. "Only snow we knows is what goes up our noses!" His entourage of fellow modern primitives laughed. "Git! 'Afore we come over and cut you up!"

The Bible preacher calmly responded with a Bible verse: *"Touch not mine anointed, and do my prophets no harm."*

Upon once again hearing the Word of God spoken, the gothic gang members grew increasingly more agitated. "Let's *whack* this cracker!"

Meanwhile, more curious pedestrians were drawn to the scene, attracted by the promise of escalating violence. Now maddened with an unnatural rage, the de-evolved primates growled, "Sacrifice this dude! Yeah!" Out of the corner of his eye, the orator saw a glint of flashing steel and sensed the imminent reality that he was about to die. Reading from the Book of Psalms, he cried out, *"Help me, O LORD, my God; O save me according to thy mercy; That they may know that this is thy hand; that thou LORD, hast done it. Let them curse, but bless thou; when they arise, let them be ashamed; but let thy servant rejoice. Let mine adversaries be clothed with shame, and let them cover themselves with their own confusion, as with a mantle."*

After he finished reading, one of the primitives came at him; drug-crazed eyes, switchblade knife in hand, wildly slashing the air.

Before the weapon could pierce his flesh, there was heard a sharp crack resounding in the cool vibrant air. To the astonishment of the lone man raised above the crowd, the following sequence of events proceeded in rapid succession:

One of the primates was now lying immobile on the pavement, while the others were moving in, lunging with knives and throwing ineffectual punches that never came close to their intended target – Tony Nichols. Now strategically positioned between the street preacher and his attackers, with mechanical precision, the champion fighter executed only five movements, one for each remaining gang member; every technique striking with a thudding force that snapped bones, causing bodies to instantly fall limp upon the sidewalk.

An hysterical woman frantically screamed, "Call the police! Someone *call - the - police!*" Another bystander, a man in a designer suit, used his cell phone to dial 911. Within the minute, two police cruisers came to a sudden screeching halt at the nearby curb. There followed the sound of four doors slamming shut. Then, four black-shirted peace officers pushed past timid spectators who moved quickly to get out of their way. When the police came to the scene of six bodies lying prostrate on the ground, and pools of oozing blood next to some of them, one of the policemen asked, "What happened?"

Someone shouted from the crowd, "It was that big guy right there. He started a fight." Pointing, he added, "He beat these guys up for no reason."

Tony glanced over at him and calmly said, "You're a liar."

The preacher confided with Tony, "You defended the Truth. I therefore know that I can rightly call you my Brother. Praise be to God!" He reached down from the stool and offered his hand. "My name is Alex Travis. Much obliged." They shook hands.

Two of the officers now moved aggressively forward, then, one of them matter-of-factly addressed Tony when proclaiming, "You're under arrest. Let's go." When the peacemaker attempted to lay hands on the skilled fighter, Tony's reflexes were cat-like quick: the first cop's head jerked sideways when a backfist slammed hard against the side of his face. Then, his partner buckled to the ground when a thrusting front kick suddenly landed squarely on his chin. Within five seconds, both cops were sprawled immobile on the concrete.

The sound of radio static now crackled in the air as one of the two remaining lawmen made a desperate call for more backup support. After pausing a critical minute to allow the dispatcher to alert all available police units, the courageous officers then drew their guns, and pointing them at the accused, stepped cautiously forward while shouting, "Down on the ground! NOW!"

"Better do what they say," said Alex, "or they just might kill you. They're like unthinking rabid wild animals."

Tony remained still, and as the crouching cops inched their way ever closer, guns held out before them, he offered no explanation and made no attempt to verbally defend himself.

With both hands clutching their lethal weapons, carefully stepping over motionless bodies lying on the pavement, the frightened policemen continued screaming like raging lunatics: "Get face down and spread your arms and legs! Do it NOW!" Approaching sirens could be heard in the distance. The crowd backed away, leaving space between themselves and the central players in the unscripted, unedited for TV, real-life drama of police-citizen interaction.

There was an icy chill calm in Tony's voice when he stated, "You kill me, you kill a servant of the Lord Jesus Christ. I go to heaven, but you go to hell, where you rightly belong."

One of the justice officers sneered, "We're not goin' nowheres but ta' take you ta' *jail*! Now git your face to the ground or we'll blow your _ _ _ _ head off!" Unnerved to see that a citizen was not intimidated by their comic police academy training, the peace officers remained safely behind their protective weapons. When coming to within seven feet of Tony's left foot – the foot that moved with lightning speed and the explosive power of a tiger's paw – the public servant's gun was swiftly kicked out of his hand, consequently throwing him off balance and directly into the line of fire of his unwitting partner. When the gun went off, the bullet missed its intended victim, but struck the faltering policeman in the shoulder. The remaining cop made a mad rush toward the unarmed man, but instantaneously fell hard onto the sidewalk when the thrusted heel of Tony's boot collided with his face.

A long trail of sirens blared. Tires screeched to a sudden halt. A succession of police car doors clicked open. There was heard the sound of boot leather scampering quickly forward. Shortly, a gang of more than 100 police officers lined up along the sidewalk, some down on one knee, all wielding short barreled shotguns or automatic military assault rifles pointed directly at the two lone men standing among ten fallen bodies. Then came the obstreperous command from a police megaphone: "Don't nobody move! Both you put your hands on top your heads and walk slowly forwards." Neither did as they were commanded, not willing to legitimize representatives of an illegitimate government. Seeing they were not cooperating according to expectations, the cop further announced: "Get down on the ground and spread your hands and legs. Do it NOW!" Alex glanced over at his companion, who smiled and paraphrased Isaiah 51:23 when saying, "We'll not bow down that they may go over." A mass of black uniforms now stepped boldly toward the unarmed men, guns intently trained on them. Meanwhile, some of the police rushed over to help their fallen comrades, supporting them to stand on unsteady legs and lead them away to an awaiting ambulance. The other six injured gang members were regaining consciousness when the stretcher arrived to load them aboard a van for transport to a hospital.

More armed police now hurried forward to encompass the two righteous renegades. A synthesized disembodied voice boomed over the megaphone: "Everyone stand clear!" Eric stepped back to blend in with the crowd, then remained unobtrusive as he helplessly observed the mob of police swarming like a Masonic beehive, maneuvering like a feverish pack of stalking wolves. The crowd of police were now six deep around the two men. In a concerted moment, they suddenly closed in and began striking with clubs until the men were beaten down. When their prisoners were incapacitated, the peacekeepers handcuffed them, and while shielded from eye witness observation, took added delight in administering electroshock torture from their stun guns. When Eric shouted, "Police brutality!" the megaphone synthetic voice responded, "*We'll do whatever we want.* Shut up or you'll be arrested!"

Soon, the two assaulted men were lead to separate vehicles, pushed into the cramped back seat of a police squad car. When the long parade of government vehicles finally pulled away, the only remembrance of the incident was the street preacher's overturned stool lying on the sidewalk, and next to it, his torn Bible, pages fluttering in the wind.

At the police station, the two captives were processed like cattle in a slaughter yard. "Book 'em both on violations of the Patriot Act: ten counts each of terrorism. Book the street preacher for violations of the Religious Freedom Act. And this one," he jerked on the complex of chains that bound Tony's hands to his feet and neck, "get 'em on

Domestic Terrorism charges, attempted murder and assaulting a police officer: four counts; assault and battery: ten counts; inciting a riot, failure to comply with a lawful order, resisting arrest, disturbing the peace, aiding and abetting violations of the Religious Freedom Act, and a … we'll come up with sumthin' more later." The two prisoners of war were fingerprinted and photographed, then led into separate small dingy concrete holding cells with vomit and pools of urine on the floor. Throughout the dehumanizing process, both men remained silent, and despite the efforts of the police to provoke them to say something incriminating in the hope of adding still more charges, they did not respond to the taunting provocations, knowing that the false accusations were baseless, and that the police were demonstrating evidence of their unrighteousness and guilt before God.

Soon they were moved to a larger holding pod with fifteen other prisoners; men without hope, dispirited and forlorn. Some of them had sustained injuries resulting from police violence: swollen disfigured faces, bloody lips, missing teeth, clumps of hair torn out, stun gun burn marks all over their bodies. One of the men had even been gang sodomized by the pervert police who used a broomstick handle. The others were defiled merely from being in proximity to legal criminals.

They all sat on the bare concrete floor with their backs against the cold block walls. Reciting verses of Scripture from memory, Alex spoke words of encouragement and comfort to the oppressed:

"Is it such a fast that I have chosen? a day for a man to afflict his soul? is it to bow down his head as a bulrush, and to spread sackcloth and ashes under him? Wilt thou call this a fast, and an acceptable day to the LORD? Is not this the fast that I have chosen? to loose the bands of wickedness, to undo the heavy burdens, and to let the oppressed go free, and that ye break every yoke? Is it not to deal thy bread to the hungry, and that thou bring the poor that are cast out to thy house? when thou seest the naked, that thou cover him; and that thou hide not thyself from thine own flesh? Then shall thy light break forth as the morning, and thy

health shall spring forth speedily; and thy righteousness shall go before thee; the glory of the LORD shall be thy rearward. Then shalt thou call, and the LORD shall answer; thou shalt cry, and he shall say, Here I am. If thou take away from the midst of thee, the yoke, the putting forth of the finger, and speaking vanity; and if thou draw out thy soul to the hungry, and satisfy the afflicted soul; then shall thy light rise in obscurity, and thy darkness be as the noonday; and the LORD shall guide thee continually, and satisfy thy soul in drought, and make fat thy bones; and thou shalt be like a watered garden, and like a spring of water, whose waters fail not."
When finished, he said, "These are God's Words, spoken through the prophet Isaiah in Chapter 58, verses 5 through 11." The incarcerated men were silent, and some understood.

During the next two hours, while the learned disciple proclaimed the gospel of Jesus Christ, the jail cell intercom periodically emitted a high-pitched beeping signal that indicated the prisoner's every word was being monitored and recorded. Occasionally, the officers in the control room delighted in raising the squelch volume to transmit a shrill high frequency blast that was intended to disrupt the tranquility of the Bible reading. But Alex nevertheless continued on:

"The wicked watcheth the righteous, and seeketh to slay him. The LORD will not leave him in his hand, nor condemn him when he is judged…. I will greatly praise the LORD with my mouth; yea, I will praise him among the multitude. For he shall stand at the right hand of the poor, to save him from those who condemn his soul. This is the Word of the LORD, spoken by David the prophet in Psalm 37, verses 32 and 33; and Psalm 109, verses 30 and 31. Praise be to God!" At the *exact moment* when he had finished saying this, there was heard the soft buzz of the cell door electronic lock. One of the jailers stood at the open door. "You and you," he said, pointing a finger at Tony and Alex. "Let's go."

Hands and feet bound with chains, they were led down a long narrow passageway, then through a series of thick metal security doors with electronic locks that vibrated as they approached near.

Eventually, they walked into the same large brightly lit room where they previously had been processed. The street preacher was not surprised when the chains were removed; and when Tony's heavy shackles suddenly dropped to the floor and the jailer said, "You're out on bond. Get outta' here," the two men shouted: "Praise be to God!"

— 5 —

A portable propane heater was the only source of warmth in the dilapidated shelter for the homeless, where there were 150 thin plastic mats laid side by side on the bare linoleum floor of a large open room. Outside, it was the dead of winter; subzero freezing temperatures and cold arctic wind blew drifting snow through the deserted byways of downtown Cleveland. On that frigid January night, forgotten denizens of the street considered themselves fortunate merely to have a roof over their head.

Early the next morning, the shelter's temporary residents lined up single file to slowly pass through the bread line cafeteria serving a limited menu of dry cereal, watered-down soup, powered eggs, and toast. Words were few among the indigent men who found themselves living materially compromised, fallen through the cracks of a prosperous society; having seemingly failed where others succeeded. In the immortal words of Victor Hugo: *Undoubtedly they seemed very depraved, very corrupt, very vile, very hateful even, but those are rare who fall without becoming degraded; there is a point, moreover, at which the unfortunate and the infamous are associated and confounded in a single word, a fatal word, Les Miserables; whose fault is it? And then, is it not when the fall is lowest that charity out to be greatest?*

Howard Conrad pondered his fate as he sat by himself at one of the shelter's battered wooden picnic tables, nibbling on a piece of white bread. He was fifty years of age, but looked much older, with long greasy hair down to his shoulders and scraggly graying beard that had not been trimmed in over two years. He wore soiled brown cloth gloves with holes in the fingertips; the same ones he had on when shuffling in from off the deserted street the night before. Upon reflection, his final conclusion, as always, was that his present situation was utterly hopeless. He had no means of support, neither financial nor emotional; no source of income, no home, no family, no friends – at least, that is, no one who would help him in a time of need. The harsh reality was that everyone had abandoned him, including his two teenage children and a wife of twenty years, who left him and married a man fifteen years her junior. In the divorce settlement, she was awarded the children, the home in the suburbs, the cars, and the money he had accumulated over a successful career as a computer design engineer. Subsequently, when he started drinking he lost his job, and soon thereafter was blacklisted and unable to secure employment in his chosen field. The economic downturn only added to his distress and made securing productive work all the more unlikely. From that juncture, the decline was precipitous, and he was unable to recover. All this, a consequence of the malicious efforts of his wife's well-paid attorney, who was now her husband.

The man sitting across from him, and loudly slurping a bowl of soup, appeared as forlorn as did all the others who ended up at the City Mission shelter. *Evidently*, Howard thought, *he had his own unique set of problems to deal with*. He realized that, for whatever reason, the man on the other side of the table had likewise been brought down to the level of base subsistence, unable to provide for his primary needs. Some of the poverty-stricken men were alcoholics, drug addicts, mentally ill, or a combination of all three; they were trapped in a cold, uncaring, hostile world that, for the most part, was the cause of their poverty, alcoholism, drug addiction and mental illness.

What am I doing here? Howard thought to himself. *I don't belong in this place. I deserve better. I used to be successful. I have a five-year college degree, for crying out loud!*

As the roomful of destitute men were finishing their brief meal, the Facility Coordinator stood up before rows of old wooden tables to deliver the daily address. "Good morning," he announced in a tone that was as cold and impersonal as the shelter itself; his unemotional words thinly disguising unconcern for the lowly and poor. "As I'm sure you're all aware by now, we only have resources to feed you for a two week period, during which time you must find work and show financial responsibility. We can continue to provide shelter and food support only until you get your first paycheck and can afford to get a room on your own. If you do not find employment during your thirteen day stay here, you will have to leave. We are a limited facility and must make room for others who are in the same predicament as yourselves. I hope you are making plans to go out and search for a job today. Thank you." He took a step to exit the room, then, as an afterthought, said, "The daily Bible study will begin immediately after breakfast, in the reading room."

"There *are* no jobs," someone muttered at a nearby table. Howard took his last spoonful of cold cereal. *That's right,* he thought. *There aren't any real opportunities except those you create for yourself.* It seemed an immutable hard reality, much like the reality dictating that the poor are not only disadvantaged financially, but socially, educationally, and sometimes also physically and psychologically. He was aware that the destitute have seemingly insurmountable obstacles to overcome. Even the most basic needs – like food and shelter – were nearly impossible objectives to achieve for those living below the poverty level. There seemed no clear direction for him to take, no discernible path to follow; there were no alternatives that would eventually lead him out of the wilderness of stifling poverty that choked him in its tenacious grasp.

When Howard rose up from the table to leave, the man across from him lifted his head and asked, "You gonna' go ta' the Bible study?"

Howard examined him for a moment; a ragged, unkempt man much like himself. "Why would I want to do that?" he asked.

The one who posed the question did not immediately respond, but only stared back at him and continued chewing, as if he still had food in his mouth. Upon Howard turning to exit the shelter, the man finally said, "Can't do it on your own, ya' know. Can't be done. Need God."

Howard paused, then turning to look back at him, replied, "Oh? And just where is God when I need him?"

There was something about the stranger that stuck him as curious. For a long while the stranger remained silent, as if ruminating for an answer. "Maybe you should go in there an' find out." He pointed the way to the reading room.

God was something that Howard had not considered in a very long time. *My situation is hopeless*, he again thought to himself. *I can't do anything about it. But maybe ... just maybe ... God can. Only problem is, I don't know anything about God; I don't even know if there really is a God. Some people seem to think there is, but they're usually the ones that are the down-and-outters, the losers, the deadbeats, the failures of this world, the ...* he stopped when noticing the reflection of a vaguely familiar face looking back at him in a dingy mirror hanging on the near wall. *Oh, I get it – that describes me.* He tried to smile, but couldn't. *What a fool I've become.* When turning back to the man at the table, and noticing that he was gone, he whispered to himself, "Where did he go? I didn't see him get up. I didn't see him leave. I ... I ... don't ... understand."

Moments later, Howard stood at the open door of the cheap plywood-paneled small room. He listened to someone reading from the Bible: "*Wisdom crieth without; she uttereth her voice in the streets; she crieth in the chief place of concourse, in the openings of the gates; in the city she uttereth her words, saying, How long ye simple ones, will ye love simplicity? and the scorners delight in their scorning, and fools hate knowledge? Turn you at my reproof; behold, I will pour out my spirit unto you, I will make known my words unto you.*" He ventured a single cautious step to cross the threshold. "*Because I have called, and ye refused; I have stretched out my hand, and no man regarded; But ye have set at nought all my counsel, and would none of my reproof: I also will laugh at your calamity; I will mock when your fear cometh; When your fear cometh as desolation, and your destruction cometh as a whirlwind; when distress and anguish cometh upon you. Then shall they call upon me, but I will not answer; they shall seek me early, but they shall not find me: for that they hated knowledge, and did not choose the fear of the LORD: they would none of my counsel; they despised all my reproof. Therefore shall they eat of the fruit of their own way, and be filled with their own devices. For the turning away of the simple shall slay them, and the prosperity of fools shall destroy them. But whoso hearkeneth unto me shall dwell safely, and shall be quiet from fear of evil."*

The speaker stopped to look up from the lectern, and noticing Howard standing in the back of the room, said, "Come in and join us, won't you?" The five men seated on steel folding chairs turned to stare, waiting for him to decide. Finally, when he sat down in a nearby metal chair, the teacher resumed his reading. "Continuing with the Book of Proverbs, we now go on to the next verse that begins Chapter 2:

"My son, if thou wilt receive my words, and hide my commandments with thee; So that thou incline thine ear unto wisdom, and apply thine heart to understanding; Yea, if thou criest after knowledge, and liftest up thy voice for understanding; If thou seekest her as silver, and searchest for her as hid treasures; Then shalt thou understand the fear of the LORD, and find the knowledge of God. For the LORD giveth wisdom: out of his mouth cometh knowledge and understanding. He layeth up sound wisdom for the righteous: he is a buckler to them that walk uprightly. He keepeth the paths of judgment, and preserveth the way of his saints. Then shalt thou understand righteousness, and judgment, and equity; yea, every good path. When wisdom entereth into thine heart, and knowledge is pleasant unto thy soul; Discretion shall preserve thee, understanding shall keep thee …"

Arrayed in a semicircle upon his office credenza were seven computer monitors positioned at a distance of seven feet from a large polished mahogany desk; each screen showing a different graphic display of a world commodity market. The man was comfortably seated in a matching high-back leather chair, relaxed and calm as he watched the price movements of several of his investments – market positions valued in excess of 300 million dollars. On the near wall, positioned directly in front of him, was a large plaque with raised golden letters, which read:

> *This book of the law shall not depart out of thy mouth; but thou shalt meditate therein day and night, that thou mayest observe to do according to all that is written therein: for then thou shalt make thy way prosperous, and then thou shalt have good success.*   *–Joshua 1:8*

When he heard the sound of the front door bell chime, he left his well appointed home office to go downstairs and greet expected visitors. Moments later, after welcoming the two guests, they all stood together in the high ceiling foyer illuminated by three stained-glass skylights. He said, "Pleased to meet you, Eric."

"It's an honor to make your acquaintance, Sir," returned the younger, half his age. The silver-haired gentleman smiled slightly and replied, "There's no need to be formal. Don't assume I'm deserving of respect simply because I live in a big house or because of the size of my bank account. Instead, realize these are things of no lasting value in themselves. They're blessings from God that have been granted to me so I can be of service to others; an instrument to fulfill His work. So honor *Him*, and reserve your deference for Someone infinitely more worthy than myself."

Eric's companion, Alex Travis, observed, "Unlike most people of means, my senior friend here understands that his life does not consist in the abundance of his possessions, but that material wealth can sometimes be a blessing from God, not a curse, as it typically is for most people."

"That was partially from Luke 12:15, if my memory serves me correctly," the patriarch replied, adding, "I remember where I came from; I know what it's like to be humbled. God blesses, or chastens, whomever he wishes. *For whom the LORD loveth he correcteth; even as a father the son in whom he delighteth.* Proverb 3:12."

Eric said, "If it weren't for you posting the bail money, Tony and Alex would still be in jail. Two hundred and fifty thousand dollars is a lot of money."

The man of seventy years still showed youthful vigor in his clear eyes and strong upright posture. Nodding, he replied, "God has abundantly provided for my needs, and now, I look after the needs of His people. Their problems are *my* problems. The children of God are always at odds with the children of Satan. As 2 Timothy 3:12 says: ... *all that will live Godly in Christ Jesus shall suffer persecution.*"

While they walked toward the den, Alex commented, "Howard Conrad is a financier, Eric. He uses his money to help the poor, widows and orphans, and to finance worthy Christian causes. He's what you might call a *True Christian Venture Capitalist.*"

"Now, what did I tell you about *that*, Alex," the well-groomed clean-shaven host objected. "No accolades, *please*. Don't give me any of the credit. I'm only doing what God has commanded all of us to do – we are to help each other; we're to bear one another's burden. My motivation is not to receive anything in return; I help simply because it's in my heart to do so. Besides, it all belongs to God. He owns the cattle on a thousand hills and all the gold; the world is the LORD's and the fullness thereof."

"That was a paraphrase from Psalm 50:10,12," appended the street preacher.

Howard led his two guests into a well-furnished room that was decorated in a rustic motif, where they took up comfortable seating near a large stonewalled fireplace. Walking over to light a fire, Howard said, "I know how it feels to be oppressed, and I know what it's like to be poor – in a material sense. But, I can assure you, to be spiritually impoverished is to suffer a far greater depravation.

"I would gladly give up all that God has allowed me to gain over these past twenty years, rather than go back to living according to the world's values. Like the apostle Paul, I consider the material things of this life to be mere rubbish, insignificant compared to the riches of the glory of Jesus Christ." He placed a log on the fire, then walked back to sit down on a cushioned chair, the flames soon flaring bright when he shortly asked, "What besides misplaced gratitude brings you two here to see me today?"

Eric candidly responded, "I've encountered a unique little problem that requires a solution. When considering the potential for a resolution, I find it is contingent upon the resources that can be applied – the right people, and, of course, necessary funding."

Howard asked, "What's the nature of the problem?"

Eric looked over at Alex, who said, "It's okay. He understands."

The chess master straightforwardly answered, "International child abduction and ritual murder."

Howard matter-of-factly replied, "Government organized kidnapping, child pornography, pedophilia, white slavery, human sacrifice on a global scale." He steepled his fingertips together, squinting eyes as he gazed off into the distance. Then, quietly he added, "CIA mind-control. Satanic Ritual Abuse. Media blackout. New World Order."

Alex said to Eric, "I *told* you he understands."

"And you require necessary funding in order to … what?"

Eric completed Howard's sentence. "Rescue a couple hundred children."

Still fixated on the vague beyond, the minister of finance muttered to himself, "Fascinating." After a long pause, he asked, "Tell me, young man, what's your stake in all this? What makes you so concerned about these children?"

Eric took a brief moment to organize a rationale, attempting to fathom his own subconscious motivations. "Who wouldn't be concerned?" he finally answered. "I mean, what kind of person could have knowledge of such an atrocity, and yet remain complacent about it?"

Howard turned his attention back to his guests and said, "Evidently, judging from the present state of this world, there are many people who can turn away from injustice without having any pangs of conscious. Yet, the question remains: Why have *you* taken this burden upon yourself? Why not simply ignore it – like everybody else; go on about your life, enjoy yourself, pretend it doesn't exist, as if it didn't matter?"

The man younger by 40 years met his gaze with steely resolve when answering, "Because I don't want to be like everybody else."

The senior pondered for a moment, then briefly replied, "I see." The room fell silent, and for a long while the only sound was the crackling flames in the fireplace.

"There are presently four of us committed to this effort," said Eric. "It's a righteous cause, but it's also dangerous." He hesitated before stating, "Mr. Conrad, we need your help and financial support to put together a rescue team to free these children warehoused in a medieval castle over in Europe. There may be two or three hundred of them being held captive, tortured and murdered in blood rituals. Every morning … another child is sacrificed."

Howard's attention was focused on the one speaking, and without breaking eye contact, he said, "Alex, what are your thoughts on this?"

"No need to ask, Howard. You already *know* what I think: Matthew 25:31-46 is my answer."

From memory the financier quoted a verse of that Scripture: "*… inasmuch as ye did it not to one of the least of these, ye did it not to me.*" He eased his head back to rest on the chair cushion, and looking up at the antique rafter ceiling, said, "You know, Gentlemen, there was a time in my life when I would have thought that you were both out of your mind. I would have said to myself, 'Now there's a couple of do-gooders.' That's what I would have said. But, back then, I was a selfish fool – like most everyone else. I was only concerned about myself; and if ever I happened to do a good deed, it was likely unintentional, or calculated to benefit me in some way. But, that *is* the way of the world, isn't it? Rarely does someone, out of pure intentions, help anyone but them self."

He exhaled a deep breath before continuing. "A couple decades ago, something … something quite amazing happened to me. Do you know what it was? … I'll bet you're thinking, *You became rich*. But no, that wasn't it – only a by-product. The astounding thing that occurred was that, for the first time in my life I genuinely cared about the truth. I wanted to know the truth. And I didn't even care what it was; I just simply wanted to know it. Well, as they say, *The rest is history*. When I understood that the Truth is not a thing, but *a Person* – literally Jesus Christ, and His Word, the 1611 King James Bible – when I began to take God seriously and to realize that He cannot lie and does not make idle promises … when I began to *believe God* … from that moment onward my circumstances began to change. I was no longer focused upon myself, upon what I wanted and needed, but instead, I saw the needs of others as being more important than my own. I had a radical change of heart; there was a new spirit in me. I suppose you could say that I was Born Again.

"Well, to make a long story short, as prophesied in Psalm 34:6: *This poor man cried, and the LORD heard him, and saved him out of all his troubles*. God chose to grant me a blessing that I was not able to contain. He first of all blessed me in the hereafter when He granted me His grace to redeem me from damnation and promise me life everlasting; and then, He gave me *even more*. Every day I still ask myself, *What did I ever do to deserve all this?* And you know what? … the answer that keeps coming back is: *Nothing!* I did absolutely nothing to merit any of it. God did it all. It was Jesus Christ – God manifesting Himself in a human body – Who paid the price for my sins when He hung on a cross and shed blood in my place. He died for me, even though I didn't merit it. No one *deserves* to be saved from eternal punishment in the Lake of Fire. That's a place reserved for the proud and the unrepentant."

Alex interjected, "*For by grace are ye saved by faith; and that not of yourselves: it is the gift of God; not of works, lest any man should boast. Ephesians 2:8,9.*"

The elder rolled his head to look over at the well-versed preacher. Now gazing forward to address Eric, he said dryly, "Alex happens to be a Bible scholar."

Refocusing his thoughts, he concluded, "So you ask if I will assist you in this venture, this most noble undertaking. James 1:27: *Pure religion and undefiled before God and the Father is this, To visit the fatherless and widows in their affliction.* That is a command, Gentlemen, not a suggestion. Therefore, what can I say? … *No, I won't help you?* Or, *Do it yourself, and good luck?*" He smiled. "Only a selfish fool would say that."

Eric asked, "Then, you mean … you'll help?"

Howard answered, "Like yourselves, I could not do otherwise."

— 6 —

"Do I think it can be accomplished?" Howard rhetorically asked, addressing the four other men who were seated in high-backed chairs – two on each side – around a polished black conference table in his home office. Positioned at the head of the table, he stated, "I'm a speculator, Gentlemen, a risk manager. Every day I deal in probability scenarios, risking tens of millions of dollars in the world financial markets. Yet, the Word of God tells me not to rely upon my own ability. Proverbs 3:5,6 advises: *Trust in the LORD with all thine heart; and lean not unto thine own understanding. In all thy ways acknowledge him, and he shall direct thy paths.* In every aspect of my life I owe any worldly achievements to the Lord Jesus Christ, Who gives wisdom and understanding to those who put their trust in Him. That Scripture is from Proverbs 2, verses 6 through 9; and James 1:5. Can we succeed in this endeavor?" he mused. "At this present juncture I can only say that if we attempted to do it through our own power, it would be impossible to achieve; we would surely fail. But, it *can* be done. *With God all things are possible.* Matthew 19:26 and Mark 10:27."

Alex cited Jeremiah 32:27: *"Behold, I am the LORD, the God of all flesh; is there anything too hard for me?"* He then commented, "Nothing is too hard for God. He can resolve this situation. His Holy Word testifies that it is His will for this problem to be resolved, and that it *can* be resolved by the will of righteous men. But realize that what we are proposing to do is engage the enemy in spiritual warfare. We're not fighting against mere flesh and blood. Ephesians 6:12. Tony and I experienced Satan's fury through his ministers, the police. As his servants, they're sometimes granted authority by God to oppress God's people, but God rescued us from them. Job experienced Satan's God-approved wrath more than once. The adversary and his demons, through the intermediary of human vessels of wrath such as police, can and do afflict us. Yet, whereas their power is *limited*, the power of God Almighty is *infinite*."

Brandon said, "Those who run the international child abduction syndicate are the very personification of evil. I *know* what these kind of people are capable of doing; I have studied them and understand how they think. And I can assure you, they are not like you and I."

Tony said in a cold even tone, "Anyone who could do what they do is an animal."

"You're quite right, Tony," the researcher replied. "They're actually less than animals, since at least animals don't torture and murder their own kind. They're a distinct breed apart from the rest of humanity. Physically, they may look like a normal human being, yet, they are of a completely different order altogether. In a material sense, they are wealthy elitists who genuinely believe they are superior to all of humanity. They are convinced they *deserve to rule* over others. In their twisted psychopathology, they sincerely consider themselves to be gods, or alien beings from another planet, which should give you some idea of just how demented they truly are. Their all-consuming desire in life is to control other people. They do not think of the rest of mankind as physical beings with a mind, soul and emotions, but as material resources to be exploited and utilized for their own benefit. They consider the world's people to be their rightful property, in the same sense as you or I might think of a parcel of land or piece of furniture. In unilaterally assuming ownership and jurisdiction over that property, they feel justified in doing *whatever they want* to it. In fact, that is one of their mottos: *Do what thou wilt is the whole of the law.* Or so they think. They believe they are somehow entitled and deserving of *worship*, and fully expect that all people should be their slaves and serve them as kings."

Eric astutely observed, "In other words, they have the mentality of a typical politician, judge, attorney, or policeman."

"Yes, exactly," answered Brandon. "The political system was created by men as a justification for its own existence. It is self-perpetuating by virtue of extortion and avarice. Those functioning within its jurisdiction consider it to be an end in itself."

Tony said, "Genesis Chapter 6 tells us who they *really are*: monsters."

Brandon experienced difficulty relating to Scriptures. "Whatever your source of reference, the fact remains they are a distinct species in a spiritual genetics sense. You are correct in observing they're not fully human."

"Or else, they're *too* human," volunteered Alex.

Eric asked, "Do they have any other identifying characteristics that we should know about?"

The scholarly Brandon replied, "The ones with occult powers demonstrate physical and mental feats beyond the range of a normal individual. For instance, some of them are said to possess enhanced visual acuity up to twenty times the norm. This is believed to be fairly common among those that have been cognitively disassociated by trauma-based programming. Typically, they have multiple personalities, convincing alter egos – an asset, I suppose, if one happens to be in politics. Many of those in world leadership positions have been mind-controlled and psychologically programmed by some form of ritualized torture. This is standard practice among the elite generational crime families of the world, and also the various secret societies, for example, Freemasonry, The Mormon Church of Latter Day Saints, Catholic Jesuits, to name but a few. The military produces some of the finest specimens of mind-controlled subjects; anyone with past military involvement has been psychologically conditioned to elicit responses reflecting their programming. Victims of cult torture frequently acquire a photographic memory: they can retain vast amounts of complex information and visual and auditory impressions. They may also be capable of Remote Viewing, which – in theory, at least – is the ability to physically transcend space and perceive distant objects and events. This is not a latent human potential, as the pseudo-science of psychology supposes, but is vicariously experienced as a heightened state of awareness. The sensation seems real, but, like all spiritual and occult phenomenon, the mechanism is incorrectly understood by science."

Alex made an observation. "We're nearly on the same wavelength, Brandon. The True Christian perspective is in agreement with your basic understanding, but where we differ is that True Christianity positively identifies the first cause of all reality as the one and only living God, the Lord Jesus Christ."

The traumatized survivor of childhood ritual abuse struggled to comprehend how a merciful God could allow an innocent little child to suffer harm. Brandon still bore the emotional scars acquired from those closest to him, the very people entrusted to guide and protect him. Because he was betrayed by those authoritarian figures in whom he placed his trust, he therefore reasoned: *How can I trust God, the Ultimate Authority?* In contrast, Eric was the product of a Biblically illiterate culture. Earning several advanced degrees from the finest Universities, he was innately intelligent and "book smart," but was ignorant of spiritual matters. Like his mentor, he had an affinity for the truth, but presently, was not able to come to a knowledge of the ultimate Truth.

"We'll need to begin doing the necessary research," said Brandon, continuing while averting the sensitive issue. "In a study I did several years ago, I was able to gather preliminary data on the Castle of Darkness. There is very little information available to the public. The place is not exactly open for tourism."

Howard volunteered, "I'll get in touch with my European contacts to obtain a blueprint of the building. We've got to know this Castle inside and out. I'll be able to supply transportation and any needed equipment."

Eric made his initial assessment. "We'll need GPS maps of the access roads and surrounding terrain. The rescue plan has to be executed with the utmost precision. We have to tactically outmaneuver them on every front. There's only one way that can be accomplished – we must thoroughly know our enemy."

"Yes," agreed Alex. "And our enemy is *invisible.*"

The room fell quiet while everyone was thinking the same thoughts, imagining what it would be like in a situation that placed them in great physical danger. Finally, Tony looked around the table at the others, and said, "And we must be prepared – each one of us – *to die.*"

—7—

The shine had long since faded on the light blue twenty-four year old Buick Electra that registered over 200,000 miles on its odometer. Although the well-worn upholstery was clean, the owner had never wasted a moment of time washing the exterior that had patches of rust on all the door panels, missing chrome trim, and a right front fender that wobbled at certain resonating speeds. Turning from the dusty back road into the parking lot of the shooting range, when driving over a chuck hole, the sagging muffler scraped the ground with a loud grating sound. "I should have that fixed someday," he said with casual indifference.

Once inside the rustic modern clubhouse, he addressed a lone man standing behind the counter. "Leeson, today I'll be shooting my nine millimeter Ruger."

"Very good, Sir," replied the sprite clerk, unlocking one of the sliding glass cases displaying an assortment of firearms owned by members of the Sportsman's Club. "Will you be firing shorts or longs, Sir?" Using a thick cloth for a cushion, he carefully placed the blued metal handgun on the counter top.

"Longs. And make it hollow points. Ten clips should do it."

"Excellent choice, Sir."

Dressed in a tweed jacket and complementing broad-rimmed bush hat, the veteran club member picked up the gun to examine it more closely. After pulling back the breach and sighting down the barrel, he said, "Fine weapon. I like it even better than my Glock 45. Every American citizen should own at least two or three of these."

Ten stacks of ammunition were placed upon the plate glass. "Will there be anything else, Sir?"

"No, Leeson, that should be all for now, thank you."

Upon turning to exit at the side door leading to the outdoor firing range, the clerk said after him, "Do have a good shoot, Mr. Conrad."

When positioned inside one of the protective stalls, Howard donned earmuffs and began firing rounds at the life-size pop-up targets of various recognizable figures. There was a South American drug kingpin, Manuel Noreiga, and Middle East CIA operative, Sadam Hussein – both long-standing oil and drug dealing business associates of the Bush Crime Family. Their mutual interests in the Kuwait oil fields, international drug smuggling, opium and cocaine production and distribution, white slavery prostitution, and domestic and international terrorism, made such Illuminati families integral to the world's largest organized crime syndicate. In terms of dismantling the U.S. Constitution and subsequent loss of U.S. sovereignty, with the possible exception of former Presidents Franklin Delano Roosevelt and Woodrow Wilson, the Bush terrorist organization were among the most notorious criminals in American history. Howard thought to himself: *The grandfather, Prescott, was Hitler's accomplice; his son, George Herbert Walker, was a German double agent during the second world war and was chosen to be a spokesman for the Illuminati's New World Order global Police State; he is listed in CIA and FBI dossiers as a pedophile who rapes little children. The grandson, George W., was CIA mind-controlled to present a convincing show to deflect public suspicion regarding Washington's involvement in facilitating the false flag September 11, 2011 planned demolition of the New York City World Trade Towers. All three of them were mass murderers, serial killers, and traitors to the American Constitution.*

Among some of his other favorite targets were Bob Cheney, CEO of Halliburton, implicated in the international child abduction network, and, by his own admission, a serial killer; Donald Rumsfeld, instrumental in carrying out directives issued by his Illuminati handlers for destroying American independence and creating a dictatorial Police State in America; and Henry Kissinger, a hold over from the Nazi Third Reich, still being used by the Illuminati for foreign relations policies that fulfill their multi-generational plans. There were a host of other neo-Nazis that forfeited America's Constitutional way of government to establish a worldwide Communist dictatorship. The sporting gun owner was delighted to fire his weapon at cardboard effigies for the imaginary cause of freedom; it was an emotionally satisfying experience shared by the rest of the club members, who were *also* defenders of the truth. While none of them would ever cause bodily harm to a political figurehead, the shooting range was an appropriate setting in which to vent their indignation against unrighteous rulers guilty of high treason. The Club's amusing motto was: *What else can you do with traitors, except shoot 'em?*

Howard's favorite targets were the cardboard image of Bill Clinton. Popular among the club's 520 members, this life-sized target was always in short supply. While the marksman's accuracy was overall rated average, his scores were consistently superior for the full-size color replicas of this New Ager witch. When a target suddenly popped up thirty yards away, he reeled to the left and fired off six shots into the CIA asset, who, through it all, continued smiling like a Cheshire cat. Positioned in the hand of the now bullet-ridden cardboard image – held near his face for all to see – was the Universal Healthcare Card that few had suspected was intended as a National ID Card, a precursor to the Book of Revelation prophesied Mark of the Beast. Had it been implemented in the 1990's, the damning plastic card would have further expedited political tyranny in America. When the last bullet blew the former Illuminati appointee's head off, Howard smiled and said to himself, "I sure like the way these hollow points hit their mark."

A barrage of guns were now firing in succession on either side of where he stood. The club members favored using a variety of weapons, including automatic military assault rifles with detachable box magazines: M-16, AK-47, AR-15, SKS, FAL type, UZI – these were the type of weaponry most feared by the globalists planning to order police to kick in citizen's doors and haul away dissident patriots and Christians to concentration camps. The members of the Sportsman's Club were aware of the true intent of so-called "Gun Control" legislation, realizing that the laws had been copied directly from the Communist Manifesto. They all knew that gun control laws were actually *gun confiscation* to disarm the American public, and were implemented as a ruse to override citizen's Constitutional right to keep and bare arms. The globalist's objective of total military control of America, and also of the rest of the world, was facilitated by first staging acts of terrorism, then creating so-called "Anti-Terrorist" laws that made it illegal for citizens to own firearms. This was the mandate of Hitler's regime just prior to declaring Martial Law in Germany. In totalitarian governments throughout modern history, before a dictatorial takeover, restriction of firearms and gun confiscation was always the first step of the standard operational procedure.

A multitude of pop-up figures, representing other infamous modern-day Nazis guilty of treason, now suddenly appeared all over the field. Like the grand finale at a Fourth of July fireworks display, thirty outdoorsmen simultaneously opened fire, each thrilled when seeing bullet holes pierce three-piece suits and military uniforms of mass murderers and serial killers posing as people's advocates. On the mock battlefield at the Sportsman's Club, True Christian patriots experienced the exhilaration of witnessing New World Order terrorists fall to the ground, symbolizing the triumph of good over evil.

Suddenly, a nearby target of the Russian dictator, Stalin, exploded. Then, a searing beam of light bore a perfect two foot diameter hole through a large tree trunk on the far side of the shooting range, 100 yards away. From the adjacent protective stall, a rugged-looking middle-aged man with short crew cut graying hair peered around the corner and said, "Sorry 'bout that, but I jus' couldn't resist demonstratin' the latest addition to ma' private arsenal: the XR Excitomer Laser. This here dandy cuts clean through solid concrete. Engineered it m'self."

Howard tried to appear unimpressed when he soberly replied, "Can it penetrate a four foot thick stone wall?"

Dressed in camouflaged kacki field attire, the multiple war veteran answered, "If I step it up a few quanta, this lil' baby can slice through tungsten steel like it's hot butter!"

Howard squeezed off a few more rounds, tearing gaping holes in the black hearts of other despots like Mao-Tse-tung, Hitler, Pol Pot, Castro. After returning the hot-barreled hand gun into its shoulder sling holster, he said, "Join me for a cup of coffee, Rex?"

Back at the Clubhouse lounge, seated across from each other, they reminisced and relived old times. Rex Marshall, former Captain in the Marines and ex-Green Beret, was an expert in advanced artillery, demolition, and explosive devices. As a member of Special Forces, he earned a Purple Heart for bravery, a Silver Star, and other meritorious awards in recognition of his wartime valor and skill in tactical guerrilla warfare, surveillance, and infiltration and egress maneuvers.

In the past, when the two friends had occasion to discuss the politics of war, they both recognized that war was not a necessary evil – as some contended – but rather, was *made necessary* by the designs of evil men. "I'm not against warfare," Howard would always say. "I only take issue with *who it is* that are to be the participants. I say: *Let there be war!* B*ut, let the soldiers stay home … and let the *politicians* kill each other. Give *them* the guns and let *them* go and slaughter each other on the battlefields! Transport all politicians, judges, attorneys and police to the deserts, to the rice patties and jungles, to die; load them onto ships, then, torpedo it! Only when all the legal criminals are finally dead and sent to hell, will wars cease on this planet."

As in the past, the war hero agreed, adding, "Yeah, after ya' git rid of the government criminal element, the citizen criminal element is so small the local folk can handle 'em. Like they did in the old West: horse thieves get hung."

Howard replied, "The crime rate significantly decreases on Sundays, the day when most police are off duty." They both laughed. "The police are creating crime! They're the criminals!"

Rex said, "Until the return of Jesus Christ, there ain't never gonna' be no peace. When He comes back at the battle of Armageddon, that's when you'll get your wish. Revelation 19 says so. Until then, the viper pit of snakes in high offices are gonna' keep on convincin' ignorant twenty year olds ta' fight their wars for 'em; sacrifice their young lives so's a few mass murderers can profiteer off the spoils of war."

Howard agreed. "These naive kids join the military because they see it as their only career option; the recruiter promising them perks if they somehow manage to come out of it alive, or with their arms and legs and their mind still intact. They're brainwashed by government propaganda into believing that 'fighting for your country' is a noble thing to do. But once they're in the military, the government owns them: mind, body, and soul. They're used as experimental guinea pigs for testing lethal biowarfare agents in sham wars; they're vaccinated with deadly viruses to give them diseases that are transmitted to their families upon returning back home; they're used as disposable cannon fodder to further the private interests of a small group of super wealthy elitists. By the time they're through with them, their young bodies are destroyed and their minds wasted and programmed to do the will of their government masters. In becoming part of Satan's New World Order army, they forfeited their life to the Beast, gave up their God-given free will and right to His protection. No point in trying to tell them the military intends to use their bullet ridden corpses as landfill." He shook his head when adding, "If only they knew what Kissinger said about them: *Military men are just dumb stupid animals to be used for foreign policy,*' they would think twice about enlisting or cooperating with any government coercion to force them to participate in the military."

His friend replied, "I didn't realize that 'til one day when I found m'self in the heat of battle – in a foxhole. That's where it finally dawned on me. It wasn't 'till I came face-ta'-face with death that I thought ta m'self, *What in the world am I doin' here? Why ain't I back home watchin' all this on TV? How come the Senators and other Washington parasites ain't here with me gettin' their arms and legs shot off?* Well, ya' know, I was just a kid over there in Nam, so I guess I didn't know much better. But I sure enough knew that at any moment I was gonna' die. I was gripped by fear so great that I was paralyzed. I mean, I - could - not - move!" He paused to take a sip from his cup of coffee. "But, ya' know sumthin'? ... when I called on the name of the Lord, I was no longer afraid ta' die. Ain't that amazin'? When I trusted my life ta' the Lord Jesus Christ, I knew, I just plain flat out *knew* in m'heart – like the thief on the cross knew – that I was Saved and goin' ta' heaven. No matter what happened after that, I was gonna' be with the Lord Jesus." Finishing his drink, he appended, "There *really ain't* no atheists in foxholes."

Howard nodded in agreement. They were alike in several important ways. Both loved the truth. Each of them came to know the Truth during a crisis period in their life; each had a conversion experience – a dramatic change of heart – at a critical juncture where everything was at stake. They both knew what it was like to be confronted with the stark reality of their immortality. They understood that death was inevitable, but in their decision to follow Jesus Christ, they also realized that the end of mortal existence was only the beginning of eternal life.

The philanthropist posed a question. "Rex, do you believe that God sometimes uses His people to execute judgment upon those who are His enemies; upon those who don't belong to Him?"

The veteran military officer paused a moment before replying. "I'd seen some amazin' things when I was in combat. Men blown to bits right before m'very eyes. And then 'agin, I've seen men who seemed invincible, like they could dodge bullets. Psalm 91 says: *A thousand shall fall at thy side, and ten thousand at thy right hand; but it shall not come nigh thee.* I believe it ... yes, I shore enough do. God protects His people, and He avenges the righteous. Luke 18:7,8 says: *And shall not*

God avenge his own elect, which cry day and night unto him, though he bear long with them? I tell you that he will avenge them speedily. The Old and New Testament Scripture is full of proof that He sometimes uses His people ta' execute justice … God's Word is always true."

"That was my thinking exactly," responded Howard. "God *commanded* the Israelites to obliterate the pagan nations that occupied the Promised Land. In fact, he *ordered* them to spare no one, not even the cattle. Since then, when has God changed His mind about His people tolerating wickedness?"

"He ain't," answered Rex. "He never did changed his mind. God don't change! He ain't never issued a retraction. In Revelation 2:2 God *approves* of those that hate evil and don't tolerate it. An' in Psalms 97:10, He says: *Ye that love the LORD, hate evil.* He's the same today as He was way back then. God never changes his Word. *Never.*"

"All right," prefaced Howard, "then what should be our Christian response when we have knowledge of the evil deeds committed by Satan's people?"

The forthright marksman grinned a toothy smile and said, "Make life-sized cardboard dummies of 'em, and then *fire away!*"

His companion maintained his focus. "We both take God's Word seriously. We don't compromise it to suit ourselves, or to please others, or to justify sin. We believe it says exactly what it says, and it says that executing righteous judgment is the divine right of God's people." He took a 1611 King James Bible from his field bag, then read Psalm 149:5-9: *"Let the saints be joyful in glory: let them sing aloud upon their beds. Let the high praises of God be in their mouth, and a twoedged sword in their hand; To execute vengeance upon the heathen, and punishments upon the people; To bind their kings with chains, and their nobles with fetters of iron; to execute upon them the judgment written: this honor have all his saints. Praise ye the LORD."*

The decorated war hero nodded in agreement. "Whenever I read the Word of God or hear it spoken, that's the one thing that kin' make me tremble."

Howard replied, "That's why I know I can count on you to assist me and four others in rescuing a few hundred children being held hostage by New World Order servants of hell."

Rex was accustomed to hearing his friend talk in expansive terms, and for that reason was not surprised by his abrupt announcement. He knew that Howard, like himself, was a man of God, filled with the Holy Spirit; a man of righteous integrity based on the Bible, who thought big, risked big, and achieved great things in service to the Lord Jesus Christ. He asked, "You mean, like vigilantes?"

Howard finished off his coffee, then firmly replied, "No. Like true servants of the most High God."

— 8 —

There are two long flights of stone steps leading down a narrow passage; the thick musty air is permeated by the stench of pungent sulfur. At the bottom of the descent, to the immediate right, is a small room containing surveillance equipment: closed circuit monitors and remote cameras used to observe and video record the ritual tortures, pedophilia, bestiality and snuff films produced for sale on the international black market. Progressing further along the subterranean corridor, the dank passageway is dimly illuminated on either side by flickering torches set in dripping wet stone walls. In the half light, an occasional rat skitters across the dirt floor. At the end of the narrow path, a metal door with a small wire mesh window glows with an unnatural light in the semi-darkness. When approaching closer, there is an overpowering sense of oppression and doom, as if the very ground itself is crying out for help.

On the other side of the thick door is a large stone-chiseled cave-like room, brightly lit with stark fluorescent lighting suspended from the ceiling. Immediately upon entry, to the right, along the near wall, is a bank of computer terminals that makes the earthen dungeon seem like a modern scientific laboratory. To the left, on both sides of the cavernous hollow, separated by a wide division, are hundreds of four foot square metal cages stacked to the ceiling, six tiers high.

The dungeon master, a human-demon hybrid of massive physical proportions, paces up and down the narrow side isles separating rows of cages that imprison infants and small children behind wire bars. Night stick in hand, he is oblivious to their constant hunger and pain, ignoring their cries for help as they plead in vain for a mother that never appears. The caged children are emaciated, bruised and bleeding from recently inflicted wounds; they are systematically tortured by frequent shocks from the electrified grids, and also from the metal-tipped electrode at the end of the dungeon master's swagger stick. "You won't be here much longer," growled the guard at a starving four year old boy lying immobile on his side in the fetal position. Weak, unable to respond, with vacant expressionless eyes, the naked child blankly stared out through the metal grates. "You're almost dead anyway," sneered the tattooed monstrosity, showing teeth filed to sharp points. Wearing a sleeveless brown leather vest, the former police officer was armed with a side holster revolver and a stun gun, which he often used on the children, just for the fun of it.

Despite the torture, there was yet light in the little boy's eyes, but, like all the other children that were taken to the Castle of Darkness, excruciating torture and imminent death was their only future.

They were dressed in floor-length black robes, walking slowly, carrying a small burning candle cradled in both hands. They were prominent men and women from the world of international politics, commerce, business, entertainment; some were aristocrats, bureaucrats, autocrats. Most of them were Royalty from old surviving European aristocracies.

As they mingled among their colleagues in the medieval foyer, they were courteous and deferential toward one another, excessively polite; not merely out of respect for the exalted title of the inherited office, but more significantly, because of rank held within the secret cabal of the International Hierarchy. Official government business was openly discussed, since, within these thick stone walls, there was no need for secrecy or to be covert, as they were in the public eye. Those among the controlling elite, having assumed authority over the world masses of people whom they oppressed, prided themselves in their use of cryptic words and phrases, doublespeak jargon that served as a buffer to hide their wicked deeds from an undiscerning public. When functioning in their public persona, they all spoke the same veiled language, using obscure hand signals to communicate coded messages to their like-minded colleagues. By force of habit, they used code words with double and triple meanings, word inversions, metaphor word plays and reverse symbolism intended to be understood only by fellow generational witches and Satanists. There were few outside the Hierarchy who recognized their vague language and symbolism, or who comprehended the hidden meaning behind what superficially passed in the media as banal chatter. Few indeed discerned that world leaders were actually communicating among themselves, the so-called *Chosen Ones* united in a Great White Brotherhood that worshipped Lucifer, the Devil, as their god.

The most influential men and women in the world were the descendants of major historical figures; they were the offspring of some of the most notably wicked human beings that ever lived. If it were possible to reconstruct their lineage, their ancestry could be traced all the way back to the Tower of Babel, man's first attempt to usurp the sovereign government of God and replace it with a corrupted version devised by evil men. In the present modern era they set themselves up to rule over the human race, using their vast wealth and generational occult power to instigate wars, establish kingdoms, depose rulers. They primarily operated through political organizations and respectable corporations, behind the scenes, concealed from public scrutiny. Their photographs seldom appeared in major newspapers and magazines, which they owned and controlled. Because each had intimate knowledge of the others' personal lives, they knew of the diabolical deeds that each was capable of enacting. It was, therefore, out of mutual fear that they postured in affectation of reciprocal respect. Otherwise, they would *literally devour* one another.

After cocktails and a sumptuous formal dinner party, the mood gradually became more somber, their conversation less animated, for they knew that the hour was fast approaching. "What do we have on the agenda for this evening, my dear Maxwell?" a high-ranking member of the Belgium royal family asked the Master of Ceremonies appointed for that night's festivities. The goateed, tattooed man with shaven head, gold ear rings, pierced eyebrows and lips; and who never seemed to change his dole expression, was by day, an elementary school teacher and politically active environmentalist; at night, he was a witch, a sorcerer in a local neighborhood coven. He casually answered, "I think, Sir, that you will be most well pleased."

"Oh splendid, *splendid!*" the old monarch replied, greedily rubbing his hands together, anxious to gratify perverse needs instilled in him since childhood; needs conditioned by a lifetime of generational Satanic rituals. Psychologically programmed by torture since his early youth, a drooping eyelid was the only visible characteristic clue to the trauma visited on this adult child of Black Nobility European rulers. "I simply can't wait," he said, licking his pallid lips in anticipation. Turning to one of his royal associates, he asked, "Sybil, are you thinking what I'm thinking?"

A member of the Mothers of Darkness Queen's Court, "Sybil" – a common pseudonym for someone trauma-based programmed – like the other female attendants, wore a glittering decorative costume mask that covered the upper half of her face. She had long glossy black hair and milky white skin, prized features among female initiates. Around her neck was a gold chain with sparkling jewelry; she adorned herself with earrings and bracelets bearing esoteric symbols from ancient Egyptian culture. When speaking, her refined demeanor was deceptively charming. "Of course you know I can read minds – *yours* included," she said with confidence. Her polished facade momentarily faded when a diabolical smile creased her carefully made-up face. "*This* night we shall *destroy wonderfully!*" When overhearing her prediction, a score of others standing nearby instantly perked up their heads; dignified world leaders from several European nations stopped all conversation to focus upon their mutual topic of interest.

The Belgium Castle of Darkness was a favored destination of the highest-ranking members of the European political elite, those generational members of an international witchcraft coven popularly known as the Illuminati. Inheriting nobility, immense wealth and political influence, most of them were blood relatives. Their marriages had been carefully prearranged, parentage selected on the basis of their occult bloodlines: the greater the evil which their ancestors had committed, the more desirable their resulting progeny. European Nobility was proud of their ancestry and believed they were worthy of their exalted position. They considered themselves to be gods, "Olympians," set far above the rest of humanity, whom they vehemently despised. They presumed to decide the destiny of nations, lording over the masses with cruel oppression. They bartered in human lives, trafficked in the souls of men. They were the most admired, the most highly praised among mankind; but they were the most debased, the most depraved, the most decadent vile creatures on the face of the Earth.

Shortly, there was heard the faint tinkling sound of a bell. Everyone immediately responded on cue, going to the dressing rooms, preparing to take their places, assuming their respective roles as they made ready to reenact an ancient ritual that was about to begin. Twenty minutes later they gathered once more, this time in the Castle's cathedral Great Room. Some were dressed in red or purple loose-fitted robes with embroidered jewels; others were clad in black ceremonial robes fringed in red, purple or silver; still others dressed in animal costumes, donning masks and skins of various creatures, for example, the ram-headed goat, or birds such as the Egyptian ibis. Beneath their attire they were naked in order to allow for sudden morphological changes in their physical stature,

The lights were extinguished; the large cathedral-like chamber room now lit only by pin-points of illumination set in the high domed ceiling, a thousand points of light forming Zodiac star constellations shining through the semi-darkness.

The invocation was recited by the Master of Ceremonies. In the center of the cathedral, a group of twenty-three formed a circle around a five-pointed black star inlaid on the white marble stone floor. Soon they began chanting in a Druidic dialect that reverberated through-out the empty hollow, invoking ancient demon spirits, calling each by name.

A high-ranking member of the European Union was then ordered to come forward and stand in the midst of the pentagram circle. After removing his robe, the onlookers witnessed the spontaneous material-ization of an inverted five-pointed star that mysteriously appeared as a raised welt on his chest. When the ritual leader took his long curved knife and cut a deep gash into the image, the others began to stir, their primitive cravings awakened by the sight and smell of human blood. Moments later, when their primordial lust for human carnage was fully aroused, they began to emit bizarre alien sounds that were un-like those of any known creature. During the orgy that followed, the entire assemblage performed every perverse sexual act forbidden unto man: male to male, female to female, adults with children, children with children; they copulated with dogs, goats, horses, and with the visible manifestation of their controlling demons. In joining them-selves with unclean spirits, they allowed still more evil to enter into them, and into their own progeny.

Afterwards, when their animalistic desires were temporarily sated, they brought out the sacrificial victims: two boys and two girls, naked and trembling, their thin undernourished bodies baring the marks of numerous previous assaults, rapes and tortures by their pedophile handlers. However, the previous systematic abuse and desecrations paled in comparison to what these children were about to experience, because shortly they would be ritually offered to the fiendish spirits of the underworld; these were the same spirits that controlled the minds of all world political leaders.

Demons feed on fear, and it was for this reason that the chil-dren had not been given mind altering drugs to numb their pain and awareness, as they usually were prior to being forced to perform in pornography, bestiality and snuff films. Consequently, the greater the cry of the innocent, the more incited was the power craving of world politicians who ritualistically raped and murdered defenseless little children, just as they raped and murdered the rest of humanity.

Eyes open and fully conscious, a quivering eight year old little girl was the first one brought forward. She was approached by a healthy well-nourished handsome twelve years old boy of Royal blood, and that was dressed in a red tuxedo, an heir to one of the Black Nobility monarchies. He casually walked up to her and offered his hand in a gesture of friendship, then, raising her limp hand to his lips, bite her on the forearm. She let out a shriek of pain, and while he continued to bite her over and over again, ripping out chunks of flesh all throughout her body, the terror-stricken child's sobbing wails of desperation served only to further excite the blood lust of the crowd gathered around. Oozing blood poured from the teeth marks of deep wounds; the child was being ravished in a pool of her own blood. When he bite her on the face and then chewed off her left ear, the level of death arousal was elevated among the European royalty.

The bleeding and disfigured child was then given over to be sacrificed. First, they used the long curved blade ritual knife to disemboweled her. Then, while she was still alive, they cut out her heart … and ate it. The taste of human flesh and smell and sight of spurting blood excited them to a feverish pitch. Next, a high ranking member of the British Parliament, while sodomizing a four year old little boy, grabbed him by the hair and violently jerked back the child's head, then slit his throat. The site of this caused other state officials to immediately go into an uncontrollable feeding frenzy, *doing whatever they want,* slurping at the free flow of blood while vocalizing otherworldly sounds. Depraved beasts, they lapped at the gaping wound with their extended tongues that dripped red with the dead children's life blood.

The third child sacrifice was a thirteen year old boy that was forced to have intercourse with a girl half his age. After watching in amusement, they cut off his genitals and stood by to observe as he bled to death on the floor. The six year old girl was raped by all the men, who then mutilated and dismembered her still living body, cannibalizing the remains. During the ensuing pandemonium, some of Europe's most famous politicians and financiers flickered crimson serpentine tongues as they feasted on the pure blood of the innocent.

They devoured the young and helpless; they consumed the great masses of people. The world was their oyster, to be plundered and pillaged. Their ancestors murdered the innocent; and now, they, their descendants, likewise destroyed life to appease their indwelling demons; to gain more occult power from the generational spirits that controlled them, their actions, and thoughts. They satisfied the demands of their underworld master by desecrating the purest form of humanity – little children. They were Luciferians, witches, bond slaves to the one who gave them power to kill, steal, and destroy. It was during the sacrificial blood rituals at the Castle of Darkness, as well as other European castles and locales throughout the world, that their indwelling demons manifested at a moment when famous world leaders shape-shifted into their true identities as the offspring of a tainted bloodline, a fallen spiritual race intermingled with the souls of men.

They were *not* superior beings destined to rule the world, as they supposed themselves to be; but rather, were quasi-humans, spiritual genetic freaks; a breed of human-demon hybrid, cold-blooded *reptiles* with scales and lidless unblinking eyes. These were the progeny of a lesser god. They were the spiritual descendents of an ancient Edenic serpent.

When the ritual bloodfest was over, now transmutated back into their human form, a mass of naked human bodies held each other in the post ritual "Embrace Predator." Afterward, they remained still, their ancient blood-lust temporarily sated; silent meditation, "Dead Stillness" of predatory spirituality.

Outside the turret-spired Castle where swirling translucent spirits howled in the still of the dead night air, helpless little children cried out in the darkness, tortured screams that nobody heard.

— 9 —

"No! No! *Nooooooo!*"

He woke up suddenly, screaming, lips feverish, panting in short breaths, in a cold sweat. It was early morning in the Western Hemisphere, yet, he had seen it all – in his mind. Now sitting upright in bed, he covered his face with his hands, and trembling, uncontrollably wept.

A short while later, he stumbled over to a window overlooking a typical middle-class suburban neighborhood, where children were laughing and playing in well-maintained yards, and where Tom Zygbowski's Irish Setter was barking at a squirrel chased up a tree. It was Sunday, and everything appeared normal; all was seemingly well. He observed his neighbor across the street mowing lawn; and the neighbor next to him polishing his shiny new sports car in the driveway. When finished, they would watch the ball game on television, have a few beers, then a quiet dinner. On Monday morning they would go back to work, put in their time, and return home to repeat the cycle all over again. And never once would they think beyond themselves; never would they look up at the sky ... and wonder. They lived for the satisfaction of their immediate physical needs; their lusts, their stomach, was their god. Slapping his hand down on the window sill, he shouted, "I *will not* be like them!"

He perceived them as walking dead, in a dazed trance. They were unconcerned about anything not directly related to their own personal needs. Their world consisted of what they could see with their eyes, or what they saw or heard on television. They lived in a state of reality denial, putting off for the moment any consideration of the *final* moment. *Eternity,* they thought, *if it even exists, was a long way off. In the meantime, I'm too busy to be concerned about that now.* Without an eternal perspective, their lives were a long series of repetitive actions that were essentially meaningless. Consequently, they existed for the pursuit of instant gratification, recreational amusements, amassing wealth for its own sake, or, more commonly, increasing their personal debt. In having assimilated the values of a morally bankrupt culture, they were committed to only one cause – *them self.* Preoccupied, self-absorbed in the pursuit of their own interests, they had no concerns that might disturb them on a deeper level; they refused to hear of anything that would cause discomfort or make them reflect upon a greater meaning to life. They were busy in their own private world, a "make believe" world which happened to be a favorite chair positioned directly in front of a big screen TV monitor. For them, *that* was the only reality they knew, or cared to know.

"I refuse to be like *them,*" he repeated to himself when turning away from the window. "There's more to life than driving a new car and living in a big house!" Walking over to the side of his bed, he knelt down, raised his hands above his head and cried out: "O LORD God … What do you want me to do? Speak to my heart and tell me. They do not love the truth. They do not call upon You. They can not feel righteous indignation because they are *not righteous*! They can not understand because *none of the wicked shall understand.* Where are Your people, O God? Where are they? Lead me and guide me. You show me things to come. Show me where can be found Your chosen Elect, Your Remnant who know You and know that You are a just and righteous God, a warrior God, a God *of vengeance*!

"God of Abraham, Isaac and Jacob; Creator of all that is; in the name of Jesus Christ I ask that You reveal Yourself to me. I, Your obedient servant, await Your answer."

He then lowered his hands, bowed his head, and opening at random his 1611 King James Bible, began reading aloud from Matthew 19:13,14: *"Then were there brought unto him little children, that he should put his hands on them, and pray; and the disciples rebuked them. But Jesus said, Suffer little children, and forbid them not, to come unto me: for of such is the kingdom of heaven."* He then closed the Bible, and upon reopening it, his eyes were drawn to Luke 9:48: *"Whosoever shall receive this child in my name receiveth me; and whoever shall receive me receiveth him that sent me; for he that is least among you all, the same shall be great."* Once more he closed and reopened the Word of God, and this time read from Psalm 2: *"Why do the heathen rage, and the people imagine a vain thing? The kings of the earth set themselves, and the rulers take counsel together, against the LORD, and against his anointed, saying, Let us break their bands asunder, and cast away their cords from us. He that sitteth in the heavens shall laugh: the LORD shall have them in derision. Then shall he speak unto them in his wrath, and vex them in his sore displeasure. Yet have I set my king upon my holy hill of Zion. I will declare the decree: the LORD hath said unto me, Thou art my Son; this day have I begotten thee. Ask of me, and I shall give thee the heathen for thine inheritance, and the uttermost parts of the earth for thy possession. Thou shalt break them with a rod of iron; thou shalt dash them in pieces like a potter's vessel."*

Reading the Word of God made him tremble in reverential fear. He was grieved in spirit, having felt the pain and suffering of the murdered children. Throughout the remainder of the day and night he continued pouring out his heart to the Lord Jesus Christ in whom He trusted. *"Arise, O LORD; O God, lift up thine hand; forget not the humble. Wherefore doth the wicked contemn God? He hath said in his heart, Thou wilt not require it. Thou hast seen it; for thou beholdest mischief and spite, to requite it with thy hand; the poor committeth himself unto thee; thou art the helper of the fatherless. Break thou the arm of the wicked and the evil man; seek out his wickedness till thou find none. The LORD is King for ever and ever; the heathen are perished out of his land.*

LORD, thou hast heard the desire of the humble; thou wilt prepare their heart, thou wilt cause thine ear to hear: To judge the fatherless and the oppressed, that the man of the earth may no more oppress."

Unknown to him, near the foot of his bed, there stood a vaguely human form of translucent Light, listening to his every word.

—10—

The flight schedule was announced over the public address system to a crowd that moved efficiently through the terminal concourse: "Passengers on United Airlines Flight 549 to Cleveland are now boarding at Gate 47A. Please have your boarding ticket ready to present to the flight attendant."

A lone man stood over by the near wall, ostensibly perusing the art fresco symbolism that was a mosaic of a centuries-long plan to create a worldwide government dictatorship ruled by dynastic crime families. He was a Delta operative, unremarkable in appearance; no one could have surmised his true identity from any outward indications. When making his way through the mass of people to wait in line and board a plane heading East, no one knew he was a man on a mission, delivering a communiqué from the Global Hierarchy chain of command.

He traveled first class in the front of the cabin, and throughout the four hour flight avoided any conversation with those seated around him. When disembarking at Cleveland Hopkins Airport, he rented a car, and thirty minutes later arrived at the downtown business district. Not bothering to deposit coins when parking at an expired meter on Superior Avenue, after striding confidently across a busy intersection, he walked up a long flight of broad concrete steps leading to the U.S.

District Courthouse, where gold letters above the entranceway bore the discrepant phrase: *The Justice Center.* Joining a busy stream of citizens moving through revolving glass doors framed in polished brass, he passed unhindered through the security check point, then took an elevator up to the sixth floor. Having received his instructions, he knew exactly what to do; it was all part of his programming.

When the number "6" flashed red, he stepped out of the elevator and proceeded to the left, then walked along a wide vacant hallway with sterile hard floor buffed to a glossy shine. Upon arriving at a specific courtroom, he turned the polished brass door handle and went inside. Unobtrusively, he then sat in a bench seat near the rear, arriving just as Judge Carrion Mason was about to pronounce sentencing.

The black-robed magistrate scowled down from his elevated throne, and with over-controlled intonation said, "Steven Daniel Jeremiah, the jury has found you guilty of sedition, as charged. Conspiracy is a serious felony offense against the state. The Supreme Court has previously ruled it a world crime, punishable in accordance with Patriot Act legislation, carrying a sentence of thirty years to life in a federal prison. Before I pronounce sentencing, is there anything that you would like to say in your own behalf?"

Clothed in a bright yellow prison jumpsuit, handcuffs on his wrists, chains binding his neck to his ankles, the accused stood before the oak podium. In a calm voice, he said, "I quote from Holy Scripture, Psalm 31:18: *Let the lying lips be put to silence; which speak grievous things proudly and contemptuously against the righteous.* I declined an attorney to represent me, and I do not speak on my own, but the Holy Spirit of God speaks through me. And what he further has to say to this court is Psalm 58." From memory, he recited the following Scripture:

"Do ye indeed speak righteous, O congregation? Do ye judge uprightly, O ye sons of men? Yea, in heart ye work wickedness; ye weigh the violence of your hands in the earth. The wicked are estranged from the womb; they go astray as soon as they be born, speaking lies. Their poison

is like the poison of a serpent; they are like the deaf adder that stoppeth her ear; Which will not hearken to the voice of charmers, charming never so wisely. Break their teeth, O God, in their mouth; break out the great teeth of the young lions, O LORD. Let them melt away as waters which run continually; when he bendeth his bow to shoot his arrows, let them be as cut in pieces. As a snail which melteth, let every one of them pass away; like the untimely birth of a woman, that they may not see the sun. Before your pots can feel the thorns, he shall take them away as with a whirlwind, both living, and in his wrath. The righteous shall rejoice when he seeth the vengeance; he shall wash his feet in the blood of the wicked. So that man shall say, Verily, there is a reward for the righteous; verily he is a God that judges in the earth."

Judge Mason's ire was aroused when sarcastically commenting, "The Christian God is not registered with the State of Ohio to practice law in this courtroom."

The accused succinctly responded, "Jesus Christ will be your Judge."

The black robe was noticeably disturbed at the mention of the Name, *Jesus Christ*. In an angry tone, he cautioned. "Are you finished? … because if you aren't, you are very close to a charge of contempt."

"The Word of God is truth, not contemptuous," the prisoner of war replied. "I have acted in good conscious when obeying my God rather than man. He commands that His servants reprove those who do evil deeds and conceal wrongdoing. True servants of the most High God openly oppose evil and publicly speak out against those who practice it.

"Terrorists arrested me for being a terrorist, for publicly speaking out against government terrorism. I was maliciously prosecuted, falsely imprisoned, assaulted by police, bankrupted by attorneys, and face a long jail term. I now stand before you, before this court of liars and thieves, among whom can be no justice. You may be able to punish me for doing good, but the Lord Jesus Christ will sentence you and your mob of legal criminals to the *Lake of Fire*."

The Judge slammed down his gavel and shouted, "*Now* you're finished!"

"It's just as well," retorted the political prisoner. "The Bible says in Matthew 7:6 not to cast pearls before swine. So, in obedience to God, I have nothing further to say to you filthy pigs."

The Master of Ceremonies again pounded his hammer. "I hereby sentence you to serve the maximum life sentence in a forced labor camp, the Bureau of Prisons government incorporated Unicor manufacturing facility!" Scowling down at him and pointing with the wooden mallet, he vehemently shouted, "Officers, take him away!"

Six U.S. Marshals moved aggressively toward the bound man, and forcefully grabbing him, ushered him out of the courtroom. Before the prisoner disappeared behind a side exit door, he shouted in a loud voice, "You can silence me, but you can *never silence the Truth!*"

The news media was there, drawing sketches, scribbling notes, snapping photographs. Reporters were already beginning to spin the story, casting the Christian investigative journalist in the standard United Nations Megiddo Report role of "*a Dangerous Terrorist,*" an "*Enemy Combatant,*" "*Right-wing Christian Fundamentalist,*" "*a threat to national security.*" Their lies were published; the courtroom testimony of the falsely accused, was not.

Afterwards, when the court-appointed Defense Attorney and Assistant Federal Prosecutor were relaxing in the Judge's chambers, the distant traveler walked in unannounced. "Afternoon," he curtly greeted. Then, nodding his head toward the court-appointed Public Defender, Victoria Verman and Prosecutor, Edmond O. Icky III, he asked the judge, "They okay?"

Judge Carrion Mason was cavalier when responding, "*Of course* they're okay."

The visitor glanced sidelong at him. "Good. Let's get started." Hopping onto the Judge's polished desktop, in an emotionless measured tone, he then began speaking in short clipped sentences that sounded mechanical and rehearsed; his perfect audio memory reproducing instructions programmed into him at the time of his most recent MK-Ultra torture session: "Public awareness is increasing. The Council of 33 has decided to expedite The Plan. Some defection is expected to occur. You are to redouble all points of contact in your sector of the 9th District, especially the local broadcast media and newspapers. Disinformation and Counter Intelligence Programs are vital to suppress any grassroots backlash. Anticipate further interference from Christian solitary opposition. Make more efficient use of your police against political dissidents. Strictly enforce the Religious Freedom Act. Prohibit Christian proselytizing on the streets and in the schools. Enforce all laws prohibiting reading of the Bible in public access areas, and especially during school functions. Give life imprisonment sentences to violations of home schooling laws. Liberally interpret the Constitution; it is no longer in force. Provide further monetary incentives for increasing citizen surveillance neighborhood watch support. Establish a local Fusion Center to act as a clearinghouse for identifying and detaining potential subversive elements that could be a threat to National Security. Broaden the definition of what constitutes a threat to National Security – for example, anyone who speaks against the government, whether publicly or in private. Ensure that your Masonic Christian pastors are using the NIV Bible version. Promote globalism rather than nationalism. Reinforce media efforts to equate gun ownership with terrorism. The citizenry must be disarmed, or provoked to a confrontation with the militarized police to expose rogue subversive elements. Offer greater incentives to kids for reporting their parents to authorities for violations of home schooling laws and corporal punishment. By restricting their right to religious freedom you take away their spiritual power; they must be completely disarmed. Their Bible is our greatest enemy. If any of your people fail, there will be consequences."

Like a talking head whose batteries abruptly went dead, he finished as suddenly as he began.

Avoiding eye contact, and while fingering his Masonic Brotherhood Fraternity ring, the Honorable Judge seemed to have lost his
authoritative edge when timidly responding, "I-I fully understand."

Switched on once again, the mind-controlled courier concluded
his trauma-induced memorized communiqué: "Seven are assembling
in this region and are presently at large. They're being fortified by the
Enemy and must be terminated. Fraternal Order of Police within your
local Masonic Lodge will keep you apprised of their whereabouts."

The Illuminati liaison pushed himself off the desk to stand before
the men. Summarily, he stated, "That's all."

Judge Mason felt a sense of relief now that the unexpected meeting
was concluded. Regaining some of his former composure, he replied,
"Tell the Grand Council that I will make certain these seven terrorists
are apprehended and brought to justice."

—11—

"Eric Thomas Rider, *that* is the most *ridiculous* thing I have *ever* heard in my *entire life!*" Deborah was infuriated. "You *can't* be serious! How can you be so *insensitive!* Risking your life on some crazy Indiana Jones expedition to – to *who knows where*? And I may never *see you again!*" She began to cry. Between sobs, she quivered, "We-are-supposed-to-be-getting-married! ... *remember*!? It ... it just doesn't make *any* sense!" When she abruptly turned in her seat to face away from him, the others present at the outdoor sidewalk cafe took up sides in the betrothed couple's dispute.

"That's *men* for you," sympathized Pamela, a veteran wife of three husbands running. "They'll find any flimsy excuse they can, just to get out of making a commitment."

Todd, husband number three, attempted to come to Eric's defense. "Now wait a minute. This has nothing to do with that ... *does it*, Eric?" Eric shook his head, still reeling from Deborah's scathing rebuke. "See. He's not trying to avoid a marriage commitment. He's marching to a different drummer ... that's all. It's a matter of principle. *Isn't it*, Eric?"

The maligned fiancé finally spoke for himself. "This is something I have to do. It's something I can't turn away from. To me, it's just one more chess game to be won – only this time, it's being played out on a much larger game board."

"And the chess pieces are *deadly killers*," said Marilyn, who sensed her Maid of Honor status fast eroding.

Connie, the nurse, volunteered an observation. "I think it's a noble thing to go over there and rescue those children. I mean, how many men do you know who would actually *do* something like that?"

Glen, her sometimes boyfriend, responded, "No one in their right mind, that's for sure." Some of the others laughed.

Jeffrey, the career student with multiple Ph.D's, joined in the conversation. "Who are you to make an assessment of his motives? Eric has a perfectly logical mind. I've never known him to make a tactical error – at least, not in any of our matches."

Sterling Harlet, the aspiring lawyer, volunteered his take on the situation. "Let's get real here for a minute, shall we? Eric is doing what he considers to be a good deed. Fine. But he's doing it to satisfy a Death Wish. I've got criminal case law to back up my assertion. For example, Mortuary Life Insurance versus Branbury. The defendant, Branbury, staged his own death in order for his crippled daughter to collect on the insurance policy. It's a scam as old as the hills: altruist does good, dies a hero, everyone lives happily ever after. Simple." He flashed a lizard-like grin. "I rest my case."

All eyes were now on the affronted bridegroom as he gave his delayed rebuttal. "Sterling, after due consideration, I have come to the conclusion that attorneys should be re-classified as an entirely new species of Invertebrates, taxonomically positioned somewhere in the food chain between Mollusks and Nematodes, bottom-feeding scavengers." Everyone laughed. "If several of them were ever in close proximity for any sufficient length of time, they would cannibalize one another." More laughter.

The proconsul sought revenge. "I'll get the last laugh when you're skewered on a spit." His crass comment instantly darkened the light-hearted atmosphere.

"That wasn't very nice," said Connie.

"But it shows how serious this is!" Deborah fumed, turning back to address her husband to be. "This *isn't* about fun and games, Eric. Wake up to reality *before it's too late!*"

In a quiet tone, Eric replied, "What I intend to do, *is reality.* It's all of you that are living in a fantasy world." He scanned their perplexed faces. "I don't have a Death Wish. This is a game played for high stakes, a game that must be won. Whether I live or die, it *must* be won."

Jeffery once again came to his defense. "Theodore Roosevelt said it best: *It is not the critic who counts; not the man who points out how the strong man stumbled, or where the doer of deeds could have done them better. The credit belongs to the man who is actually in the arena, whose face is marred by dust and sweat and blood; who strives valiantly; who errs and comes short again and again ... who spends himself in a worthy cause; who at the best, knows in the end the triumph of high achievement, and who, at the worst, if he fails, at least fails while daring greatly.*"

Eric said, "Thanks for the vote of confidence."

For a long while the group remained silent. Then, Eric's fiancé made a last desperate appeal. "What *on earth* has gotten into you lately? You're not the same person. You haven't been yourself ever since you heard about this ... this *Castle!* You're willing to risk our future on some crazy cloak and dagger escapade, and ... and ... *for what?* The place probably doesn't even exist!"

Eric replied, "There are greater issues at stake than just our future."

In a confidential whisper, the three other women tried to console her; there was mention of the wedding shower, the gowns, the floral arrangements, the photographer. Meanwhile, Todd asked Eric, "So you're really going through with it, huh?"

"Sure."

"What's your game plan? I mean, how will you pull it off?"

Eric smiled and replied, "*Very* carefully."

Marilyn's husband, Jack, conceded, "You've got guts, I'll give you that much."

The strategist's reply was tongue-in-cheek. "Appreciate it."

Throughout the remainder of the evening, the mood remained overcast, conversation strained. Further discussion of the troublesome topic was conspicuously avoided.

During the previous dialogue, no one took notice when a man walked into the cafe and sat at a table in the far back corner. "What can I get 'ya?" the perky waitress asked, setting a folded square napkin upon the tabletop. He seemed annoyed when gruffly replying, "Draft Beer." When she left to get his order, he directed his attention to the large front window, peering out onto the sidewalk, at the group of ten people animatedly conversing. Casting a quick glance at a photo from the National Security Agency's dossier on Eric Rider, he made a positive ID.

"Here you are, sir," the waitress abruptly announced when setting a tall glass of beer before him. "That'll be three ninety-five."

He held out his right hand, palm down, and said, "Scan it."

"Huh?" She looked puzzled.

"I guess you can't do that yet," he said. Reaching into his pocket for a wallet, he presented her with what looked like a credit card, then said, "In that case, I'll use *this*."

"Sure, we take Biometric ID cards," she affirmed.

The patron replied, "Works same as this Mondex microchip in my hand. Go ahead and run it through your scanner."

— 12 —

Hovering two feet above the floor, a three dimensional holographic miniature replica of the Castle of Darkness slowly rotated in space, allowing those present to view all four of its sides. "The Castle is located in the extreme South of Belgium, in the region of Bouillon, near the village of Muno. It's in a heavily forested area close to the borders of Luxembourg and France. It was built in 1877. It's made of red brick and of timbers from the surrounding terrain. The façade is the Romantic style of architecture with corner stones, widow and door frames in white limestone. It was constructed by local peasants, under the direction of Freemasons who used it as their regional headquarters, and possibly still do, since Belgium is one of the principal occult centers in Europe. From this same general locale, Adam Weishaupt's Illuminati infiltrated the European Masonic Lodges, which later became the power base for certain of the European Dynasties, including the Rothschilds, which control politics here in America."

All six men were present as Howard stood behind a lighted control panel directing a computerized life-like Virtual Reality reconstruction of the medieval Castle in the middle of his living room. "The building configuration is L shaped, with the Castle main tower at the end of the long wing. Exterior dimensions in feet are 366 by 166; height: 133. There are 366 windows. The structural dimensions are based on occult numerology. The interior volume is roughly equivalent in size to that of a Renaissance cathedral." He used a penlight pointer to highlight details of the scale model. "Notice the two open drive-through tunnels that enter at the front of the building and exit out the back sides. They serve to load and unload vehicle occupants under the cover of secrecy. The left tunnel circles back in front of the building to connect with the main drive. The straight through drive continues onward to eventually exit at a main road.

"The Castle and surrounding terrain are situated in the Muno Forest, owned by Prince Philippe of Saxe-Cobourg-Gotha of Belgium. My European informants have reported that he owns an international business that manufactures children's play yard equipment."

"The perfect cover," said Eric.

Howard replied, "Yes, and I've received reports of organized hunts on young children in the woods surrounding this Castle." After typing commands into the computer keyboard, a virtual landscape suddenly appeared, showing the nearby grounds and local access roads. He highlighted the forested region in the vicinity, then set the Virtual Reality program to show a series of images on the approach from the long driveway leading up to the Castle, which appeared like this:

"And this is a view of the backside shorter wing of the Castle, showing the drive through and connecting walkways."

Lounging comfortably in an overstuffed chair near the stone fireplace, Rex said, "These mutants think children are like wild game. I'm lookin' forward ta' doin' me some turkey huntin'… and the game I'm after ain't got no wings."

Howard nodded in agreement. Then, continuing, he said, "The next three frames are from ground-level photographs obtained from one of my sources. Starting at the main road, the long driveway proceeds along a wooded area until it branches into a Y about half the distance to the Castle. He used the light pointer to trace the driveway. "Notice the road diverges right here; the left drive leads directly to the Castle, the right side is the return exit. Alex, since you'll be driving the bus to pick up two loads of children, just remember to always stay to the left. In Europe they drive on the left side of the road."

"A short distance up ahead, the drive splits again where there's a house off to the right, just before the juncture." Using the light pointer he indicated the second fork in the road and the 2-story building.

"The house appears to be vacant, but it could be a secondary level of security guarding the surrounding grounds. There's high-powered electric utility poles coming from the structure, and which feed an electrified fence, to dissuade trespassers."

Eric commented, "We'll simply cut the lead wire and make it non-electrified."

Howard replied, "Good. I'll be sure to pack insulated wire cutters." He moved the penlight to the left of the drive, encircling a pasture that extended to the border of the forest. "I've gotten some intel on there being booby traps set over in this area. So look for anything that might be a snare."

Rex commented, "I spent the better part of a year in the steamin' jungles of Nam, so I can tell ya' what ta' look for in the way of booby traps. These are probably the non-explosive kind, otherwise they'd be blowin' up animals all over the place. I seen plenty a 'booby traps in Nam. They're usually small black stakes, about a foot high stickin' outta' the ground, and with a run of wire fence the same height. When your foot hits the short fence it trips the mechanism and sets off a silent alarm. We'll be on the lookout for 'em."

Howard continued his discovery, next highlighting the front gate. "Note the iron bar security gate, and on the other side of the gate this small gatehouse over here to the right." He zoomed to enlarge the image. "Observe the wrought iron detail and the ornate ironwork in the letter M." A close-up view looked like this:

"What does the "M" stand for?" asked Eric.

Howard replied, "Not sure. Could represent the village of Muno, or have some other significance that we don't –"

"It stands for *Mothers of Darkness*," interjected Brandon. Everyone focused their attention on the new speaker. "The colloquial name is the Mothers of Darkness Castle, but the actual formal name is

Chateau des Amerois, or the Castle of Kings. An Illuminati matriarch is at the top position in the Castle hierarchy. That would be the elderly Grande Dame, the Queen Mother. Her son is a Luciferic Highpriest. She presides over the occult ritual ceremonies held in the cathedral-like Great Room that was the inspiration for George Herbert Walker Bush's cliché, 'A thousand Points of Light.' The sacrificial room is reportedly lit by numerous lights in the high domed ceiling, like a planetarium."

"Points of light?" resounded Eric. "Is that a reference to the Illuminati?"

"Yes," Brandon answered. "They think of themselves as individual points of illumination, an occult reference to esoteric knowledge. But, of course, they hate the truth, and everything they believe is lies."

Alex observed, "Matthew 6:23 explains it: *But if thine eye be evil, thy whole body shall be full of darkness. If therefore the light that is in thee be darkness, how great is that darkness!*

Neither Eric nor Brandon offered a reply.

"The Illuminati was not established in 1776 by Adam Weishaupt, as many believe," continued the researcher. "Rather, their origin can be traced back thousands of years, to the Middle Eastern Babylonian Mystery Religions."

Howard proceeded to highlight a clearing about 100 yards distance from the Castle. "This area over here appears to be a helicopter landing pad, a convenient and efficient means for transporting the kind of high level people that frequent this place. It could also be used for transporting abducted children."

Rex said, "The fact that it's so secluded is gonna' provide us cover. That's gonna' work ta' our advantage during the final approach and exit."

With focused attention, Eric made some observations. "We'll need to know where surveillance cameras are positioned at all points leading up to the target. We'll need to know the number of guards, how they're armed, and exactly where they're located. They'll outnumber us, so a direct assault is to be avoided. The mobility of our small group will be an asset for outmaneuvering them. Stealth and surprise will be crucial elements to victory. We'll need superior weaponry and instruction in how to use it. We'll need multiple contingency plans for all stages of the approach, entry, and exit."

"You'll have plenty of time to work out the strategic details," said Howard.

Rex added, "I'll take care of the high tech weapons. We ain't gonna' be out-gunned – that's for dang sure."

Tony reclined on a brown leather sofa; muscular arms crossed, long legs resting on the cushions. "God taught my hands to war and my fingers to fight – like he did David. I don't need any other weapons."

Howard replied, "Before this is all over, big guy, I have a feeling you're going to come in handy."

Brandon spoke next. "In regard to the issue of surveillance cameras, I can assure you these people do not require modern technology in order to know your whereabouts. The reason is because they can simply use their occult powers – remote viewing – to determine your exact location at any given time."

"He's right," Alex replied from the other side of the fireplace. "Their demons will tell them. We have to keep in mind who we're dealing with here: the servants of hell. That's where they get their marching orders. But o*ur help is in the name of the LORD, who made heaven and earth.* Psalm 124:8. We must trust in God to provide for our safety and the success of this mission. As soldiers in the army of Jesus Christ, we need to petition Him to go before us and deliver the enemy into our hands. The weapons that will ultimately prevail against these people are not physical, *for the weapons of our warfare are not carnal, but mighty through God to the pulling down of strongholds* … Second Corinthians 10:4."

"Praise be to God!" arose an enthusiastic confirmation, but Eric and Brandon did not participate.

Alex said, "We're about to engage the enemy in *spiritual warfare.* We must ask God to make us invisible to them; hide us under the shadow of His wings, as His Holy Word says in Psalm 91:1,4. We are *not wrestling against flesh and blood, but against principalities, against powers, against the rulers of the darkness of this world, against spiritual wickedness in high places.* Ephesians 6:12. Know without any doubt whatsoever that the true enemy is invisible to us, concealed in a non-material dimension. But we *will* prevail – not because of our planning or superior capability – but because Jesus Christ has already won the war, and He has given us the victory! Amen?"

"Amen!" the others responded in unison. Alex observed that Brandon and Eric had again remained silent.

After Howard entered more commands into the keyboard, the virtual image displayed a schematic representation of the Castle's interior design; thick walls now made transparent to reveal its internal features. "Remember, Gentlemen, this is only a computer simulation based on the original blueprints I was able to obtain from my sources. It may not be representative of the Castle exactly as it exists today." He pointed the laser light at a large centrally located room. "This is the cathedral Great Room that Brandon made reference to, where they conduct their blood rituals. It's ornately decorated, high walls, balconies; side banks of candles – an allusion to Lucifer, which means, *Light Bearer*, as previously suggested. That's their god. The building is in the form of an L, again, signifying Lucifer.

"The entrance from the main drive-through leads to a central corridor that transverses the short leg of the L-shaped structure, then branches to the left to follow the longer section which leads to the Great Room. There are a number of bisecting hallways along the corridor: here, here, and here, which go to the second, third, and fourth floors." The laser pointer sequentially highlighted adjoining hallways. "The upstairs rooms appear to be smaller than those on the first level, so they might be living quarters for servants and staff, and they might also be where mind-control torture sessions are conducted. To the extreme right of the entrance is the stairway leading down to the lower basement level." He used the light beam to trace two flights of steps to the basement. "It's here in the ground level that the holding dungeon is located. Note this side room, over here … looks like some kind of utility storage. The electrical wiring schematic of the Castle shows plenty of juice going there, indicating the presence of electronic equipment."

Rex commented, "I'll bet I could lob a grenade and knock it out in a jiffy."

Eric asked, "What's that open area in the basement floor, to the left, directly beneath the Great Room?"

Howard highlighted it. "Can't tell. I'll zoom in for a closer look." He increased the magnification to 10X. "It appears to be an entrance to some kind of sub-flooring." He further adjusted the resolution to bring the darkened area into sharper focus. "Still can't tell."

"I know what it is," offered Brandon. "Satanists perform a ritual they call the *Black Hole Ceremony*. They dig a deep pit in the ground. In this case it happens to be under the Castle itself. The idea is for evil spirits to rise up out of the hole when they're offered a human sacrifice. During the actual ceremony, a child is impaled on a large metal hook in the groin area. The victim is cut near the genitals so the open wound produces a free flow of blood from the femoral artery; the sight and smell of human blood supposedly attracts spirits from the underworld. When the children are suspended by a long rope down into the hole, they're physically and sexually assaulted by the denizens of the deep. The trauma is so intense that few children survive it. Most of them die a horrifying death."

Tony stirred, the vivid description hit a raw nerve that caused him to become visibly agitated.

Alex said, "I've heard of it. They're known as *Satan pits*, and they *aren't* dug by human hands. It's a tunnel opened *by demons*; a literal portal to hell."

Howard's light pointer continued following the narrow stone wall passageway that eventually led to the dungeon. "As you can see, there's only one route to the children – along this route, right here, which ends at the door to the torture chamber. Who knows what we'll find in there … it's best to be prepared for anything."

"Y'all should expect confrontations at all points along the way," said the war-hardened veteran. "We'll be ready. There ain't gonna' be no surprises."

There followed a moment of silence, during which time each of them tried to fathom horrors that exceeded the comprehension, or even the imagination, of most people.

Their disturbed thoughts were interrupted when Eric finally spoke. "This place is like a maze. Each of us needs to be carrying a pocket-size electronic tracking and communication device of some kind so that we can instantly locate our exact position within the Castle, and in relation to each other, in case we get separated."

"Noted," said the financier. "Global Position Satellite transceivers will be included in the equipment package that each of you will be issued. Also, computer-generated micro maps. With secured communication and advanced weaponry, we'll have the best resources available. Rex will brief us on weapons deployment and military assault maneuvers; he's an expert with over twenty years hands-on experience. We'll be working with him during an intensive two week basic training program to prepare us for the rigors of what we're likely to encounter. Also, Tony will provide instruction on close range hand to hand combat techniques. Needless to say, there's no better teacher." He paused. "Any questions so far?"

In a menacing tone, the champion fighter asked, "Who are these uncircumcised Philistines?"

Brandon answered. "Visitors to the Castle are mostly from top European Illuminati families. But they're actually all one family – a lineage of inbred generational occult practitioners. Some of them are instrumental in global politics, international business and banking. The Global Hierarchy consists of a 3 Tier system. At the top are the Black Nobility, which are old surviving European aristocracies and their financiers. 'Black Nobility' is a term sometimes used when referring to their European lineage that can be traced back to the Roman Emperors. This bloodline is like a race unto themselves. For literally thousands of years their ancestors were deeply involved in ritual black magic and ceremonial human blood sacrifice. Some examples of these aristocracies are the Royal Families of Belgium, France, England, the Netherlands, and the Hapsburg Monarchy of Austria, Hungary, Switzerland and Spain; their financiers are primarily the Rothschilds. The next lower level is the Second Tier, which consists of rich and politically powerful courtiers to the First Tier dynastic families. The Rockefellers fall into this group, as do other familial Illuminati crime cartels such as Dupont, Collins, Astor, Van Duyn, Krupp. The Third Tier serves the Second Tier, and are not permitted to approach those in the First Tier. A primary example would be the Bush family, of which George Herbert Walker Bush is the main representative. Members of the First Tier refer to those of the Third Tier as 'Useful Idiots.'

"I brought along a list of names that will help to familiarize everyone with who the major players are in the Belgium Castle of Darkness. They're an illustrious lot; I have a research file *this* thick. Keep in mind it is only a partial list; there are many others who frequent the Castle and participate in the human sacrifice rituals. Some of those on the list are deceased." Brandon passed out to the others a typed sheet of paper with the following information:

I.) MAJOR BLACK NOBILITY
   – King Albert II and Queen Paola: Saxe-Cobourg-Gotha, Belgium
   – Count Maurice Lippins: Satanist, Criminal Elite
   – Prince Alexandre: Saxe-Cobourg-Gotha, Belgium
   – Princess Stepanie de Windisch-Graetz
   – Wladimir de Russie Paris
   – Comtesse Dolores
   – La Comtesse de Paris
   – Princesse Amory
   – Philippe Cruismans
   – Monsieur Ygor Chaperon

- Monsieur Pierre Cardin
- Konrad Lorenz: Nobel Prize, Biology: Vienna
- Gerhart Egger: Professor
- Madame Kris Krenn: Director of Television, Vienna
- Comte Andre Batthiany
- Baron Daniel Janssen: Children and Drug Trafficking
- Count Jean-Pierre de Launoi: Children and Drug Trafficking
- children heir and heiresses of the royal monarchies

II) MINOR BLACK NOBILITY
- Pope Benedict XVI Joseph Ratzinger
- Prince Laurent: Saxe-Coburg-Gotha, Belgium
- "Prince" Henri de Croy: Embezzlement, Human Trafficking
- Michael Nihoul: Child Trafficking, Rape, Murder, Sociopath
- Baron Aldo Vastapane
- Queen Fabiola: Belgium
- Queen Elizebeth II: England
- Prince Phillip: England
- Queen Beatrix: Netherlands
- Prince Phillipe: Saxe-Cobourg-Gotha, Belgium; Castle owner

The researcher continued. "Leading the rituals are the First Tier Royal Families of Europe. The Second Tier lacks blood status to conduct the human sacrifice ceremonies, and the Third Tier stands further back during the blood rituals and is reduced to the status of an observer. They all share a common belief in their own immortality and right to rule over the masses. Some of them are integral in the formation of a worldwide government. Participants in the cannibal feasts at the Castle are a Who's Who of recognizable faces seen in the media. No one would suspect they are involved in such a sordid affair; they hide behind apparently ordinary lives while directing the global government takeover agenda and participating in human sacrifices.

"European Royalty enjoy participating in a bloodletting now and then and are not squeamish about carrying on centuries-old traditions of witchcraft and ritual black magic. Names like Evelyn de Rothschild, Guy de Rothschild, and Phillip Eugene de Rothschild are involved in mind-control experimentation, and are known shape-shifters."

Only Eric had been informed about shape-shifting, but for the others it was a foreign concept. Brandon explained. "Human morphogenesis is not a mythological idea, but has substance in verifiable fact. It's a real phenomenon."

Alex affirmed, "The first shape-shifter was in the Garden of Eden, when Satan transmutated into a snake. His descendants still do it to this very day." He then quoted Scripture. "Second Corinthians 11:14-15: *"And no marvel; for Satan himself is transformed into an angel of light. Therefore it is no great thing if his ministers also be transformed as the ministers of righteous; whose end shall be according to their works."*

Most of the others nodded in agreement with the Word of God. Rex said, "I'm gonna' be doing me some lizard huntin'."

Brandon resumed with his exposé. "Prince Phillip of England is at the pinnacle of leading rituals at some castles, but not necessarily at this Belgium Castle. Select super wealthy European and American families are blood-related descendants of the Merovingian Dynasty, the world's major occult bloodline representing highly secretive familial representatives of international high-level witchcraft. The family tree includes virtually every head of the European establishment, in addition to most American Presidents since John Quincy Adams. As I said, they're all blood relatives, therefore, incest is widely practiced.

"The United States is reportedly not without representation at the macabre galas. Researchers have documented the likes of the Rockefeller clan: David and Jay; George H.W. Bush, Al Gore, Henry Kissinger, Alan Greenspan, Warren Christopher, William F. Buckley Jr., and an occasional member of Congress or the Senate. Videotaped murders and various sexual perversions involving children can later be used to blackmail Washington's many pedophiles and sexual deviants should they hesitate to commit high treason by violating the U.S. Constitution. Notables from Hollywood have also reportedly participated in human sacrifice rituals, though not necessarily at the Belgium Castle. The motion picture industry is one of the Illuminati's favored devices for mind-control programming the world masses. "These people can be classified as Pedophile Homosexual Sadists. Like the ancient Roman Empire, this perversion is characteristic of the later declining stages of all human civilizations.

"The modus operandi of the supra-government Hierarchy is to infiltrate the media, education, government and the financial system. The North American main headquarters for the Illuminati is the San Diego area in San Bernadino County in Southern California, a region of the country where Satanism and witchcraft is especially rampant. On the East coast, Pittsburg is their spiritual power base, and Alexandria Virginia is the location for their administrative headquarters. In several Western U.S. regions are local groups of witches covens that are affiliated with the San Diego main branch and consist of thirty members each; likewise, similar 'sister groups' outside the Pittsburgh region are comprised of five to fifteen members per major metropolitan area.

"The Vatican in Rome Italy is near the top of the world occult power structure. The Illuminati Council of 13 is positioned directly above that ancient occult center, and functions through the Black Pope, below whom is the CIA. Child sacrifices have been reported to take place in large underground catacombs beneath the Vatican. The next level down in the International Hierarchy is occupied by twelve European 'Fathers' who rule over the several U.S regions. You might be surprised by some of the names on the official roster, representing the world's most notorious mass murderers. It's safe to assume that anyone holding a high position in government is a child-sacrificing blood-drinking serial killer."

Alex commented, "The super rich are always involved with the occult in some way."

"Yes, that is true," the researcher replied. Continuing, he revealed, "There are a number of other Castles throughout Europe, which the Black Nobility Illuminati – also known as the Moriah – use for conducting ritual sacrifices and for mind-control programming children. For example, there's Balmour Castle in England, and the Exen Castle located in Strasbourg, France, which, in the native language is called Dreien Eguisheim. This is where the Grand Druid Black Council – the main Illuminati controllers of Europe – meet to perform child sacrifice blood rituals. There is also the Chateau du Sautou, near the Belgium border, where children's corpses have been exhumed on the park grounds. All the Dynastic Castles throughout the world serve the same purpose.

"It is said that a major world leader, the Biblical Antichrist, will be christened during a meeting at the Mothers of Darkness Castle, which is reportedly the Illuminati world headquarters. The Belgium Castle is essentially a fraternity of high-ranking female witches, but politically powerful male witches are also in attendance. For them, it's a dress rehearsal for violently assaulting and destroying all of humanity."

Eric matter-of-factly stated, "When they're not orchestrating international wars or flying commercial airplanes into buildings, they're ritually sacrificing little children in dreary castles."

Brandon registered a faint smile, "That's probably not an oversimplification. These depraved creatures have an extraordinary need for blood, especially human blood. They believe that the blood of a still living child gives them an extra boost of occult power. But, of course, it's actually more evil spirits indwelling them. They require a steady supply of fresh human blood to prevent themselves from shape-shifting back into their reptilian form in public. They can lose their human form while sleeping, or the women can spontaneously transmutate during periodic menstrual cycles."

Howard stated, "The vampire myth is not a myth, after all."

Brandon replied, "It's based on the lifestyle of these very same kind of brute beasts. They not only kill to live; they live to kill."

Alex inquired, "Tell us more about the mind-control aspect."

Brandon replied, "The female witches – all of whom are the offspring of top-ranking Illuminati families – were indoctrinated into the familial satanic circle during early childhood by the use of trauma-based mind-control techniques. The intensive physical and psychological trauma induced in them what is known in the occult-based pop psychology vernacular as Disassociative Identity Disorder, abbreviated DID; and formerly termed Multiple Personality Disorder, MPD. Each of the major witchcraft covens, as represented by the world's wealthiest families, have ranking members within the supra-government Global Hierarchy that rules from behind the public spotlight. The Castle of Darkness is one of their favorite haunts where they conduct human sacrifices and perform mind-control experiments on children. Other key human programming centers are England's Travistock Institute and Canada's Wackenhut Corporation. Most U.S. military bases and some U.S. University college campuses have mind-control programming facilities.

"The rank and file Hierarchy of the international Illuminati Brotherhood, as identified by occult title, includes: Queens: *Queen Mothers*; Kings: *Luciferic High Priests*; Princesses: *Mothers of Darkness* and *Sisters of Light*; Princes: *Princes of Darkness*. The presiding head of the Castle of Darkness, the Grande Dame, affectionately known as the *Queen Mother*, receives her directives from the Findhorn Institute of Scotland, which is another major Illuminati headquarters. It's at Findhorn that reptilians, or extraterrestrial aliens, or whatever they are, impart to world political leaders their instructions for bringing about a global dictatorship and the selective eradication of the world population. The end result of this process is euphemistically known as the New World Order."

Howard asked, "Can you tell us anything about how all this ties in with secret societies, like Freemasonry?"

The scholar replied, "My research on the subject indicates a concerted worldwide movement to create an international government for the purpose of enslaving all of mankind by the use of an implantable microchip. The criminal elite at the top of the Illuminati are planning and carrying out government-sponsored acts of international terrorism for the intended purpose of terrorizing the citizenry into giving up their rights as a free people; promising to keep them safe by taking away their freedom. Their ultimate goal is to microchip every person on earth. When they accomplish that feat, they will have achieved their long range objective of a New World Order consisting of servile obedient human drones. Free Will, as we know it, will have become a thing of the past.

"The major players in the global conspiracy consist of some of the same people we're talking about here at the Castle of Darkness. They're primarily the world's Nobility that hail from the highest echelons of international banking and commerce; their sordid ancestry goes back centuries. The world's super-wealthy elitists consider themselves to be chosen to rule over the rest of humanity. In their power-crazed delusion, they view the world masses as mere objects to fuel their perverse dreams of attaining absolute control over this planet, its resources, and people. Compared to the many lower level members of the power Hierarchy – for instance, the 33 degrees of Freemasonry – at the top there exists only a relatively few of them in positions of global political influence. Familiar names like Cheney, Rumsfeld, the Clintons and Blair, are superficial front men acting on orders from their First, Second, and Third Tier Illuminati superiors. As to the secret societies themselves, in addition to Freemasonry, there are many of them. Names of modern representatives are redundant in the various secret and semisecret societies and organizations that form the shadowy Illuminati web of human control. Some examples are The Order of the Red Garter, Club of Rome, Bilderbergers, Knights of Malta, Priory of Scion, Royal Institute of International Affairs, and the exclusive Pilgrim Society that includes only 1800 members worldwide. Among organized religion, key examples are the Vatican and its order of Catholic Jesuits, as well as Gnostic theologies such as Mormonism, Unitarianism, Jehovah Witness, Cabbala Judaism and Islam.

Government agencies and organizations such as the CIA, FBI, and Council on Foreign Relations also function for bringing about a dictatorial planetary government. Various highly select Councils comprise the upper levels, including the Committee of 300 and Council of 33. The Council of 3 are reportedly 3 Rothschilds who occupy the next higher tier."

Rex added, "We all know who it is at the top o' that rotten garbage heap, and that's Lucifer, the Devil."

Brandon resumed without comment. "Among the highest level key members of these groups is what has become popularly known as the Illuminati, which are a vaguely defined body of world controllers spearheading the totalitarian world takeover. They basically consist of the Three Tier Global Hierarchy, entire families that have been crossbred to concentrate their occult power, and represent the puppet masters pulling the strings of the figurehead political puppets that have no real power or authority. Positioned at the top of the pyramid of global control, the Illuminati has long made its invisible presence known by such overt symbolism as the all-seeing eye displayed on the reverse side of the Great Seal of the United States, and also on the back of a U.S. one dollar bill. From the illuminated eye filters down orders for executing the global enslavement campaign ..."

Brandon continued explaining the interrelated connections of the few that controlled the many; the wealthy crime families of the world who terrorize the global population in the name of freedom to bring about their political-spiritual agenda. The focus of conversation eventually returned back to the matter at hand.

"So, when we leaving?" Tony eagerly asked.

"We'll have made all the necessary preparations within thirty days," answered Howard. "In the meantime, I'll arrange for transport to and from our destination." When he turned off the holographic VR projector, the virtual Castle instantly vanished. Now joining the others near the stone fireplace, he took a seat, then said, "We're going up against the most ruthless men in the world. They'd kill anyone without thinking twice."

Tony replied, "But they're going up against servants of the Lord Jesus Christ, the Creator of the universe. And this time, *they're* the ones that will die."

The street preacher addressed the two men that were not True Christians. "Eric, Brandon, what the rest of us believe may sound foreign to you. Howard, Tony, Rex and myself have all had personal encounters with the living God; each of us has experienced the power of His anointing. It's real. We *know* it's real because we see it operating in our daily lives. We're not *church people*; were not *Professing* Christians that talk a good game for appearances. We're True Christians who don't just talk, but *do*. That's why we responded to God's call to rescue these children. We do good deeds – not because we want to appear righteous before men – but because it's in our heart to do it. We believe this mission is something worth fighting for, and, if necessary, dying for. But beyond that, what we're proposing is more than simply confronting wicked men; it's in obedience to God's command for His people to obey His Word to execute righteous judgment upon those who blaspheme the image of God. We know that both of you feel the same way, otherwise you wouldn't be among us." He paused to wait for a response, but none was forthcoming. "We also know that you have not yet accepted the Truth."

Howard said, "We realize that you two guys are here for a reason, and that reason is the conviction you have in your heart. You're willing to put your life on the line for those children. There are few men today who would do that. That's because they are without the Spirit of God. We believe you have God's Spirit, otherwise you wouldn't have gone this far. You could have thought that this sort of thing doesn't happen, and go on with your life. But then you wouldn't be who you are." He rose up from his seat to stoke the fire. "No one can come to God unless He draws them," he declared with poker in hand, repositioning logs. "Your commitment to this cause is evidence that God is drawing you to Himself." He finished what he was doing, and after returning to his seat, declared, "He loves little children and pronounces terrible vengeance upon anyone who harms them. I know you feel that same righteous indignation, and that's why God has included you in our little army for carrying out His will to save those who are precious in his sight. We hope you will join with our Spirit as we go forward as instruments of God's righteous wrath in driving out the heathen and warring against His enemies."

The searing fire popped and fizzled with glowing flares during the silence to follow.

"There's *no way* we 'kin do this unless we're all united by the same Spirit!" proclaimed the decorated war veteran. "I'm not much for makin' speeches, but I'd just like to tell y'all a little story about how I came ta' know the Lord. When I was in Nam, everyday I seen my buddies get blown to bits. You ever see someone step on a landmine? ... One second they're there; the next second – poof! They're gone! Just like that! Clean blown into eternity. I always wondered why it was I never stepped on a landmine, or got shot by a sniper, or taken prisoner. Sure, I got shot at – pret'ner all the time ... had plenty of opportunities ta' die. Almost every day I was out there in that mosquito-infested hell hole. That's how I know I was bein' protected. You see, I asked God – and I was about ta' die when I said this – I asked God that if He would keep me alive, I would serve Him the rest of m'life. I really did say that! I said it out loud so's everyone around me heard it. I told Jesus Christ that I didn't wanna' spend an eternity in hell; I didn't wanna' be ashamed ta' face Him after I closed my eyes for the last time on this here 'ole earth. A few of the other guys thought I went coocoo, you know – nuts – but there was a few who thought like me, and besides m'self, they were the only ones in ma' platoon that made it back alive. The others didn't. Since then, I've lived m'life for the Lord. From that moment on, I ain't *never* been afraid ta' die. Amazin', ain't it? ... Without the Spirit of God – even though I was physically alive – I was dead; but with His Spirit – whether I die physically or not – *I'm alive!* Praise be ta' God!"

Tony sensed that it was now his turn to be a witness to the Truth. "Our faith isn't for show; it's not to impress anyone," he began. "The reason I was undefeated in the ring wasn't because of anything that

I was physically, but because of what I was *spiritually*. There's a lot of tough guys out there, but they all eventually lose. It was the power of God Almighty that enabled me to win. I never went into the ring by myself; I never won a single fight on my own. God beat them all; He wouldn't allow my opponents to prevail. He went before me and beat down my adversaries before my face. He defeats my enemies, which are also *His* enemies. The LORD God gave me superior fighting ability, superior strength, and superior endurance that was unmatched by anyone. It was supernatural. I was unbeatable only because *He* is unbeatable. Throughout my career it was my mission, my ministry, to hold up the name of Jesus Christ before the entire world. I was a role model for all the millions of little children that looked up to me. That's why I never missed a chance to proclaim to the world – on international TV, the newspapers and magazines – that *it's Jesus Christ that gives the victory!* I knew the reason that I always won was because of *Him*, and that's why I never took the credit. He knocks down giants and cuts their heads off! The evil that's in this world trembles in fear of the name *Jesus Christ*. No one can stand against Him. *No one!* There is no power in heaven, or on earth, or beneath the earth that can defeat Him. Proverb 21:30 says: *There is no wisdom nor understanding nor counsel against the LORD.* These wicked men – I have nothing but contempt for them – no fear, no nothing. Zero. They're all going to fall; they will surely die by the instruments in the hand of an angry God."

Eric and Brandon's analytical minds tried to comprehend the meaning of what was said by these four credible witnesses. They *intellectually* understood their testimonies, but did not grasp the deeper *spiritual* significance. "I don't doubt your sincerity," Eric said. "You all seem to have knowledge of something that's real for you." He exhaled a forceful breath of air. "Yet, since I've never had your experiences, it's difficult for me to relate to what you're saying."

Brandon ventured to comment. "Frankly, I find it somewhat disconcerting that I can write on matters pertaining to spirituality, but yet, have only the faintest idea of what you're talking about." He paused thoughtfully. "I don't exactly know how to reconcile that."

Alex responded. "We're not talking about spirituality, which is a New Age term not relevant to the living God. Don't try to intellectualize God. He's as far above us as the heavens are above the earth. He's infinite; we're finite. But if you must analyze, consider this: God created us as multidimensional beings with a physical body, mental apparatus – our brain or mind – and a spiritual aspect that is our eternal soul, which never ceases to exist. God is a spirit, and His Holy Spirit wishes to have fellowship with our soul spirit. When we fail to make that connection by a free will decision to obey God's Commandments, our consciousness is severed from the source of all truth, wisdom, and life. That *life*, quite literally, *is* Jesus Christ Himself. Jesus speaking in John 14: 6, said: *I am the way, the truth, and the life: no man cometh unto the Father, but by me.* The Way, the Truth, and the Life, are all synonymous with the personhood of the Lord Jesus Christ.

"This severing or separation is called sin. Since the wages of sin is death, because of this disconnection of our spirit with God when we transgress God's laws, we die spiritually. When this occurs, we become blinded to spiritual truths; we lose the ability to discern the difference between absolute right and wrong. In this unconnected state, it is impossible for a human being to know God, and a person therefore becomes incapable of recognizing the truth when they hear it. Consequently, their moral sense deteriorates, the distinction between good and evil is blurred, and their soul is cut off from God." He paused briefly to wait for a reply, but again, there was none.

"Since separation from God results in a lack of Godly wisdom and spiritual discernment, anyone that has not accepted Jesus Christ – Who is The Truth – will not be able to correctly understand the truth concerning matters of good and evil, right and wrong. Such an individual needs to repent, turn away from their sins, and toward the truth of God's Word, the 1611 King James Bible. Those that have

not repented of their sins are in a state known as *Spiritual Blindness.*
This is the present condition that both of you find yourself in, and it's
the reason why you're having difficulty relating to what we're saying.
Satan is hindering you from acting on the truth and receiving the
Spirit of Truth that God gives to all those who receive Him as their
Lord and Savior. 2 Corinthians 4:3,4: *But if our gospel be hid, it is hid to
them that are lost: In whom the god of this world hath blinded the minds
of them which believe not, lest the light of the glorious gospel of Christ,
who is the image of God, should shine unto them.* Isaiah 44:18 further
explains: *They have not known nor understood: for he hath shut their
eyes, that they cannot see; and their hearts, that they cannot understand.*
Until you have a complete change of heart – until you repent – you
will continue to be opposed by an invisible enemy; you will remain
blinded to what is easily understood by even a child. You will be, as
it says in 2 Timothy 3:7: *Ever learning, and never able to come to the
knowledge of the truth.* Most people remain in darkness their entire
life, never coming to a knowledge of the truth about who they are
spiritually and their true purpose for being here on this earth.

"The unsaved, the Spiritually Blind, oppose those who love the
truth, and in so doing, give evidence of their allegiance – that it is not
with God. Unless they repent before leaving this material existence,
they will incur the just wrath of the Almighty at the Final Judgment.
At that time, the unrepentant are judged according to their unrighteous deeds, and the Lake of Fire is their eternal destiny. But those
redeemed by the shed blood of the Lamb of God are not judged by
their *deeds*, but rather, by their *faith* in the Lord Jesus Christ. They
believe God's Word – Jesus Christ, the Word of God, the 1611 King
James Bible – and live by His Word, and are Saved by grace, not by
works. Ephesians 2:8,9 tells us: *For by grace are ye saved through faith;
and that not of yourselves: it is the gift of God: not of works, lest any man
should boast.*

"To partake of the spirit of Truth, you must be Born into the
Kingdom of God. As John 3:3 says: *Verily, verily, I say unto thee, Except*

a man be born again, he cannot see the kingdom of God. Revelation 3:20 explains: *Behold, I stand at the door, and knock; if any man hear my voice, and open the door, I will come in to him, and will sup with him, and he with me.* All that you have to do is open the door and let Him in. It's really that simple."

The two men were pensive during the protracted silence to follow. Suddenly, the standoff was interrupted by a soft rap on the front door. All eyes were immediately drawn in that direction. The room fell silent. No one spoke a word. Then, there came another quiet knock. Everyone remained frozen in place. Finally, Eric said to no one in particular, "Aren't you going to answer it?" His eyes met those of his confident associates.

Brandon's gaze remained downcast as he quietly muttered to himself, "Interesting," marveling at the well-timed synchronicity. "Very interesting indeed."

Howard cleared his throat. "Well I … I suppose I should go see who it is." He then rose up to walk the distance to the open foyer. When there, after taking a quick glance at the remote security monitor, he unlocked the door and turned the knob.

Standing outside on the cobblestone steps was a middle-aged man of slight build, Latino complexion and crystal clear diamond blue eyes. "Excuse me, Sir," he said. "As to why I'm here … all I know is … I should be."

— 13 —

"Men, this is Adam," Howard announced, re-entering the room five minutes later, an unexpected visitor now at his side. "Adam, over there is Eric, Rex, Tony, Brandon and Alex." Each acknowledged with a nod or wave of the hand. "It seems that … a … Adam here has something he would like to tell us." The host directed him to a nearby chair, where the visitor took a seat and hesitantly began to address the small group.

"Uh, yes … as you all know, my name is Adam – Adam Vistajaarta. I was the first born child in a family of Mexican migrant workers. We were very poor. Both my parents were Christians. Before I was born, they consecrated me to the Lord Jesus Christ. At an early age I began to tell of things that were to come. Later, when I grew older, God sent me dreams and visions; I can sometimes know the future. It is a spiritual gift of prophesy. Praise be to God." Their gazes were now riveted upon the stranger who commanded their full attention. "I saw in a dream … this house, this very address. It is why I knew to come here. The reason is to tell you what God has shown me.

"In this dream, I saw that you were all in very great danger, and have terrible enemies seeking to kill you. They are wicked men, servants of Satan, who is coming against you to prevent you from doing the will of God. Then, I saw the little ones, the children. They were suffering greatly and caused to die because there was no one to stand up for them in the gap. Daily they are offered as a sacrifice – to the evil one, yet there is no one to help them. These children are very precious in the eyes of God; they cry out, yet, everyday more are slaughtered as are sheep."

He then began to prophesy: "Thus saith the LORD: *They cried unto the LORD in their trouble, and he delivered them out of their distresses. He shall judge the poor of the people, he shall save the children of the needy, and shall break in pieces the oppressor.*

"You are not to fear these men; they are subject to you because of the power that you have in the Most high name of the Lord Jesus Christ. Thus saith the LORD: *Fear thou not; for I am with thee: be not dismayed; for I am thy God: I will strengthen thee; yea, I will help thee; yea, I will uphold thee with the right hand of my righteousness. Behold, I give unto you power to tread on serpents and scorpions, and over all the power of the enemy; and nothing shall by any means hurt you. Thou shalt not be afraid of them: but shalt well remember what the LORD thy God did unto Pharaoh, and unto all Egypt; Thou shalt not be affrighted at them: for the Lord thy God is among you, a mighty God and terrible.*

"You will be delivered from all evil. Thus saith the LORD: *Surely he shall deliver thee from the snare of the fowler, and from the noisome pestilence.... There shall no evil befall thee, neither shall any plague come nigh thy dwelling.*

"You are chosen vessels of God's wrath poured out upon the heathen, upon those who hate God, and whom God hates. Thus saith the LORD: *The face of the LORD is against them that do evil, to cut off remembrance of them from the earth. O LORD, when thou awakest, thou shalt despise their image. Know therefore that the LORD thy God, he is God, the faithful God, which keepeth covenant and mercy with them that love him and keep his commandments to a thousand generations. And repayeth them that hate him to their face, to destroy them: he will not be slack to him that hateth him, he will repay him to his face.*

"God has delivered them into your hands; they have no power over you, and none of their lives are to be spared. Show them no mercy, for the Spirit of the Lord goes before you to give you the victory for the glory of God. Thus saith the LORD: *Behold, all they that were incensed against thee shall be ashamed and confounded: they shall be as nothing; and they that strive with thee shall perish. Thou shalt seek them, and shalt not find them, even them that contended with thee: they that war against thee shall be as nothing, and as a thing of nought. And when the LORD thy God shall deliver them before thee; thou shalt smite them, and utterly destroy them; thou shalt make no covenant with them, nor show mercy unto them. But thus shall ye deal with them: ye shall destroy their altars, and break down their images, and cut down their groves, and burn their graven images with fire.*

"You are instruments of God's righteous judgment. Thus saith the LORD: *Thou whom I have taken from the ends of the earth, and called thee from the chief men thereof, and said unto thee, Thou art my servant; I have chosen thee, and not cast thee away.*

"You are to deliver these children, and God will go before you and grant you the victory. Thus saith the LORD: *And I will beat down his foes before his face, and plague them that hate him. And thou shalt consume all the people which the LORD thy God shall deliver thee; thine eye shall have no pity upon them: neither shalt thou serve their gods; for that will be a snare unto thee. But the LORD thy God shall deliver them unto thee, and shall destroy them with a mighty destruction, until they be destroyed. And he shall deliver their kings into thine hand, and thou shalt destroy their name from under heaven: there shall no man be able to stand before thee, until thou have destroyed them.*

"There are two among you that do not have the Spirit of Truth. They must come to Jesus Christ. Only *then* will God be with you in all that you do."

When Adam had finished with the outpouring of God's Holy Spirit, the others sat quietly in stunned amazement. Alex tentatively inquired, "Is there … anything else, Adam?"

"That is all that the Holy Spirit has revealed to me at this time."

Eric was studying him carefully, noting his every movement and gesture. "How do we know this hasn't been staged for the benefit of Brandon and myself?"

Before anyone could answer, Brandon replied, "I don't think that's what we're seeing here. He's obviously not rehearsed this. There's been no indications in his mannerisms or micro-involuntary reflexes to suggest he's lying. I think we should take what he has to say at face value."

"Gentlemen, this is not a game," said Howard, coming forward to stand in the midst of them. "God can, and does, speak through His servants. We're living in the last days, a time foretold of in the Bible – in the Book of Joel – when this sort of thing is supposed to occur."

Alex appended, "That's in Chapter 2, verse 28."

Rex added, "If you two guys wanna' play Russian roulette with your life, just keep on resistin' God's Holy Spirit when He calls ya' to repentance. You ain't got no guarantees that you'll ever get another chance but right now."

Brandon's focused mind reviewed each item carefully, sorting every detail, every piece of information, weighing it against a lifetime of disciplined learning and worldly experience. "I can see no logical inconsistency in any of what's been said. Does that mean I'm beginning to be convinced?"

"The term is *convicted*," said Howard, resuming his seat. "Convicted by the Holy Spirit."

"All right, so there's even a name for it," the author replied. "What makes it official?"

The street preacher said, "You first of all need to realize that this isn't some sort of ritual formula or exercise where you repeat magic words and then you're Saved and on your way to heaven. There has to be a heartfelt deep inner conviction, or it's meaningless in the eyes of God. Psalm 34:18 assures: *The LORD is nigh unto them that are of a broken heart; and saveth such as be of a contrite spirit.* If your decision to follow Jesus Christ is genuine – and only you and He know that – you'll experience a significant change in your spirit, in your actions, words, and thoughts."

Eric pondered for a moment. "And if we don't decide in favor of Jesus Christ … what are the stakes?"

Tony answered succinctly. "Eternal damnation. And eternity is forever."

"High stakes," the strategist blandly responded. "Real place … this hell?"

"As real as it gets," returned the fighter.

His childhood friend said, "Tony, I've never known you to lie."

"It has nothing to do with me personally," corrected Tony. "It's God's Word that you can trust. It's *He* that's never lied."

After a brief pause, the chess master concluded, "The premises appear to be irrefutable – that is, if God cannot lie, and if He said what you're telling me, then, given the consequences, I would have to be extremely foolish to reject it as untrue."

"Either that, or *Spiritually Blind*," said Brandon, who further confirmed when saying, "I think I'm now beginning to understand the true meaning of that phrase."

Eric then asked, "Where do I sign?"

"In your heart," answered Tony. "Just invite the Savior, the Lord Jesus Christ, to come into your life, and ask His Holy Spirit to live within you. State your commitment to the living God verbally; say it out loud. That way, heaven, earth, and hell will be a witness."

Eric seemed disappointed when saying, "You mean … that's *it*? That's *all* there is to it? Sounds too easy."

"No, no, no," answered Rex. "That's only the first step. If ya' mean it, God's Spirit'l show ya' the rest of what ya' gotta' do ta' be Saved into His Kingdom."

"Do?" questioned Brandon.

Howard explained. "Most people think they're Saved by simply saying the sinners prayer. But that's not true; that's not what the Bible teaches. A profession of faith *is only the beginning* of proving one's sincerity toward God. Although we're not Saved by our works – that is, there's nothing we can personally do to gain salvation – yet, there is still the issue of *obedience* to God. The gospel of salvation is *conditional*; God's Word instructs that *If* we truly love the Lord we will keep His

Commandments. That's found in John 14:15. Jesus also said that *If you persevere until the end, you will be Saved.* Revelation 2:26. We're Saved by *hope* in the Lord's mercy. Romans 8:24. Although individuals professing Christianity believe they are Saved, relatively few actually are."

"That's found in 1 Peter 4:18; Matthew 7:14; 20:16; 22:14," offered Alex.

Howard nodded in appreciation. "Thank you." He continued clarifying the popular doctrinal error of 'Once Saved Always Saved.' *"Ye shall know them by their fruits.* Matthew 7:16 and 20. That's one of the evidences of the Spirit of God working in your life – the fruits – or good works, which are a testimony that you have been reborn into the Kingdom of God. So then, if there are no outward indications of a change of heart, no evidence that someone claiming to be Saved is, in fact, Saved, that person is not regenerated, not Saved, but is only fooling them self."

Adam said, "Also, to be Saved, you must repent of all sin in your life. *Repent* means *to turn away from,* to stop sinning. Jesus commanded us in Mark 1:15: ... *repent ye, and believe the gospel.* Also, you must remain faithful to the Word of God and persevere in obedience to God's Laws *until the end.* That means, until death. If you turn away from sin and persevere, you will be Saved. Ezekiel 18:21,22 tells of that which I have said." He took a small 1611 King James Bible from his shirt pocket and read: *But if the wicked will turn from all his sins that he hath committed, and keep all my statutes, and do that which is lawful and right, he shall surely live, he shall not die. All his transgressions that he hath committed, they shall not be mentioned unto him: in his righteousness that he hath done he shall live.* This teaching is again in the verses of 27 and 28."

Alex further instructed, "Another evidence of being Saved is having a zeal for God's Word. In regard to the dead works of Roman Catholicism, or Judaism, or other Jesus Christ rejecting philosophies or religions, Romans 10:2 warns us *they have a zeal of God, but not according to knowledge.* In Matthew 15:8,9, Jesus said: *This people draweth nigh unto me with their mouth, and honoureth me with their lips; but their heart is far from me. But in vain they do worship me, teaching for doctrines the commandments of men.* In other words, they have a *different Jesus.* Eternal salvation has nothing to do with religious observance of man-made laws and traditions. Religious institutions are full of pious hypocrites. Those who are truly Saved believe that God is not divided, but is One, and therefore has only one written Covenant with man: the Old and New Testament of His Holy Word, which is the 1611 Authorized King James Bible. Psalm 119:89 declares: *For ever, O LORD, thy word is settled in heaven.* A person who is Saved will reject all other Bible versions as changed manuscript perversions. He upholds and defends the 1611 KJV to be the only true Word of God for the English-speaking people. Anyone who denies the 1611 King James Bible to be the only true and incrrant Word of God has committed the unforgivable sin of *blasphemy against the Holy Spirit.* They have not only denied Holy Scripture, but have also blasphemed God by denigrating His Word to a generic status. In equating the only true Bible with all the many Satan-inspired versions that are available today – apostate renditions such as the NIV, NAS; the Catholic, Mormon, Jehovah Witness, Masonic, and many other false versions – the unsaved give evidence of their antichrist spirit. The complete and correctly transliterated Old and New Testament is found *only* in the 1611 King James Holy Bible, and not in any other popular facsimile."

Howard noted, "Compared to the Authorized 1611 King James, the NIV has 64,000 missing words and entire verses deleted. One of the manuscript editors was an avowed lesbian."

Alex appended, "The so-called *Christian* publishing industry is thoroughly corrupt to the core, totally sold out to the Devil, and not in the least bit interested in publishing the truth. Disinformation and lies is what sells well for them. Nearly all books offered in Christian book stores were written by authors who compromised the truth and deny the Word of God.

"The modern apostate churches, which includes nearly 100 percent of so-called Christianity in America today, are much like the first century Laodicean church described in Revelation 3:14-18. These churches are *social clubs* peopled with lukewarm individuals who give their allegiance to the Beast government. They are not Churches of Jesus Christ, but 501(c)3 tax exempt *government corporations*. They are not the body of Christ, but have joined themselves in spiritual adultery to the Revelation Chapter 17 Whore of Babylon, where Satan dwells. The leader of these so-called *churches* is the government; they are *government churches* headed by the state's Attorney General, *not* Jesus Christ. The pastor signed a document to confirm this, and in so doing, agreed not to speak against Satan's New World Order or any of its worldly domains or agendas, such as homosexuality, abortion, Martial Law, citizen surveillance, processed food additives, chemically doped drinking water, Chemtrail aerial spraying, vaccines, planned genocide and terrorism, and so on. The Bible tells us in Colossians 1:18 that Jesus Christ is the Head of the *true Church*. Therefore, 501(c)3 churches *are not* True Christian Churches, but are spiritual whore houses that commit fornication with the unclean Beast government of man. The Holy Spirit does not reside in *any* of them."

"They're all spiritual fornicatin' whores," reiterated Rex. "They fornicate with the world, the Great Whore of Babylon. There ain't a bit a difference between them and a nonbeliever. Synagogues of Satan is what they are."

Howard agreed, then said, "Today's *Professing* Christians don't dare speak out against the wickedness of human government and its Jesus Christ-rejecting leaders. By their silence, they are partakers in the evil done by organized governments. Their silence is betrayal. They deny the Word of God, which instructs in Ephesians 5:11: … *have no fellowship with the unfruitful works of darkness, but rather reprove them.* Instead, pseudo-Christians have abdicated any resistance to wrongdoing and are merely hoping to save their own yellow hides by holding out for a nonexistent *Pre-Tribulation Rapture* to bodily remove them from the earth so they won't have to suffer Antichrist government persecution for the cause of Jesus Christ. Nearly every person who walks into the church building of an organized religion on Sunday *hates the truth*. The Truth is Jesus Christ. John 14:6. If they loved the Truth, Jesus Christ, they would be in obedience to God's Word, which says in John 14:15: *If ye love me, keep my commandments;* and Revelation 18:4: *Come out of her, my people, that ye be not partakers of her sins, and that ye receive not of her plagues.* Also, Second Corinthians 6:17: ... *come out from among them, and be ye separate, saith the Lord, and touch not the unclean thing; and I will receive you."*

Tony said, "The mark of a false Christian is someone who says, 'Jesus loves you,' but does nothing to bear another's burden. They smile and profess to be righteous, but in their heart they're whitewashed tombs full of hypocrisy."

Alex said, "Professing Christians don't know God, but *only profess* to know Him. Titus 1:16: *They profess that they know God; but in works they deny him, being abominable, and disobedient, and unto every good work reprobate.* They fear man and his Beast government, not God. Professing Christians do not publicly speak out against evil; and neither are they willing to suffer persecution from the police, politicians, judges and attorneys that are the earthly foot soldiers in Satan's army. Revelation 21:8 warns these *fearful* Professing Christians that they will be the *first ones* to be cast into the Lake of Fire."

Tony pointed out: "The Church of Jesus Christ is not a building or the people who go to a building which they call a church. The *True* Church is the body of *True* Christian believers in all the world, throughout all of human history. They recognize each other, but, a phony Christian cannot recognize a True Christian. You can always tell when you're talking to a fake Christian because when you use God's Word to reprove them of their false beliefs, they'll attack you. As Isaiah 59:15,16 says: ... *he that departeth from evil maketh himself a prey.* It's a Saved person who does as the LORD has commanded by standing up for the truth, instead of defending a lie."

Alex expounded: "The basic teaching of the gospel message is to believe that Jesus Christ is God, the Messiah, sent by the LORD God – the first person of the Godhead trinity, and Who is an eternal Spirit – to redeem mankind from their fallen nature. Even Professing Christians believe this, and most of them will affirm that all Scripture is inerrantly true. However, from that juncture they fall away from the truth of the gospel, which is prophesied in 2 Thessalonians 2:3, and which false Christians wrongly believe refers to a non-existent Pre-Tribulation Rapture. Those who are resistant to the 1611 KJV, or who otherwise deny *any* part of the Scriptures, or believe another gospel or use another Bible version other than the 1611 Authorized King James, have denied God according to Galatians 1:8,9; they have *another gospel* and do not have God's spirit of Truth. Without the spirit of Truth they cannot possibly be Saved, but are perishing and condemned according to 2 Thessalonians 2:10-12: ... *with all deceivableness of unrighteousness in them that perish; because they received not the love of the truth, that they might be saved. And for this cause God shall send them strong delusion, that they should believe a lie: that they all might be damned who believed not the truth, but had pleasure in unrighteousness.*"

Rex summarized when saying, "What they're trying to tell ya' all is that ya' gotta' be *Born Again*. That's in John 3:3. You gotta' be changed from the *inside* – in your heart spirit. If your spirit ain't been changed, then you ain't Born Again. In that case, you're just plain flat out *not Saved*. Period. Ya' just think ya' are, and that won't cut it on Judgment Day when standin' before the Great White Throne of a righteous Almighty God pourin' out His wrath upon sinners."

"For now, don't worry about all the details," appended Tony. "Just trust God that your past sins are forgiven and covered by Jesus Christ's shed blood. Read His Word every day and keep His Commandments; talk to Him in your thoughts and out loud. His Holy Spirit will do the rest. Salvation is a heart thing, not a mind thing."

Eric looked over at Brandon, then at the others. "No way we can lose – right?"

"No way," assured the high stakes risk manager, Howard. "When you're playing on God's team, it's *absolutely impossible* to lose out in eternity."

"I've read the Bible," said Brandon. "Until now, I haven't given the matter of salvation much thought. The historic and scientific evidence in support of the Bible's veracity and authenticity is beyond reproach. It actually confirms history and science. But even more than that, I realize there is a larger issue here, something more than mere printed words on a page. Our consciousness does not cease at the moment of physical death. Therefore, any rational, thinking person must address the issue of eternity. The universe could not have come into being of its own accord; Whatever or Whoever created it must have also created us. Evolution is a silly myth believed only by those afraid to confront the ultimate questions concerning life and death. It has no scientific basis in fact. Those in support of it trust in Darwin rather than God, because to reject evolution leaves a void in their mind that can only be filled by God, Who's condemnation they wish to evade for as long as possible."

Alex observed, "What you just said tells me you're not far from the Kingdom of God."

Brandon shifted in his seat, let out a sigh of resignation, then said, "If I can know that these globalists are wrong in what they do, and that you men are correct; and know that the Bible is true, and that anything contradicting it is false; and if I realize the severe consequences of denying what the Bible has to say in regard to the eternity destiny of the soul … then I can only hope that God is as merciful as He says He is, because I am going to need a great deal of mercy."

Howard replied, "We all need God's mercy. Acknowledgment of your transgressions against God's Law is the first step toward receiving that mercy. It sounds to me like you've just taken the first step."

Everyday throughout the world, people like Eric and Brandon – those who love the truth and will not compromise it – experience the convicting power of God's Holy Spirit. They went on to make an open profession of their faith in Jesus Christ, acknowledging Him as

God, their Redeemer, Lord, and Savior. They asked for His forgiveness of their sins, and vowed to repent of their unrighteous deeds. When finished, they were congratulated by the others, and with a sense of renewed camaraderie, there was now present among them a Spirit of unity.

The seven bowed their heads while the elder, Howard, led them in a prayer. "LORD God, in the name of Jesus Christ, we come before Your throne to offer our thanks for what Your Holy Spirit has done for Eric and Brandon this day. We know that they are now our Brothers in faith in You, and that all of us are one spirit with You. May Your blessing be upon us as we go forward to do Your will in this matter that You have laid upon our hearts to accomplish. O Lord, we claim all Your promises and believe them to be true. We look to You for all that we need. You are our strength, our protection, the Rock of our salvation. We will obey You and do as Your Word has commanded us to do. We stand firm on Your Word because we know that Your Word is Truth. All praise, glory and honor be to You, Almighty LORD God, the Lord Jesus Christ, Lord of lords and King of kings. Amen."

All the others gave a resounding, "Amen."

The room then fell silent; there was a peaceful calm pervading the small assembly. The placid tranquility was punctuated by the crackling hearth blazing with tongues of fire. Shortly, there was heard the faint sound of soulful whimpering.

"Hey, what's the matter, lil' buddy?" said Rex to Adam, who was blankly staring into the flames, weeping.

Brandon was quick to comprehend the significance. "Adam, tell us what you see."

In his mind, Adam witnessed the hook – the large barbed meat hook dripping blood red from the pierced corpse of a five year old little boy, battered and bleeding, dangling from a long rope suspended down a deep dark hole.

Alex shouted, "Adam! *Adam!* What do you see? Tell us what *you* see! ... *Tell us!*"

Eyes unblinking, tears streaming down his cheeks, the visionary remained perfectly still, except for twitching facial muscles that were unable to suppress muffled sobs. With great effort he articulated an eyewitness testimony of the event as it was now occurring in real time. In a faint whisper, he responded, "I see them crucifying the image of God."

— 14 —

First, the police closed off the main roads, setting up barricades to stop local traffic. Then, six Department of Homeland Security military transport vehicles – black box trucks with a large white five-pointed star on the side doors – rumbled down the quiet suburban street, roaring past strategically positioned armed guards. Curious bystanders in front yards were ordered inside their homes by police shouting through megaphones, creating a sense of emergency among confused and frightened citizens who ran back inside, then peered out through windows to watch with fearful eyes from behind half-drawn curtains.

When the convoy came to a halt on the side of the street, scores of armed soldiers jumped out the rear of the trucks and ran to the front lawn to get into position. Wearing black ski masks and black uniforms lettered on the back with: "Anti-Terrorist Task Force," they threw themselves onto the ground in standard military posture, preparing for an offensive attack. Some of the militarized policemen were former BATF, FEMA, or FBI operatives prior to the Department of Defense merging with UN global peacekeeping forces. The rest of the assault team consisted of regular duty policemen from local police departments, and foreign soldiers trained on U.S. military bases for paramilitary citizen confrontations such as this. As non-citizens, they had no allegiance to America, and consequently, were not sympathetic toward Americans and would not hesitate to fire upon them when ordered to do so.

While more police troops continued pouring out of armored carriers to conceal themselves behind trees and shrubs; overhead, quaking vibrations from a hovering UN black helicopter pummeled the air.

Within five minutes the siege was set up and ready to commence. The intended target: a small clapboard-sided bungalow, now surrounded by more than 250 foot soldiers pointing military assault rifles and various artillery directly at the modest abode. Each peacekeeper was thrilled by the prospect of being the one who's bullets tore into the body of the object of the government act of war: Rex Marshall.

Inside the house, Rex was considering his options. He realized they could route him from his home – tear gas bombs might come crashing through the windows at any moment. Since the enemy had the overwhelming strategic advantage, he knew it would be futile to resist, just as he was also aware that government raids on citizen's homes nearly always ended with the death of the occupants. The Randy Weaver family at Ruby Ridge, the Branch Davidians in Waco Texas, the Brunswick Ohio murders, Oregon's Embassy of Heaven siege, Indianapolis Baptist Temple demolition – these were only a few examples of government military acts of war against peaceful citizens. Rex understood that the American government had long since declared war on its citizenry, and that the Constitution was no longer in effect, and that unlawful decrees were being dictated by a supra-government to a puppet regime in Washington D.C. In America, God-given rights had now been subordinated to rule by force; Judge-approved search and seizure warrants were no longer necessary; everyone was a potential "terrorist," guilty until proven innocent. Whether gun confiscation, religious persecution, or retaliation against citizens exercising their right to free speech, the criminal actions of the federal government encountered no resistance from terrorized Americans, a people easily manipulated into believing that government was good and protected them against terrorists. But what the brainwashed people failed to understand was that *there are no terrorists* ... the only terrorist was *the government itself!*

The former combat veteran lived alone, without the responsibility of a family, so the consequences of taking action would impact only himself. Rex was not afraid to die, and so he did not fear the police terrorists. He was a child of God, Saved into the Kingdom of heaven, and therefore understood that those who opposed him were servants of hell. Now looking at the door of his personal arsenal, he realized this was what they wanted – a collection of state-of-the-art weaponry: citizen armaments; some of the most advanced and sophisticated munitions and artillery known to man. Even though he had taken the precaution of lining the vault with lead sheeting to prevent detection by low-flying x-ray imaging aircraft, he yet suspected that surveillance technology could penetrate his concealed armory.

Unlocking the tungsten steel reinforced door, he walked into the large storage room and thought to himself: *I could wipe out the whole dang front lawn with just one of these fragmentation imploders.* He held the grapefruit-size bomb in the palm of his hand. *Or, I could take 'em all out with this here sonic wave cannon.* He hoisted the bazooka-like device onto his shoulder, and said, "Yeah, I could kill 'em all if I really wanted to." This was not an idle boast, but the confidence of a jungle guerrilla warrior who survived 153 consecutive days of intensive combat in Vietnam. Setting the one-man army back onto the shelf, he shook his head and thought, *But then, there'd be more of 'em. They're like cockroaches. They'd be here in droves, swarmin' the place. Can't kill 'em all.* His eyes darted around the compact room, then, slowly raising his head to focus on the ceiling, he said, "Lord, if I'm gonna be taken out, let me die for somethin' better than *this*. Let it bring glory to You .... This ain't worth it."

Just then, he heard the disembodied megaphone. "We - have - you - surrounded. Come - out - with - your - hands - above - your - head."

The vault was left open when he walked through the front door and stepped outside. Upon surveying the four military units that were now joined by an armor truck division and three helicopters hovering low overhead, he smiled and shouted, "One man of God against a couple hundred filthy heathen … looks like ya'all gonna' need some more help!"

"Put - your - hands - up - and - walk - slowly - forward," announced the anonymous amplified voice that could be heard throughout the suburban housing development.

With enough firepower behind them to destroy a city, six members of the citizen terrorist team rushed at him. Pot-bellied, steroid-pumped thirty year olds wielding M-16's enacted a well-rehearsed citizen assault protocol when maniacally screaming: *Face down on the ground. Do it Now! Now! NOW!*" Rex was slow to comply, and remained standing until the mind-controlled soldiers were upon him. Four of them maliciously attacked and held him face down on the ground, the others clamping steel shackles onto his wrists and ankles. Straining to look over his shoulder, the prisoner of war said, "What's this all about?"

One of the government terrorists answered, "Unregistered weapons violation."

"What about ma' rights?" asked the former decorated officer, a jack boot now stomped on the back of his head, pressing his face into the dirt.

"Shudup!" the squat UN drone sneered. "You don't got no rights!"

With another military assailant sitting on his back, compressing his lungs and making it difficult for him to breathe, Rex managed to mutter, "What about ma' Constitutional right ta' keep and bare arms?"

Standing over him with feet set wide apart, breathing heavily and nostrils flared in orgasmic delight, a robotic servant of the Police State yanked on the chain shackles and said, "We're in control. *We'll do whatever we want.*"

Another vociferated, "You be a terrorist. You go to Camp FEMA. Welcome to the New World Order!"

While the inner city street preacher was reading Holy Scriptures to a small gathering assembled on the sidewalk at 9th and Carnegie Street in Cleveland's downtown business district, he noticed the two police cruisers parked on the other side of the street. Alex had recently observed more police squad cars than usual roaming the city and the surrounding suburban vicinity. As a result of anti-terrorism laws and Patriot Act legislation, the police ranks were doubled in every metropolitan area throughout the country. On that hazy Chemtrail overcast day, he was disturbed in his spirit, and felt directed by God to read the following appropriate verses to the indigent homeless: *"He sitteth in the lurking places of the villages; in the secret places doeth he murder the innocent; his eyes are privily set against the poor. He lieth in wait secretly as a lion in his den; he lieth in wait to catch the poor; he doeth catch the poor, when he draweth him into his net. He croucheth, and humbleth himself, that the poor may fall by his strong ones.* That was from Psalm 10, verses 8 through 10," he announced to the forlorn and hungry, most of them standing there for no other reason than because they had nothing better to do, no where else to go. The City Mission provided for their basic material needs, while Alex contributed to their greater requirement for spiritual sustenance. Throughout the previous months that he had been preaching on the streets, as he read from the 1611 King James Bible, many wandering vagrants had the opportunity to hear the Word of God. Some had even come to a knowledge of the Truth.

"This is Psalm 64: *Hear my voice, O God, in my prayer; preserve my life from fear of the enemy. Hide me from the secret counsel of the wicked; from the insurrection of the workers of iniquity; who whet their tongue like a sword, and bend their bows to shoot their arrows, even bitter words. That they may shoot in secret at the perfect; suddenly do they shoot at him, and fear not. They encourage themselves in an evil matter; they commune of laying snares privily; they say, Who shall see them? They search out iniquities; they accomplish a diligent search; both the inward thought of every one of them, and the heart, is deep. But God shall shoot at them with an arrow; suddenly shall they be wounded. So they shall make their own tongue to fall upon themselves; all that see them shall flee away. And all men shall fear, and shall declare the work of God; for they shall wisely consider of his doing. The righteous shall be glad in the LORD, and shall trust in him; and all the upright in heart shall glory."*

Upon finishing, when gazing up, he saw them – two black uniformed policemen crossing the street, headed his way. Alex continued with the Bible reading: "*The angel of the LORD encampeth round about them that fear him, and delivereth them. Psalm 34, verse 8. And this is Psalm 12, verse 8: The wicked walk on every side, when the vilest men are exalted.*"

"You got a license to preach?" one of the government agents said, now standing nearby.

Alex responded, "I don't need a license to preach the Word of God. In fact, Jesus Christ commands His people in Mark 16:15: *Go ye into all the world, and preach the gospel to every creature.* I must obey God rather than man."

The slack-jaw citizen terrorist flippantly replied, "Well, God don't make the laws in this precinct. So, if you're not registered with the City, you're in violation of the Freedom From Religious Persecution Act."

Alex laughed at the contradictory statement.

"Unless you're registered with the City and State and according to Federal law, you're also in violation of a hate crime," said the other public servant.

The street evangelist replied, "I will not disobey the Commandments of God for the sake of unrighteous man-made laws created by an illegitimate government."

The justice officer immediately countered, "You're under arrest." He then grabbed hold of Alex. "Git' over there and put your hands on the wall." He pushed God's servant against the brick building, and then frisked him. When finished, the other justice officer twisted the prisoner's arms behind his back and ratcheted down handcuffs tightly onto his wrists. "That's what ya' get for back talkin' your superiors, boy."

They led him away toward a line of squad cars now parked on the curb. "We're takin' 'em in and bookin' 'em," the shaven head ten year police veteran announced to his comrades.

His black-suited accomplices smiled, and one of them gloated, "Yeah, get the garbage off the streets."

Brandon was in his library study, reading from Genesis 4:7: *If thou doest well, shalt thou not be accepted? and if thou doest not well, sin lieth at the door. And unto thee shall be his desire, and thou shalt rule over him.*"

Loud pounding on his front door disturbed the peaceful tranquility of the spacious Victorian house. Observing the surveillance monitor, he saw the six policemen standing on the threshold, and wondered, *How did they get past the security gate and alarm?* Switching to another remote camera, he discovered the answer. *Cutting torch.* Another series of bold raps resounding hollow throughout his home. Brandon's mind worked quickly to evaluate contingency alternatives that he had previously devised for just such an emergency. *I could release the dogs*, he thought, *but the psychotic cops are trained to shoot them.* He then considered doing nothing at all, not responding, allowing them to think that he was not home, and hope they would give up and leave. Yet, since he had not determined the reason for their visit, he knew they would come after him again, and perhaps at a less opportune moment, such as while driving his car. He realized there was no avoiding them; they intended to do him harm, and he knew they would not desist until accomplishing their objective. Taking a deep breath, he exhaled slowly, thinking, *I'll confront them.*

Switching on the intercom, he announced, "You are trespassing on private property and have committed additional crimes, to wit: malicious destruction of property, breaking and entering, menacing, and other violations of my Constitutional rights. State your business, then leave."

An authoritative reply came back: "We have a warrant for the arrest of Brandon Dietrich Wells. Come outside. We only want to talk to you."

"What's the disposition of the warrant?"

"Are you Brandon Wells?"

"Regardless of my identity, I'm ordering you to leave the premises at once." Through the monitor he saw them drawing their 40 caliber pistols and calling for more backup help.

A sarcastic voice crackled over the speaker. "Is *that* right? And we're ordering *you* to open this door or we'll break it in!"

The scholar calmly replied, "I wouldn't do that if I were you. All portals are wired to deliver 1 Million volts of electricity upon breach of entry. Come any further and you'll be fried pigs."

He saw them conferring among themselves, then watched as they walked back to their police cars to radio for additional backup support. While they lingered, Brandon knew the confrontation would soon escalate. *They'll shut down power to the utility main*, he thought, unconcerned, since auxiliary electric generators supplied a security grid on backup independent circuits. Fifteen minutes elapsed, yet still nothing transpired. He paced the floor. Finally, half an hour later, on the closed circuit gate monitor he viewed a police convoy escorting an eighteen wheel tractor-trailer; on the flatbed was *a bulldozer*. "Insane fools!" he muttered, envisioning a replay of the Branch Daividians and Brunswick Ohio murders. In a matter of minutes, a mob of armed government terrorists were again at his door.

"Sure hope you got homeowners insurance," the ring leader mockingly spoke into the intercom.

Another jeered, "You comin' out, or we gonna' have ta' knock down your house? What's it gonna' be?"

A pudgy steroid-injected junior officer gleefully proclaimed in a sing-song shrill voice, "Somebody's goin' ta' ja-il … Somebody's goin' ta' ja-il," thus confirming the mandate for new police recruits not to exceed an Intelligence Quotient of 98.

At this juncture, Brandon realized his alternatives were limited. He could resist and be taken captive, incurring physical harm and possibly murdered. Or, he could surrender and be taken captive, perhaps with minimal physical and emotional trauma, and survive to consider a further course of action. His research taught him about the psychological makeup of all those associated with the criminal justice system. When sensing the imminent destruction and death of those whom they oppressed, police were like a pack of wild hyenas, mindless rabid jackals, blood thirsty serial killers, brute beasts without a conscious. Over the intercom, Brandon announced: "I'll be recording everything on video and audio digital CD from several concealed cameras. A permanent record will be made of all that transpires. A copy will be transmitted to a remote computer retrieval system at various locations for posting on the Internet, where a YouTube video will be instantaneously uploaded. Should there be any violations of my Constitutional and Civil Rights, you will be prosecuted on criminal charges in a court of law." He said this without much conviction, realizing that the courts were merely an extension of the Police State barbarism made possible by collusion among a fraternity of legal criminals. Brandon knew that judges, attorneys and police were the ultimate expression of lawlessness, and were the worst kind of criminals – unrighteous men masquerading as lawful government; armed psychopaths that were part of a system that did not abide by its own laws. Because they knew they would not be held accountable for their actions, legal criminals had no fear of any consequences.

The reply that came back was chilling. "We own the Internet. Ha, ha, ha, ha, ha, ha. Your video won't see the light of day."

When he finally went downstairs to open the door, a sudden wave of black uniforms raced inside; sixteen cops swarmed him, throwing him to the floor, pinning him down. The scholarly intellectual could smell their rancid steroid breath; he heard them laugh with delight while four of them pinned him to the floor, one holding down each appendage, another sitting on his back, meticulously applying a stun gun to his prone body that vibrated when electricity coursed through his frame. Brandon screamed in agony each time they shot him though with yet another paralyzing jolt of electric voltage. For five prolonged minutes they continued the torture, performing ritualized sodomy, desecrating a temple of God by surrogate rape. As was true of all rapists, the more the tortured victim cried out, the greater was their perverse satisfaction. The physical violations he suffered at the hands of the police were reminiscent of his childhood abuse, and consequently, he went into a catatonic seizure to compartmentalize the trauma.

After their power lust was temporarily sated, they lifted Brandon off the floor, shoved him against the wall and frisked him. "What's this?" the patting officer asked the corpse-like Brandon when discovering a miniature cassette recorder in his shirt pocket. The author was too traumatized to speak. "You *don't need* this," sneered one of the assaulting officers when he confiscated the incriminating evidence. Switching off the record button, he tossed the device over to one of his criminal associates who, like himself, was also a three week graduate of the UN Police Academy. Emitting a feminized giggle, the rotund testosterone-deficient deputy announced, "I think it's funny!"

Dazed, as if in a dream, Brandon was led from his home in hand cuffs. Along the way, the police continued taunting him, hoping to elicit a response that would warrant further charges. When opening the back door of the military transport vehicle, they pushed him inside, and one of them said, "Git in there, pervert."

It was almost dusk, and Tony was driving down the road in light traffic when he noticed the multicolored flashing lights in his rear view mirror. After pulling off to the side of the road and stopping, two State Highway patrolmen approached from behind. Soon, one stood at the driver side, the other at the passenger window. "I need to see your Drivers License, registration, and proof of insurance," the nearest officer said.

Tony asked, "Why did you stop me?"

"We don't need a reason," said the patrolman. "And I can see you're not wearing your seat belt."

The occupant of the pickup truck replied, "I'm touched by your concern for my safety and well-being, but it doesn't have anything to do with why you stopped me. The insurance companies lobbied for the seat belt law so they could reduce their expenditure in payout claims."

The armed highwaymen ignored him, demanding, "You got two choices: either show us your ID, vehicle registration, and proof of insurance, or you're goin' ta jail. Now, what's it gonna' be?"

Tony answered, "There's another choice ... you can both go to hell, where you rightly belong."

The peace officer glared at him, and from the look of his bulging eyes and lawless demeanor, Tony could tell that he was demon-possessed.

As one of the policeman went back to his cruiser to call for reinforcements, the other spoke into his lapel microphone in coded language: "4662 ... Unit 66 requests backup for a TCR91 ... 0651 ... Suspect driving a blue Chevy pickup truck, license plate JC33AD, hostile, armed and dangerous." Having alerted the dispatcher, who could find no previous record of the suspect, and who issued back a "Clear" report, the courageous officer then waited a short while, timing his planned citizen assault to coincide with the soon arrival of fellow partners in crime.

When his comrade returned to join him at the detained truck, he perfunctorily shouted, "Step out of your vehicle and place your hands on the hood – do it NOW!"

Tony calmly answered, "Servants of Satan's illegitimate government don't have jurisdiction to command a servant of the Lord Jesus Christ. Just the opposite. Luke 10:19 gives me authority to *command you*! So get out of my face before you're evicted from trespassing on God's private property." When he saw them going for their guns, he stepped on the accelerator, floored it, the truck burning rubber and throwing a spray of gravel.

The justice officers ran back to their policemobile, and within minutes were followed by a long line of other State police patrol cars flashing lights in hot pursuit. "He's turning onto the Interstate," they communicated over two-way radios that spewed out the following alerts: "Calling all available units to set up road blocks at exits along I-71 Northbound from 82. Suspect is a terrorist, armed and dangerous. Advise use of deadly force."

The truck sped down the four lane highway, traveling 110 miles per hour, weaving between slower traffic, several times averting a collision. By skillful maneuvering and quick reflexes, Tony managed to keep some distance between himself and the now more than thirty police cars from three different counties. During the twenty mile race to freedom, two black helicopters followed close overhead. A half mile before reaching the ramp where he planned to exit, Tony could see the roadblock, and when glancing through his rear view mirror at the long procession of flashing lights coming up from behind, realized he was trapped. He had to make a quick decision: stop, or crash through the barricade. He prayed, "Lord, don't allow Your enemies to triumph over me. Yet, not my will, but Yours."

Exiting the road, he reduced speed when approaching closer to the barrier. Hypnotic colored lights sequentially flashed in the early twilight, appearing like UFO materialized demons. The helicopters were now stationary directly overhead. His truck came to a halt fifty feet in front of a line of Homeland Security militarized police that stood shoulder-to-shoulder, wearing body armor and wielding sawed-off shotguns and automatic rifles pointed directly at his windshield. A megaphone voice commanded, "Come out with your hands up!"

Tony realized that if he obeyed the demands of terrorists, they would physically assault him and transport him to jail. He understood that police are psychologically unstable and were societal parasites who produced nothing and lived off the live blood of productive people. Tony's Godly discernment enabled him to perceive they were manifest evil. Silently, he asked, *Lord, what should I do?* Then, he waited.

During the interim, it grew darker, and shadowy black forms now encircled his truck. The megaphone boomed: "You are hereby commanded to step out of your vehicle. This is your last warning."

The driver cracked opened the side window and shouted: "You don't have the jurisdiction to command God's people to do anything!"

Another disembodied voice spoke with authority: "This is Captain Swiney. I'm a duly sworn officer of the law."

Tony yelled back, "And I'm a servant of the Lord Jesus Christ. You're outranked!"

The police terrorist responded, "You are in violation of failure to comply with a lawful order. Come out with your hands up. We only want to talk to you."

Tony replied, "Your order isn't lawful, and I don't have any legal obligation to obey representatives of an unconstitutional, illegitimate government."

The standoff continued.

His doors were locked, so when the mad police violently yanked on the door handles and found they were not able to force an entry, it made their anger rage all the more. Using clubs, they smashed the window on the driver side, and when a uniformed terrorist reached for the inside door handle, Tony grasped the hand and quickly twisted it, dislocating the intruder's arm at the shoulder.

Suddenly, the windshield exploded into a spray of glass all over the truck cab interior. Two feverish cops quickly scampered onto the hood, and as one of them reached across the dashboard in an attempt to grab hold of Tony, the fighter used both hands to seize the armed terrorist by the hair and slam his face into the steering wheel. When the other public servant likewise moved aggressively to trespass upon private property, the servant of God pulled him inside and flung him against the opposite door, then followed through with a savage punch that snapped the policeman's head back against the passenger window, shattered the glass. An instant later, Tony felt the numbing thud of a rifle butt on the back of his head, and everything went black.

Adam was pacing the floor. He stopped to pick up the phone and start calling. When there was no answer at Brandon's house, he tried to reach Alex, who also was not home. After several more unsuccessful attempts to contact other members of the group, Howard answered. He was reading the Bible, his back turned away from the seven computer monitors across from his desk when he replied, "… What? … Are you sure?"

"Servants of Satan have captured some of the others," said the seventh member of the team. "The Lord has revealed this to me. We are all in great peril."

———•◆•———

It was a favorite pastime of high-level politicians who devalued life and made sport of human beings. In jest, they referred to it as "The Most Dangerous Game," but, they were deadly serious.

A pack of starving hunting dogs accompanied the four men as they rode horse back through a field of tall grass on the 20,000 acre Montana ranch. Eventually, they came to a halt upon reaching the high chain link fence marking the peripheral boundary of the enclosed forested retreat. Appearing relaxed, they engaged in small talk about politics, guns, their specially trained dogs, and other inconsequential items of conversation. "Well, George, what kind of shot are you using for load this time?" said the man with a cocaine bulbous nose, and who wore an Air Force cap inscribed with the words: *Aim High*.

His former colleague strained a crooked grin when casually replying, "Thought I'd try some of that new plastic buckshot, you know, the stuff we got legislation passed for police riot control. It rips a bigger hole through the flesh; does maximum damage at close range."

With a disarming perpetual smile that was part of his mind-control programming for convincingly lying to the public, the former Chief Executive waxed nostalgic. "And to think we actually *instigated* those riots, *and* the school shootings and sniper attacks." He held in his hand a small vile containing white powder, which he snorted up his nose. "They sure are stupid to believe whatever we tell them."

George sighted down the gun barrel, seemingly not listening to his friend's comment. "Yeah, can't get much dumber than the American people. If they ever found out what we did to them, we would be chased down in the streets and lynched. We let them think they have a choice – ha! Some *choice* when both parties belong to us! Even if the elections weren't rigged, no matter who they vote for they still vote for our people. They wanted freedom, so we told them that slavery and subservience to *us* – the ruling class elite – is freedom. And if any of them ever got half a brain and enough guts to oppose us, we simply charged them as terrorists and hauled them off to prison."

A former Vice President said, "We've got 'em brainwashed to believe anything – anything at all!" Bearing the crazed look of a serial killer, he peered through the high-powered rifle scope. "They're so conditioned by our news media, they handed over their guns without an argument. Nothing. Not even a whimper. They'd put on their own handcuffs if we told 'em to." Everyone laughed contemptuously.

The fourth Capital Hill career criminal said, "Well, partner, that's what I call good obedient slaves who know how to please their masters. Too bad none of them are smart enough to figure out we're just public servants."

The past Vice President replied, "They didn't call you the Great Communicator for nothing, Ronnie. We put 'em in a deep sleep so that it was Bedtime for Bonzo."

"That's right, Dickie. And the media made you look like a star too. After you were notified at the Bohemian Grove that you were due a promotion, no one in the media mentioned your naughty little habits that were publicly exposed in that book written by one of our programmed operatives, Cathy O'Brien. After she wrote *Trance:Formation of America* with the assistance of one of our defected CIA handlers, Mark Phillips, we had to deal with her again."

George said, "After that, she was useful only as a Containment Agent. It's our game, and we control the flow of information. The dumbed-down public only gets to know what *we* want them to know."

The former Hollywood stage mime said, "I'll bet you miss all the tricks our people programmed into her, don't you, George?"

"It's her little eight year old daughter that I miss," the famous pedophile replied with a wicked smile. "Can't remember how many times I had that one in uncompromising situations. Her frightened screams are what really turned me on."

Dick mimicked the voice of the Wicked Witch of the West from the mind-control movie, Wizard of Oz: "… and I'll get your little daughter *too*, my pretty!" Everyone laughed. "I musta' beat the living _ _ _ _ outta' her mother a hundred times. Broke her jaw, messed her up real good. It's amazing she survived it."

"Maybe it was the drugs," offered Bill, sniffing more white powder. "Both of them worked out fine for our purposes. But now, it's almost a shame we have to get rid of these …" he used his gun barrel to carelessly point down to the three naked people shivering in the cold mountain air. Below them stood a thirty-five year old mother, her nine year old daughter, and a forty one year old army Captain."

George said, "They need some more programming." He quickly jerked the pump lever on his shotgun, injecting a shell into the chamber, now made ready to fire. "Back to business," he said. Raising his voice, he ceremoniously shouted, "Is everyone ready to play The Most Dangerous Game?"

The three naked bodies were the quarry, Delta Slaves, owned and handled by CIA government agents who mind-control programmed them using MK-Ultra trauma-based techniques. They had been subjected to long-term torture and addicting drugs that scrambled their minds so new personalities were created that would make them useful for government espionage, as drug couriers, or human sex toys available for abuse by Washington politicians. Like thousands of others, they had been abducted for psychological experimentation, targeted for ritual torture, and for use as agent provocateurs to foment terrorism in service to the International Hierarchy. Since early childhood they had suffered unspeakable horrors, rending their minds, irreparably damaged. Now, mere skeletons of their true selves, they were physically and mentally too weak to resist; so severely traumatized they were beyond the point of comprehending that the object of the game was *death*.

"You know the rules," Bill said to them. "First we give you a head start into the woods, then we let loose the dogs. If they don't get to ya' first," he paused to flash a sneering smile, alluding to his fondness for bestiality, "we shoot ta' kill…. Got it?" Clinically, he was a *Charming Psychopath*, explosive and extremely dangerous, who boasted a long list of murders to his credit. His perverted charm suddenly changed to reveal a rapist mind, a depraved killer, when snarling, "Remember, there's no where to run, no where to hide. Now … *Run!*"

Ten minutes later, they let loose the dogs. Then, in pursuit of their human prey, the four mass murderers set their horses to a slow trot.

Naked, running barefoot, stumbling often from physical exhaustion, the released slaves could hear the distant baying howls of the ravenous dogs approaching ever closer. To them, it was merely another nightmare, one more never ending terror-filled dream. Their fractured minds could hardly grasp the mentality of the human monsters who used them for sport, expendable objects for their perverse amusement. Too weak to run any further, slowing to a mere walk, panting in feverish anticipation, they repeatedly glanced over their shoulders to witness the horrifying fate that was fast closing in. The dogs were nearly upon them.

When the riders had sighted their prey desperately running for cover, they increased their pace to a quick gallop. When arriving at the scene, the old soldier was on the ground being mauled by the dogs; the mother and her child had climbed up a small tree and were clinging to a low hanging limb, just barely out of reach of the frothing hound's snapping jaws.

Reagan casually said, "Well … I guess party time's over."

With amused smiles, the four horsemen patiently observed as the snarling dogs ripped chunks of bloody meat from the howling military man. Unmoved by the spurting blood and gore, Cheney gazed up at the mother and said, "Yeah, and now it's *our turn* for some fun."

Clinton wore a demented grin when he stepped off his horse to pat one of the killer dogs on its head. "Good boy. You helped us round up terrorists, just like our police do to citizens who try to escape us."

FBI documented pedophile and serial rapist, George Herbert Walker Bush, leered at the trembling child and said, "I'll first have my fun, then let the dogs have at 'em."

—15—

The police dispatcher's voice could be heard above the grating static from the squad car's 2-way radio: "Travis, Alexander, Gregory; DOB: 8/27/58; Social: 921-43-9882; Last known address: 714 Thirty-second Street, Collinwood; No priors." The arresting officer looked over at his partner seated next to him in the squad car, and said, "He does now." Slightly turning his head to gaze over his shoulder, he spoke to the prisoner in the back seat when adding with derision, "Ain't that right, nigger?" The biting sarcasm coming from the other side of the heavy gauge wire mesh divider had no affect on the battered and handcuffed man lying on his side in the cramped rear seat. When he failed to respond, the other policeman taunted, "Hey Allie! Hey alley cat! What's matter, cat got yer tongue? Speak up, *boy!*" The public servants enjoyed a hearty laugh, then, one of them shouted, "Hey alley boy! You gonna' preach to us? Huh Allie? Huh alley *boy?*" They continued the harassment throughout the duration of his transport to the downtown headquarters, during which time they took a circuitous route in order to prolong the three minute trip, their audio recorder selectively turned on and off, hoping to provoke a response so they could bring further charges against him without incriminating themselves.

Thirty minutes later, the shiny black cruiser finally descended a steep ramp to the lower level of the metropolitan police station. "Open number two," the driver mumbled into his lapel microphone.

"Number two clear," a voice crackled over the car's speaker. The overhead corrugated metal garage door opened to allow passage of the state vehicle into the subterranean parking area. Displayed over the cave-like portal was a sign that read: SERVICE ENTRANCE. One of the policemen broke the phrase into syllables when pronouncing: "SERVE US IN TRANCE." The uniformed wards of the state chuckled over this coded Masonic cliché. With car audio recorder turned off, he said, "Hey alley boy! How'd ya' like ta' serve us in a trance? Huh boy? How'd ya' like us shootin' ya' so full o' drugs that ya' can't preach no more? Huh? How'd ya' like us to do that to ya? Huh? Answer me ... *boy*!" Alex remained silent while they continued to scorn him with their crass banter. "Nobody knows and nobody cares about ya; and even if they did know, nobody can do anything about it, because *we do whatever we want*. Better get used to answering your superiors, boy, 'cause you're now our *slave!*"

Alex's body was wracked with pain. He was having difficulty breathing, and realized they had broken several of his ribs when repeatedly kicking him after he was thrown down onto the cement sidewalk. Squeezed into the small cramped space of the patrol car's rear seat, arms twisted behind his back, tightened handcuffs cutting into his wrists, he yet managed a smile. He smiled because he perceived that his situation was not merely one of being arrested by criminally insane simpletons, but rather, he was being persecuted by those having a spirit different from his own. Alex understood that he was suffering for the sake of the Bible truth of Jesus Christ. Silently, he quoted appropriate Scriptures, which included Philippians 1:28: *And in nothing terrified by your adversaries: which is to them an evident token of perdition, but to you of salvation, and that of God.* He smiled because, like all true saints of God, it was a privilege to be worthy of cruel treatment for the glory of his Lord, Who had been likewise tortured by worthless ignorant men. Alex was aware that his persecutors were the enemies of God; that all police were servants of Satan, indwelled by the same spirit as the Roman soldiers who, nearly 2,000 years ago, mocked, brutally assaulted, then murdered Jesus Christ. He realized that, since then, nothing had essentially changed; the spiritual lineage of police had continued on to the present time. Alex knew that God Himself, Jesus Christ, had referred to them as "dogs" and "swine" in Matthew 7:6; and as "beasts" in Ezekiel 34:28. God well knew their heart, and considered them *the basest of men* in Daniel 4:17. Alex smiled because he was aware that their fate as Romans 9:22 *vessels of wrath fitted to destruction*, would be the same as their demon-possessed counterparts throughout all of human history: the Revelation 21:8 Lake of Fire.

Once inside the jail, he was ordered to strip. Then, as he stood there naked, the officer sprayed his head and private parts with a toxic pesticide. "Got any lice on ya'?" derided the jailer. "Don't move or I'll have ta' spray ya' again." The public servant seemed to enjoy his life work. "Aw, too bad, ya' moved! Gotta' do it *all over again*." He reapplied the spray to the prisoner's hair, further punishing him when directing the burning stream toward his face and eyes, forcing him to inhale the carcinogenic mist. "Now, you go on in there and take a nice hot shower." The prisoner walked into the open bathroom stall that was without a privacy curtain, then stood in freezing cold water as several grinning police officers watched in amusement. When finished, dripping wet, they threw at him coarse, loose-fitting, bright orange prison fatigues. He was subsequently photographed, fingerprinted, iris scanned, injected with a Tuberculosis virus; a DNA sample taken from his urine, blood and skin. After being processed by the Beast, the sanctity of his biometric personhood having been stolen from him, he was led in handcuffs down a long corridor that passed through a series of heavy metal doors, an electronic buzzer activating each of the remotely controlled locks.

His handler, a bald-headed obese jailer, eventually stopped at a side door that led to a large open room known as a "Pod." Passing into a small glass-enclosed pre-cell, after removing Alex's handcuffs, another electronic door was opened, and instantly, he was met with a torrent of dissonant sound, a wave of chaos and confusion that spewed forth from an assemblage of fifty other prisoners. Two racially segregated television sets boomed with noxious repetitive rap music; most everyone was playing cards or vacantly stared at the violence on the overhead TV screens. Alex walked across the bare concrete floor, past the several tables where prison garb inmates sat dealing hands of gin rummy all day long. When arriving at his assigned cell – a nine by twelve foot bare concrete room – upon opening the heavy steel door, on the lower bunk there sat a large man with shaven head, gray handlebar mustache, and tattoos depicting demons and dragons on all exposed areas of his body. His piercing stare indicated to the discerning preacher that he was totally demon-possessed. The repeat felon eyed his new cell mate, then gruffly said, "Let's get sum em' straight right from da' start … you gonna' be my girlfren'."

Rex, Brandon and Tony had endured similar abuses from the police and jailers. Tony sustained a concussion, while Rex and Brandon were bruised, cut, bleeding, and had third degree stun gun burns on their bodies. The prison doctor, an attractive middle-aged woman with short blonde hair and stern features, did a rough cursory inspection of their open wounds before summarily declaring they would not require any medical treatment. Carelessly, she probed contusions and lacerations, responding to their concerns with aloof disinterest. Upon noting the hemorrhaging from the back of Tony's head beginning to subside, she flippantly said, "You're okay." With a reckless swipe of a gauze pad, she wiped some excess blood, and then, looking over at the several police-men who stood nearby like vultures awaiting a corpse, the jail house lesbian casually announced, "Take him. He's all yours."

The four prisoners had been processed separately and were un-aware that the other members of the team were inmates at the same jail, and were in fact now held behind locked doors in nearby cells. From the sound of an echoing voice down the long sterile corridor, Brandon overheard one of the prison guards say, "The other three are being rounded up. We'll have 'em in here before too long." Immedi-ately grasping that it was not merely a personal vendetta to silence him from publishing government exposés, but rather, a planned conspiracy against the group, he thought, *Remote Viewing. That's the only way they could have known of our intentions.* Yet, the other members, being more spiritually mature, had a better grasp of the implications of what had occurred. Because of their greater degree of spiritual discernment, they recognized that what had transpired was *spiritual warfare*, and understood that the apparent earthly battle was merely a manifestation of the conflict taking place in the higher dimensional invisible realm. They realized that they were involved in a continuously raging war between good and evil, where the ultimate outcome was measured in terms of won or lost human souls.

In the stark bright lighting of the jail intake room, sitting at a small metal desk, one of the officers was talking on the telephone. "Nope, there ain't no one here by that name…. Nope, ain't got him here either. Can't help ya'."

After Howard ended the cell phone call, Adam said, "He's lying."

Gathered together in Howard's home office, Eric observed, "They'll set a Bond. We have to find out how much it's going to cost and get them out of there."

Howard thought for a moment. "No attorneys. Are we all in agreement?"

"Absolutely," affirmed Eric. "We're not selling out to those prostitutes in three piece suits. They're *liars*, not *lawyers*. Besides, they're part of the corrupt system and would be fighting against us, not for us."

Adam commented, "They serve the kingdoms of this world: the government, which is ruled by Satan. They are therefore his servants. There is no such thing as a *Christian* attorney."

The senior let out an exasperated breath of air. "They'll want a sizable chunk of cash, for sure. That's what it's all about for these government extortionists – money. The court system is legalized racketeering. It's a criminal enterprise that has nothing to do with justice, but with embezzlement at the implicit point of a gun."

"How much do you think they will want?" questioned Adam.

"I don't care how much it is," the financier confidently replied. "Whatever the amount, I can cover it." While the others remained silent, he pondered the dilemma, strumming his fingertips on the polished mahogany desktop. Abruptly, the phone rang. Howard checked the caller ID before answering. Then, after listening for a moment, he said, "Good work, Jimmy. Thanks." He hung up.

"Important?" prompted Eric.

"That was one of my informants," Howard explained. "He told me what we suspected, and what Adam already knew … the police have them. They're being held at the Municipal Jail in downtown Cleveland." He paused before adding, "And there are warrants issued for the rest of us."

"Oh yeah?" Eric said with a faint laugh. "What's *the charge*?"

Howard was busy rummaging through a desk drawer. Finally, he pulled out a thick roll of $100 bills and a 45 caliber automatic pistol. Standing, he answered, "First Degree Murder. Let's get out of here."

—16—

"I'd like a double room," said Howard to the Holiday Inn hotel clerk.

"That will be $98, plus tax. How would you like to pay for that, Sir?"

Howard snapped a Visa card down onto the counter. "Just go ahead and ring it up for a week," he replied.

"All right, Sir." The girl behind the counter ran the card through a scanner. "Your total will be $734.02. I'll also need to see your driver's license, please."

He produced a photo ID, complete with a social security number and residential address. The sales clerk jotted down the license number and other personally invasive information, then returned the card, along with two magnetic stripe plastic key cards. "Your room number is 752. Enjoy your stay, Mr. Langley."

Howard turned and walked through the lobby, then proceeded along a short corridor leading to the elevators. The clerk was not able to view Eric and Adam when Howard opened a door further down the hallway to let them inside. While in the elevator, on the way up to the seventh floor, Howard signaled for them to remain silent, pointing to what appeared to be a stereo speaker in the elevator ceiling.

Once in the hotel room, they sat at a small round table next to a window that provided a view of the parking lot below. Adam quoted

Scripture from Proverb 28:28: *"When the wicked rise, men hide them-selves: but when they perish, the righteous increase."*

Howard said, "We've got to lay low for a while; Satan's people have been alerted to oppose us." He took out of his pocket a stack of plastic cards. "I knew someday these custom ID's would pay off. A few years ago I had a whole bunch of Driver Licenses made, including passports and birth certificates. Cost me a grand a piece. It was a good investment."

"Fake ID: don't leave home without it," Eric dryly said.

Howard noted, "In today's Police State you have to be prepared for anything. The whole system is gone mad. If I had paid for the room in cash, the clerk would have immediately alerted the police." He smiled. "It's just one of those things you learn from having lived a long time."

The conversational tone quickly changed to become more serious. Eric analyzed the situation. Thinking out loud, he said, "We can't directly confront them with the truth. The reasons are obvious, especially because of the fact that cops are Masons, and therefore, Satanists – the very ones warring against us in the spiritual realm. Yet, we have to spring our people from their gulag." He was pacing the floor. "They want us. They also want money. Their own laws mean nothing to them, so, they could refuse to release their political prisoners." He walked the short distance to the end of the room, and turning, had already devised a workable plan. "Our gambit is to distract them with the payoff bail money long enough for us to accomplish our goal. Presently, there are only two relevant questions. First: How much money will they want? Second: How will we get it to them without being captured ourselves?"

Seated at the table, chin resting on cupped hands, Howard said, "We can expect the bail to be set at an outrageous sum. Regardless, I've got the funds to handle it. As far as the transport of the payment … I'll have a reliable courier make the delivery."

Adam spoke prophetically. "These people are acting on orders from their superiors, who receive their orders from the top of the demonic hierarchy – ultimately, direct from Lucifer himself. I also know they will not give up their captives easily. The outcome will be decided in another dimension. We must pray to the Lord to disable their demons operating within the guise of civil law."

Upon rising, Howard said, "There's no question that these are totally reprobate people who play by their own rules and don't observe their own laws. They're in it strictly for the thrill of the power grab and their aberrant spiritual need to control others. Fighting this in court would be a total waste of time, money and effort. All of them have the same mind, the same spirit: the cops, the attorneys, the politicians, the judges. They're a fraternity of legal criminals."

"*Especially* the judges," confirmed Eric. "As Orwell stated in his futuristic book, *1984*: *What can you do against the lunatic who gives your arguments a fair hearing and then simply persists in his lunacy?* In a courtroom, that's the kind of psychotic mentality you're dealing with."

"I agree," replied the elder. "For now, all we can do is wait. Hopefully, tomorrow we'll see something in the newspaper about the arrests and the bail amount."

The master strategist said, "The media is part of government criminality. They'll only print what their controllers will allow them to report. If the police department has orders to block news coverage, our friends could vanish from off the face of this earth, and nobody would ever know what happened to them."

"Such occurs," affirmed Adam. "People disappear. They end up in federal prisons; forgotten, forsaken by their family and friends. They waste away in tiny rooms for years, and nobody cares about them."

"I see your point," said Howard. "I better make a phone call." He dialed a coded number into his secure cellular phone. "Alonzo … make a recording of the following: … I need to have press releases sent to all the news networks and major national newspapers. The issue concerns the false arrest and incarceration of Eric Rider: R-i-d-e-r; Brandon Wells: W-e-l-l-s; Tony Nichols: N-i-c-h-o-l-s; and

Rex Marshall: M-a-r-s-h-a-l-l; that are being held at the Municipal County Jail in Cleveland, Ohio. You can add details as you feel are appropriate. Send it out to UPI, Associated Press, Reuters, as well as international media. I need full coverage on this. Make it good; we have to get some hungry young reporters to sniff at it. This is a rush job, so I need headline copy in *tomorrow's* papers." He then hung up, exhaled a deep breath and said, "Well, at least now we have something to look forward to – tomorrow's edition of the Cleveland Plain Dealer."

The next day, while they were having breakfast in the hotel room, the newspaper was delivered to their door. Eric quickly scanned the cover stories, then began paging through the rest of the paper. "I don't see it," he said, turning the thin pages. He continued searching. "Wait! … Here's something … on page six!"

"Of course," Howard commented knowingly. "They always try to bury the truth."

Adam observed, "The number six is Satan's spiritual signature."

Eric began reading: "… *the four member team, believed to be part of an international terrorist organization, were arrested on conspiracy charges yesterday …* He paused to interject, "What a laugh! Imagine being accused of terrorism by a terrorist government!" Continuing, he read: "… *and were taken into custody. A cash Bond of one million dollars has been set for each of the dangerous Right Wing extremists …*"

Eric threw down the newspaper, venting his anger. "Lying thieves!"

Howard seemed unconcerned.

Adam was moved to quote Psalm 2:2: "*The kings of the earth set themselves, and the rulers take counsel together, against the LORD, and against his anointed …*"

Eric sat back down and quickly recovered his usual calm. "Okay. So now that they've committed to their position, we make a counter move. Can we meet their demands?" he asked the man who was on the cell phone making another call.

"This is Howard Conrad. Give me a price on the September

S&P." He waited a moment for the response. "Sell 900 contracts at the market." Another pause, then he said, "Thanks Brad." Flipping closed the phone cover and putting it in his shirt pocket, he leaned back in the chair.

"Well? …" prompted Eric. "What did you do?"

The accomplished futures trader casually answered, "Oh, a … I just closed out a fifty million dollar position for cash. That should be sufficient to cover our immediate expenses."

"Fifty *million*?" repeated Eric.

"We might need some extra spending money," Howard replied. "The Lord provides."

They were all smiles when saying in unison, "Praise be to God!"

—17—

A tall distinguished-looking gentleman, with horn-rimed glasses, a short trimmed beard, and dressed in a black three piece Armani designer suit with white silk tie, walked confidently into the police station. Passing through a revolving door, he soon arrived at a small glass enclosed reception counter where a shaven head police officer was sitting behind a bullet-proof translucent partition, munching on a bag of Fritos. Upon noticing the new arrival standing there, he brusquely asked, "What'd you want?"

Stooping lower to speak into a small circular metal grid, the visitor replied, "Greetings, my good man. I'm here to remit bail money for the release of certain persons whom you have rooming here in your, a … establishment."

The pointed head, heavy jowled peace officer replied, "Whaaat?"

The guest cleared his throat, then said, "Actually, there are four individuals."

The civil servant stared blankly at the visitor while stuffing a handful of chips into his mouth. He then asked, "You a attorney?"

"No, Sir. I would never resort to that base level of existence."

The officer demanded, "What's their names?"

"Brandon Wells, Tony Nichols, Alex Travis, and Rex Marshall."

Without breaking eye contact the cop clerk stuffed yet another handful of dry chips into his mouth, and masticating loudly, responded. "Nope. Ain't got no one here by those names."

SEVEN WHO DARED 183

"But perhaps you are mistaken, my friend. I'm certain that an astute fellow such as yourself is able to reconcile any disparity that may inadvertently –"

"Hey man!" he interrupted, "Why can't you just speak plain English?"

The genteel visitor returned, "May I suggest that you check your inmate roster. Surely you have read the daily newspaper? It is public knowledge that these four named individuals are being detained at this particular facility."

The seated guard suddenly stopped crunching, his eyes widened, and throwing down the Frito's bag, he exploded, shouting, "Don't you go tellin' *me* what to do! Understan'? Or you be endin' up wif' 'em!"

The cultured sophisticate raised an eyebrow. "So you affirm they are here. I believe the bail amount is set at one million dollars each. Here is a cashier's check for their release, in the sum of four million dollars." He slipped the check through a narrow slot beneath the thick bullet proof glass.

The public servant snatched it up greedily and demanded, "And jus' who are *you*?" Without verbally responding, the patron slid him a State photo ID. "This here, *you*?" queried the observant policeman.

"That's what it says," was the immediate response.

"You got more ID?"

The dignified gentleman reached into the inside pocket of his tailored Italian suit and pulled out a stack of plastic cards and folded papers. "What is it that you wish to see: credit cards? bank statements? birth certificate? utility bills? ... fishing license?"

After loading a handful of chips, the ward of the state belligerently replied, "Gimme' 'em here." Snatching up the documents, he examined each item, and when finished, made a telephone call, turning his back to ignore the waiting citizen standing in the lobby. During the interim, he resumed munching even more chips. Several minutes later, another uniformed officer entered through a back door of the transparent room. After a brief conference, the second cop approached the window and said, "You Julian Quincy Kensington?"

The suited man replied, "The documents are right there in front of you."

"This here cashier's check says it's drawn on City Bank here in town. How do we know if it's any good?"

"You might try calling them," suggested the visitor.

The customer service policeman turned his back to make another phone call. Meanwhile, the gentleman was careful to conceal his nervous apprehension. Several minutes later, the same officer announced, "We can't accept a check for a cash bond." He slid the bank note and identification back under the glass.

"But this is as good as cash. If you called the bank, they will confirm this check was purchased there less than an hour ago. Surely you don't expect me to simply walk in here with that amount of cash on my person?"

The contemptible government bureaucrat shook his head and issued a power-based ultimatum. "We don't take no checks."

After gathering up the documents, the refined ambassador casually straightened his tie, then, confidently replied, "Very well." Soon after exiting through the revolving door of the legal racketeering enterprise, he gradually increased his pace, and while heading toward a parking lot across the street, was keenly aware that his every move was being monitored by surveillance cameras. When less than half way there, he abruptly turned 90 degrees to the left and ran along an adjacent walk for two city blocks, then slipped down a side alley, where he jumped into a red Ferrari and sped away.

From the car, he made a telephone call. "The Masonic morons didn't buy it," he said, now with a slight Jersey accent, his speech no longer formal. "They wanted straight cash. For a minute there I thought they had me."

"Where are you now?" replied Howard in a reassuring calm voice.

"Just crossed Superior Avenue. Should be back there in about thirty min – uh oh … got company." Gazing into the rear view mirror, he saw the flashing multicolored lights of three police cruisers in hot pursuit. Downshifting, he raced the powerful engine, then quickly accelerated past a line of cars up ahead.

"Lose them," said his employer. "You're not being paid twenty grand to deliver the mail."

"Right, Boss." Immediately after ending the call, he floored it, the high performance Testosterossa fishtailing when he swerved in and out of congested downtown traffic. Skillfully maneuvering, the driver was alert to the oncoming cars that were forced to veer off the street and onto the sidewalk; he was unfazed by their sustained horn blasts and the look of frenzied terror on the multitude of faces that streaked by his limited field of vision.

Flashing lights reflected off his side mirrors; the shrill sound of sirens were closing in from behind. In the overhead mirror he could see a motorcycle cop join the lengthening convoy. "Cockroaches!" he exclaimed. "Let's see you follow *this!*" The engine roared as he raced through a series of red lights, then, upon turning onto Euclid Avenue, traffic was bumper to bumper, almost stationary. Up ahead, he saw more opposition. "This is where we part company," he said with a determination born from a lifetime of overcoming adversity on the streets of New York City. Cutting the wheel sharply to the right, the sleek low profile machine burned rubber when he drove over the curb and onto the sidewalk, wild-eyed pedestrians leaping to get out of the way, the police now left behind, remaining stationary in stalled traffic, unable to follow. The awaiting ambush had been efficiently circumvented.

Now speeding down the concrete walkway, he raced the short distance to the end of the block, then made another sharp right turn, fishtailing and screeching tires to maintain a narrow course that was impossible to follow. When on the other side of a massive abandoned department store, and heading in the opposite direction from his pursuers, he traveled along a desolate narrow byway, then streaked past a row of stationary garbage trucks to finally emerge near the Interstate entrance ramp. Once on the multiple lane highway, he pushed the speedometer needle to the far right, then maintained it for the next fifteen minutes until finally arriving on the West side of town, where there were fewer government terrorists in sight. Abandoning the false ID rented car in the parking lot of a crowded shopping mall, he unobtrusively boarded a bus to the hotel.

"Nice try, Nick," said Howard, when the courier entered the hotel suite and handed his employer the multi-million dollar check.

"*Now* what?" asked the former confidence man, no longer wearing his glasses, mustache, and beard disguise.

"The three of us here will continue praying," Howard replied. "You're welcome to stay and join us. Tomorrow, I'll get this converted to cash, and then our wicked little adversaries will be in for a big surprise."

—18—

"Wish I could have been there to see the look on their faces when they opened the back door of that armored Brinks truck stacked with bundles of cash," said Eric, now joined by the other six members of the team comfortably lounging in the hotel suite. "The cops were disappointed they couldn't keep some of the money for themselves, as they often do in drug busts and when seizing citizen property."

Howard added, "And the mock television crews filming the whole thing – that was sheer brilliance on your part, Eric."

The one who masterminded the government coup replied, "We had to keep them honest. Local TV coverage would have been prohibited; they're whores for the government."

Adam said, "Satan's people fear exposure more than anything else. There is nothing the servants of darkness hate more than having the light shined on them."

Still reeling from multiple brutal assaults during the two day ordeal, Rex was sporting bandaged wounds from stungun burns all over his body. "The prisoners oughta' be set free and the cops locked up in those jails," he commented. The combat-hardened war veteran shook his head. "They're nothin' but filthy pigs wallowin' in a pig sty that's called government."

Alex was favoring the side where they kicked him and fractured three of his ribs. "Our persecution and suffering is for the cause of Jesus Christ," he proclaimed. "Because of it, we're told in Luke 6:23 to leap for joy. They hate us – not because of who we are personally – but because of Who we represent spiritually. Let's try to keep that in mind."

Tony said, "They're Satan's people; we're children of the King, born of the Spirit of God, which, by divine right, makes them our mortal enemies. 1 John 3:7-10. They're *not* the brethren, and we're commanded not to welcome them or to pray for them. 2 John 10; 1 John 5:16. We're to hate evil and love good. Amos 5:15; Romans 12:9; Psalm 97:10; Proverb 8:13; 2 Chronicles 19:2; Revelation 2:2,6 … let's keep *that* in mind."

Howard affirmed, "*Woe unto them that call evil good, and good evil…* Isaiah 5:20. Sounds like you took a few lumps while in there, Tony. An undefeated world champion fighter who downed four of their fellow Luciferian Masons, and now vulnerable in handcuffs and leg irons – they must have savored the opportunity."

Tony laughed without emotion. "That was just round one. A cop can only act tough when he's got a gun and the whole U.S. militia backing him up. On his own, he's a sniveling coward."

Howard agreed, "The government-owned media never allows that truth to be seen by the public. If they did, people would lose confidence in the power that enslaves them. The masses are fed a steady diet of Hollywood propaganda portraying the police as benevolent protectors, upstanding men and women with high moral and ethical character. But, as we all know, that's a patented falsehood. Police are more criminal than the so-called criminals they incarcerate. Psalm 17:13 reveals their true identity: *Arise, O LORD, disappoint him, cast him down: deliver my soul from the wicked, which is thy sword.*"

Rex confirmed, "God uses the unjust cops to do His dirty work!" Everyone laughed.

Tony asked Brandon, "How did you weather the storm, Brother?"

Appearing to be deep in thought, the introspective scholar answered, "It was everything I expected it would be. I've researched and written about the social and psychological effects of imprisonment – both civilian and wartime. The sentiments expressed by the others corroborate my findings. The police uniform serves as a cover for their psychopathology. They're perfectly well suited for their role as revenue collectors for the government. Cops decided upon their chosen career in order to fulfill aberrant pathological needs. Essentially, they're the grown up version of the school yard bully, the misfit that no one liked, and who never got better. In adulthood, they simply continue a lifelong pattern of dysfunctional behavior, choosing a career in law enforcement that would provide them a socially acceptable venue in which to enact their psychopathology. Dumb thugs are exactly what an illegitimate government needs for demanding extorted funds from terrorized citizens and to bring them into subjection to the New World Order Police State.

"When the Great Tribulation is underway, we should all fully expect to be tortured, maimed and murdered by this same class of barbarians. Until then, consider seriously the possibility that no one can act with such unrestrained malice unless they are utterly mad." He casually shrugged his shoulders. "Accounting for the demonstrated madness of police is easily attributed to their indwelling demons."

"It sounds like you've been reading your Bible," observed Alex.

"Yes, that's correct," said the author. "For all these years I've overlooked the world's most valuable source of truth and wisdom. It appears I was remiss in my research."

"You weren't remiss," corrected Adam, who sat gazing out the window. "You were Spiritually Blind. But now that you've been Born Again by the Spirit of Truth – Jesus Christ – the truth has been revealed to you so that it now seems obvious."

"I know you're right," Brandon replied. "The infinite wisdom of God's Word far transcends the collective vain mutterings of mankind."

The visionary stated, "The conflict we now face is a battle *against principalities, against powers, against the rulers of the darkness of this world…*"

Alex finished the verse of Scripture, "… *against spiritual wickedness in high places.* Ephesians 6 implies not only the spiritual, but also the physical realm. It's not just *their* demons against our Lord's protecting angels, but also the wicked government itself against us. Man's government is the physical manifestation of Satan's invisible demonic kingdom. Human government is Satan's religion."

Brandon added, "Man's government is like an enormous detritus magnet that draws unGodly men seeking to fulfill their wicked desires in a safe context that insulates them from the consequences of their criminal actions."

"Well stated – all of you," the elder complimented. "We're of one accord, and are in agreement over what we believe and know to be true. We all have the same Spirit, the same mind, in obedience to God and likened unto Him. That's why we seek the truth from the Word of God, the 1611 King James Bible. Gentlemen, we are not part of this world system; we have been called out from it, made separate from it, having been chosen by the Lord Jesus Christ from before the foundation of the world to fulfill His will. We are the enemies of the unrighteous; and they are God's enemies, which makes them our enemies."

"Praise be to God!" everyone acknowledged.

Upon passing the hotel room King James Gideon Bible, in turn, each read verses appropriate for the discussion. The street minister began with Proverb 28:4: *"They that forsake the law praise the wicked; but such as keep the law contend with them."*

Eric read Proverb 24:23-25: *"It is not good to have respect of persons in judgment. He that saith unto the wicked, Thou art righteous; him shall the people curse, nations shall abhor him: But to them that rebuke him shall be delight, and a good blessing shall come upon them."*

Tony recited Scripture from Daniel 11:32: *"… the people that do know their God shall be strong, and do exploits."*

Brandon then received the ancient Text and read from Psalm 78:65,66: *"Then the Lord awakened as one out of sleep, and like a mighty man that shouteth by reason of wine. And he smote his enemies in the hinder parts: he put them to a perpetual reproach."*

The Holy Book was given to Rex, who paged to Psalm 139:21-22: *"Do not I hate them, O LORD, that hate thee? and am not I grieved with those that rise up against thee? I hate them with perfect hatred: I count them mine enemies.*"

Howard read from Psalm 37:30: "*The mouth of the righteous speaketh wisdom, and his tongue talketh of judgment.*"

Adam was the last to read the Word of God, concluding with a passage from Matthew 18:6: "*But whoso shall offend one of these little ones which believe in me, it were better for him that a millstone were hanged about his neck, and that he were drowned in the depth of the sea.*"

When he closed the sacred Book and said, "Amen," they all enthusiastically responded, "*Amen!*"

It was late evening, almost midnight, and the men were still awake and discussing their plans, analyzing every detail in light of the recent new developments. "We'll have to expedite our schedule," said Eric. "The supplies must be purchased under cover, and we'll have to forego the basic training. There's not enough time."

Howard announced, "I bought enough storable food provisions to feed 300 starving children for seven months. It's all organic, the best that money can buy. And also plenty of warm blankets and enough clothes for each child to have seven changes of attire. I even bought $20,000 worth of toys. Everything is already loaded onboard a cargo plane that I recently purchased. It's capable of making a transatlantic flight with a load capacity able to transport us and our precious cargo."

"Who's going to fly it?" asked Tony.

"I'm a pilot," the elder replied. "Rex will be the copilot; he flew a Hughy chopper in Vietnam." Upon a sheet of paper the financier sketched a crude diagram of the flight plan, then briefly explained the risks of flying a noncommercial aircraft to a foreign country. He concluded, "The plane is unregistered, so it can't be traced."

"How soon before we're ready to leave?" inquired Alex.

Eric answered, "I've calculated the minimum time to obtain the necessary provisions. Barring the unforeseen, the earliest possible departure will be in three days."

"Three days. That ain't much time," commented Rex.

Adam said, "In a dream last night, I saw a cloud – large, black, casting a shadow over a tall mountain. A storm broke out: there was thunder and also lightening and hail stones. Then, I saw the sun break through the cloud, but it was only for a brief moment."

"That's our cue," deduced Brandon, interpreting the mountain to symbolize the hotel where they were staying; the storm signifying the raging battle between good and evil. "The light shining through the darkness represents a window of opportunity; but it's only going to be opened for a short while. I suggest we make haste, before that window closes."

—19—

At the base of the pyramid, the lowest level of the International Hierarchy, security clearance was restricted. The bottom of the satanic triangle is were clusters of government representatives openly engaged in criminal activity: judges, attorneys, State and local politicians, police, government-funded researchers and medical doctors, as well as other unwitting operatives comprising the vast body of individuals that were useful for achieving the goals of the New World Order. Both, individually and collectively, they contributed to making the global takeover a current reality.

The next higher level was occupied by federal agencies and non-government organizations that served as a "buffer zone" between the citizen population and the legal/medical components of the Criminal Fraternity network. This Brotherhood consisted of the print and broadcast media, organized religions, intelligence agencies, illegal drug cartels/legal pharmaceutical companies, government-owned institutions and corporations; and, at the primary level of organized crime, the judicial court system. Above these fraternal organizations were the super-wealthy Luciferian families of the world: for example, the Rockefellers, and above them, the Rothschilds; as well as the Federal Reserve Bank, World Bank/IMF, and other global financial institutions. At the next higher level was the *supra-Government*, the "shadow government" Global Hierarchy that ran the political machinery in Washington, London, Paris, Tokyo, and other major world centers of human control. The United Nations General Assembly ostensibly operated at this level. The next higher tier was occupied by secret societies, exclusive membership in high-level generational witchcraft and Satanism, the Black Nobility, global Illuminism.

With each successively higher level, more pertinent information was declassified and made available to the initiates. It was only in the upper echelon that integral elements of the global conspiratorial "Plan" was revealed. Throughout the various hierarchical strata there was vertical integration, some groups and key individuals among the super-wealthy international crime families were granted considerable latitude to participate at all levels within the satanic pyramid of human control.

It was in the upper half of the occult triangle that spiritual power was most heavily concentrated; where the aspirations of the planet's most wicked men and women were conceived and filtered down to the lower levels. Among the principal world decision makers were the Committee of 300, which was superseded by the Council of 33 representing the highest ranking Freemasons in the world. Beyond them was the Council of 13 Illuminati Druidic witches, many of whom performed their blood sacrifice rituals at the Castle of Darkness and at other secret locales throughout Europe. These were subordinate to the Council of 9 unknown men: exceedingly wealthy individuals who created wars and insurrections, manufactured plagues and diseases in laboratories, planned economic booms and global financial busts. They were directly responsible for collapsing the New York City World Trade Towers in 2001, just as they planned to collapse the U.S. Stock Market to bring down the world financial empire. They manipulate and control all national governments; they depose Presidents and raise up the Antichrist. But, even these politically powerful individuals were subordinate to the 3 Rothschilds who presided above them, and who some insiders considered to be non-human. At the top level, positioned at the apex of global control, was the all-seeing eye, the Eye of Horus – *Lucifer* – also known as Satan, the Devil. With a thousand disguises and assuming a thousand different names, he was the spirit master of the multitudes of human slaves that did his bidding in ruling the world. It was he that was the ultimate source of evil, the progenitor of death and destruction. Human beings were his willing or unwitting servants. All those who participated in human civil government were the spiritual progeny of the father of lies and the master of deception.

It was not often that it happened at the higher levels, but defection occasionally *did* occur. Such rogue individuals were expediently dealt with, punished in particularly gruesome ways. They were controlled by various means: blackmail, family members taken hostage, microchips implanted in their body and that were programmed to terminate them should they fail to cooperate with any aspect of the Plan for a global dictatorial government.

"… Mr. Oppenheimer, this Committee demands an explanation for your failure to include the U286 primate virus in our latest version of Flu Vaccine in our protocol to inoculate the North American continent with terminal disease pathogens. The disappointing epidemic had a kill yield of only 33 percent of the test population, totaling 47 million human lives, which was far short of our projected mortality of 113 million. What do you have to say for yourself?"

The Committee consisted of 300 of some of the most influential people in the International Hierarchy: European Royalty, world politicians, international bankers, media representatives, scientists. They were an exclusive group of powerful men and women who bowed the knee to their dark underworld invisible master.

The Nobel Prize winning microbiologist trembled uncontrollably as the assemblage of his peers looked on. The amplified voice of the Committee Chairman reverberated within the confines of the large private chamber. "Mr. Oppenheimer … Mr. Oppenheimer …"

When the scientist finally replied, his frightened quavering voice sounded pathetically weak, like the bleating of a lone sheep among an assemblage of ravenous wolves. "You're mad – all of you – mad! T-This is treason … taking over America … destroying U.S. sovereignty! D-Destroying the world! B-Billions of lives! You – you poisoned the food chain … the water … even the air! MSG, Aspartame, Genetic Engineered plants and animals, Fluoride … Disease transmitting vaccines … Chemtrial nanofibers … human implanted microchips … weaponized synthetic food … slow kill genocide … citizen surveillance … prisons … concentration camps … hundreds of millions of people in slavery – this is insanity! I-I can't take it anymore. I won't do it. No! No! I can't … no more … no more death … no more destruction … no more killing … no more murder … precious lives – the innocent children … no more! I won't be a part of it! I – I quit! I refuse to be controlled by your microchip technology. I refuse to cooperate … I will expose you … I will … aghhhhhhhhhh!"

When administered directly into the neck carotid artery by one of his colleagues, the hypodermic injection, containing a triple dose of U286 monkey pox virus – in combination with Mercury, Aluminum, MSG, Aspartame, Lead; and other lethal vaccine, processed food, and Chemtrail components – caused a cerebral embolism and cardiac arrest. He died instantaneously.

A disembodied menacing guttural voice resounded over the speakers. "No one ever quits The Family, Mr. Oppenheimer."

— 20 —

By the second day, the seven had procured most of the necessary supplies and equipment. Arranged upon twin beds in the hotel room were seven sets of black camouflage fatigues and an assortment of paraphernalia, including communication and GPS devices, specialized weaponry, precooked MRE food rations, and various other items of survival gear. Rex picked up a slender pen-like object. "This here's actually a laser," he said, instructing the others in its use. "Direct it at someone's face, flip this here little ole' switch on the side, and within a millisecond, they'll be blind as a dang ole' bat." When he demonstrated the device on the far wall, an intense beam of coherent blue light seared a three inch diameter burn mark into the plaster. "Instantly burns out the retina." He clicked off the device and set it down upon the bed. "Effective range up ta' twenty yards. Y'all got one. Be careful how ya' use it." He then selected another weapon from the arsenal. "This long knife is razor sharp. Use it for close range combat. Attach it to yer' outside shin with these here Velcro straps." He fastened the knife in its holder onto his lower leg. "An' for longer strikin' distance, we got these lil' babies – special edition 44 magnum pistols with silencer, infrared night scope, an' a heat-seekin' laser dot sight mechanism that'll guarantee ya' can't miss. These extra ammo clips are ta' be carried on yer' belt. I'll be handlin' the explosives, since they require a good bit more know-how." He grabbed the quantum laser gun. "Still got ma' ole' Betsy. Good thing I keep her at the shootin' range, or else the pigs woulda' got it when they trashed m'house."

Howard rose up to stand before them and explain the function of a pocket-size communication transponder. "Once inside the Castle, we'll be dividing up into two groups. We'll locate each other and monitor our relative positions at all times with this LED display on the front cover that shows the location of each member of the team. When you press *this* button, it can be used as a two-way radio. There's a lot of room to roam inside that place, so we need to constantly stay in touch."

Eric said, "By this time tomorrow we should have secured the remainder of our provisions. How's the transport plane coming along, Howard?"

"It's a real beauty," he replied. "DC-7C cargo carrier; quad engine, post World War II vintage, capable of air speeds up to 500 mph. It's got plenty of room for hauling a few hundred children and a store of food provisions across the ocean. The long distance fuel storage capacity will enable us to traverse the Atlantic both ways without refueling. Perfect for what we need it for. It was a bargain at only ten million."

"What's the maintenance record look like?" the strategist asked.

"Low air-miles on the Rolls Royce engines; shouldn't have any problems. I've got a team of aviation mechanics working on it right now giving it a thorough once over."

"How well did you screen them?"

"They're all hand picked personal confidants that I've worked with for years, and can be trusted."

Eric thought for a moment, reviewing every contingency detail in his mind. "Have them double check all the back-up systems, especially the hydraulics. Also, the circuit board control panel and connecting wires and electrical systems. These are the most likely points of failure."

"You got it," answered his senior, who was immediately on his cell phone to issue the new directive: "Jared, I want you to do a through retest of all the back-up systems, hydraulics, electrical systems, control panel and wiring. Spare no expense to replace whatever it might need. Tomorrow I'll be departing for Australia, so get the crew on it right away. Have it ready by 7:00 AM sharp."

"*Australia?* …" whispered Rex, a wry smile on his rough, unshaven face.

Pocketing the small phone, Howard replied, "Just in case there's a security breach. God commands us to be wise as serpents."

Eric appended, "Be sure any record of a flight plan reflects that destination."

"Already done," answered Howard. "Within twenty-four hours – God willing – that plane will lift off. We'll go direct to Luxembourg, then land in its capital, known by the same name."

Brandon gazed around the room at all the others, the reality now beginning to loom large in his mind. "We're actually going to do it, aren't we?" he said with subdued amazement.

Tony confidently replied, "You *bet* we're going to do it."

Rex affirmed, "It's time for some street justice."

Later that night, sleeping on sofas and upon the carpeted floor, they were abruptly awakened by a series of loud knocks. Rex instantly jumped to his feet, pistol in hand, aimed at the door. Eric turned on a small lamp to light a corner of the dark room, then motioned for everyone to stay down. Seven pairs of eyes darted about the hotel suite, ears straining to hear, yet, there was only silence. Brandon whispered, "Sharp rapping sounds of the nature we just heard are an indication of a spiritual presence."

"It sounded like it came from the wall, not the door," observed Tony.

Adam was quick to add further insight. "Their demons were sent to hinder us."

Alex commented, "It's the spiritual equivalent of the harassment we endured from their human counterparts, the police. We're engaged in an invisible war."

Howard said, "Psalm 34:7 tells us that *The angel of the LORD encampeth round about them that fear him, and delivereth them*".

"We are surrounded by a protective wall of impenetrable fire," perceived Adam. "The enemy can do us no harm."

With that assurance, they turned out the light, then, periodically throughout the night heard abrupt noises – unexplained footfalls, strange dissonant sounds of swirling whispers in the darkness.

At the first light of dawn, while loading their gear into duffel bags, the men recounted events of the previous night. "We can expect more of the same as we get closer to our target destination," instructed Alex. "The nearer one draws to doing the will of God, the greater are the attacks from the hordes of hell."

Brandon further observed, "We're experiencing the conflict simultaneously on two levels – material and spiritual. Yet, because the enemy is invisible, the spiritual realm is even more deadly."

Adam discerned, "But we've got *twice* as many on our side as they've got on theirs."

By late afternoon, the final load of supplies was delivered to the room by a trusted courier. "That's the last of it," said Howard, using cash to pay yet another confidant at the door. After phoning the crew supervisor at the airport hanger to confirm that the plane was fueled and ready for takeoff, he then made another call to bring the windowless extended cargo van to the back of the hotel for loading. "I'll go down to the front desk and check out," he said to the others as they familiarized themselves with any new items of equipment.

"Don't!" warned Eric. "It's a contact point for potential exposure. Let them think you're still here. We'll leave in stages; some taking the stairs, others the elevator."

"Okay," Howard replied. "The van is white and unmarked, and will be parked around the back."

Eric said, "We'll go out the South exit door and enter from the front passenger side. I'll be the driver. Adam, you and Howard go first.

Tony and Alex next. Then, Brandon and Rex. I'll exit last. Everyone got it?" They all nodded.

When leaving the room, each was toting a large canvass bag slung over their shoulder. The first two exited and headed in opposite directions. Five minutes later, two more left the room. After they had all vacated, shortly, when Brandon, then Eric, emerged from the back door of the hotel and joined the others already in the cargo van, they immediately knew something was wrong. "Where's Rex?"

"He took the elevator," Brandon said.

"I'll go check it out," volunteered Tony, who, with cat-like reflexes, quickly moved to the front and out the passenger door. Meanwhile, Eric got behind the wheel, started the engine and pulled up closer to the hotel.

On the descent to ground level, the elevator had abruptly stopped. Rex was the only passenger in the sealed compartment, which made it apparent to him that the well-timed malfunction was intentional. Combat ready, he remained poised under pressure, having faced life and death situations many times during his military career. But, he was unschooled in battling against a spiritual adversary that was unseen. Avoiding the elevator's emergency telephone, he activated his communication transponder. "Houston … looks like we got us a little problem," he calmly spoke into the wrist-mounted device. "This here rocket ship ain't goin' nowheres. Please ad-vise."

Answering the alert signal that beeped in his shirt pocket, Tony replied into the GPS receiver, "I've got your position located." Moments later, when standing in front of a row of closed elevator doors, he noted that one of the red lights remained stationary between the sixth and seventh floors.

Eric coached from the van. "Tony, see if you can find the circuit breaker. It's probably down in the basement."

"I'm on my way," replied the versatile athlete, swiftly running toward the stairwell, then down four flights of steps, and finally bursting through a metal door. Once in the basement, he flipped on a light switch that cast dim illumination throughout the expansive room cluttered with rolls of carpet, beds, and other hotel furnishings.

"Check the walls for a large grey metal box."

"I see it," Tony acknowledged, striding over to a rectangular cabinet fastened on the near block wall. "Now what?"

"There should be a labeled diagram on the inside door cover. Find any reference to elevators, then look on the opposite panel grid for a corresponding breaker switch or fuse."

Tony paused a moment to study the hotel's complex electrical flow chart. Soon he announced, "Here it is: E1, E2, E3; E must stand for elevator. Looks like number two fuse is miss –" He abruptly broke off in mid-sentence.

"Tony? … Tony!" several of the others in the van were now shouting into their transponders. "Tony – you okay? …" During the next fifteen seconds there was no audible reply, only muffled sounds of shuffling feet and a series of electric sharp cracks. "Tony, you still there? … Come in, Tony …"

A moment later he was back, a slight pant evident in his voice. "There's no problem. Just a couple chumps that needed a boxing lesson."

Eric said to the others, "They know we're here."

Ignoring the bloodied bodies lying motionless on the cold bare concrete floor, Tony went about his task of removing one of the fuses to transfer into the vacant elevator slot. "How's that, Rex?"

"We got contact. I'm movin'," he answered, the elevator car now beginning to descend.

Minutes later, with the van in motion and sliding side door wide open, the two running men jumped inside. Rex commanded, "Let's get outta' here – *fast!*"

The loaded vehicle responded to the accelerator pedal as they quickly exited from the hotel parking lot. "We're twenty minutes from the airport hanger," said Howard, as everyone braced them self against the side walls when the truck made a sharp right, then a left turn onto the main road.

Eric looked in the side mirrors and shouted back to the others, "Cop car behind us!"

Instinctively, Howard and Rex made ready their guns. "I was hoping it wouldn't come to this so soon," the elder said. "I mean, I don't want to waste any ammo before we get there."

"Consider it jus' target practice, Brother," replied Rex, pulling back the breech of a spare Luger pistol. "Make like it's a turkey shoot."

Howard was quick to address the apparent reluctance of the others to take up arms. "This is *war*, Gentlemen." He glanced intently at each one of them in turn. "Does anyone here doubt that our mission is the will of God?" The others shook their heads. "Psalm 97:10: *Ye that love the LORD hate evil.* And, in a God-hating Luciferian government, are not the police the very embodiment of evil?" More unanimous assent. "We know that the police would gladly kill us if God allowed them. When entering the Promised Land, the Israelites were instruments of God's wrath upon the heathen. Even now, we too are His instruments of that same wrath. So let's not shrink back and allow them to hinder what God has appointed us to do."

Rex added, "The Bible says that murder is the shedding of innocent blood. But the blood of these bags o' dirt *ain't innocent!* So's killin' 'em ain't murder. It's Scriptural ta' kill the enemies of God that murder His people. In Matthew 22:7, it says: ... *the king sent forth his armies, and destroyed those murderers, and burned up their city.*"

Alex confirmed what Rex had said, adding, "We have an obligation to fulfill. We are living Bible prophesy. Right now. In this place. In this time. What is happening to us is for the glory of God. Let our bravery be to His honor, and to their shame."

The others were in unanimous agreement. Now, they were not only physically and mentally prepared for war, but were also spiritually prepared.

Howard commented, "Satan's people think Christians are passive and non-confrontational, and would never resist tyranny. That only makes cops act all the more tyrannical. Remember, they're paid cowards, and a coward does not want a confrontation. But that's not what a True Christian should be. God's people despise the wicked, and throughout Scriptures, His anointed battled against the human hosts of hell."

Rex stated, "We're the stones of God that will knock down Goliath and cut his head off!"

"More company," said the driver. "There's now five police cars following us." In the side view mirror, Eric could see them gathering like crouching lions, lurking, lying in wait to ambush their prey.

The six in the back had their loaded guns drawn and ready. Adam said, "Satan's people are under orders to make a final effort to stop us before we get to the airport."

"Lights *are on*," announced Eric, noting the growing line of revolving colored lights behind them. "It won't be long now." As soon as he said this, shrill sirens began to blare.

Sensing a replay of the recent abuses he suffered at the hands of the police, there was evident tension in Brandon's voice when he said, "I've written about this sort of thing for years, yet, until one has actually experienced the reality of spiritual warfare, the encounter can be quite unnerving." While the police approached ever closer, he thoughtfully added, "The realm of the spiritual manifesting in the physical is a most interesting phenomenon to observe."

"You ain't seen *nothin'* yet, Perfessor," said Rex, focused, ready for action. "This here's jus' kid's stuff. Wait till we get ta' the Castle – that's when you're *really* gonna' see sparks fly."

"I suggest we all pray," said Alex. Then, as the servants of darkness closed in for the kill, the men bowed their heads and opened their King James Bibles. The preacher began by reading Psalm 54: "*Save me, O God, by thy name, and judge me by thy strength. Hear my prayer, O God, give ear to the words of my mouth. For strangers are risen up against me, and oppressors seek after my soul: they have not set God before them. Selah. Behold, God is mine helper: the Lord is with them that uphold my soul. He shall reward evil unto mine enemies: cut them off in thy truth. I will freely sacrifice unto thee: I will praise thy name, O LORD, for it is good. For he hath delivered me out of all trouble: and mine eye hath seen his desire upon mine enemies."*

Adam was next to read, selecting Psalm 27:1-3: *"The LORD is my light and my salvation; whom shall I fear? the LORD is the strength of my life; of whom shall I be afraid? When the wicked, even mine enemies and my foes, came upon me to eat up my flesh, they stumbled and fell. Though an host should encamp against me, my heart shall not fear: though war should rise against me, in this will I be confident."*

The new True Christian, Brandon, cried out to God from Psalm 144:7,8: *"Send thine hand from above; rid me, and deliver me out of great waters, from the hand of strange children; whose mouth speaketh vanity, and their right hand is a right hand of falsehood."*

A kaleidoscope of flashing red and blue lights – appearing much like materialized demons masquerading as alien space craft – were now reflected in the side mirrors.

Rising above the blaring sirens, God's infallible Word was spoken by Tony, reading from Psalm 21:8-13: *"Thine hand shall find out all thine enemies: thy right hand shall find out those that hate thee. Thou shalt make them as a fiery oven in the time of thine anger: the LORD shall swallow them up in his wrath, and the fire shall devour them. Their fruit shalt thou destroy from the earth, and their seed from among the children of men. For they intended evil against thee: they imagined a mischievous device, which they are not able to perform. Therefore shalt thou make them turn their back, when thou shalt make ready thine arrows upon thy strings against the face of them. Be thou exalted, LORD, in thine own strength: so will we sing and praise thy power."*

Rex recited Psalm 22:16: *For dogs have compassed me: the assembly of the wicked have enclosed me."*

Finally, Howard read Psalm 35:1-6: *"Plead my cause, O LORD, with them that strive with me: fight against them that fight against me. Take hold of shield and buckler, and stand up for mine help. Draw out also the spear, and stop the way against them that persecute me: say unto my soul, I am thy salvation. Let them be confounded and put to shame that seek after my soul: let them be turned back and brought to confusion that devise my hurt. Let them be as chaff before the wind: and let the angel of the LORD chase them. Let their way be dark and slippery: and let the angel of the LORD persecute them.*"

At the very moment that Howard finished reading, Eric shouted, "Hey, guys! You're never going to believe what just happened!" The men sat in rapt attention, anticipating his next words. "One of the cop cars just slammed into a telephone pole!" They all broke out into a rousing cheer. A moment later, alternately gazing at the side mirrors, he excitedly added, "And look at *that*! … Two more just crashed into each other!" Another ecstatic round of cheers. "The rest are now falling back … they're losing ground. They're - *actually* - slowing - down!"

Shortly, after they passed through the next intersection, the sirens of their pursuers became a faint distant echo. For no apparent reason, some of the police cruisers had pulled off the side of the road; the remaining others had stopped dead in the middle of the highway, and were now backing up traffic.

A score of police car hoods were raised, their drivers perplexed and angry while standing near overheated engines spewing dark billows of thick hot smoke.

Enshrouded within a mass of swirling rising steam, the flagellating peace officers cursed their bad luck, and each other: "You're responsible for keeping this _ _ _ _ thing serviced!"

"No, _ _ _ _ , YOU are!"

Meanwhile, as the van continued cruising leisurely down the road, inside, the celebration was well under way:

"God has granted us the victory!"

"He has delivered us from the enemy!"

"His Word is alive! It's alive!"

"The Lord Jesus Christ is Faithful and True!"

—21—

Howard phoned the ground crew using an encrypted microwave frequency on his cell phone. "I want an additional back-up of armed guards on the runway until we leave the ground – understood?" Pausing for the confirming reply, he then added, "Stand by, we're on our way."

An half hour later, they drove into the parking lot of Cleveland Hopkins International Airport, then to a rear terminal where a row of massive 747 airliners were docked for refueling. "Our plane is near Gate 15A," he instructed Eric. "Just pull to the third ramp up ahead. My people will get rid of this van."

While driving by, the van was dwarfed by the size of the huge jumbo jets. "The DC-7 isn't quite as big as these," said the pilot, "but has as great a carrying capacity. It's a piston engine prop, one of the earlier models built by McDonnell Douglas. They designed it for use in wartime transoceanic flights. It's a cargo carrier, perfect for what we need it for." Up ahead, they could see the unmarked silver aircraft. "Well, Gentlemen … what do you think? Told you she was a beauty."

"When did you learn to fly?" inquired Adam.

"About fifteen years ago," replied Howard. "It was an avocation, really. I assisted in some Christian relief projects, flying to remote parts of the world – Asia, South America, the Philippines. Did an air drop mission to the Sudan not too long ago. Don't worry about a thing. I'm well qualified to fly this bird."

The copilot smiled when nudging his senior with an elbow and saying in jest, "If y'all fall asleep at the helm, I'll be there ta' drive us back home." Some of the others were tense and could only manage a brief smile.

Working on the plane, awaiting their arrival, were a twelve member crew dressed in navy blue jumpsuits. When the van came to a sudden halt at the boarding ramp, the seven men quickly exited. "The maintenance check hasn't yet been completed, Sir," said the mechanic supervisor. "We were pressed for time."

"We'll trust in God," was his employer's curt response. Immediately addressing the other members of the ground crew, he then said, "Everyone is on top security alert regarding disclosure of our Australia destination, and also concerning my traveling companions that you see here."

"Yes, Sir," they all responded.

Nearby stood another group of Howard's employees. Nodding at the ten well paid guards armed with machine guns, he then said, "Your orders are to use deadly force to defend this plane and its occupants from anyone – and I do mean *anyone* – who attempts to hinder our departure. Is that clear?"

They all responded: "Yes, Sir!"

Carrying their gear on board, the seven quickly took seats near the front of the spacious cabin. Minutes later, Howard and Rex were in the cockpit, at the flight controls. Through his headset Howard heard Rex when he said, "Let it rip!" Propellers began turning, whining engines warming up. Soon thereafter, an airport tow vehicle was transporting them out to the runway. The air traffic control tower radioed their clearance. "Flight 777 to Sidney, proceed to Airstrip G, now ready for takeoff."

"Roger," the pilot answered into his headset microphone. "Proceeding to G."

While they were being towed to the runway, when nearly in take-off position, a procession of six TSA airport security vehicles suddenly appeared from around the corner of the terminal building; colored lights flashing, sirens blaring. "They're back!" someone shouted from within the cabin.

Howard communicated with the man operating the tow hyster. "Disengage tow."

He waited. No response.

The trail of black cars were fast approaching. Above the engine roar, they heard the first shots fired. The pilot repeated, "Disengage *now!*" Again, no reply.

"The cops musta' contacted the airport," noted Rex.

Upon realizing that the tow driver was intentionally ignoring him, Howard was forced to make a quick decision. "So you want to come along for the ride? ... Okay, here goes." Increasing the throttle, the four massive Rolls Royce engines cranked the propellers faster, creating a powerful whirlwind turbulence. The pilot announced his ultimatum: "This is your final warning to disengage. Liftoff will commence in thirty seconds." While the plane remained bound on the tarmac, threatening government vehicles were closing the distance.

Howard's security team had interposed themselves between the menacing rivals and the plane. The government agent's wore black ski masks to conceal their faces, and black jackets with *TSA Patrol* printed on the back in large red letters. During the first exchange of gunfire, one of the approaching vehicles spun out of control and rolled over, suddenly bursting into flames.

The other cars screeched to a halt, unloading two TSA agents from each car, and commencing a volley of gunfire. One of Howard's men fell wounded. The remaining nine guards were able to stall the escalating attack for a needed few seconds more, during which time, six agents of the New World Order fatally dropped to the ground.

The metal link on the tow vehicle creaked and strained under accelerating engine RPM, until finally, with a loud bang, the holding pinon broke away, the pilot quickly maneuvering to avoid a collision with the hyster tow truck.

Once again the enemy was mounting an assault on the aircraft that was now lumbering down the airstrip, moving under its own power. "Step on it!" the copilot said above the sound of the whirling engines. Howard shoved the throttle forward, the plane gaining more speed, and within seconds they were outdistancing the trailing line of policemobiles that had breached the armed buffer zone. Rex pointed to the end of the runway, directly up ahead. A flashing police car was coming straight at them!

The pilots could see the occupants through the windshield – guns drawn – two government agents with deadpan expressions; mind-controlled assassins programmed to kill. The aircraft steadily increased momentum racing down the runway; the distance between the car and plane rapidly diminishing: 300 yards … 200 … 100 … Rex shouted, "Run the bastards over!"

Howard maintained his composure when noticing the agent's guns pointed out the side windows. "Fasten your seat belt!" At the last moment, he pulled back on the flight control and the heavy craft slowly began to lift. "It'll be close …"

An instant later, the wheels barely cleared the top of the car, and now airborne, the massive plane was steeply inclined, the ground quickly dropping away from below them. Powerful engine thrust forced them back in their seats as the copilot said to the pilot through headphones, "They didn't fire a dang gone shot." Meanwhile, in the passenger cabin, a rousing cheer could be heard from the men seated in the empty cargo carrier. "The glory be to God!"

An hour into the flight, the initial euphoria had waned, their mood was now more gravely serious. The awareness of what they were about to commence was now beginning to impact their consciousness. The pilot's voice came over the speakers: "We're flying at an altitude of 40,000 feet. Weather conditions are stable. Down below, you'll see the Eastern coastline as we leave the United States. At our present air speed of 480 miles per hour, we should make Europe in approximately

16 hours; Luxembourg in two more. So, Gentlemen, sit back and relax as much as possible. I suggest you try to get some rest."

The five in the ample cargo compartment maintained a vigil, passing the time in an effort to quell their anxiety. Adam said, "Courage isn't being fearless. It's persevering in spite of the fact that you're scared to death."

"*God hath not given us the spirit of fear*," announced the street preacher, quoting 2 Timothy 1:7.

Brandon once again expressed his bewilderment. "I just can't believe we're actually going to do it."

Alex replied, "This is real, Brandon. We can, and we *will* prevail. God's Word tells us in Proverb 20:18: 'Every purpose is established by counsel; and with good advice make war.' Our Counsel is God. Therefore, we *will* succeed."

"No fear," added Eric.

"Yeah," was the fighter's curt response. "And it's *them* who better be afraid of *us*."

Alex added, "By the strength and power of Almighty God the Lord Jesus Christ."

Tony declared, "We're not going all the way over there to negotiate, but to carry out the Lord's vengeance. The wrath of God be upon them, and His mercy upon us."

The others affirmed. "Amen, Brother!"

A moment later, Adam said, "I feel sorry for those guys."

Rex said, "I don't."

The plane glided silently through the vast starry expanse of the night sky, surrounded by a halo of radiant light.

During an ensuing discussion, Brandon provided additional information gathered from his research. "The Castle of Darkness is also known as the *Mothers of Darkness Castle*. The locals refer to it as *Chateau des Amerios*, or *Castle of Kings*. It's appropriately situated in Belgium, since that small country was established in 1831 for the purpose of proliferating Satanism. Brussels is the world headquarters for the European Union and NATO – organizations created by the Illuminati to facilitate world unity and today's antichrist world government. The massive mainframe computer, known as *The Beast*, is located in Brussels. It's databanks store information on every person in the world that has been assigned a Social Security Number. That universal numbering system is presently being replaced by a human implantable microchip. The SS number is merely a precursor to the computer chip Mark of the Beast."

Alex said, "Numbering people has always been the means by which Satan tries to control God's people. His servants – government bureaucrats – track people by requiring them to register. I haven't signed my name to a government document for over twenty years. Anyone who submits to the scrutiny of Satan's people becomes their property, a slave, as Romans 6:16 tells us: *Know ye not, that to whom ye yield yourselves servants to obey, his servants ye are to whom ye obey; whether of sin unto death, or of obedience unto righteousness.* "

"Isn't the whole Belgium government like a secret society?" asked Tony.

"Yes, it is," replied Brandon. "There are certainly high concentrations of Luciferians operating out of Belgium. It's the world capital for Satanism and heads the European Union. In fact, the country has been named after the one it serves. In ancient pagan cultures, the word, *Bel*, was synonymous with the Devil, or any of various pagan deities cryptically signifying that name. It is also seen written as *B-a-a-l*, or *B-e-l-i-a-l*. The fallen angel, Lucifer, has many aliases."

"What's the American connection?" inquired Eric.

The erudite scholar responded, "Since the 1950's, the Defense Intelligence Agency and CIA developed genetic and trauma-based mind-control programs designed to shatter the will and personality of experimental subjects, most of whom were children recruited from incestuous families that were steeped in witchcraft and Satanism. The psychological principles employed were developed by Hitler's SS black art occultists who used these personality disintegrating techniques on prisoners of war in Nazi concentration camps. At this present time, a principal objective of the controlling elite is to apply these same trauma-based programming techniques to *the entire human race*; using political terror to traumatize the masses into a mindless robotized state. What happened after September 11 is a classic example of that; a mind-control response was deeply entrenched into modern world culture, especially in America. The result is that nearly everyone today has become a docile, terrified, non-critical thinking zombie who views everyone as a potential terrorist and loves to be told what to do by their government handlers.

"Children are being taken from their own back yards – not by rogue criminals and pedophiles operating in our communities – but by government employed operatives hired to procure children for ritual sacrifices. The controlled media then spins the truth to make everyone suspicious of everyone else so the general public remains in a constant state of irrational fear and obeys the government while it steals more of their freedoms and personal privacy.

"Mind-control programming of select children is being conducted at research facilities on college campuses and key U.S. military bases, for example, MacDill in Tampa; Kennedy Space Center in Titusville, Florida; Fort Cambell, Kentucky; Fort McClellan in Anniston, Alabama; Offit Air Force base in Nebraska; Redstone Arsenal; and Marshall Space Flight Center in Huntsville, Alabama.

"Even before birth, while still in the mother's womb, these unfortunate children are traumatized, subjected to physical and psychological torture that exceeds the human tolerance threshold for enduring pain. Any number of programming techniques are used, including electroshock; sleep, food and water deprivation; hypnotic and neurolinguistic programming; sensory deprivation; virtual reality simulators; hallucinogenic drugs; and other forms of extreme emotional and physical torture. The children are sexually abused by adults and subjected to the most perverse forms of human desecration. As a result, their minds become fractured, their personalities fragmented in order to cope with the severe physical and emotional pain. Their subconscious mind compartmentalizes to create separate identities which are able to deal with each subsequent trauma. Consequently, they develop multiple personalities. For example, there may be a personality that copes with incest, one for mind-control programming, another for bestiality and various other forms of Satanic Ritual Abuse. The victims maintain a separate identity that functions more or less normally in everyday life. Amazingly, the personalities, or alters, are often not even aware the others exist. This should give you some idea of the severity of the trauma.

"The shattered personality of the children makes them like a hollow shell, an empty vessel filled by selective programming that induces them to respond on cues issued by their handlers, which are agents of the federal government assigned to systematically traumatize them. Without a mind of their own, these children are used for government-sponsored drug running, prostituted to pedophile politicians, or mind-numbed as consciousless lethal killers – adolescent terrorists programmed to carry out assassinations and mass executions, such as school shootings."

"How do these children end up at this Castle?" asked Tony.

Brandon answered, "Many are from orphanages – children that nobody knows or cares about. Some were kidnapped by local or State police, or federal agents – FBI, CIA – who sell them as sacrificial victims to satanic and witchcraft covens. Others were conceived during SRA rituals by females impregnated by their biological father; the incestuous offspring are later ritualistically murdered, no record having ever been kept of their birth. During Mothers of Darkness rituals conducted at the Castle, the first born of the young daughter must be sacrificed to Satan. Since no birth record exists, there can be no follow-up investigation.

"Many of the abducted children are procured through adoption agencies, such as those controlled by your friendly neighborhood government social services. The international child abduction network obtains its victims from community crisis centers, child care agencies, women's abuse shelters, pre-school and daycare centers, and from advocates for children involved in divorce disputes. Another fertile source tapped by the various branches of the government-sponsored organized crime network is international adoption agencies, which prove to be lucrative commercial enterprises for their pedophile operators, especially in America. These organizations and the individuals directing them are protected from prosecution by local police departments, all of which are headed by Satanists. Hospitals – and in particular Children's Hospitals and Trauma Centers – are complicit in providing blood ritual organizations with young human bodies to torture, mutilate and murder. Child-related organizations and hospitals are infested with Satanists and witches; a significant portion of doctors and nurses are active in local covens. Career professionals have the advantage of a respectable public image and legal backing by the Masonic courts, which is the reason why some professionals are Freemasons. This enables them to cover their tracks so no one seriously suspects they and other health care workers are a vital link in supplying SRA children for satanic blood rituals.

"Of course, there are the parents themselves, who sell their own offspring. Some of the children being kept at the Castle of Darkness are from multi-generational cult families that sold them to the government. In the deal, the federal government grants these parents immunity from prosecution for pedophilia, pornography, rape, drug dealing and murder. Their ranks are populated by Freemasons, mobsters, judges, politicians, attorneys, police officers, and other societal parasites. Not surprisingly, among this underbelly of humanity, the most notorious of them all are holders of high-level government office. Documentation exists to prove that Gerald Ford procured children for the CIA and was a pornographer and Mafia Capo until the Illuminati appointed him a U.S. Presidency; likewise another famous sexual predator, pedophile and serial killer, George Herbert Walker Bush.

"Children not sacrificed in rituals, such as those at the Belgium Castle, may circulate in the worldwide Delta Slave network. For instance, North of Belgium is the city of Amsterdam, where child prostitution is legal, and the enslaved mind-controlled children are displayed openly behind a neon glass partition. Southeast Asia is famous for ritual child abuse; SRA is rampant in the so-called Golden Triangle – a geographic region circumscribed by Thailand, Indonesia and the Philippines. Children trapped in the international ritual abuse web are considered by their handlers to be a *lucrative and disposable commodity.*

"The few children who survive the physical and emotional trauma may eventually be groomed as government operatives for a variety of tasks, as I previously mentioned: school terrorism, snipers, provocateurs, drug couriers, political messengers, or as sex toys for the many homosexual sadists occupying all levels of government. Nationally, the operation is run and covered up by politicians in Washington DC; the planned terrorism of children can be traced all the way down to the lowest level of community police departments. Since all police are members of the Fraternal Order of Police; and since the FOP is a semisecret organization within Freemasonry – which, according to its own documents, is a Lucifer-worshipping cult – therefore, all police are Satanists. Female police officers, as well as women in the military, have been psychologically damaged from the time of young childhood to assume the male dominance role in today's society. Some of them are same sex perverts and Wiccan witches.

"As you can perhaps see from all that I've said, the compartmentalized organizational structure of government facilitates secrecy among the international child abduction network."

"Scum floats to the top," said Tony.

"Or sinks to the bottom," appended Brandon, "depending on your perspective. Election to a public office appeals only to those that are already mind-controlled to some extent, or otherwise psychologically imbalanced. To see this more clearly, ask yourself: *How mentally stable can someone be if their principal goal in life is to usurp the God-given freedom of others and exert power and tyrannical control over peace-loving people?*"

Alex observed, "It's no coincidence that their master, Satan, *also* seeks power and control over human beings. They're following in their father's footsteps. As the old saying goes: *Like father, like son.*"

Eric commented, "You mentioned *genetic mind-control.* That implies there's a spiritual component to this trauma-based programming."

Brandon answered, "There is indeed. Generational ancestry is of crucial importance to families of the International Hierarchy that rule the world. The inheritance of what I call *spiritual genetic traits* are the basis for establishing the hierarchical chain of command among the global satanic network. Since the physical and spiritual inextricably interrelate – i.e. *life is in the blood,* as the Bible states in Leviticus 17:11 – the inherited biological blood of wicked ancestry has corrupted the spiritual blood, or the soul, of their progeny. The selection of world leaders is determined on the basis of this demonic gene pool."

Eric laughed when light-heartedly jesting, "You mean our *votes don't count?*"

"Sure they do," the author replied. "They count as a means for government intelligence agencies to gather information on their citizen-slaves and track them to their doorstep."

On a more serious level, Alex interjected, "What Brandon is really talking about is inherited generational curses. Exodus 20:5 explains: *... I the LORD thy God am a jealous God, visiting the iniquity of the fathers upon the children unto the third and fourth generation of them that hate me....* That Scripture is also found in Exodus 34:7; Numbers 14:18; and Deuteronomy 5:9."

Brandon acknowledged with a nod, then continued. "Super wealthy multi-generational Luciferian families, such as the European Royal Dynasties, strive to retain their satanic blood in the family genealogy. Incest and inbreeding are one of the primary means which they employ for accomplishing that. Consequently, all the major players in world politics are blood relatives. For example, nearly all past and present U.S. Presidents are direct descendants of the chief blood-related Black Nobility Monarchies. Key individuals from this same family tree will one day replace their cult parents to rule the world. At a very early age, usually by the sixth year, they are forced to participate in satanic rituals, human sacrifice ceremonies where murder and mind-control programming are the primary objectives. Jimmy Carter, for instance, in preparation for his Presidential placement by the Illuminati, was trauma programmed at England's Tavistock Institute, a known mind-control torture facility founded by England's equivalent of the CIA, the Royal Institute of International Affairs. It was Tavistock that formed NATO, which is yet another political ploy for creating today's global Police State. Until recently, Carter's sister was the highest ranking witch in North America. It's also noteworthy to mention that the English Monarchy is blood-related to Gengis Khan and Count Dracula.

"As you can see, blood is very important to these – dare I say – *people*. The ruling elite have bastard children that are given a different name to conceal their true blood geneology from the public. The important ones, in terms of satanic bloodline, are sometimes adopted and raised by another Illuminati family. It's not until the biological father comes forward – usually during a blood ritual ceremony – that the child's true lineage is revealed.

"Everyone in top levels of world government is an Illuminati witch or practicing Satanist; they would not have been permitted to attain their high-level position if that were not the case. As bond slaves to Lucifer, they no longer have a free will of their own, and have no choice but to do what their master commands them to do – that is, murder and enslave the world masses of people in preparation for the arrival of their New World Order global leader, the Antichrist.

"What we'll be dealing with at the Castle are Lucifer's children; people that have consigned themselves over to serving Satan. He owns them. They sold their birthright to the Devil in exchange for worldly wealth and power to rule over others. And this is where the government mind-control operation involves the spiritual element. The idea

– at least in their warped way of thinking – is to plant *evil spirits, demons, into children* during occult rituals. The children are sexually impregnated by demon-possessed adults, and also by the literal demons themselves. The Bible informs us in Genesis, Chapter 6, that this is how the early human bloodline became corrupted after the Edenic fall of man. This sexual transference of demons to humans is yet another means by which the soul of men becomes corrupted by *spiritual genetics.*"

"Isn't that what Hitler was trying to do?" questioned Adam.

"Yes, of course," answered the researcher. "Hitler was a Communist politician, a Satanist, and a Catholic Jesuit – all at the same time. The doctrines of all three are mutually inclusive. The Vatican supported his eugenics campaign and provided him financial aid and sanctuary for his Nazi SS murder squads when Catholic Rome enabled them to escape capture and criminal prosecution after WWII. The Vatican, and more specifically, the Jesuits, are heavily involved in the occult and government mind-control operations. They not only deal with covert projects, such as MK-Ultra, but also spread religious propaganda on a global scale. This is largely directed at indoctrinating children into their Mystery Babylon pagan belief system, otherwise known as the *Roman Catholic Church.* Operating under the guise of Christianity, Catholic religious doctrine is one of the most insidiously dangerous forms of pagan occultism. The Bible specifically identifies it in Revelation 17 when referring to *The Great Mother of Harlots and Abominations of the Earth.*"

Alex commented, "The Pope is unmistakably the False Prophet spoken of in Revelation: 11:13-17; 16:13:19:20."

Brandon affirmed, "Catholicism is only one among many satanic religious systems promoting itself as *Christianity.* Because its followers reject the authority of the Bible, they are not True Christians at all, but only profess to be. They're actually neopagans, and are blinded to the realization that they do not serve the God of Heaven, but the god of this world – Lucifer. Like its twin sister, Islam, Satan uses these two religious giants to send billions of unsuspecting followers to the Lake of Fire.

"It's important to recognize the synergy that exists between the worldwide religious ecumenical movement and global politics. Both of them are integral to the spiritual-political agenda of the New World Order. This organization is comprised of some of the very same individuals we are about to confront at the Belgium Castle."

Tony concluded, "So, it looks like we're caught in the middle of something that's bigger than all of us. What we're about to do has a deeper spiritual meaning than just routing a bunch of sadistic perverts. It's no accident that we've been gathered together to fight this thing."

While gazing out one of the darkened side windows, in a voice that sounded distant and detached, Adam replied, "It was no accident. It was planned. God knows our hearts and drew each one of us here." He then prophesied: "Eric, you were convicted by the Holy Spirit on that day when you first heard of the Castle of Darkness and the terrible things being done to the image of God. Brandon, ever since you were a child you have been preparing for this moment. Because you have lived the pain, none of us feels the hurt to the depth that you do. Tony, you are God's anointed servant of the warrior class. You hate evil and unrighteousness as does He. The Lord has granted you the commission to be an instrument of His consuming wrath. Alex, as a minister of God's Holy Word, the Lord has given you a heart for the poor and oppressed. You came when He called you to free those in bondage; the little ones that He loves above all His creation."

As silver wings soared on into the dark night sky, for a long while they remained silent, pondering their destiny, and what soon lie ahead.

— 22 —

They flew nonstop the remainder of the night and throughout the next day, touching down at 7:00 PM, just as darkness was covering the land. While the plane rolled to a gradual stop near a terminal refueling bay, Howard announced over the intercom, "We've got a rental van on reserve and a room booked for the night." Before disembarking, he said, "Tony and I will go inside to check that our transportation is secure. The rest of you stay in here. Have your weapons ready to fire at all times."

The two men made their way through the crowded airport concourse, then paid for the vehicle using alias identification. Soon, they drove the windowless cargo van up close to the plane and quickly transferred their essential gear.

"The hotel is only a couple miles away," said Howard, as the group drove out of the airport and onto a dimly lit narrow street. Upon their soon arrival at the hotel, using aliases, each member of the team checked in separately at the front counter, then met later in one of the double suites.

After dining on canned rations, they reviewed their plan. Howard flattened out a map upon a small coffee table as the others gathered around. "This is our present location," he pointed, using a pen. "We're approximately fifteen miles East of the Belgium border. Here's the route we'll be taking ..." He traced the road previously marked in yellow. "We head Northwest toward Arlon, which is just across the border. Then, we drive South about twenty miles, along this road paralleling a forested area. The Castle is near the French border, in the vicinity of St. Leger and Virton, and close to the village of Muno." He drew a circle around their ultimate destination.

"Muno, Belgium," commented Brandon. "Appropriately named. It means *Satan's Moon.*"

"They don't miss a thing," replied the elder. "From Muno, we travel North to Highway 83, then West on a road called Les Amerois. The Castle is in the immediate vicinity. Just look for the gate." He circled a wooded area, then said, "My French contacts have already leased two school buses. Each has been specially equipped with seating to accommodate us and approximately 140 small children. Eric and Alex will be the drivers. Eric has worked out the rest of the details, so I'll let him take over from here."

The brilliant mind of the strategist was focused, his calculated words spoken in an even measured tone. "We'll travel at dusk and make the final approach in the dark." Using his penlight as a pointer when referring to the map, he said, "Along the fringe of *this* heavily wooded area we'll look for a side access road to park the buses, traveling far off the main highway, driving to about a mile from the Castle. It will serve as our base camp. Alex, you'll stay and guard the buses; the rest of us will proceed on foot.

"The element of surprise gives us a strategic advantage. By stealth and evasive maneuvering we hope to approach the Castle grounds undetected. If not, we have the firepower capability to put down resistance. Once we gain entry into the Castle, we'll divide into two groups. Team One will be the rescue team, and will consist of Tony, Adam, and myself. Team Two will be the seek and destroy team: Rex, Brandon, and Howard. Confrontation is inevitable. We shoot to kill on sight and take no prisoners. Our primary objective is to locate and take the children out of there as quickly and efficiently as possible; our secondary objective is to destroy the enemy, and ultimately, the Castle itself." He paused to look at the others. "Everyone got it?" They all nodded.

Rex advised, "It's kill, or *be killed* – simple as that."

Eric continued. "Team One proceeds directly to the basement, while Team Two sweeps the main floor to knock out any interference. Both groups are to have their radio transmitters tuned to the preset frequency that's an encrypted secure channel allowing us to remain in continuous radio contact. If either Team is in trouble, the other must respond immediately. The transponder's digital micromap will provide a diagram of the Castle interior, so you'll know your way around. Once the children are located, they are to be led outside to an awaiting bus for transport back to base camp. Team One will have radioed Alex at least ten minutes in advance for him to be there waiting when they exit out the front main entrance."

Now referring to a photo enlargement showing an aerial view of the exterior grounds, he illuminated the guard house located just beyond and to the right of a wrought iron gate between two stone pillars. After circling the gate with a pen, he said, "It's approximately ten feet high and is directly off the main road. The guard house will likely be occupied with one or more guards. Alex, you'll have to eliminate them, then use plastic explosives to open the gate to allow access for the buses. Timing is crucial. We may only have a brief period of time to secure the children and make our exit before reinforcements arrive. It's imperative that our advance and departure not be impeded. When the first load of children are returned to base camp, Alex, you'll then bring the second bus to retrieve the remainder of the captives, and us."

Howard produced a blueprint of the interior of the mansion, and when spreading the scroll upon the table, said, "Let's once again review the layout of the building." Using the penlight, he said, "As you recall from the view of the holographic image, access to the interior is through either of these two portals." He illuminated the two open tunnels that allowed for vehicle entry and exit. "The one on the left side could be a garage entry and exit; the other one, the main portal, goes all the way through and out the back of the building. Eric has calculated the probabilities of a successful entry for each possibility and concluded that the main tunnel is the better choice for gaining access." He then shined the light to follow their subsequent intended path. "This is the most likely route to the children." Tracing a marked dotted line superimposed on the floor plan diagram, the point of light proceeded to the right of the main entrance, then down two flights of steps to the basement dungeon. He went on to review the design for the remainder of the Castle. "On the first, second, and third levels, these are the rooms, halls, and connecting passageways." He highlighted each in turn.

Eric prompted, "Take careful note of the relative position of the rooms and passageways. We have to know every square foot of this place like the back of our hand. Study it thoroughly, burn it into your memory, make it second nature so that you could walk through it in the dark … because, you just might have to."

Brandon commented, "The final approach seems workable, but there's still a wild card: we won't know until the last moment how many there are of them, or where the guards are located."

"Just expect the unexpected," cautioned Tony.

Rex said, "I'll be plantin' explosives all along the way, settin' the timers ta' go off ninety minutes after we breach the entry. That should give us enough time ta' do what we gotta' do, and then clear outta' there."

Eric's disciplined mind calculated every move they were likely to make: the time required for each maneuver, and the needed time delay on the bomb fuses. Allowing a margin of error for unexpected contingencies, he spatially envisioned – as if on a chessboard, calculating 20 moves in advance – the movement of all the pieces. Shortly, he advised Rex, "Make it one hundred and twelve minutes."

"Hundred and twelve it is," replied the decorated demolition expert. "When it detonates, the whole dang buildn'll be reduced to a pile a' rubble within sixty seconds."

They all stayed in the same room for the remainder of the evening, resting, checking equipment and supplies, going over specific details of the plan. Later, while relaxing, Brandon read from a courtesy copy of the daily newspaper. "Listen to this ..." he announced. "Here's a front page story obviously intended by the Belgium government to promote the globalist's agenda of weapons *confiscation* from the citizenry. They call it *gun control*, just like the media propaganda does in America. The news report recounts an incident of a school shooting. Does this sound familiar? ... It's about a six year old first grade student who pulled a gun on one of his classmates and shot her in the heart at close range." Brandon translated the article that was written in French. "I'm quoting: '*The child showed no remorse. The murder was performed with military precision.*' That was yet another Delta Slave – an Illuminati programmed mind-controlled assassin. Undoubtedly, a product of the Castle of Darkness."

"Create the problem; offer the solution," said Howard. "Standard procedure for any government dictatorship."

Brandon explained further. "The children-killing-children syndrome is used by the world controllers as a pretense for legislating more gun control laws. They realize they can't overthrow an armed populace, and fear that well-informed citizens will not voluntarily surrender their personal weaponry. Therefore, they psychologically manipulate the undiscerning masses by staging terrorist antics *like this* in order to entice the people to *want* to give up their guns. I guarantee you this child was mind-controlled by trauma-based programming. Governments produce trained killers that are undetectable as mind-controlled slaves. Gestapo agents posing as D.C. politicians legislate gun confiscation laws, then use media hype to make their fascist rule seem like a public service. It's all orchestrated to appear as a needed civil service, yet, they're following the Communist Manifesto script for establishing a global dictatorship."

Howard said, "You'll never hear a news anchor person talk about *that*, and you'll never read it in Time Magazine, The New York Times, Washington Post, or any other –"

"Or any other major media in America," concluded Brandon. "The reason is because all print and broadcast media is being controlled by the Illuminati agents of disinformation. Whether the source is newspapers, TV, radio or Hollywood; their goal is always the same: *Mold public opinion to conform to the New World Order agenda*. Staged acts of terrorism rank at the top of their priority list. Severely psychotic men suffer from the delusion they are somehow our masters, and that we are their undeserving slaves. Anyone with even a base level intellect should be able to see right through their smoke screen. But, unfortunately, people today have lost the capacity to think critically; they have no ability to recognize the truth."

Alex commented, "Second Thessalonians, Chapter 2, verses 9 through 12 explains the reason for that: it's because they hate the truth ... and *The Truth* is Jesus Christ."

Eric said, "The political elite regard the people as mindless sheep for slaughter. Their propaganda has nearly everyone brainwashed, mind-controlled and dumbed-down to the point where people today are like vegetables."

"Mass hypnosis," observed Alex.

"Global madness," volunteered Adam.

"Of course it is," Brandon confirmed. "Simply by watching television or playing certain video games, nearly anyone can be programmed to become a cold-blooded serial killer. Computer video games are designed to train children to be expert marksman assassins. Role-playing games and popular books and films like the Harry Potter witchcraft series, condition young minds to an uncritical acceptance of sorcery as being normal and good. Television programming is just *that – programming*. Watching TV, or viewing a movie, will subtly change a child's attitudes and perceptions to create a monster. I seriously doubt if there exists a single child's television program or major motion picture today that has not been crafted by Hollywood witchcraft for use as a tool of propaganda and mass mind-control. The Disney films illustrate this point; those cutesy Cinderella themes are actually sophisticated programming instructions specifically targeting indoctrinating children into the occult. American, European, and Eastern culture are now immersed in witchcraft and occultism. A little boy or girl sitting in front of a television set is a captive audience for being mind-manipulated by the mesmerizing spell of the Luciferian Hollywood sorcerers.

"Upon further considering the fact that the air, water and food supply has been chemically and genetically doped; and that modern medicine is essentially voodoo; and that the primary goal of public school education is to produce lockstep socialists; it's not surprising that the world population has been dumbed-down and conditioned to be subservient to the emerging global government."

"Bad is now good, and good is now bad," added Howard.

Tony said, "Most people wouldn't lift a finger to help a child in their own neighborhood who's being mistreated by abusive parents or a guardian, much less travel halfway around the globe to do it."

The researcher agreed. "Statistics indicate that as much as eighty percent of children are silent victims of some form of childhood abuse at the hands of their parents, or single parent – which is the norm today – since very few children are raised to adolescence by both their biological parents. Divorce rates are sixty percent, and rising. Consequently, one of the legal guardians is typically not the biological father or mother, which makes it increasingly likely that incest and other forms of child abuse will occur. The figure for daughters sexually abused by their fathers is over fifty percent, which can't be much different from what it was in the days of Sodom and Gomorrah. Ours is a sick culture, and it's getting sicker every day."

"That's what the Bible says," affirmed Alex. Second Timothy 3:13 warns: *Evil men and seducers shall wax worse and worse, deceiving, and being deceived.* We're not headed for an era of renewed prosperity, as the New Agers believe, but instead, a literal hell on earth is about to break loose."

Eric commented, "This Castle of Darkness ... the children being mind-controlled and tortured by demon-possessed people with a global agenda – it's actually a microcosm of what the *whole world* is becoming as we approach the time of the Great Tribulation. It's an obvious parallel that should leave no doubt that human governments are controlled by a supernatural being with a supernatural hatred for God's children."

Recognizing that his lifelong friend was demonstrating evidence of spiritual regeneration, Tony slapped him on the back and complimented, "Well stated, Brother." The fighter then said, "What the seven of us are about to experience is the story of True Christian believers during the coming Tribulation. It's God's people against Satan's people; good versus evil; us verses them ... and *they will lose!*"

It was late at night when the group finally retired, once again sleeping on sofas or on the floor. Nerves taunt, their dreams were disturbed by a war raging in the heavens, and they were in the middle of the battlefield.

During the small hours of the morning, Tony suddenly sprung to his feet, startled. He was immediately followed by Rex, having also heard the scraping noises that sounded like the rending of bone and sinew. Eric whispered, "What was *that?*"

In the semi-darkness, the former military commando was poised with gun ready to fire. "Dunno."

The others were now stirred and awakening. "What's going on?" asked Howard, groggy with sleep.

Adam responded, "There is a spiritual presence here in this room, and it is hostile." The diffuse glow of the oil lamp cast the room in gray shadows. "Listen! ..." The visionary's face was set like stone in the half-light. "Can you not hear it? ... Horrible." He abruptly stifled a sob, then, in a voice filled with emotion, said, "They are *killing yet another one of God's little ones!*" In his mind's eye he could see the ritual as it was actually occurring – a vivid impression of a large room whose dimly lit ceiling lights created a thousand pin points of illumination. He was able to view the robed figures standing around a black leather altar; the drone of their monotone chants echoing in the chamber of darkness. "Listen! …"

While the others stood shock still, the hotel suite was permeated with mysterious swirling sounds that were the blood lust of transdimensional spirits aroused by the last gasps of life from a dying child. When a glistening long curved knife was plunged into the little girl's beating heart, the God-ordained visionary cried out, "Nooooooo!"

— 23 —

In the morning, Adam was the first to rise, and was sitting at the kitchen table by himself when Brandon came in and sat across from him. "Are you all right?" he asked.

Supporting his head with one hand, while he wrote with the other, without looking up, the visionary feebly nodded.

"What are you writing?"

"Oh, it's just a poem."

"Mind if I see it?"

Adam slid the paper over to him. Brandon took a moment to read it, then, noticeably disturbed, said, "Is this what you saw last night?"

Again he nodded.

"It's quite moving," said the erudite scholar, struggling to suppress memories of his traumatized past. He then silently read it once again:

> *The evil ones killed an angel last night,*
> *Took a life that was once aglow;*
> *They desecrated a temple of the most High God,*
> *They bent her halo.*
> *They killed yet another child last night,*
> *In a musty room, dark and cold;*
> *Where there was no one to love and protect her,*
> *When they tore out her heart and scarred her soul.*
> *Innocence was murdered once again last night,*

They defiled her body, broke her wings;
They chanted while her life blood slipped away,
Tortured her while she screamed.
Now the laughter in her voice is heard no more,
The twinkle in her eye is gone;
Broken body lying motionless,
Her smile now a frown.
One eye of the universe was closed last night,
And the world is now a darker place;
With the death of that sweet Angel,
Spattered blood, dried tears upon her face.

The word imagery triggered vivid impressions in Brandon's mind as his photographic memory replayed flashback sequences before glazed eyes. Now feeling detached from his own body, he could view the past: the sadistic torture, the depravations, humiliations; all of it now triggered to suddenly flood his consciousness. He saw the dark basement where his parents had confined him in a cold damp closet-sized room, the place where he was ordered to go after school. He could see them coming out of the shadows – the smiling angry faces of the past were haunting him, back once again.

He was forbidden to speak with, or even look at his brothers and sisters, and was not permitted to eat dinner with his family, nor was he allowed to use the bathroom. His adoptive parents squandered government welfare checks and food stamps to purchase drugs and alcohol for themselves. Tortured cries were now faint echoes in his mind; his pleas for help drowned out by his guardians' threats: "Shut up!" they demanded, while cutting his arms with a razor blade, and telling the starving eighty pound teenager to drink his own blood. "That'll keep you alive for awhile."

His siblings were abused in much the same manner: his stepfather prostituted his nine year old sister to friends. His stepfather, who often raped her, and whose heavy footfalls could now be heard descending the wooden steps … on his way to administer yet another senseless beating. Someone in the neighborhood was righteous enough to be concerned and call Child Protective Services. But that was a mistake. The CPS worker was a paid informant of the underground Child Abuse network. She made recommendations to the court for having children removed from homes where abuse was suspected, but also from homes where a well-meaning parent called 911 for an unrelated incident – the neighbor's dog bite, for example. Prior to the social worker arriving at the home to interview the family, his mother had sternly warned the children not to tell of the abuses. Because the government employee had been instructed by her handlers not to intervene in most cases of legitimate Child Abuse, she made no false claims to remove the children, even though she suspected abuse was occurring. Later, his parents added yet another adopted child to the family – another Welfare Check – a two year old little boy, who would *also* be abused by his new parents. When the child's stepmother swung a wood two by four and severed his spine so that he became a quadruphelegic, the doctors believed her when she said he slipped on the sidewalk. But the doctors were part of the cover-up … and the police – FOP Freemasons – squelched an investigation.

"Brandon! *Brandon!*" Eric was shouting as he grabbed him by the arms, recognizing that he was once again in a trauma-induced trance. "*Brandon*! It's over! *You're out of it!* It's okay! *It's okay!*"

The victim of domestic child abuse was rigid, his face contorted in a deathly pallor as he breathed in quick shallow gasps. After being led to sit down at the table, he incoherently mumbled to himself, "Most of the hospital staff were witches or Satanists. My stepfather was a Mason and … he was also a Baptist preacher."

Everyone gathered around to offer emotional support. Howard gave him a glass of water to drink.

"He read this," Eric said to the others after perusing the poem, then handed the paper to Alex, who gave it to Rex, who passed it on to Howard, and then to Tony. A moment later, the fighter slammed the palm of his hand down hard upon the table. "If only we arrived here *one day sooner!*"

"Take it easy, big guy," Howard said. "We can't do anything about it now … she's in heaven."

An undercurrent of irrepressible rage was evident through clenched teeth when the formidable undefeated world champion replied, "Yeah. But soon – *very soon* – they'll all be *in hell!*"

Rex was livid. "Who do they think they are? … Huh? … Just who the bloody hell - do - they - think - *they* - are?! They think nobody's got the nerve ta' stand up to 'em! They think there ain't no real men left anymore! … That we're all a buncha' gutless cowards that'll let 'em *do whatever they want ta' us!*" He kicked his foot into an upholstered chair. "They think they can destroy our children, and nobody's gonna' do anything about it!" He shook his fist at the darkened window, presumably in the direction of the Castle, and shouted, "You bastard sons of Belial! You're goin' down! … Ya' hear me?! … We're comin' for ya'! We're comin' ta' *git ya!*"

After breakfast, the two buses were ordered and delivered to the hotel. Weapons were inspected and guns were loaded; the plan was now submitted to the careful scrutiny of a final examination. Afterwards, Eric stressed, "There's no margin for error. We *cannot* afford to make *any* mistakes."

"Listen up, y'all," commanded Rex, standing before them. "I'm not braggin' when I say I've been in close range combat once or twice before. The hand of Almighty God preserved me from death many times. I learnt' this much for sure: When ya' encounter the enemy, *don't hesitate!* Destroy 'em. The kinda' situations we'll be in are gonna' be life and death. That split-second indecision is all it'll take ta' get ya' killed." He stepped to the middle of the room and proceeded to demonstrate guerrilla tactics. "You don't just waltz on in there like you're on some kinda' Sunday stroll in the park! You gotta' be aware of yer' surroundings at all times and cover your backside! That means you gotta' have eyes in back o' yer' head! Sweep your field of vision three hundred sixty degrees. Play heads up, or you'll find yerself lyin' flat on yer face after takin' a bullet."

Alex next came forward to provide counsel. "Men, in case you have any lingering doubts concerning the righteousness of what we're about to do, let me remind you that *it is Scriptural* to destroy the enemies of God. Exodus 22:18 commands us: *Thou shalt not suffer a witch to live.* Old Testament Scriptures were written to serve as an example for the New Testament believers. Acts 5:29 tells us: *We ought to obey God rather than men.* God's Word warns of the consequences of allowing evil to flourish. Ancient Israel was commanded to destroy the pagan nations and to drive out the heathen from their midst. When they tolerated evil, it proliferated, and they consequently lost their righteous standing before God. The same happened to King Saul. For Israel's disobedience, they suffered the wrath of God, four times brought into bondage by their enemies, made slaves by Assyria, Babylon, Rome, and Nazi Germany. As happened to Israel, the modern world will soon go into captivity because those professing to be God's people *tolerated wickedness;* the people claiming to be righteous have allowed witches and homosexuals to overrun our society. This time, it is Professing Christians that will be taken captive by an antichrist Police State dictatorship – a government run by child-sacrificing servants of Satan. *These* are the kind of people we are about to exterminate." He paused to observe the conviction in their expressions before continuing.

"The *unrighteous* allow evil; the righteous hate evil and *will not* tolerate it. In Revelation 2:2 Jesus *commends* the church at Ephesus for not tolerating evil: *I know thy works and thy labour, and thy patience, and how thou canst not bear them which are evil….* Ephesians 5:6 tells us the consequences of not executing vengeance upon God's enemies: *Let no man deceive you with vain words: for because of these things cometh the wrath of God upon the children of disobedience.* Those who advocate tolerance toward the blasphemous heathen *are themselves* blasphemous heathen! They cannot feel righteous indignation because *they* are not righteous! They call evil good, and good evil; their false humility is a cover for their pride. Isaiah 29:13 and Mark 7:6, describes them as *This people honoureth me with their lips, but their heart is far from me.*

They have a form of godliness but deny the power of God. Second Timothy 3:5. And Revelation 21:8 gives assurance that they will be cast into the Lake of Fire *even before* the unbelievers! By their lack of outrage and action taken against the wicked, Professing Christians pronounce their own condemnation. Let us not be guilty of that same fatal error."

The men were in unanimous agreement when they all responded, "Amen, Brother!"

"*Let God be true, but every man a liar!*" exclaimed Eric.

Adam said, "*The fear of the LORD is the beginning of wisdom. The fear of the LORD is to hate evil. Ye that love the LORD, hate evil.*"

Next, Rex and Howard gave a crash course on the use of the firearms and high-tech attachments. While installing the muzzle silencers and heat-seeking infrared night scopes onto the oversized handguns, Howard said, "This silencer will reduce the effective range of these high-powered magnum pistols to about a hundred and fifty yards. For proper use of the laser dot sighting mechanism, note how the internal computerized indicator light will signal when the target is sighted and in range. It does the aiming for you, so it's impossible to miss."

Within the hour, they were all adept at handling the guns; loading, sighting, and firing techniques. The veteran jungle soldier then took out his shotgun-sized Excitomer Laser from one of the duffel bags. "They wanna' play rough? ... Okay. Let's play *real* rough! One blast from this'll send them sons of hell ta' the Lake of Fire ahead a schedule!"

They were fitted with a shoulder strap gun holster and military issue utility belt containing extra ammunition clips, transponder communication device, and a pen-sized laser weapon. "Remember," coached Rex, demonstrating the miniaturized pocket laser, "score a direct hit in the face, and the enemy'll think they're lookin' directly at the sun. They'll be instantly blind as a bat, totally disabled."

When displaying the sheathed long knife for use in hand to hand combat, Howard explained, "It may prove convenient in close range situations." Finally, as they laid out the dark camouflage fatigues, he said, "We'll change into these later tonight. In the meantime, I suggest we conserve our energy and try to get some sleep." He glanced at his watch. "It's now 01700. We'll be leaving in a couple hours."

As they lounged in the hotel suite, the tempo of their mood gradually escalated. Adam's vision and his subsequent poem did much to heighten their awareness and intensify their righteous anger, dispelling fears, and gave them an even greater sense of purpose and urgency. They were being impelled by the Spirit of God.

Rex paced the floor like a caged tiger. "They're the same ones who wanna' force world government on us! They sold their souls ta' the Devil, and that's why they do what they do – damn 'em! *Damn 'em all ta' hell!*"

Tony sprang up from the sofa, agile as a jaguar. "They want us to fear them because they're murderous cold-blooded serial killers. But they better *fear us* because we're the sons of Almighty God. We're princes of *the Creator of the universe!* Remember who we are, Brothers! *Remember!*"

Alex calmly stated, "Thanks guys for putting it into perspective. We are not to feel intimidated by stupid worthless men. We are not to fear the children of a lesser god. They haven't gone up against the likes of us before, so they think they're invincible. But we come prepared in our spirit, and we bring with us their *death warrant*: the Holy Scriptures Word of God. *That* is our power, and it's the *only* justification we need."

Brandon said, "Anyone who disagrees with what we have been commanded by God to do is justifying their own unrighteousness."

"Or cowardice," appended Howard.

Tony commented, "Our plans are righteous in the eyes of God. If anybody has a problem with it they should take it up *with Him.*"

Rex declared, "The only way what we do ain't righteous is if the Word of God ain't true … an' that ain't *never* gonna' happen."

Alex read Revelation 19:11-16: *And I saw heaven opened, and behold a white horse; and he that sat upon him was called Faithful and True, and in righteousness he doth judge and make war. His eyes were as a flame of fire, and on his head were many crowns; and he had a name written, that no man knew, but he himself. And he was clothed with a vesture dipped in blood: and his name is called the Word of God. And the armies which were in heaven followed him upon white horses, clothed in fine linen, white and clean. And out of his mouth goeth a sharp sword, that with it he should smite the nations: and he shall rule them with a rod of iron: and he treadeth the winepress of the fierceness and wrath of Almighty God. And he hath on his vesture and on his thigh a name written, KING OF KINGS, AND LORD OF LORDS."*

He then said, "Our Master is the KING OF KINGS, AND LORD OF LORDS – Jesus Christ, the Warrior God! What we do, we do for the glory and honor of *The KING!*"

They all shouted: "For The KING!"

Alex then handed the Bible to Brandon, who said, "I read from First Corinthians 3:17: *If any man defile the temple of God, him shall God destroy; for the temple of God is holy, which temple ye are.*" He then turned to Job 34:24-28: "*He shall break in pieces mighty men without number, and set others in their stead. Therefore he knoweth their works, and he overturneth them in the night, so that they are destroyed. He striketh them as wicked men in the open sight of others; because they turned back from him, and would not consider any of his ways: so that they cause the cry of the poor to come unto him, and he heareth the cry of the afflicted.*"

He gave the ancient holy Text to Eric, who read Proverb 21:22: "*A wise man scaleth the city of the mighty, and casteth down the strength of the confidence thereof.*"

Howard was next to read the following Scriptures from Zechariah 4:6: "*Not by might, nor by power, but by my spirit, saith the LORD of hosts.*"

Adam read from Psalm 82:3,4: *Defend the poor and fatherless: do justice to the afflicted and needy. Deliver the poor and needy: rid them out of the hand of the wicked.*

Tony recited Psalm 60:12: *Through God we shall do valiantly: for he it is that shall tread down our enemies.*"

Rex said, "This one here's from Deuteronomy 33:27: *The eternal God is thy refuge, and underneath are the everlasting arms: he shall thrust out the enemy from before thee; and shall say, Destroy them.*"

In unison, they all shouted, "Destroy them!"

— 24 —

"The angel of the LORD killed 185,000 Assyrian soldiers in a single night," said Tony, as they prepared to leave the hotel room. "I wonder how many more of God's enemies will die tonight?"

While slipping on a sling shoulder gun harness, Eric ventured to answer. "No way to know. Yet, because it's Saturday, a weekend, the probabilities favor a crowd."

Brandon slid his long-barreled handgun into its holster. "Expect to see some familiar faces."

After packing their duffel bags and changing into their fatigues, they were ready to depart. "It's now 01900 hours," said Eric. "The drive should take less than an hour. While it's still daylight, we'll establish our base camp in a concealed wooded area, then hike to the Castle on foot. If my calculations are correct, we should be within viewing distance by dusk."

Without further dialogue, they filed out of the room. Brandon was the last to leave, and when about to shut the door, he hesitated, then called out to the others. "Wait. Look at this." They all walked back and gathered around. "Notice the door knob…. See anything unusual?"

"Looks kinda' wet and greasy," observed Rex. When he reached for it, Brandon quickly blocked his hand.

"Don't touch it!" Moving closer, Brandon sniffed it. "As I thought. Hypogaine."

"What's that?" asked Howard.

The researcher replied, "A lethal nerve poison made from a South American root. It's been mixed with gum arabic to make it sticky, and DMSO so it penetrates the skin within seconds. Touch it, and the electrical impulses in your brain will be short-circuited. Result: You'll experience epileptic seizures, then die within a few hours." He folded the DO NOT DISTURB sign and crushed it over the doorknob. "There. Now no one will have to die."

Eric said, "They hoped to eliminate some of us before we made our move. How thoughtful of them to pay us a visit."

Tony coldly replied, "Let's go return the favor."

The two buses were parked at the back of the hotel. The drivers were Eric and Alex. Tony and Adam rode with Eric; Rex, Howard and Brandon, with Alex.

Storm clouds loomed large in the late afternoon darkened sky as they drove West toward the border of Luxembourg and Belgium. From the driver seat of the lead bus, Eric spoke into his secured frequency radio transmitter. "I hope the border patrol won't ask too many questions."

In the trailing bus, Howard replied, "If they do, just say we're picking up a load of school children to take on a field trip."

"At *this* hour?" questioned Eric.

"Tell them it's an over-nighter."

"I hope they buy it."

"They better."

A light rain began to fall on the windshields as the two transport vehicles proceeded down the mostly vacant stretch of highway, the wipers slapping back and forth as rumbles of approaching thunder could be heard in the distance. Referencing his wrist-mounted computer, Howard spoke into the transponder microphone to announce to all the others, "We're now heading Northwest. Once we get through the border patrol and pass into Belgium, we head South at Arlon to Muno, then, another thirty minutes and we're there. The global positioning satellite will provide the coordinates that should get us to within walking distance of the Castle."

Eric communicated, "We need to locate a drive somewhere off the road that trails into the woods for cover. Can the GPS get a detailed read on the micro-terrain?"

Howard keyed another map into the viewing screen. "Looks like there could be some paths overgrown with dense vegetation leading off the main road. I have no idea where they go, but we could try one and find out."

Brandon dryly remarked, "Let's just hope the one we pick isn't someone's driveway."

As they advanced, the intensity of rain was increasing; on the near horizon, jagged flashes of lightening electrified the overcast sky. Soon, wind-driven rain and large hail descended upon the two vehicles, making a rhythmic tapping sound like dancing fairies upon the sheet metal roofs. When seeing the short line of traffic slowing down up ahead, Eric advised from the lead bus, "Border in sight."

Adam prayed out loud, "Lord Jesus, blind their eyes and make them overlook us and allow us to pass through."

"Amen," the others acknowledged.

As the first bus slowed to a gradual stop at the road block, two men dressed in military uniform, and armed with uzi machine guns, approached the driver's side window. "Where you go?" one of them curtly demanded in broken English.

"To pick up a load of children," responded Eric.

"Children?" the skeptical guard questioned.

"Yes, school-aged children."

"Ah-uh," said the jaded customs official, trained not to believe anything. "An' jus' where you take dees loado' children?"

"They're foreign exchange students," Eric truthfully replied. "We're going on a field trip."

"Ah-uh. Field treep."

Tension was mounting by the second as the other guard walked over to the opposite side of the bus and shined his flashlight through the door window. When the small circle of illumination revealed a corner of one of the duffel bags, he said, "What's *that* on floor?"

The silence that ensued was deafening. Adam quickly answered, "Toys."

The others anxiously anticipated the guard's delayed reply. "Ah-uh. *Toys*. Let me see *dees toys*." The Captain then abruptly demanded, "Open door!"

Eric glanced at his passengers, realizing that the entire plan could fail at this critical juncture. Slowly, he cranked open the mechanically operated folding door.

When the intruder brusquely forced his way inside and reached down to open the bag, there emerged a white soccer ball, bouncing as it rolled down the steps and out the door. The chagrined border patrol inspector tried to save face when he said, "Aw yes. I once play soccer as a boy." Now stepping out, he reached down, picked up the ball, then playfully drop-kicked it back inside. He next did something else quite unexpected when he motioned to the guard operating the gate. A moment later, the barricade lever was raised. As they drove through the bottleneck, Eric smiled and said to the Captain through the open door, "I'm sure the children will be thrilled to know that you play soccer. We'll be coming back in a few hours, and look forward to seeing you all once again."

The rifle-wielding border guards returned the courtesy with an uncharacteristic smile; and when the second bus approached, they waved it through without any further hindrance.

Now entering into Belgium, while speeding down the highway in the pouring rain, shouts of joy rose up from both buses. The men were elated when communicating with each other over their radios. Someone quoted Proverb 16:7: "*When a man's ways please the LORD, he maketh even his enemies to be at peace with him.*"

They all shouted, "Amen Brother!"

Howard said, "God's ways are higher than our ways, and his thoughts than our thoughts ... *For in him we live and move and have our being.*"

Alex appended, "Isaiah 55:9 and Acts 17:28."

As they drove on, Brandon asked, "Where did the ball come from?"

In the other bus, Tony shrugged his shoulders. "Good question."

Eric then spoke into his transmitter. "Hey, Adam. Would you happen to know anything about a ball?"

The visionary replied, "All I know is that is what God showed me in my mind. The Lord delivered us."

The passengers let out more ecstatic cheers and gave thanks to God for the miracle He had performed before their very eyes.

Rain was now coming down in torrents, reducing visibility to about twenty yards. Howard said, "We're traveling on a road called Les Amerois, it's the final leg of our journey." He checked the directional indicator on the LED readout. "We're getting close. The entrance should be somewhere along here, off to the right."

"If there *still is* an entrance," remarked Eric. "They could use air lift to gain access."

"There's *definitely* a main entrance gate," replied the senior. "It was confirmed by my Luxembourg contact. That was the source of the ground-level photograph."

"You can bet it'll be monitored and guarded ta' the teeth," said Rex. "Closed circuit; the works."

Eric observed, "And that's why we have to first knock the electric utility room out of commission. Only *then* does Alex approach the main gate to destroy it."

The old soldier advised, "Eric, after you plant some explosives in the dungeon, on 'yer way back out, blow up their generators and shut down power ta' the whole dang place."

Brandon quipped, "I'm certain they'll have plenty of spare candles."

The others were too intently focused to respond to his off humor, each scanning the rain slick black road up ahead for signs of a turnout. When they passed what appeared to be a high gate, Alex announced over his transmitter, "Three guesses what *that* was."

Tony said, "I saw a guard house, but no guards."

"There was a vehicle parked on the other side of the fence," observed Brandon.

Rex said, "Alex, that means ya' gotta' be ready ta' shoot."

"We're right on track," noted Howard. "Now to locate a side road to conceal the buses."

Adam suddenly exclaimed, "Up ahead! Turn right."

The rain was now pelting the windshield so heavily that visibility was reduced to less than ten yards. "Where?" questioned Eric, slowing down. "I don't see anything." Straining his vision to penetrate the translucent liquid veil, he flashed a right turn signal, alerting the bus behind him.

"*There!*" Adam pointed.

The buses slowed to a near stop. "I *still* don't see anything."

Adam quoted Scripture: "*The just shall live by faith*. Turn *now!*"

Eric said, "No car headlights in sight. Let's go!" He swung the oversized vehicle wide to the left, then immediately back to the right and into a ten foot high stand of dense vegetation.

Alex's bus followed closely behind through the overgrowth, and after traveling a short distance from the main road, he said, "You sure this is a path?"

They drove through the protective cover, surrounded by a thick veil of steamy mist that rose up from the ground to create a surreal other-worldly effect. Slowly proceeding forward, the oversized vehicles advanced cautiously along the unmarked trail, staying parallel with the dark forest edge. Despite the rain, the ground was yet firm. Eric said, "Howard, I need some feedback on our position. Please advise."

Before Howard could answer, Adam said over his transceiver, "This is the way. Stay on course."

The elder navigator said, "God's Word is true. We live by faith…. Continue forward, Eric."

Traveling along the wooded fringe for about 300 yards, they came to a small clearing nestled among a stand of oak trees. Eric said, "This is as far as we go."

The rain was beginning to subside as the buses finally came to a stop, and when the men exited, they marveled at their strategic position. Brandon asked Eric, "What do you suppose is the probability of finding this fortuitous route strictly by chance?"

Looking back at the concealed way they had just traversed, and considering the limited visibility, unfamiliarity with the terrain, and the close proximity to their destination, he replied, "Chance? God only deals in certainty. As Einstein said, 'God doesn't play dice with the universe.'"

Brandon then said, "You realize, of course, that the heavy rain was no coincidence. That is, it enabled us to make our entry undetected."

"I know," agreed Eric. "And we should have gotten stuck in mud … but we didn't, did we."

"No, we didn't," Brandon pensively replied. "Jesus walked on water."

Ten minutes later, after a final check of the equipment, in a light drizzle, six men prepared to set out on foot, leaving Alex behind with the buses.

"Use these ta' open the main gate," said Rex, reaching into his duffel bag and handing the street preacher three plastic explosives. "I gave ya' extra on the fuses, so after ya' set 'em, you'll have enough time ta' stand back a ways." He then handed him the detonating electrodes. "Can't take a chance with wet matches."

Eric said to Alex, "The guards at the gate will probably be contacted by the Castle guards when we storm the grounds. Therefore, a high probability exists you'll find the gate house vacant and can proceed with the demolition without confrontation."

"You should be all right here," Howard said to him. "Expect a communication from us by no later than 02200 hours."

Alex replied, "In the meantime, I'll turn the buses around and be ready to pick up the first load of children." He shook hands with them all, then bade farewell. "You guys take care of yourselves, and … Godspeed."

The ominous evening sky was cast in massive billowy black and white storm clouds that rose up like megalithic battling giants. A thin layer of white Aluminum oxide Chemtrails blanketed the lower atmosphere with particulate toxic metals and an oily smear of jet fuel that filtered the moon's sickly yellow rays like a dim light in a smoke-filled room. The rain had stopped shortly after they left the camp only moments ago, and now, walking through a knee-deep layer of thick fog, the troop neared the edge of the meadow clearing. From his lonely outpost, Alex watched as they disappeared into the engulfing mist of a foreboding dark forest.

The soggy leaf-covered ground cushioned their steps when entering the mysterious silent domain. Vague silhouettes of black tree trunks stood like silent sentinels in the misty grove. The last reluctant rays of sunlight filtered through leaves still dripping wet from the recent storm. "Old growth Oak-Hickory," observed Brandon. "Must be several hundred years old."

Quantum laser gun slung across his back, Rex took the point position in the single file row. "Keep yer' voices down and conversation to a minimum. The woods might be patrolled."

They traveled in the same general direction as the adjacent meandering driveway that was occasionally visible off to the right through breaks in the timberline.

Within half an hour they had trekked over a mile. "It'll soon be getting pitch dark in here," said Eric. "We should be coming to the forest edge soon."

Tony spotted something up ahead. "What's *that*?"

Approaching closer, they came upon a large flat rock that rested on four cornerstone boulders approximately three feet high, and that was partially concealed among a tangled overgrowth of arching branches. "It's an altar of some kind," discerned Brandon. Moving closer, he pointed and said, "See these symbolic carvings on the side? It's ancient Druidic. This was undoubtedly a ceremonial site used for ritual sacrifice."

"Look!" Adam exclaimed. Beneath the thick stone slab were the charred remains of the victims – bones, bits of clothing and human skulls partially buried in the red-stained soil.

"Fiendish killers," muttered Howard.

"Innocent blood calls out from the ground," said Adam. "Many generations of evil men and women have brought a curse upon this land." While standing there in the filtered dim light of the emerging full moon, they felt a sense of overpowering oppression. Suddenly, a chill breeze wafted through the gnarled tree boughs cast in black relief.

Rex commanded, "Let's move on," and they headed off, deeper into forbidden territory.

The ancient forest was now immersed in near total darkness; strange unearthly sounds of chirping night-watches echoed in the ebony gloom. The men pressed forward, moving silently through the woods, maneuvering over fallen tree trunks and forest undergrowth. "How close are we?" Howard asked Adam.

"It's near," the Godly seer affirmed.

Shortly, a lightened horizon was becoming visible through the trees. Upon their soon arrival at the wooded edge, they came to a partial clearing enshrouded by a thick layer of fog. When standing on a rocky precipice, and gazing out into the distance, they could see the lights of the imposing turreted Castle, the cathedral tower and multiple spires rising up to the heavens appearing like a many-headed Beast emerging from a sea of misty gloom. In silence they gazed upon the curious spectacle, feeling as if they had gone back a thousand years in time.

"Medieval," remarked Brandon.

"So … *that's* the Castle of Darkness," commented Howard, at long last viewing the infamous stone hewn structure.

"Appropriately named," said Eric. "I almost expect to see a unicorn."

— 25 —

Rex viewed the distance using infrared night vision binoculars. While scanning the Castle grounds, he said, "It's heavily guarded, for sure. Looks like they got four rifle tottin' goons out front … an' two more walkin' the outskirts. There's probably a few others on patrol out there in the woods."

"It's not exactly a fortress, I take it?" offered Howard.

Rex replied, "No, but these freaks o' nature don't encourage tourism either. They'd kill anyone ta' keep their dirty little secret from the world."

Eric commanded, "Our first move is to get within striking distance without being detected – at least one hundred and fifty yards from the main entrance. Between here and there, we take out any interference, and do it silently."

"That's the idea," said Rex, eager for action.

Gazing out over the gloomy terrain that was before them, Adam prophesied when reciting Deuteronomy 12:2,3: "Thus saith the LORD: *Ye shall utterly destroy all the places, wherein the nations which ye shall possess served their gods, upon the high mountains, and upon the hills, and under every green tree: And ye shall overthrow their altars, and break their pillars, and burn their groves with fire; and ye shall hew down the graven images of their gods, and destroy the names of them out of that place.*"

In a quiet unified solemn tone, they all bowed their heads and agreed, "God's will be done."

The strategist continued his analysis. "We have to time the elimination of the four in front to precisely coincide with dropping the two roaming guards. Otherwise, if they have a chance to become entrenched and return fire or to relay a communication, we'll lose our strategic advantage. Once those six are out of the way, we wait to see how many more cockroaches come out of the woodwork. Only after they're all disposed of, are we clear to make our entry into the Castle."

"It's .753 miles away." Howard gave the triangulation reading from his wrist-mounted miniature computer. "Everyone check to make sure your communication transponder is operational." The five others pressed the reset button that immediately gave a visual LED readout of *Ready*.

Dressed in camouflage darken hues, while they applied lamp black to their face and hands, Eric asked, "Any last comments or observations before we begin the first phase of the assault?"

No one replied. Their varied expressions were seen in the dull light of the half moon, and ranged from Brandon's anxiety to Tony's cool confidence. Eric was the epitome of concentrated focus; Adam seemed distant, in a world of his own; Howard was fully engaged in the moment; Rex was fearless, like an indomitable pit bull. "This is *it*," said the old soldier. "There's no more rehearsals, no turnin' back. Keep yer' eyes open, stay close together, use hand signals ta' communicate, and shoot ta' kill. Any questions? … Okay, let's go."

They moved out into the unknown of a blood moonlit night.

In semi-darkness the men walked single-file through an open field that had few trees for cover. Rex was in the lead, retaining a single formation to minimize the chance of setting off a booby trap. "What's that – over there?" Brandon pointed at a shadowy figure about 100 feet away. They all stopped, then remained frozen in place. Using their infra-red gun scopes, the indistinct shadow materialized to reveal it was merely a farm animal, a small pony grazing in the grass pasture. Remaining on high alert, they continued moving forward.

Soon, they came to a wire fence.

Rex bent down and shined a penlight near to the ground. "See this here wire comin' off the fence … means it's electrified." He took out a rubber insulated wire cutter from his utility belt and carefully severed the lead wire, disconnecting the high voltage current. "There, now we can cross over without gettin' fried."

From that point onward they advanced more slowly, moving cautiously through the heavy night air as they entered and emerged from a series of low-lying pockets of fog. Maintaining a distance of about 100 yards from the driveway, off to the right they could see the first fork in the road leading to the Castle. "Keep your eyes on the ground, men," said the experienced jungle warfare soldier. "This here area's where the booby traps are supposed to be."

Shortly, Adam stopped abruptly and pointed at a nearby grassy patch of ground. "That's one," he said.

Rex walked ahead, then crouched low and shined a narrow beam of light. "Yep, it's a trip fence," he confirmed. "An' over here's the stake." He clipped off a connecting wire using the wire cutter, then stepped over the ankle-high fence. "Now they can't know we're here."

They moved forward once again, and within another fifteen minutes passed the second fork in the road, noticing the grey stucco house faintly visible in the reflection of the moon's glow. "It's not much further," said Howard, checking his wrist-mounted GPS map.

Within twenty minutes they had taken up a position at the forest edge, upon an elevated knoll, to the left of the Castle, slightly less than 100 yards from the towering edifice. The main access road was a short distance to the right, terminating in the L-shaped concrete half-courtyard before continuing to pass through the entrance to the rear of the building. Concealed by the thick darkness, all six men now lay flat on the ground, positioned in a row. Rex whispered, "When the two on patrol come within range of the others, I'll give the command and we open fire." He waited several minutes longer as the guards made their surveillance rounds of the perimeter and were now beginning to return back along the front drive that half-circled the enormous structure.

"See those small black attachments on their lapels?" said Howard. "Two-way radios. We can't allow them the chance to use them. If they do, no telling how many more they can summon to the scene."

The two roving guards were now in close proximity to the other four sentries.

"Everyone ready!" Rex announced in a hushed tone. "Numbering from left ta' right: Tony, you take out number one; Eric, number two; Howard, number three; Brandon, four; Adam, five; and I'll git number six. Activate the infrared laser dot sight just before ya' pull the trigger." Elbows resting on the ground, everyone's long barreled pistol was in the ready position, held steady with both hands. "Take aim, men, the sightin' computer does the rest. Shoot for the upper body, right side of the chest. Second and follow up shots go ta' the head." Like a trained battalion, each of them had one of the guards sighted in the cross-hairs of their night scope; six high-powered magnum pistols with silencers, directed at their designated targets. "Activate laser site … Targets locked on … Ready. On three: One … two …"

"Wait!" cautioned Adam. They held their fire. "Cars are coming."

"I don't see nothin'," said Rex.

Seconds later, headlight beams preceded the appearance of a state-registered black stretch Cadillac limousine silently driving up to the Castle, stopping just before entering the furthest tunnel entrance. When the occupants stepped out, Brandon remarked, "Well, well, well, who do we have here?" Sighting through the magnifying gun scope, he said, "No less than the Grande Dame Queen and her Luciferic Highpriest son, the Prince. They rank near the top of the

Global Hierarchy, and are in high positions of leadership on the Committee of 300 that's largely responsible for determining world political, economic and religious policy. Both are major New World Order players and serve as honorary members of several secret societies, most of which tie in with the U.S. Council on Foreign Relations. The CFR basically runs the puppet government regime known as the United States of America." The Queen was carrying a staff with the emblem of a white dove positioned on top. "The white dove symbolizes death and destruction," Brandon explained. "It's an example of *reverse symbolism* among the Luciferian elite, for whom everything is inverted, turned upside-down, and means the opposite of what seems apparent to the general public."

"Evil is good, and good is evil," commented Tony.

"Precisely," replied the researcher. "The world's satanic leadership use cryptic language to confuse the masses, employing esoteric symbolism, words and phrases that mean the opposite of their conventional meaning. When they say *peace*, what they really mean is *war*; to them, the word *truth* means *lies*; *freedom* means *slavery*; *justice* is *tyranny*, and so on. The mind-controlled public never catches on; they're so brainwashed by television programming and media propaganda they believe every word of what the shadow government allows them to hear.

"The members of the international political cult lead secret lives apart from their beneficent public persona. These two unsavory individuals are, first and foremost, generational witches positioned near the very pinnacle of the International Hierarchy. They're also the world's major opium, cocaine, and pharmaceutical drug dealers; and are among the principal movers behind instituting an international dictatorial government, global religious unity, and the Middle East peace process. Genghis Khan and Count Dracula are both in their direct ancestral blood line. And ... they are cannibals."

The team waited patiently undercover while the occupants of the vehicle made their way into the Castle and the limo drove through the tunnel to park around the back. Almost immediately, another black stretch limousine pulled forward, and more high-ranking members of the New World Order stepped out into dim illumination. Brandon commented. "That's Sir Richard Garner, a well-known shape-shifter and pedophile."

Eric spotted another luminary advancing into the cool night air. "*That one* looks familiar."

Brandon responded, "Rupert Murdock. He's a Hollywood pornographer, tabloid magnate, and chairman of Zondervan – a Christian book publishing company that produced the NIV Bible. He presumably owns the copyright to the Word of God."

Lowering his voice, Howard said, "The NIV is *not* God's Word, even though it's the version used in most so-called Christian churches today."

"They ain't True Christian churches," clarified Rex in an uncharacteristic whisper. "They're government-owned, bought and paid for by their 501(c)3 tax exempt status that says the preacher can't criticize the government. They're just spiritual whore houses, that's all."

Brandon offered further commentary on the next to emerge. "*There's* the infamous Windsor Canadian Satanist, Pierre Trudeau: child molester, mind-control programmer – you name it, he's done it. And the guy following after him is Zecharia Stichen, New Ager who writes books on extraterrestrials being the origin of humans on Earth. He too is a famous shape-shifter. And here comes yet another one – William F. Buckley, from the Rothschild-owned American media. My research quotes witnesses that say he's very mean when shape-shifted, and enjoys biting his victims repeatedly."

"Does anyone recognize *that* guy?" asked Tony, sighting the man next to exit.

The author thought for a moment, mentally reviewing a long list of blood-feasting world politicians that he uncovered from his studies. "Edward Heath is the name that comes to mind. In English Parliament high society he's known as a particularly vicious shape-shifting reptilian; one that enjoys kinky sex acts with little boys. This monster is famous for slitting their throats while in the act of sodomizing them."

"He ain't gonna' be famous for *nothin'* after tonight," declared Rex. "We're about ta' do us some serious gator huntin'. These lizards are *all* goin' down!"

Meanwhile, another long black limousine emerged from out of the shadows. The occupants read like a Who's Who of Capital Hill. The expert on the occult proceeded to expound upon the hierarchical chain of command. "These are all lower level Illuminati functionaries. They're basically high-ranking Masons who act as CFR window dressing and are merely power brokers behind Satan's diabolical world government. Only one of them even ranks in the lowest level Third Tier.

When two U.S. Senators and erstwhile Presidential hopefuls came forward, Adam perceived their spiritual identity. "Those are sorcerers who are being groomed for placement close to the Antichrist."

A forth luxury sedan pulled forward, and when the passengers began to disembark, Howard chuckled with surprise, "A major Christian Evangelical leader! And there's his partner in crime – the Pope of Rome!"

"Makes perfect sense," replied the learned Brandon. "Two religious world figures – representing Protestant Christianity and Pagan Catholicism – are both working toward the same goal of world unity through the ecumenical movement to establish a One World Religion."

A high-ranking Rockefeller was the next to exit. The author explained: "His family funded global genocide programs to eradicate most of the people on this planet. Numerous eyewitnesses at blood sacrifice rituals have identified him as a shape-shifter. He's positioned below the Pope in the supra-government Hierarchy.

"The Vatican leader is a devout Luciferian working closely with the Antichrist. He's likely to be the False Prophet of Revelation 13. The Christian media celebrity is a 33rd degree Freemason with a multiple personality. As a mind-controlled dupe of the Illuminati, he sincerely believes he's a man of God, but is on record for having denied that Jesus Christ is the only way to salvation. The European Illuminati funded his evangelical crusades starting back in the 1950's. They also continue to finance his and his children's millionaire lifestyle. Like many professing Christian preachers today, he's an impostor. Yoked with Harlot Babylon – the Catholic Church – he's merely an errand boy for the Illuminati. They use his global crusades as a front for maintaining diplomatic relations between world political figures. Essentially, he's a double agent working to establish an antichrist global government."

Following the religious celebrities there appeared two young children, three and five years of age. Tony instantly reacted with violent rage. "Give me ten seconds – *just ten seconds* – and I'll kill any of those servants of hell *with my bare hands!*"

"Take it easy, big guy," Howard advised. "You'll soon get your chance."

Standing in the courtyard in the half-light, before stark brick walls; pedophile, drug lord, serial killer, mass murderer, former Illuminati-appointed head of the CIA and U.S. President, George Herbert Walker Bush, said, "If the American people had ever known the truth about what we have done to this nation, we would be chased down in the streets and lynched."

Standing nearby, former Prime Minister of Canada, Brian Mulrouny, replied, "The only way to world peace is through mind-control of the masses."

Ronald Reagan, another Illuminati-promoted political figurehead, replied, "We did what Hitler did, by brainwashing the youth."

The three global leaders enjoyed a hearty laugh, then Bush said, "We've got them so doped up, dumbed-down and buffaloed, they're too stupid to even know they're alive."

Before going inside, former Secretary of Defense and Vice President, Dick Cheney, *triggered* a mind-control programmed response from one of the children when he said in a harsh demanding tone, "*Tinkerbelle*! Where did *you* come from?"

Conditioned by ritual torture, in a drug-induced trance, the five year old blond hair blue eyed little boy automatically responded on cue, "I rode the Freedom Train, Sir!" The child could not realize that the term – *Freedom Train* – in characteristic reverse symbolism, was a cryptic code phrase for *Project Monarch*, a subprogram of MK-Ultra, the Nazi-originated trauma-based mind-control experiment conducted by the CIA, British Secret Service MI6, England's Tavistock Institute, the Vatican, and numerous other factions operating the worldwide Satanic Ritual Abuse network.

The career politician contorted his hard features into a diabolical sneer, then forcefully grabbed the child by the arm and jerked him closer to himself. Crouching down so they were face to face, just inches away, he snarled, "*That's* right. The *Freedom* Train – where you're free to be *our slave!*" He then shoved the small child against the nearby stone wall, and with bulging eyes and drooling saliva, maniacally hissed, "I could kill you, *kill you!* You're not the first, and you won't be the last. I'll can kill you anytime I _ _ _ _ well please!"

— 26 —

The four limousine chauffeurs were the last to go inside. The Castle grounds were once again occupied by several roaming guards. Two of them were now stationary along the right side of the building; the other four, standing near the walkway in front of the main tower, had just lit up cigarettes and were engaged in animate conversation when they noticed a small bright red dot on their comrade's chests. They all froze in place. An instant later, soundless bullets punctured their hearts, then, two more high speed projectiles pierced their foreheads. Six lifeless bodies slumped to the ground.

"We'll wait a few minutes ta' see if anything happens," said Rex. Shortly, he commanded, "Let's go." They moved forward with the stealth of a practiced SWAT team.

Soon after emerging from the forest shadows and into the diffuse lighting, upon approaching near to the Castle, suddenly, a shower of bullets streaked over their heads and ricocheted off the back wall. They threw themselves down onto the dew-soaked lawn, and lying prostrate, peered out into the damp misty gloom. "Where they at?" said Howard, his heaving breaths visible as they all scanned the pitch black horizon with their infrared scopes.

"The mathematical probability increases by fifty percent that they'll hit on the next attempt," stated Eric. "We have to locate them *immediately!*"

Just then, Rex squeezed off three muffled rounds in rapid succession. Plunk! Plunk! Plunk! "Bagged me another one!" he pridefully announced. "This is more fun than a turkey shoot."

Adam cautioned, "There are two more to the left of the road, up the embankment, near the forest edge."

They all pointed their weapons in that general direction; gun scope heat-seeking sensors glowing bright. "There they are," announced Howard. Just then, another round of sizzling bullets whizzed only inches above their heads.

"They're in my sights," alerted Howard.

"I'm zeroed in also," confirmed Brandon.

"Let it rip!" said Rex.

The simultaneous convergence of multiple red laser beams on their targets was followed by a concerted burst of stifled gunfire. Plunk! Plunk! Plunk! Plunk! ... Plunk! Plunk! Plunk! Rex said, "That makes it *nine."*

Two sets of headlights were now seen fast approaching up the long driveway. The men remained flat on the ground. "It's probably the guards at the front gate and half way house," said Eric. "When they get to the edge of the woods, shoot out the headlights and the windshields on the driver and passenger sides. Also get the tires."

Ten seconds later, Rex commanded, "Now!" They opened fire, bullets exploding glass and tires of the 4 wheel drive SUV's that suddenly went out of control and careened off the road; one of them collided with a tree, the other flipped over and into a ditch.

"There are no more," advised the prophet of God.

Through a secured frequency channel, Howard contacted Alex. "Check to see if there's any more guards at the gate house. If not, you're all clear to blow the gate. But wait until we give you the signal."

Alex replied, "You guys are busy."

"We're jus' gittin' started," returned Rex.

They stood up and reloaded with new ammo clips. Eric commanded, "Let's move these bodies out of the light." The men drug the six dead guards off into the shadows. "Now, let's get into this place. Commence Phase Two." The six men ran across the paved court-yard, then into the tunnel that was in a direct line with the drive. An entrance door was located to the immediate left. Upon trying the latch and realizing it was locked, Eric said, "Rex, it's all yours." The demolition expert unslung the photon gun from his shoulder, then motioned for the others to stand back. Seconds later, a beam of coherent light bore a fist-sized hole through solid oak, melting the internal lock mechanism with a burst of searing energy. He then pushed open the door, and they boldly went inside.

—27—

The entranceway was cast in semi-darkness; a dismal gloom pervaded the stale air that was permeated with the stench of death. Lurking nearby were hideous medieval gargoyles perched on the door entablature; wild-eyed grimacing winged demons cast in marble, like those atop the Cathedral of Notre Dame and State Capital buildings throughout America. Esoteric occult symbols were etched into the torch-bearing stone walls: sunbursts and images of human-demon hybrids; ancient deities, lesser gods. The immediate area was vacant; there was no one in sight. Using only hand signals, they silently pointed the way, dividing into two groups, bidding each other a last minute farewell with a thumbs up.

Eric, Adam and Tony ran off to the right, toward the dungeon stairwell; Rex, Howard and Brandon cautiously proceeded along the short wing to begin the room to room search. Each group navigated the way using their wrist-mounted micro-maps to confirm their position and plan a course.

The Rescue Team went down the narrow passageway that was bordered by rough-hewn side walls, the temperature becoming noticeably cooler as they descended the second flight of stone steps into the subterranean level of the old mansion. At regular intervals along the way, sulfur-burning torches cast eerie flickering shadows onto the wet rocks. At the bottom of the stairwell, off to the right, Eric pointed at the side door which they had previously identified in the hologram as a possible electrical control room. "We'll hit it on the way back," he said.

Leading the Search and Destroy Team, Rex held the photon gun at waist level; his two companions, guns drawn, flanked slightly behind him on either side. When opening the door to the first room, they found it vacant except for a solitary high-backed wooden chair, wired to deliver high voltage electricity. "Used for trauma-based mind-control programming," whispered Brandon.

Standing at the threshold of the small room painted all black, Howard rhetorically asked, "I wonder how many children have been tortured and died in this room?"

"Somethin' tells me we ain't seen nothin' yet," replied Rex, stepping further inside to plant a pre-timed plastic explosive.

They quickly exited, then advanced down the hallway, storming room after room, only to discover more torture devices and implements designed for inflicting pain and misery. Several of the chambers had been utilized as wardrobe change rooms; there were expensive suits draped on hangers, or neatly folded on the sheetless bloodstained mattresses. "Let's get ta' where the action is," said Rex, leaving behind yet another percussion bomb synchronized to detonate with all the others.

Following a short hall that connected with the longer leg of the L-shaped Castle configuration, when about to emerge into the open corridor, they stopped short upon hearing the sound of approaching footsteps. Rex motioned for the others to take up positions on the left side of the narrow alley, and as the footfalls come closer, they heard two men speaking in a foreign dialect. When they had passed by, Rex suddenly leapt out at one of them from behind, and with choking forearm under the enemy's neck, plunged his long knife into his back. The other guard turned and immediately fell when Howard and Brandon's silencers each emitted a stifled pop. The bodies were dragged into the concealing side hallway, and after Rex had placed yet another timed explosive, they continued toward the cathedral Great Room.

The suffocating damp basement air was saturated with a putrid stench, like that of a cattle rendering yard. Now standing at the juncture of two narrow low ceiling tunnels, Eric glanced down at the illuminated dial of his navigation computer, then pointed straight ahead to silently indicate the most likely direction of the holding dungeon.

Nerves taunt, the trio moved cautiously forward, guns poised, expecting someone, or something, to jump out at them at any moment. "Look!" said Adam, pointing down the torch-lit corridor off to the left, at the several long ropes that hung down from above. Traversing the distance that led to an open area in the dirt floor, he shined a flashlight down the hole. At the end of the ropes he saw the large curved steel meat hooks stained blood-red. "It's an opening to hell," he grimly observed, and they realized this was the Satan Pit seen in the hologram. Overhead, directly above them, coming from the top of the hole that emerged into the cathedral Great Room, they could hear the low droning sounds of ritual chanting.

The 3-member team returned to the main underground passage, following the illuminated readout on their wrist computer, until, up ahead, they saw a metal door set deep into the black stone wall. Tony ran to peer through a small wire mesh window positioned just below eye level, then, after exhaling an emotionally-controlled quivering breath, he abruptly turned away.

Moving cautiously along the first floor corridor, Rex held up his hand, signaling the others to stop. "Hear that?" he whispered. A low chanting sound reverberated from within the cavernous bowels of the Castle. Continuing onward, with every step, the dissonant murmur grew louder, drawing them like a beacon to its source. Upon proceeding further, he pointed to large wooden double doors at the end of the main hallway. "That's gotta' be it," he said, readying the laser gun to force an entry. "This'll send 'em ta' hades."

Suddenly, they were knocked to the floor by an invisible force.

— 28 —

The door to the dungeon was unlocked. Tony entered first; the others were close behind, guns drawn.

The inside was like a chiseled stone cave; high dome ceiling illuminated by stark bright fluorescent lighting that created a macabre sterile effect in the large tomb-like chamber. A bank of electronic equipment was to the immediate right, against the near side wall; computers that regulated the electroshock voltage. Immediately upon entering, they paused to survey a scene that left them speechless and stunned in utter disbelief. Intermingled with the constant low hum of electrical current was heard the faint cries of hundreds of little children imprisoned in small wire mesh cages stacked to the ceiling. Ranging from infancy to early puberty, their emaciated undernourished bodies were bloody, soiled, and naked.

The three men walked slowly forward, then to the left, down the wide dirt floor central isle. They were deeply affected as they gazed upon the children who were like trapped animals blankly staring out through the metal grates. Eric was profoundly disturbed in his spirit; Tony was moved to tears that streamed down his face; Adam was besieged with conflicting emotions, torn between caring compassion for the children and a seething hatred for their oppressors. When Eric tried to open a small door to one of the cages, he quickly withdrew his hand upon being shocked with a mild jolt of electricity. "I'll go locate the switch to turn off the power," he said. Just then, three jailers appeared at the far end of the elongated cave.

Tony instantly reacted by sprinting at them in a violent fury. Bullets whizzed by his head, just missing him; and when 20 feet away, he leapt into the air, tucked his leg and side kicked the first guard in the face with such force that his adversary's neck was broken. When another drew his gun, the skilled fighter kicked it out of his hand, then, in a single continuous motion, thrust the heel of his boot into his opponent's leg, snapping the knee joint, felling the howling killer to collapse disabled onto the floor. The third guard was a gargantuan human-demon hybrid; six-fingered, over seven feet tall and weighing more than 400 pounds. Wearing a leather vest that exposed his massive arms and torso, his body was pierced and tattooed, head shaven, teeth filed to sharp points. Emitting a low monstrous grunt when he charged like a raging bull, the electric prod-wielding behemoth lunged at the undefeated world champion, who, with cat-like reflexes, directed a powerful front thrust kick that met him half-way, square on the chin, repelling the colossus and buckling him onto the dirt floor.

In the interim, the other downed assailant managed to retrieve his gun, and when about to shoot Tony, a muffled rapid burst of gunfire was heard. Plunk! Plunk! Plunk! The jailer fell face forward, dead. A short distance away, Adam stood with gun held tightly in both hands, his bullets having hit their mark.

The brute beast was now rising from his stunned fall, a look of pure evil on his face when Tony delivered a lightening fast whirl kick that smashed the heel of his boot into the side of the giant's head, and once again he toppled to the ground. Using both hands, the anointed warrior grabbed him by the front of his leather vest, and with supernatural strength, raised him up and threw him across the isle like a rag doll. Dazed, the titan crawled on all fours in a vain attempt to escape, and after a short distance, clung desperately to a stone pillar, using it to support his hulking frame while standing on unsteady legs.

Now walking slowly toward him, face set hard as flint, there was fire in Tony's eyes when he said with deadly calm, "This is for all my little buddies." He then unleashed a swift flurry of paralyzing blows, each thudding with the force of a steel sledgehammer; snapping bones, splattering blood. Tony shouted, "This is what it feels like to be small and helpless! How do *you* like it! How do YOU like it!" As the massive carcass sunk lower against the supporting column, the enraged instrument of God's wrath continued his merciless pummeling, rock hard fists striking a mass of quivering flesh.

Moments later, from behind him, Adam said, "He's dead, Tony," yet the fighter would not relent. "Tony!" he yelled, "He's *dead*!" Adam reached forward and touched his shoulder, and God's avenger of blood was brought back to an awareness of the present moment.

When the brutal onslaught had finally ceased, the limp lifeless form lay in a broken heap upon blood-soaked ground. Breathing heavily, the valiant defender of the innocent was trembling from deep-seated emotions arising from an eternal wellspring of righteous outrage.

Eric came running back from the other end of the long isle. "I shut down the power," he said. "Let's hurry and get them out of here!"

When the three men began opening the metal doors of the cages and saw that the starving prisoners were near to death, listless and weak, they knew the children were unable to grasp the reality that they were being set free. Carefully, one by one, their abused bodies were gently lifted out and set upon the floor. "I estimate there's between two hundred and two fifty," Eric said into his wrist radio, notifying Alex to prepare to bring the first bus. "There's some here that are barely able to walk."

While Adam and Eric released the children from the lower and mid-level cages, Tony used a tall step ladder to reach those imprisoned at the higher levels.

A four year old little girl with large vacuous brown eyes stared out from within the steel bars. "What's your name, sweetheart?"

whispered Adam, as he reached inside and took her up in his arms. But the severely traumatized child was unable to speak, or to realize that Adam was an ally. He saw her many scars, and carefully touched a fresh burn wound on her arm. "I'm going to name you, Angel," he said, kissing her gently on the forehead. Then, suddenly overcome with grief, he hugged her close to himself, and bitterly wept.

They moved quickly and efficiently. Barred doors swung open to set the captives free. Soon, more and more children were standing in the crowded passageway. Many were so emotionally traumatized they had to be coaxed out of the cages, and in several instances, when reaching in to remove what appeared to be a sleeping child, they discovered that the still body was a corpse.

"That's the last one," said Tony, gently handing yet another small child to the men below. Now stepping down from the ladder, he proclaimed to the large crowd of boys and girls gazing up at him with subdued wondrous awe: "Okay, little buddies, by the power of Almighty God, we're walking out of here. We're going to leave this place forever, and go where the sun is shining and there's lots of good food and toys to play with." Somehow, the physically and mentally damaged children were vaguely able to comprehend what was said. "Follow me through the door," he directed, and they all began to move forward. Eric trailed behind and planted a timed explosive before exiting.

Departing from a real-life hell, guns drawn and ready, they emerged out into the darkened passageway. Tony was in the lead, Adam in the middle, Eric followed from the end of the long procession of small children. "Let's walk fast," the men continually prompted the many feeble ones lagging behind.

While progressing through the dismal dungeon, Eric once again radioed Alex. "Move into position to blow up the front gate."

Alex immediately responded, "Did you knock out the control room yet?"

"It'll be done within the next one hundred twenty seconds. You're approximately a mile from the Castle. It's clear all the way. Hurry."

Before the children reached the control room at the base of the stairs, Eric ran ahead and took a cylindrical plastic explosive from his belt, then, setting the timer to detonate in fifteen seconds, he rolled it beneath the door. When the bomb went off, it blasted out the metal door and extinguished electric lights throughout the Castle.

Led by Tony, when the long trail of children began to climb the narrow torch-lit stairway, he heard the sound of rushing footfalls coming down from the top. Laser pen ready, he flashed a beam of coherent light into the angry faces that suddenly appeared from around the bend. An excruciating cry of pain rang out; the four men fell to their knees, hands to their faces, blinded by the intensity of the searing radiance. Quickly rushing up the steps, the champion finished them off with a brutal series of thudding kicks. The train of children once again advanced onward; Adam and Eric guiding the rescued survivors over the lifeless fallen enemy.

Minutes later, when the double line of children filed into the entrance foyer, Tony cracked open the door to get a glimpse outside. "It looks okay," he said, and standing in the drive-through tunnel, he stood guard as they began to exit the building.

When the last of the children had left the Castle, Eric spoke into his transceiver. "Team One to Team Two. Over." He paused. "Come in Team Two." There was no response, only radio static. He said to the others. "They're in trouble. We've got to help them."

Tony replied, "Alex will be here any second. Adam – you get the first load safely on board, then stand guard over the others while me and Eric go back inside."

———•◆•———

Located deep within the bowels of the Castle was the cathedral room of 1000 points of light. Set in the high domed-ceiling, pinpoints of illumination symbolized the multitudes of enflamed black souls that were the servants of Satan – his *shining dark minions*, world leaders who masqueraded as the lights of the world.

Rex, Brandon and Howard had previously been led away by a squad of six black-robed guards that pushed them forward at gun point. Upon being ushered into the ceremonial Great Room, they found themselves in the company of world leaders; most of them European Black Nobility; but some were of the lower caste financiers and courtiers of the Royal bloodlines; fewer still were representative of the next lower level of Dynastic Families who served the financiers and were prohibited to approach the upper echelon Illuminati. They were all blood relatives of an ancient race that long ago forfeited its soul. Two in attendance were of the exclusive Council of 33, the world's highest ranking Freemasons; one was a member of the even more restrictive Council of 13. The cabal of European Royalty, influential politicians and banking elite, were dressed in ceremonial black robes lined in silver or crimson red, and were seated in the balconies or stood around a black leather altar in the middle of a white marble floor.

Sitting on an elevated throne near the altar, dressed in all black, except for gold slippers, was the Queen Mother, the aged matriarch leader of the Castle's coven of Illuminati witches. The royal seat was pure gold and black ebony; the arms were carved into the image of a cobra's head, red rubies for the eyes. Just behind the high-backed chair, extending four feet above her head, were several columns of gold spires appearing like the rays of the sun, and which she was able to manually rotate by means of a foot pedal. Behind her throne, seated on Louis XVI French Renaissance-style red velvet chairs, were thirteen members of the Grande Druid Council, coven chieftains who were among the highest ranking Wiccan witches in the world. The stern-faced Grande Dame, wearing an abundance of gold jewelry and precious stones, presided over the global Luciferian Hierarchy of Witch Kings, Witch Queens, Mothers of Darkness and Princes and Princesses of Darkness hailing from the world's top Illuminati families. Ruby-eyed cobra-head scepter held in her right hand, evil scowl upon her wrinkled face, her slitted serpentine eyes grew wide in anger upon seeing the strangers that preceded the armed guards, and that had interrupted the ritual ceremony. "How *dare* you profane the unholy!" a deep masculine voice quavered from within her diminutive frail body.

In a loud voice, Howard boldly announced, "We stand against you in the name of the Lord Jesus Christ, and by the power of His shed blood!" At the mention of the name, *Jesus Christ*, a shock wave of terror and seething hatred circulated throughout the expansive room, eliciting reptilian hisses and gnashing of teeth.

"Oh, you *do*, do *you*?" the old crone mockingly replied, pursing pallid lips, as if ready to explode. Quickly rising to her feet, she pointed the cobra scepter at them and let out a piercing screech. "You will all *die!*" The guards immediately complied with her order, leading their prisoners in the direction of the far wall equipped with heavy chains for binding sacrificial victims.

The Queen Mother then sat back down, coal black eyes reflecting the dark inner void that was her soul. Upon resuming the coronation ceremony of the coven's future Sisters of Light and Mothers of Darkness, she proclaimed, "Bring forth the next generation!" Dressed in floor length white robes, there walked out onto the arena seven teenage girls who were pre-selected candidates from Illuminati generational Satanist families. Upon standing before the Grande Dame, each set a small one ounce bar of pure gold at her feet, then paid homage by lying prostrate before her. When the Queen Mother moved the snake head wand up and down over the bodies of the supine mind-controlled subjects, upon striking each one of them in turn, a jolt of electricity was discharged from the cobra's fangs. Later, after the approval ceremony was over, seven captive children would be sacrificed; a quill pen dipped in their blood would be used to sign the names of the approved girls into the unholy record book of the international Illuminati coven.

Rotating her throne to face the Grande Druid Council, the Queen Mother announced: "This is tomorrow's generation, a chosen few!" Now turning back to her underlings – the world political leaders, European Monarchs, international bankers, and other elite despots of high-ranking Illuminati society – she said in an unnatural other-worldly voice, "Let evil reign supreme!"

Members of the Global Hierarchy then openly discussed the current progress of "The Plan," their centuries-long scheme for creating a world culture based upon ancient witchcraft and their hope of ushering in the ultimate politician, the Antichrist. "We shall do it using mind-control and terrorism to coerce the seven billions of world masses to submit to *us*, a mere few," said one of the Dynastic leaders who stood among the group of illustrious world controllers. Upon concluding the brief conference, they commenced with their ancient blood rites.

The first ritual was called the Moonchild Ceremony, where a human fetus was tortured in the mother's womb. Amid a background chorus of monotonous chanting, the black-robed Master of Ceremonies inserted long needles into the uterus of a pregnant twelve year old girl lying naked on the raised black leather altar. Months earlier, during a Mothers of Darkness ritual, in an occult marriage she was impregnated by her biological father; the subsequent child of the incestuous union destined to be ritually sacrificed to Satan. The more the young girl struggled and screamed in pain, the more the world leaders vicariously derived perverse satisfaction; the bloodlust of the elite spectators aroused by the sound of her terrified helpless cries. Mixed blood from the mother and the unborn infant soon began to flow in crimson rivulets that were collected in silver basins beneath the altar, and later to be consumed by the highest ranking members of the Black Nobility coven. With a glistening long blade knife her father made a careless jagged incision into her abdomen, and reaching in, pulled out the writhing human life, then held up the wailing blood-dripping infant for all the others to see.

The three prisoners witnessed the horror as they stood side by side, shackled with heavy iron chains, spread-eagle against the far stone wall. Rex shouted, "You're all gonna' pay for this!"

As the chanting droned on, Brandon said to the others, "The top Illuminati families are involved in creating Monarch slaves. They program their mind-controlled children to one day be their successors, fashioning them to become remorseless consciousless fiends like themselves. They torture victims to the point of death, stopping just before they die – it's called Death Door Programming. When a sacrificial child is killed, they believe they are granted supernatural power by drinking the shed blood which contains an adrenaline-like substance called Adrenochrome. It's secreted by the pineal gland of a terrorized victim just before the point of death." The men watched helplessly as the life blood of the beautiful young girl slowly drained away.

The face of the blood ritual conductor was now only an inch away from the girl as he gazed into her eyes with an hypnotic stare to draw out her soul essence at the moment of death. It was then that human-demon hybrids are known to lose their human shape and become transformed into monstrous proportions.

While the Druidic feast proceeded, the three bound men witnessed the physical change taking place among some of the world's most influential men and women. They observed with their own eyes what numerous eyewitness testimonials have confirmed: *renown world leaders transmutated into creatures from another dimension.* The bound men saw respected public figures mysteriously morph into alien creatures; shape-shifting into birdlike reptiles with unblinking eyes and flickering forked tongues, appearing as mythical chimeras who grew to stand over eight feet tall. These, the men and women who presumed to rule the world, were, in reality, the spiritual genetic progeny of an ancient reptile being, the Great Red Dragon, otherwise known as Lucifer, Satan, the Devil.

Aghast, Howard whispered, "This explains how those in power can be such heinous monsters."

In a restrained tone, Brandon replied, "Yes, they *are indeed* monsters. Quite literally."

"They're damn devils," said Rex. "Serpent seed of hell!"

The high-ranking Luciferic Highpriest, the Prince, a key figure in the European Union, lurched forward with elongated iridescent scaled neck, drawn by the scent of fresh human blood and the promise of the much prized Adrenochrome. When he suddenly plunged his toothy snout into the open wound of the mangled still living child-mother, the New World Order tribal leader shook his reptilian head in a blood-thirsty feeding frenzy while violently tearing off and consuming whole pieces of her flesh. Soon he was joined in the blood fest by other high-ranking members of old European dynastic monarchies; eviscerated parts of the sacrificial victim apportioned on the basis of privileged rank within the Illuminati Hierarchy. First choice of the sacrificial human flesh was allocated to the First Tier European Royalty; then, the Second Tier Rockefellers, Warburgs and Schiffs were allowed to feast on the leftovers; finally, the Third Tier timidly crouched forward to devour any remaining scraps that spilled onto the floor. They imagined themselves superior to the rest of humanity, but were, in fact, the most depraved form of sentient life on Earth. With bulging lizard-like eyes and flickering tongues, they competed for access to the endorphin that was more powerful than heroin, ripping into the abdominal cavity of the fully conscious screaming teen mother, consuming internal organs and slurping at pools of blood collecting on the altar and upon the floor. Experiencing the death throes of the most horrifying trauma imaginable, the mother and her infant were being consumed piece meal, cannibalized by those who devour and cannibalize the nations of the world.

The souless eyes of the Queen Mother were like a black abyss as she looked on with casual indifference. When the Grande Dame shook her scepter, a low-ranking Illuminati surrogate offspring – reportedly the progeny of a Mother of Darkness witch – came forward. He pleaded with his superiors: "Because I was faithful in carrying out orders to destroy America's sovereignty and abolish the Constitution, I'll be given a high position within the New World Order global government … *won't I?*"

Standing nearby, his mind-control programming handler snapped, "Oh, stop groveling, you sniveling miserable worm! You'll be lucky if the Council of 9 allows you your ration of cocaine and diseased hookers. I have more generational occult power than you do, and that's why I'm further up in the International Hierarchy, and that's why you answer *to me*! They groomed you to be the consummate liar that we all are. Your job is to sell out America to the European financial establishment!" She then used a hot cattle prod on his back side to further make her point.

When the Ahab and Jezebel stage show concluded, next, a representative from the House of Rothschild came down from a high balcony to stand before the crowd of his fellow Luciferians. Dressed in the ceremonial regalia of purple robes studded with jewels, he seemed oblivious to the blood and gore spilled on the altar and pooled upon the white floor. Nonchalantly he cleared his throat and said, "My fellow distinguished colleagues, it is an honor and a privilege to present to you on this very special occasion commencing the year long Feast of the Beast, someone that is near and dear to us all. We know him as our leader, our counselor and confidant; that deceptively charming, wickedly clever, seductively convincing and temporary ruler of this planet – his evilness: our lord and master ..." He swept his hand in a wide arch, and when bowing low, everyone solemnly did likewise.

Appearing from out of nowhere, from another dimension, an elegantly dressed gentleman in white tuxedo walked out onto the floor; the step of his cloven footfalls echoing hollow in the large open room. The appreciative audience of European Monarch shape-shifters demonstrated their approval with serpentine hisses, clicking tongues, and reptilian caterwauls. Like his criminal fraternity of human protégés, he was articulate, persuasive, and cunningly deceptive when stating: "You are to pass down through your chain of subordinates at Levels Four and Five, the orders which I now convey to you. Your unholy bloodlines contain the essence of my spirit, which is the spirit of murder and deceit that your ancestors selectively bred into you ...

under my supervision, of course. As always, your goal is to further the great deception.

"Your unceasing labors will soon allow my evil to more fully manifest when I indwell my chosen one to rule the global government which you have so diligently prepared for him. This was made possible by my interlocking corporations and organizations that form a matrix web of absolute control over the world masses who serve me with unquestioning allegiance. In addition, the media – over which I also have total control – has enabled me to mold public opinion, and even the very thoughts of our billions of slaves. It is through the press that we have gained the power to influence while remaining ourselves in the dark. The television, the newspapers, Hollywood, the wonderfully decadent culture, has allowed us to create fabrications to serve our own agenda of mass mind-manipulation, terrorism, and behavior modification. We have succeeded in anesthetizing the group mind to such an extent as to lead it away from serious reflection, and to distract it towards a sham fight of empty eloquence. For example, the ignorant masses *actually believe* in our so-called political process, trusting that it is *they* who elect my politicians into public office. How naïve. They think that the media has a concern for reporting the truth, or – hell forbid! – truthfully informing the public *about us*! I wonder if the mind-numb masses will ever wake up and realize that it's all a charade, a staged circus to make them believe our lies are the truth. Ha! *Nothing* we ever tell them is the truth!

"Yes, our press has been very good to our cause. Since we own and control it, there is no opposition to our propaganda. Of course, we ourselves create the illusion of an opposing view by *also* taking the other side. That's how we control the flow of information and direct the public attention away from issues of any real importance. This works to make the servile sheep believe in free speech. And, as we all know, it is *we* who decide who or what is free.

"I ... uh, that is, *we*, have been so very clever in using official organizations to cover our operations and stand guard over our interests.

For example, what could we have done without our NEA that mind-controlled the sacrificial little goats – I mean, *kids* – who grew up to become our brainwashed loyal slaves? And, praise hell for the vital role our AMA played in lending credibility to our long-term vaccine campaign that inoculated nearly everyone on earth with incurable diseases! It was sure genius on my part, I mean *our* part, to add live cancer cells, toxic metals and stealth viruses that their doctors would never think of injecting into themselves or their own kids, but they have no problem whatsoever shooting up every little goat that wanders into their office or hospital emergency room. And you *also* have me to thank for all the other thousands of groups and organizations that fronted for us. If the citizen-fools would ever have realized that the truth is the *exact opposite* of whatever we told them, they might have had a chance … but no, they *trusted* us! Imagine *that*! To them, the truth was whatever they saw on TV, or were told by our people dressed in lab coats or three thousand dollar suits." He shook his head and hissed, "Stupid!"

The cloven-footed host paced several steps to rest a bejeweled hand on the bloody altar, then announced, "I need not further elaborate upon the many details that I devised over the centuries past, details which I have personally communicated to your forefathers, and that my clockwork elves conveyed to you in your wide-eyed bemusement." He let out a contemptuous laugh. "I dare say that some of you still think they are little men from outer space!" A confused reaction quickly shot though the gathering of trillionaire elitists. "Even so, there are one or two small points that may require some illumination. And they are as follows:

"I command you to continue feeding the … uhg," he paused with a look of disgust, then said, "… *humans* … a steady diet of lies. Don't worry about how ridiculous your lies may seem, since those who hate the truth will uncritically accept all that is untrue. Thanks to my centuries-long propaganda campaign to encourage their ignorance of that …" he once again gulped uneasily, "… *Book*, … they are more than willing to go along with whatever you and I tell them. Like your-selves, most of them have my spirit, and consequently, they too are liars and deceivers and will only believe to be true that which is false. You need never fear they could possibly one day hear the truth, be-cause – *even if they did* – they wouldn't recognize it as true! Therefore, they would consider it to be *a lie*. Remember our motto: *Liars believe lies.* For instance, when you say that evil is good, and good is evil – they will believe it. Tell them darkness is light, and light is darkness – they will enthusiastically agree. Say that bitter is sweet, and sweet is bitter – they will applaud you for your genius! But, if quite by accident, you should ever be so foolish as to tell them *the truth*, they will think it is a lie; and moreover, they will hate you for it.

"Just like us, they love lies, love darkness, love their sins, and do not want to give them up. Because of this, they have lost any ability to discern the truth. *He* allows us to hide it from them. They only want to be *comfortable*; they simply want to be at ease, and will not take a stand on matters of principle. Regardless of what we do to them, they will not oppose us. In other words, they are *cowards*. And that is how we like it: a whole planet of quivering, obedient, subservient, cowering slaves. Most of those who profess to be *Christians*, and especially their pastors, are actually working for us. On this point I must commend you on your excellent job of infiltration. I'm so looking forward to them all joining us in my glorious eternal kingdom." More clicks and hoots rose up from the appreciative audience. The Grand Master of Ceremonies continued. "But, sorry to say, there is always the problem of the *True Christians*." Menacing hisses oozed from the mostly shape-shifted crowd. "I don't quite know what to do about them – they're always messing up my plans. But, since there are so few, I suppose it doesn't really matter." The lizard people hooted and clicked their approval.

"When they allowed me to corrupt their wisdom and take away their spiritual strength – that is, their …" he again paused uncomfort-ably, "… *Book* – they lost all their spiritual power. After the King James

Version was rejected by their *social clubs* – which they call *Churches* – the rest was easy. My job was simplified after that. Our job was nearly done when they didn't know enough to even become outraged at what we were doing to them. Why, if they had any righteousness at all, we would all be – if you'll pardon the expression – in a hell of a lot of hot water!

"As it turns out, it is I who *owns* their spiritual whore houses, I mean, their churches. They signed them over to me. Yes – *to me!* And I've got the 501(c)3 tax exempt corporation papers to prove it!" He waited for an applause, which came in an assortment of animalistic howls, snorts, and grunts. "Thank you, thank you. In so doing, they swore their undying allegiance to me, which, of course, I deserve. They wouldn't *dare* speak out against me and my religion – which is human civil government – because, if they *did*, they would have to suffer persecution, and *that* is something religious hypocrites do not wish to experience. I know all those who belong to me, because they hear me and agree to go along with whatever I tell them to do. They're scared to death of us, actually, and have no fear of *Him* that could squash them like the little pests that they are. That's not real smart. They're so spiritually ignorant they obey the government that wars against their God." He perfunctorily straightened his flaming red bow tie. "Dogs don't bark at their master.

"Their million dollar church buildings are dead. The churchgoers are choir boys who would rather sing hymns than study their *Holy Book*. Thank evilness they don't, or else our goose would be cooked … if you know what I mean. Fortunately, all they have is a dumbed-down version rearranged by one of our own people – a lesbo, if memory serves me correctly. Anyway, since the book they have is not *The Book*, we have nothing to worry about. The NIV version is, of course, pure malarkey; it's the kind of watered-down doctrine we thrive on. After all, it was written on an eighth grade level of comprehension, so even *they*, the self-Saved church-goers, could understand it. The Never Inspired Version, and the scores of other rearranged Books, keep them from hearing the true Word that can save them *from us*! We reversed all the verses, transposed the sentence structure so they no longer had *His Words*, but *my* words! We changed the word meanings and provided false interpretations so they wouldn't become enlightened to the fact that it *is I* who controls them! It *is I* they are serving by not speaking out against our government system of tyranny – which, as you all know, is for *my* glory. They've become so stupid they believe our pastors when they tell them Romans 13 is a command from Him to *obey us!* Most of them are *that* dumbed-down! Remember, there is no danger of them opposing you, since they will never die for the truth … but, be assured, one day they *will* most certainly die for a lie." Without using a match, he paused briefly to ignite a cigarette.

"How foolish they are! When they agreed to go along with my program, they lost any wisdom which their God had given them from the beginning. By rejecting the truth, which, needless to say, we do our best to conceal from them, they demonstrated their willingness to follow me. Consequently, since they cannot serve two masters, the Spirit of their God has departed from them and they are cut off." He took a deep drag from the cigarette, not exhaling, the smoke retained within his infernal being. "Even though they made a free will decision, I would still like to take some of the credit … well, all right … what I mean to say is that I want to take *all of the credit.*" He again puffed on the smoldering ember, and then, holding it up for closer inspection while turning it in his fingers, said, "I've destroyed millions of lives with these little things. I suppose congratulations are in order to the Reynolds family. It's been a great front for our drug trade." He inhaled deeply on the carcinogenic smoke. "Ah, but I digress. More to the point….

"To illustrate, using only one example from among thousands, consider the fact that they are so spiritually dead as to allow us to lace their food and water with *wonderful* poisons! We tainted their drinking water with Fluoride, Chlorine, Lithium, radioactive isotopes, toxic metals, pesticides, and over 75,000 other health destroying substances. Into their processed foods and beverages we put Aspartame, MSG, genetically modified organisms, and a whole lot of other nervous system destroying chemical compounds. And then, the coup d'grace ... I even managed to poison the very air they breathe! Spraying them with Chemtrails was a stroke of pure genius, if I must say so myself. And, I must. I remember the day, not too long ago – in 1997 – when I put the thought into the mind of Edward Teller to saturate the lower atmosphere with tons of Aluminum oxide. (He's the guy who came up with the atomic bomb, in case some of you aren't old enough to remember that wonderful invention.) We dump all kinds of stuff on them these days, and what's truly amazing is they never even notice! Why, there are so much toxic metals, disease-causing fungi, bioengineered bacteria and infectious viruses floating around in the atmosphere, they're too sick to even care! The air they breathe is totally saturated with nanofibers that regenerate inside their bodies to create every kind of disease imaginable. Evil is so wonderful ... it's like a nightmare come true! I can alter their cellular genetics by their mere act of breathing! And they haven't got a clue!" More grunts and appreciative hisses. "Even when you tell them, they don't care!

"And let's not forget my idea to vaccinate them with deadly diseases! They thought we were helping them when they went to my medical witch doctors to get a *harmless Flu shot*. Ha! Or our government mandated school vaccinations. Imagine their naiveté! We inoculate them with the very disease they think they're being protected against! The horrible beauty of it all is they actually approve of the death vaccines administered to their kids! They even thank us for it! Doped food, Mercury vaccines, poisoned water and air ... they absolutely *love* the stuff!

"Once a human gets a little money, a big house and a new car, they throw away *that Book* and join me ... uh, I mean, *us*. Then, they'll gladly believe our disinformation agents: the doctors and news anchormen; the politicians, the TV documentaries, Hollywood films and guru How-To books. After they were programmed with decades of television – which, as we planned, turned their brains into silly putty – I knew we had them. Even if a small minority managed to figure out what we were doing to them, they could never penetrate our controlled media to warn the rest. By the time some of them finally wised up, it was *too late* – the damage had already been done!" More sounds of drooling slurps and clattering teeth from the Royal audience.

"The Plan worked perfectly! We attacked them from so many different areas, their heads were spinning. If our disease-transmitting vaccines didn't kill them, our pharmaceutical drugs *did*! And if *that* didn't do the job, we doused them with everything from Chemtrails to carcinogenic mosquito spray! We even dumped pure manure on them from above – and amazingly, they didn't seem to care! We all know why. And, best of all, they *paid us* to do it! Yes, we stole their money through taxation, then used that very same money to destroy them with it! They were too afraid of us to even let out a whimper, and cower in fear of anyone with the righteous integrity to oppose us and tell us to go to hell. Imagine *that!* In fact, they're such miserable little wretches, they'll report the one righteous enough to stand against our tyranny. We so programmed their minds with HAARP/ VLF/ ELF microwaves and a continuous stream of television news propaganda, it's amazing they can even think at all! Now, at long last, we have them right where we want them – an entire planet of spiritually ignorant slaves! Because they rejected knowledge, their God rejected *them*. By now, they're so far gone, *they no longer care what we do to them*! Isn't sin marvelous?" More hoots, cackles, and clicking beaks.

"Just think … with a little help from me, I mean, *us*, what could have been a child with above average intelligence, by the time it becomes a teenager, will be a complete *imbecile*! It's so much easier to control docile idiots than it is to deal with the ones who ask questions and who just might have enough brains to shoot you if you try to take away their guns … or inject them with vaccines … or prevent them from home schooling their kids. What I mean is, suppose even a few of them ever got together and all at once decided to stampede us like a thundering herd of mad buffalo? Like they did in 1776. Well …"

he gulped nervously, "… perish the thought, because *that* will *never* happen. But, just for a moment, let's suppose it *did*." He anxiously clomped his hoofs on the floor. "In that case, the gig's up." He threw down the cigarette butt onto the floor, the burning coal sizzling when extinguished in a pool of blood.

"Yes, they could easily overtake us, the relatively small number that we are. After all, they have our ranks outnumbered by 100 to 1. So, we really wouldn't stand much of a chance. I don't think I could bare another replay of what happened to my servant in Germany, poor fool that he was; or to my other associate in Russia – he did twenty mil the first year. And not to overlook all those who remain loyal to me in America – they too will get their reward, as will you. If the American people had ever known the truth about what we have done to them, we would be chased down in the streets and lynched." The iridescent scales of the world's shape-shifted elite flushed crimson red in sudden alarm. George H.W.Bush slunk behind a high-backed chair, ashamed for having blundered when publicly making that very same statement on national television. In standard Police State protocol, the Illuminati-controlled media had immediately suppressed it.

"What I want is a whole planet full of slaves; two-legged creatures who worship me through my religion – human government. I want weak, emasculated slaves that are so docile and naively trusting as to believe that politicians are their savior. I want mindless drones incapable of independent thought; poorly educated, or overeducated – which amounts to the same thing. I want slaves who think that a piece of colored cloth symbolizes something noble, as if there were any distinction between what they consider to be *their country* and those who control them – *us*! I want mind-controlled pheasants incapable of recognizing that we tossed out their Constitution and replaced it with the Communist Manifesto! I want groveling sycophantic government bureaucrats bowing the knee to me; and a society too dumb to realize they no longer have any rights, except, of course, the right to be our slaves. Yes, I want slaves who get their information from watching television *programming*, from reading our propaganda newspapers, from believing our lies! I want slaves who *actually enjoy being subservient!* I want slaves *who vote!* These are the kind of humans who will serve me, because when they obey the government, they *are* serving me! I want slaves who love their slavery and look to me … I mean, to you, for help. We've conditioned them to believe they *need* us, and … they *love* us! Yuck! Makes you want to just kill them all, doesn't it?" There followed an extended round of Jurassic jungle sounds. After a long interlude of basking in their praise, the guest of dishonor held up a bejeweled hand to dampen their enthusiasm.

"They exchanged their God-given freedom for the illusion of false security which I offered them after we created military conflicts and fake acts of terrorism, then passed even more oppressive laws to enslave them. They trusted us. Big mistake. Give them a full belly, and they're happy; give them a television set, a shiny new car, a big house, and they'll sell their souls to me! They appear perfect on the outside, but on the inside – like us – they're full of darkness and deceit.

"Oh, I could go on reminiscing about how I … I mean, *we*, destroyed the minds and morals of their little goats when restructuring the educational system so that schools became nothing more than occult institutions of mind-control propaganda. If only they would have realized that it was our witches and Satanists, our Change Agents, our Facilitators, who were teaching their sacrificial kids when they went off to school each day. How *easy* it is to dupe those who hate the truth! I made sure they stopped learning any spiritual truth by the time they were ten years old. Thanks to my television, my Internet, my Hollywood movies, my music industry, my popular culture, and my controlled press, most are so brainwashed by the time they graduate from high school – that is, *if* they graduate from high school – they never again have an original thought for the remainder of their paltry little lives!" More praise from the human-demon hybrid fringe. "And, just as an aside, I'm also happy to report that the Docilase enzymes, genetic modification of their foods, and laboratory bioengineered pathogens in vaccines and Chemtrails, have produced excellent results. It's official: by one year of age they now have heart disease and cancer!" Further reptilian kudos, after which, he proudly added, "If an entire world culture inundated with TV *programming* and mind-controlling HAARP frequencies, doped food and water, and enslaved by *you* – my loyal elite government masters – didn't destroy them, the educational system *did*! Yes, it's true – they *will do whatever we want*. We own them, we control them; and they want to be controlled, almost as much as we *crave* controlling *them*. They won't resist. They won't question. They'll go along with whatever we say. They won't stand up and defend the truth, because *there's no truth in them*! They'll permit you to take away their Constitutional rights, their guns, and their Bill of Rights! They'll even allow you to take away their children! They'll believe *anything* you tell them; the more ridiculous it is, the better! And get this … they'll - even - put - on - their - own - handcuffs. In fact, they'll *thank you* for them! I ask you, ladies and gentlemen, is it possible to get any dumber than that?!" More hoots and clacking beaks.

"In closing, I must once again remind you that mind-control and staged acts of global terrorism are the key to implementing our New World Order plan of tyranny and human enslavement. You are Olympians, the Chosen Ones, having inbred among your own accursed kind to carry within your spiritual genetic bloodlines the evil deeds that you and your ancestors have faithfully committed to appease me throughout the millennium. I need not offer reassurance that each and every one of you will be given a place of some importance and honor in my kingdom. How I do look forward to our kingdom – our mutual reign as co-rulers of the universe. Oh, it will be a grand and glorious future, will it not? You that have served me will live forever. *Ye shall not surely die. Your eyes shall be opened, and ye shall be as gods.* The universe will be our oyster! At long last we shall walk upon the holy mountain, among the fiery planetary stones. We shall be like the most High! I promise … and I always keep my promises."

A high-ranking Level 6 Prince of Darkness, having destroyed many lives, now stepped forward to receive his coveted reward – more power. As the sophisticated white-tuxedoed gentleman, the Father of

Lies, began to walk toward him, the echo of cloven-hooves sounded hollow on the polished hard floor. When a short distance away, his visage spontaneously changed to reveal his true identity as a hideous, grotesque reptile; a loathsome draconian winged serpent. Without pausing, it walked directly into the body of the Illuminati initiate; the spirit of ancient leviathan merging with the mortal flesh of a coven high priest, who's eye color changed to pitch black at the moment of possession.

During the ritual to follow, a section of the floor mysteriously vanished to reveal a bottomless pit, a deep abysmal sulfurous netherworld far below. Seven children were made ready to be impaled on large metal hooks. "You lousy sons of Belial!" shouted Rex, his booming voice echoing throughout the cathedral room. Violently disturbed, the limbs of his flagellating body yanked on the chains. "You'll all burn in hell for this!"

The Queen Mother slowly turned her sinister gray head in his direction. In the deep masculine voice of her many indwelling demons, she commanded her guards, "Bring – him – to – me."

Eric studied the screen of his wrist-mounted GPS micro-map displaying the interior layout of the Castle, observing the three flashing red dots indicating the location of Team Two. "They're in the cathedral Great Room," he said, noting the shortest route. "Let's go." Turning abruptly, he and Tony ran down the main hallway, leaving Adam at the front entrance to await the arrival of Alex for loading the children onto the bus.

Adam shouted after them, "For the glory and honor of The KING!"

Without stopping or looking back, the two valiant warriors raised the clenched fist of their right hand and shouted, "For The KING!"

They ran down the short leg of the L-shaped corridor, then left at the longer wing that was tainted with the scent of sulfur from burning side torches which appeared as streaks of light in their peripheral vision. "It's checkmate time," said Eric, while they ran side by side, anticipating the dangers they were likely to encounter.

Tony said, "Let's crash their party."

Eric replied, "I hope we're not too late."

Soon after turning at the bend in the hallway, they heard low frequency monotone chanting, and upon seeing the closed double doors up ahead, slowed their pace to a fast walk. When coming to a halt before the oversized entrance, they took brief notice of the symbols engraved into the black oak timber: sunbursts, pyramids, triangles, the all-seeing eye, olive branches, pentagram stars, goat heads, and other familiar Luciferian representations commonly seen in modern cultures. Guns drawn, they now stood outside the portal through which passed some of the most wicked men and women in the world. Eric exhaled a deep breath, then said, "Ready?"

The undaunted world champion firmly asserted, "I'm *always* ready."

When turning the crystal door knob and discovering the entrance was locked, the anointed warrior stepped back ten yards and proclaimed, "By the power of Almighty God, these doors *will* open!" He then rushed straight forward, and within an arms-length away, thrust out his hands, palms striking the sturdy oaken partition with an explosive force.

— 29 —

Skulking among dark shadows cast by the flickering flames of side banks of numerous candles were the spiritual genetic progeny of post-flood creatures born of demonic lineage. Emitting a cacophony of animalistic sounds, many of them were transmutated to reveal their true demon-indwelled form; shape-shifted Black Nobility world leaders reveling in the blood fest of human carnage.

It was only moments ago that a famous religious figure had sodomized a screaming three year old little boy who was about to be impaled with a large meat hook and lowered into the crater-like opening through the floor which led down into the depths of a bottomless subterranean pit. Standing nearby, stoop shouldered like vultures, fellow Luciferians greedily awaited the stream of free flowing blood.

A long flickering forked tongue preceded a slithering spectacled Federal Reserve Chairman who slinked on his stomach across pools of blood in search of more hapless prey. Meanwhile, a birdlike carnivore occupying a high executive position in Washington D.C. used his elongated reptilian snout – dripping red with the grisly remains of tortured children – to slurp spilled leftovers beneath the bloody altar. Prowling in the vicinity of the most recent sacrificial offering to their demon masters, grotesque humanoid lizard people fought over scraps of human remains.

On the far side of the Great Room, Rex was tied to a pole, tortured, battered and bleeding, nearly dead.

When the doors suddenly burst wide open, reptilian heads quickly jerked around to flash alien green eyes at the two bold intruders.… Eric and Tony instantly commenced firing.

The semi-dark room was blanketed with a spray of bullets. Unearthly beasts roared, teeth gnashed, tainted blood spurted; some of the eight foot tall creatures instantly fell to the floor. "Die, you bastard sons of Lucifer! Die!" shouted Howard and Brandon, cheering them on while chained to the wall.

Howard quoted Isaiah 14:15 when he yelled, "You're *brought down to hell, to the sides of the pit!*"

After periodic brief pauses to reload, each of the ministers of God's justice let loose yet another round of gunfire that sent more howling beasts on a premature departure to the Lake of Fire.

While a small group of Illuminati-appointed U.S. Communist political agents feasted on the bullet-ridden flesh of their executed colleagues, the two avengers of the Lord stepped forward, guns trained on them. Preoccupied with consuming the carnage, mass murdering elite remained seemingly oblivious to their imminent peril; vicious, animalistic carnivorous usurpers to the very end. Using the deceptive powers of indwelling demons to thwart their inevitable fate, each made a vain attempt to obfuscate his way out of the harsh destiny that awaited him. A Washington Illuminati shill was the first to pontificate, but, an instant later, both he and a fellow pedophile homosexual sadist and serial killer were quickly dispatched; each receiving two bullets that pierced their rudimentary reptilian brain. Next, a pornography czar and D.C. drug kingpin offered the promise of illicit wares in exchange for sparing his sordid life. He too met with a sudden ultimatum that was fitting for his many crimes against humanity. Another recognizable D.C. pedophile and mass murderer then made a token confession upon revealing that he and Saddam Hussein were business partners, and that he personally profiteered from oil rich countries during Middle Eastern wars. He went on to further admit that the war was a staged theater for testing biological weapons on a civilian population and unsuspecting American soldiers who would later be diagnosed with Gulf War Syndrome, an incurable terminal disease. "It's unfortunate that thousands of young kids were intentionally exposed to deadly depleted uranium; injected with vaccines containing experimental biowarfare agents, laboratory-engineered viruses, toxic chemicals and fatal diseases," he said through thin reptilian lips, with the sincerity which only a congenital psychopath could muster. "But, what's a few thousand more murders to someone like me?" He pleaded to be allowed to live and see the fulfillment of the global dictatorship that he worked all his life to promote. It was shortly after mentioning that it was he that planned the Kennedy assassinations, including the murder of JFK Jr., that they shot him, point blank; streams of thick green blood oozing from beneath the scales of this exceedingly wicked creature.

Now turning their attention to the next serial killer – for the first time on record – he told the truth. Kneeling before them, in a raspy tone, the slimy reptile hastily implored: "While in office I murdered hundreds of people who tried to expose me. I ordered terrorist attacks by Delta mind-controlled school children as a pretense to legislate more gun confiscation laws for disarming the American people so we could take over America. I made treaties with Communist nations, opening up America's borders to create a world economy for facilitating globalism. I did everything my Illuminati handlers told me to do. My associates and I blackmailed members of Congress to pass Bills to remove God and the Bible from schools and from public readings, calling it a Hate Crime. We took the Ten Commandments out of the courthouses and replaced it with New Age witchcraft. We single-handedly restructured children's education to reflect an occult-based curriculum for insuring they would be non-critical thinking, docile, pagan servants of the New World Order. I was mostly responsible for the loss of American sovereignty; I committed treason *every day* I was in office. It was I who legalized abortion and legislated gay rights and gun confiscation laws. I who mandated the hepatitis B vaccine be given to twelve hour old infants as a ruse for injecting them with Mercury, Aluminum, diabetes, delayed onset cancer and AIDS. I circumvented the Constitution and replaced it with the ten Planks of the Communist Manifesto. Yes, I admit it – I'm a Communist! I was installed into office by the European Monarchs who trained me in how to mind-control the American public so they wouldn't realize that I was stealing their freedom. But yet, it really wasn't me at all – it was my handlers behind the scenes telling me what to do. All I did was carry out what they told me. That's how it is with everyone that's put in my position. The American people are just too dumbed-down to realize it's all a sham. They vote!" He made an attempt to laugh, but his barred long pointed teeth made it seem like a twisted snarl. "Everyday, I raped, pillaged and plundered. Everyday, I sold another piece of America's soul." His dark reptilian eyes stared without blinking, incapable of tears. "But I did it for *them*! For my Illuminati superiors, the Committee of 300, the Council of 33, who promised me more power, more money, more illicit sex, more cocaine. Please, *Please*! Don't kill me! I repent!" His bulbous snout seemed to have grown longer.

Upon hearing him say that he repented, the two Deuteronomy 19:12 Godly avengers of blood paused in a moment of indecision.

Making a desperate appeal, the shape-shifted humanoid summoned the full force of his mind-control programming, and with a crooked grin on his lizard lips, pleaded, "Remember what the Bible says: *Blessed are the peacemakers.*" The scaled caricature knelt there on the blood-slick floor, his oversized red snout glistening from candle light reflected off the many standing pools of blood.

Tony calmly replied, "Yeah, the Holy Bible *does* say that…. But, those who destroy the wicked *are* peacemakers. Therefore, by destroying someone like you, we're blessed."

Eric smiled when pulling back the breach of the high-powered long barreled handgun that was now aimed directly at the lizard head. Without emotion, he blandly said, "Go to hell." Then he shot the venomous reptile between the eyes.

When each member of the satanic cabal had breathed their last, their serpentine body shape-shifted back into their more recognizable human form. A rictus of horror was perpetually etched on their faces from the approaching reality of bobbing up and down in a pool of boiling sulfur, which they would now occupy for all of eternity. The burning Lake of Fire was their immediate destiny. They exited this world unceremoniously, cold-blooded eyes transfixed in a stunned expression of absolute terror upon meeting the Ultimate Terrorist – Jesus Christ.

The two men then unleashed a long series of gunfire in rapid succession, metal bullet casings continuously ejected onto the floor as they razed a widening swath of death throughout the candlelit Great Room. Amid loud wild shrieks of pain and torment, moment by moment, it grew increasingly silent, and after several more minutes of sustained slaughter, those who remained standing were an assortment of cosmic zoo animals, consisting of leftover European Royalty and various lower-tier political miscreants of the Merovingian bloodline. Descendants of the founders of large tax free Trust Funds dropped without fanfare to the floor when terminal velocity bullets pierced glossy hides to rip gaping holes through their black hearts. When the last quasi-human was translated into eternity, the servants of God's righteous vengeance finally turned their attention to the one who sat upon the raised throne, and who epitomized the supreme embodiment of evil – the Queen Mother.

Standing among many slain corpses, Tony's words echoed in the hollow of the lifeless chamber when he shouted, "It's time to answer for all the evil you've done!"

The hag-like croaking voice of the Grande Dame mockingly replied, "Oh, *really*?" Passing a withered hand before her wrinkled face and in front of her small shriveled body, she pointed a bony finger and said, "Now, it is *you* who will *die!*"

Leveling their automatic weapons at the coven High Priestess, when they opened fire, amazingly, it was as if their bullets were striking an impenetrable wall; the lead slugs stopped short, then fell to spin upon the floor. The witch queen stood up quickly and shook the ruby-eyed cobra scepter at them. Immediately, two howling whirlwinds proceeded forth from her black cloaked body, her manifesting guardian demons quickly rushing toward the servants of righteousness. Like miniature cyclones, the swirling dark vortexes encircled the two men, approaching close by, yet, were unable to trespass through their invisible hedge of protection.

"You are powerless to work your sorcery against us!" shouted Eric. "Your puny demons are no match for the Almighty Creator of the universe – the Lord Jesus Christ!" A moment later, the Queen's demon guardians lost their whirlwind fury and vanished without a trace.

Once again she pointed the scepter, and this time, up from the opened chasm arose a cloud of swirling smoke that preceded the appearance of the white tuxedo gentlemen. Summoned from the darkest recesses of the underworld abyss, when materializing, he announced in a cultured tone, "Good evening. It appears we have a slight disagreement." When he came forward, the clomping of his hoofs echoed in the silence of the lifeless chamber as he stepped over the prostrate bodies of his former minions. "Perhaps we can arrive at an understanding. *Come now, and let us reason together.*"

"Quoting Scripture doesn't become you, Satan," challenged Tony. "Besides, we don't make deals with the Devil."

"Ah, yes. That, you don't," rejoined the ancient diplomat. He then cocked his head knowingly. "Or … *do* you?" Stomping closer, the accuser of the brethren added, "There yet remains the little problem of your recent slaughter. For your Book says *Thou shalt not kill.*"

Tony countered, "It is written in Matthew 19:18: *Thou shalt do no murder.* Murder is the shedding of innocent blood, and their blood wasn't innocent. God's anointed servant, the prophet Samuel, obeyed God and was blessed when he hacked King Agag to pieces with a sword!"

A fleeting look of defeat shot across the deceptively winsome face as he stroked his black goatee. "Hmmm."

Tony added, "And have you not read in the Books of Deuteronomy and Joshua, where the LORD God commanded his people to destroy all the pagans; to kill everyone who practiced witchcraft, sorcery, and sacrificed children upon your altars?"

Howard's voice boomed from across the room, "It's also written: *Thou shalt not suffer a witch to live.*"

The nemesis of the truth, father of all politicians, was again dumbfounded. "That was a misprint," he said. "In the version which I edited, the NIV, it doesn't mention anything about witches. Besides, I come as a friend. I want to *help* you. Let's talk. Can we at least agree to disagree?"

"We have no agreement with death," replied the undefeated warrior. "We don't want your help, and we're not your friend, and we're not going to dialogue to a consensus with you. You're an enemy of God and of all those who are righteous in Jesus Christ. Of you it is written: *He was a murderer from the beginning, and abode not in the truth, because there is no truth in him. When he speaketh a lie, he speaketh of his own: for he is a liar, and the father of it.* You and your servants have made *lies your refuge,* according to Isaiah 28:15, and *under falsehood have hid yourselves.* God hates and opposes you and all those who serve you. And so do we."

When the great deceiver clicked his tongue in exasperation, the forked end briefly flickered between parted lips. "Ah, *that* – Bad PR," he casually replied. "Yet, let us return to the matter at hand.... You see all these dead bodies?" he made a wide sweeping gesture with his jeweled hand that encompassed the many slain. With a laugh, he said, "Fools. Are they not? I wasn't going to give them *anything.* I was simply using them, and when I had finished using them, I would have done the same as you did and kill them all. I promised them a place in my kingdom, but, well, you know how the expression goes ... *promises, promises.*"

Soul Esprit

Pain was etched upon the face of Rex when he shouted, "Your kingdom is an eternity in hell fire!"

The sophisticated orator – father of all attorneys – challenged, "Ah, so *you* say. However, I prefer the *other* scenario, the one in which *I* rule and reign over the earth *for ever*, and not just for a pittance of six thousand years."

Tony responded, "Your days are numbered, Satan, just like they are for all your duped slaves. The only reason that God allows you out of your cage is to give people a choice between choosing good or evil, life or death. If anyone is foolish enough to choose *you*, they die a double death."

"But death is life and life is death," obfuscated the world's consummate philosopher.

"That's *another* lie!" corrected Eric. "Jesus Christ is Life. Death is separation from God and confinement with you in hell for eternity."

The denizen of darkness winced upon hearing the name that he despised above all others. "You're *so* judgmental," he replied in mock disapproval when using a trite phrase parroted by his many New Age Professing Christian followers. Arms folded, he causally asserted, "I could kill all of you right now, if I choose to do so. And, like my many servants in human government, I would do it – if for no other reason – than simply because, *I can*. And thus have I always instructed my criminal fraternity: *Do whatever thou wilt is the whole of the law.*"

"Wrong *again*!" returned Tony. "You can do nothing without God's permission. In 1 John 5:18 it is written: ... *he that is begotten of God keepeth himself, and that wicked one toucheth him not.*" Hearing the spoken Word of God rocked the Devil back on his hooves, knocking him temporarily off balance by the Sword of Truth.

Tony immediately pressed the attack, "In Luke 10:18,19 it is written: *I beheld Satan as lightening fall from heaven. Behold, I give unto you power to tread on serpents and scorpions, and over all the power of the enemy: and nothing shall by any means hurt you.* You, your demons, and everyone that's your servant, are subject *to us!*"

Wounded, the ultimate impostor was becoming increasingly weakened by hearing the spoken Word of God. Panting in shallow uneven breaths, he uttered, "I can see that ... you are hard ones to convince.... Not at all like ... those two ... in the Garden."

The skilled fighter moved forward to inflict more damage. "In Proverb 14:19 it is written: *The evil bow before the good; and the wicked at the gates of the righteous.*"

As if struck by an invisible blow to the mid section, the masquerading angel of light suddenly buckled in pain and collapsed onto the blood-slick floor. Dazed, now on his hands and knees, in short tortured gasps he proclaimed, "Bow down ... to me ... and I ... will give to you ... whatever you want.... For all the kingdoms of this world ... are mine ... to give to whomever ... I wish."

Brandon's loud voice rang out in the morbid chamber. "*Get thee hence, Satan: for it is written, Thou shalt worship the LORD thy God, and him only shalt thou serve.*"

Disabled by the sword of the Spirit, the enemy of the truth slowly crawled on all fours, and as the invisible battle raged on, he reeled each time he was confronted by the irrefutable truth of God's Holy Word:

"*... whosoever shall gather together against thee shall fall for thy sake. Isaiah 54:15.*"

"*When the wicked, even mine enemies and my foes, came upon me to eat up my flesh, they stumbled and fell. Psalm 27:2.*"

Buffeted by the continued spiritual onslaught, his white tuxedo now torn and smeared with blood, the progenitor of the ungodly rich men of the world slumped face down onto the floor, then shapeshifted into his original draco-reptilian form of a winged dragon. The outpouring of truth continued:

"*Through God we shall do valiantly: for he it is that shall trend down our enemies. Psalm 60:12.*"

"*Thou shalt tread upon the lion and adder: the young lion and the dragon shalt thou trample under feet. Psalm 91:13.*"

Continuously pummeled by the unrelenting attack that echoed true throughout the high ceiling room, the hideous creature made desperate attempts to rise and lurch forward, but each time fell short, once again dropping face down into a pool of blood. Tortured by the piercing truth of Scripture, the Red Dragon covered it's scaled ears and hissed, "Stop it! Stop it! No more truth! I hate it! I *hate* it!"

"*He shall judge the poor of the people, he shall save the children of the needy, and shall break in pieces the oppressor. Psalm 72:4.*"

"*Only with thine eyes shalt thou behold and see the reward of the wicked. Psalm 91:8.*"

"*Through thee will we push down our enemies: through thy name will we tread them under that rise up against us. Psalm 44:5.*"

In torment, the Beast of Revelation prophesy roared like a lion.

"*… your adversary the devil, as a roaring lion, walketh about, seeking whom he may devour … resist, stedfast in the faith. 1 Peter 5:8,9.*"

"*Resist the devil, and he will flee from you. James 4:7.*"

"*And the beast was taken, and with him the false prophet that wrought miracles before him, with which he deceived them that had received the mark of the beast, and them that worshipped his image …*"

The old Serpent pleaded, "No! Stop it! Not *that verse*! No! Don't read anymore of *that one*! I don't want to hear it! I - don't - want - to - hear - it!"

"*… These both were cast alive into the lake of fire burning with brimstone. Revelation 19:20.*"

The unclean spirit indwelling all those in human government, shouted, "Stop it! *Stop* it! No more truth! No more from *that Book*! I can't stand it … I hate hearing the truth! No more … please, no more TRUTH!"

Eric continued assaulting him with the Word of God, reciting Revelation 20:1: "*And I saw an angel come down from heaven, having the key of the bottomless pit and a great chain in his hand …*"

The ancient slithering serpent let out a shriek of agony "Oh, no! You're not going to read *that verse too*! I especially hate that verse. I can't bear hearing it! I *hate* it! Please! Don't read it! Not that! No, NO, NOOOO! … aghhhhhh!"

Tony finished him off with the rest of the Scripture passage. *"And he laid hold of the dragon, that old serpent, which is the Devil, and Satan, and bound him a thousand years, And cast him into the bottomless pit, and shut him up, and set a seal upon him, that he should deceive the nations no more, till the thousand years should be fulfilled.* "

Subdued and exhausted, the wounded master of deceit feebly muttered, "I will return to kill, steal, and deceive. Until the end, I will take as many humans as I can down with me to the pit." The injured leader of beastly human governments slithered away, crawling over many fallen corpses to pass through the gaping hole in the floor and disappear into another dimension. From out of the depths of the bottomless pit, the guttural sound of his voice was heard to say: "I will soon return to indwell my chosen one … and he will destroy many."

There followed a brief pause of peaceful silence, the empty chamber still as the calm before a storm. The two men once again turned their attention to the Queen Mother of Darkness who sat upon the throne – the lone surviving servant of Satan that yet remained. "It's payback time," Tony's booming voice filled the cathedral room. "All those little children that you murdered … they're in heaven now, and Psalm 116:15 testifies against you: *"Precious in the sight of the LORD is the death of his saints."* He clenched his fists and began walking forward.

Sinking lower in the ornate black and gold high-back chair, she glared at him through slitted rheumy eyes.

As the avenging warrior approached ever closer, he said, "Your subjects are all dead. Your demons are bound. Your master has retreated. You have lost the war. You are powerless. There's no one that can save you now."

When he was nearly at the foot of the throne, she suddenly sprung down from her seat, black cloak unfurled, frothing mad, gnashing teeth; a rabid animal lunging in a wild fury. Legions of her indwelling demons spoke through her when she maniacally screeched, "I'll *kill* you!"

While she was airborne, Tony quickly skipped one step back-
ward, then leapt off the floor and spun around to deliver an explosive
kick that violently flung her against the steps of the elevated dais. Her
supernatural powers were in evidence when she rose up once again
from a blow that would have disabled most men. Now clutching the
crimson-eyed snake scepter in hand – its hollow fangs dripping with
a deadly venomous poison – she pressed forward once again with
renewed vigor, a woman possessed, driven by the spirits of ancient
beings with a seething hatred for all who are righteous in Jesus
Christ. Using the cobra electric prod like a sword, the Queen Mother
slashed at him in uncontrolled arcs, lethal weapon whistling through
the air. With fluid reflexes, the skilled fighter repeatedly averted
her attacks, swiftly moving clear of the deadly weapon each time it
streaked to within inches of his face. When perfectly timing the wide
swings, he suddenly stepped forward to arrest her motion, and grabbing her arm at the wrist, crushed it in a viselike grip that forced her
to drop the scepter to the floor. Now, lifting her over his head, with
a running heave, he tossed the struggling writhing body toward the
mouth of the nearby gaping fissure. Kicking and screaming, the witch
flew headlong through the air, sent catapulted for seventy feet, and
landed among the large metal hooks that were attached to ropes at
the entrance to Satan's Pit. When one of the hooks pierced her back,
the coiled rope on the large overhead pulley bore the full weight of
her body, the cord quickly unraveling downward into the precipitous
beyond. During the rapid descent into a bottomless dark oblivion, her
piercing terrified screams trailed off as she was cast deeper and deeper
into eternal damnation. When reaching the end of the tethered rope
and it suddenly become taunt, she now found herself suspended over a
cavernous pitch-black hole; the free-flowing blood from her torn flesh
attracting the denizens of perpetual gloom.… They were there waiting for her; abysmal otherworldly creatures with large luminescent
eyes peering out from the murky darkness.

As the sorceress remained dangling in the pitch black void, hideous lurking monsters were closing in all around. Her frantic cries of

desperation could be heard in the cathedral room above; horrifying screams, the faint echoes of tortured shrieks that would never cease – no, not for all of eternity.

Tony and Eric walked over to the well-like opening in the floor, where two small children – a little boy and a girl – sat in a pool of their own blood. The valiant warrior picked them up, one in each arm, and said, "You're going home now, little buddies." They gazed at him with their vacant expressionless eyes. "No one is ever going to hurt you again."

Eric ran over to release Rex from the torture post. His face was cut and bleeding; one eye was nearly shut. There were electric prod burn marks all over his body. In a faint voice, he mumbled, "Glad y'all could make it ta' the party."

Eric unsheathed his long knife and cut the ropes. "This place is set to blow sky high," he said, throwing off the last of the binding cords. He helped the battle-hardened war hero stand on his feet, and leaning together, they shuffled over to assist Tony in releasing Howard and Brandon.

"The laser pen should sear right through these chains," said Tony, and seconds later, they were both set free.

Eric planted the last remaining explosives throughout the Great Room. Returning to join the others, he said, "They're synchronized to detonate with all the rest …" he then glanced down at his watch, "… which will be in exactly twenty minutes, nineteen seconds. That doesn't give us much time. Let's get out of here."

Before exiting, Rex pointed over at his photon gun resting against the wall. "Take Betsy," he weakly said. Howard grabbed the weapon, then he and Brandon assisted Rex, one of them on each side, and they all ran out the cathedral door.

The five man entourage jogged down the main corridor that was vacant of guards. Holding a small child in each arm, Tony spoke into his wrist radio transmitter. "Alex, come in."

After a brief pause, the street preacher responded. "You guys all right?"

"A little bruised," Tony replied, "but still breathing."

Sitting in the bus driver seat, Alex said, "Adam and I have all the children here with us. There's two hundred and seventy-five of them. They're suffering from malnutrition, and most are physically injured; all are emotionally hurting."

"We've got two more on the way," said Tony, smiling at the new additions. "Let's pray they all be covered with the shed blood of Jesus Christ."

The driver responded, "Amen, Brother."

Running, Eric said into his transmitter, "Alex, empty one of the buses. Have Adam stand guard over the children, then, drive back here to pick us up. Hurry. We've got about seventeen minutes before the bombs explode."

Alex immediately rose up to help usher the children out of the bus, replying, "I'm on my way!"

— 30 —

A faint glow from the full moon filtered through churning dark clouds in the ominous night sky.

The group emerged from the drive-through tunnel on the short side of the Castle and filed outside into the semidarkness. Rex was supported by the others as they scrambled across the courtyard. Eric directed, "Let's stay off the road and head for wooded cover." Rushing to the nearby hill embankment, they had just entered the forest fringe when there was heard the sound of pulsating vibrations in the air.

Brandon turned around and pointed. "Look!" Appearing from over the near horizon were two helicopters hovering above the tree line, red lights flashing, their forward projecting search beams scanning the dense forest below.

"Armed military aircraft," noted Howard. "And they're heading this way."

The group ran behind an outcrop of large boulders.

Grabbing the photon gun, Howard asked Rex, "What setting do I put this thing on?"

Barely conscious, he mumbled, "Flip the side switch all the way forward. Maximum quanta."

One of the choppers maneuvered sharply, abruptly adjusting its course. "They must have just now located us on radar," said Eric. A broad circle spotlight illuminated the tree tops, then advanced rapidly to work its way across the Castle grounds. Steadying the bazooka-like weapon, Howard took careful aim. "What's the effective range?"

Rex feebly answered, "Hold off till I say when."

Thumping rotor blades pounded the still night air. Suddenly, a spray of machine gun bullets fanned the nearby ground in front of them. Instantly, the hunted men dropped down lower, wedged behind the rocks.

"Git ready," mumbled Rex. Another barrage of bullets ricocheted off the granite boulders. "Now!"

Computerized sighting mechanism locked onto one of the flying machines, Howard pulled the trigger and released a high energy particle beam of light that traced a perfectly straight trajectory to the hovering craft. A moment later, it glowed fluorescent white, then, suddenly, burst into a fireball explosion.

"YEAH!" the men cheered above the powerful blast repercussion that quaked the surrounding terrain.

Rex faintly muttered, "One down. One ta' go."

The second helicopter was still at a distance, lights now extinguished to conceal its position. "Press that little top button ta' activate the infrared scope," advised the wounded soldier.

"Here comes Alex!" Far down the long driveway, they could see the headlights of the approaching bus.

Whirling pulsations were once again bearing down on them.

"I can't find the button," said Howard, passing the weapon over to Rex.

Eric excitedly cautioned, "Hurry! It's within range."

"That's it right *there*," the weapons expert said, activating the scope switch. Just then, a rocket streaked close overhead, then exploded in the hill behind them.

Howard positioned the laser gun against his shoulder. "I've got it in my sights."

Tony announced, "Do it!"

Just as the aircraft emerged from behind the Castle's main turret spire, Rex coached, "One … two … three – *Now!*"

A narrow beam of brilliant white light engulfed the hovering craft in a glowing effulgence. Seconds later, it exploded with an echoing boom, burning fragments scattered over the courtyard and nearby landscape.

"*YEAH!*" The team let out another rousing cheer.

Howard closely examined the makeshift firearm and said, "This is *definitely* better than my Ruger nine millimeter."

In a pained whisper, Rex joked, "You get ta' have all the fun."

Eric warned, "We only have two minutes and eleven seconds until this place is history." He spoke into his transmitter, "Alex, we're up ahead, in the trees, about a hundred yards to your right."

The driver asked, "What's with all the fireworks?"

Eric replied, "Hopefully, it was the last of the aerial death squad. In a few more seconds you would have been toast."

By the time they made it down to the road, the driver had already turned the bus around and was waiting. The men quickly loaded inside. "Floor it, Alex! Put some distance between us and the Castle!"

"Right!" He accelerated, and shifting gears, was soon pushing the speedometer needle past 60 mph. Tony quoted Jeremiah 20:12: "*But, O Lord of hosts, that triest the righteous, and seest the reins and the heart, let me see thy vengeance on them: for unto thee have I opened my cause.*"

Looking at his watch, Eric counted down the remaining seconds: "Five … four … three … two … one …" A low rumble began to vibrate the ground, then the atmosphere quaked from the chain reaction of a resounding tumultuous blast when the many-spired Castle suddenly exploded in an earth-shaking eruption that ejected flaming debris, raining down huge chunks of rock throughout the surrounding countryside.

"YEAH!" They all celebrated. Alex recited Psalm 58:10: "*The righteous shall rejoice when he seeth the vengeance: he shall wash his feet in the blood of the wicked.*"

After the percussion bombs had ignited the building and the Cathedral of 1000 points of light was propelled into the darkness of the night, there could be heard in the wooded glen, tortured shrieks of souls of the damned. Brandon offered to explain. "Their demons no longer have a dwelling place or human bodies to possess. What you hear is the sound of them fleeing into the darkness, looking for another home – more wicked people to inhabit and destroy."

The hour was midnight when they gazed back in the distance, at the ruins set in flaming silhouette against the dim light of a cloud-swept moon. As they receded further from the demolition, they witnessed a billowing curl of black smoke rise up from the destroyed edifice; a turbulence of darkness ascending high above the trees, signaling the Castle's demise.

"Mission accomplished, Gentlemen," said Howard.

"*Hell hath enlarged herself,*" said Alex, easing up on the accelerator, and quoting Isaiah 5:14.

"Thank God they're all dead," replied Tony.

"That was only the tip of the proverbial iceberg," Brandon observed. "There's plenty more Castle rats from where those vermin came from."

Eric pointed. "Look!" The malignant plume began to take on the indistinct form of a human face with distorted features, a mysterious visage that went through a rapid series of transformations, spontaneously changing into the faces of recognizable Black Nobility of the First, Second and Third Tier; successive images that, in the final denouement, shape-shifted into the horrifying specter of the one who indwelled them all – Satan himself. Howard quoted Psalm 37:20: "*But the wicked shall perish, and the enemies of the LORD shall be as the fat of lambs: they shall consume; into smoke shall they consume away.*"

Alex quoted Isaiah 49:25,26: "*But thus saith the LORD, Even the captives of the mighty shall be taken away, and the prey of the terrible shall be delivered: for I will contend with him that contendeth with thee, and I will save thy children. And I will feed them that oppress thee with their own flesh; and they shall be drunken with their own blood, as with sweet wine: and all flesh shall know that I the LORD am thy Saviour and thy Redeemer, the mighty One of Jacob.*"

Brandon read from the sacred Text, Deuteronomy 7:19: *"The great temptations which thine eyes saw, and the signs, and the wonders, and the mighty hand, and the stretched out arm, whereby the LORD thy God brought thee out: so shall the LORD thy God do unto all the people of whom thou art afraid."*

Tony then read Deuteronomy 19:11,12: *"But if any man hate his neighbor, and lie in wait for him, and rise up against him, and smite him mortally that he die, and fleeth into one of these cities: Then the elders of his city shall send and fetch him thence, and deliver him into the hand of the avenger of blood, that he may die. Thine eye shall not pity him, but thou shalt put away the guilt of innocent blood from Israel, that it may go well with thee."* He closed the Holy Book and stated, "Innocent blood has been avenged."

Rex glanced at his watch. "Hundred and twelve minutes," he said in a voice barely audible. Addressing Eric, he whispered, "That was some pretty good timin' young man."

Eric replied, *"A man's heart deviseth his way: but the LORD directeth his steps.* Give the glory to God."

At the end of the drive, after passing the demolished main gate and then looping back along the adjacent trail, by the light of the head-lights they could see Adam and some of the children standing outside the bus, waving their arms at the sight of the rescuers approaching through the high undergrowth.

Darkness all around them, after a brief reunion Eric commanded, "Let's get out of here; we don't have a moment to lose. The roads will soon be swarming with police." They guided the children onto the buses, and within minutes, were slowly traveling down the fog en-shrouded high grass lane that paralleled the dark forest. When the two oversized vehicles emerged out onto the unlit road, they turned left and sped toward the border.

Transported along the deserted highway, by the light of a full moon the children sat strangely quiet in the darkened bus. Rex lay across a triple wide seat, weak, but stable. Next to him, in the front row seat, Howard exhaled a weary sigh. "These children have been so severely abused, I don't see how they can ever be normal again. There will probably be long-lasting psychological effects from the ritual torture and trauma-based mind-control programming."

Driving the bus, and without taking his eyes off the road ahead, Alex confidently replied, "The Great Physician will heal them."

From the same trailing bus, Brandon spoke into his radio transmitter for all to hear. "So, now what? … What are we going to do with them? Where are they going to go?"

Eric radioed to the others from the lead bus. "Border guards up ahead. Brace yourselves."

Adam advised, "Don't worry about what to say. God's Holy Spirit will give you utterance."

There was a foreboding sense of doom as they slowed down to pass beneath the brightly-lit arched terminal where two armed border patrol guards stood waiting. When coming to a stop, the military police walked over to the door of the first bus, then commanded it to be opened.

Eric was hesitant, and when he pulled the lever to crack the rubber seal and slightly open the retractable door, he said, "Hello there! As you can see, we're back, and we have with us the children, as promised. I'd like to invite you in, but they're sound asleep, and we wouldn't want to awaken them."

In broken English, one of the officers gruffly ordered, "Show me your papers!"

Eric calmly reached up to the visor and unclipped a document that was specially prepared by Howard's forgery experts. Without opening the door any further, he handed it to him, and smiled. "Here you are, my good fellow."

The guard greedily snapped it up, and after close examination, said, "Where you go?"

"Back to where we came from, of course."

Without changing his deadpan expression, the officer mocked, "Of course."

Put on alert by the driver's vague reply, the guards conferred briefly, then suddenly returned to aggressively force open the hinged doors and step inside.

Tony sat in the front seat, ready for a confrontation. "Looking for something in particular?" he asked, not a trace of deference in his bold tone.

They rifle-wielding soldiers ignored him while proceeding to shine a flashlight at the many small passengers on board; the bright circle of illumination surveying one row at a time. Eric attempted to ease their suspicion. "We're on a field trip ... remember?"

"Ugh," one of them grunted. When moving further inside, his foot stumbled against one of the duffel bags. "What's this?" As he reached down to open it, Tony's nerves were taunt, ready to spring.

Shortly before this incident had occurred, in the nearby glass-enclosed office, the police Captain had picked up a telephone receiver and paused to listen, all the while, his steady gaze focused on the detained school buses. From within the second bus, Alex, Howard and Brandon had intently watched him engaged in the phone conversation. "I hope that isn't what I think it is," Alex had said. Finally, the Captain hung up the phone, then briefly spoke into his lapel 2-way radio and went outside to slowly amble toward the lead vehicle.

Inside the bus, before the guards could search the weapons bags, they had suddenly been intercepted by a radio communication from the Captain. The two armed men promptly stepped off the bus.

When the superior joined his subordinate guards, Eric whispered over to Tony, "Two more seconds and it would have been deja vous all over again." The battle weary champion nodded in agreement.

Moments later, the Captain stepped on board, and before closing the door, said in a loud controlled tone, "I have orders to search this vehicle. I have further instruction to kill you, and to kill the children, if you resist."

Tony, Eric and Adam exchanged furtive glances; they knew what they had to do. In realizing the inevitability of a physical confrontation, they understood there was no other choice but to take the offensive and attack. Just as they were about to spring out of their seats, the chief guard closed the door behind him, then, in a lowered tone, said, "I know where you come from. I also know where you been … and … you men are to be commended."

Amazed, Eric asked, "Are you a Believer?"

The Captain replied, "If you mean, do I believe that Jesus Christ is the Way, the Truth, and the Life – *absolutely* yes."

Tony said, "Then, peace be with you, Brother."

The military officer changed his hardened expression when he said, "Those evil men, they deserved to die a thousand deaths. Our God is a God of war; a God of righteous vengeance. He is well pleased." Then he cautioned, "But now you must leave immediately this place. A battalion of soldiers are dispatched and on their way down from Namur, only sixty kilometers from here. I will stall them as long as possible."

"And what about you?" asked Tony.

The border guard had already begun to leave, and turning, he said, "No one can take the children of God out of His hand – *no one!*" The men's gaze was fixed upon him as he exited to stand out on the road and wave them forward. Moments later, the draw gate was raised, and moving once again, both buses went through unhindered.

As they left the border zone behind them, from the trailing bus, Brandon spoke to Eric over the tranceiver, "Eric, what do you suppose is the probability of finding someone in satanic government who is actually a True Christian? And further, for that rare someone to be here – *right here,* at this crucial juncture?"

Now on their way to Luxembourg, from the driver's seat Eric replied though his transponder, "The statistical probability is infinitesimal. Especially when considering the extremely low probability events that had to coincide at precisely the right time *and sequence* in order to allow for what we just experienced." He paused thoughtfully before concluding, "I admit that I don't know how to calculate the odds on a miracle."

Adam perceived, "The battle is seemingly being fought in the physical realm, but the outcome has already been decided in the realm of the spiritual."

Within half an hour they were back at the airport, where the children were efficiently transferred from the buses into the cargo plane. Many of them were so weak or injured they had to be carried on board. "They need immediate medical attention," said Eric.

"We can't risk it now," replied Howard, sitting in the cockpit, adjusting the controls, readying the plane for take off. "Every hospital and doctor in three countries is anticipating us walking through their doors. It'll have to wait. I may have to buy a hospital and staff it myself. In the meantime, we'll trust in God." He then started the engines, the propellers cranking, whirling, building momentum as the powerful motors increased RPM. "As soon as we level off, feed the children a good healthy meal from the stored provisions," he announced over the speakers. "Then, give them the blankets and clothing and help them get dressed. Make sure they're all buckled into their seats.... We're going home."

The men worked their way down the isle, fastening safety belts, speaking soothing words of comfort to the physically and emotionally scarred passengers. "We're on our way back home, little buddies," said Tony, deeply affected when noting their expressionless faces and battered listless bodies. Disturbed by the grim prospect of returning to the States, he thought to himself, *But where is home? We can't go back.*

When Adam secured the last child – a three year old little girl with sad large brown eyes and dried blood on her face – she gazed up at him and asked, "Will the aliens hurt us anymore?"

The prophetic visionary reached out a hand and smoothed her matted hair. "No, little Angel," he said, tears welling up in his eyes.

"They won't hurt you anymore." He gently kissed her on the forehead and whispered, "God's promise." He then prophesied when reciting from Ezekiel 34:28: *"And they shall no more be a prey to the heathen, neither shall the beast of the land devour them; but they shall dwell safely, and none shall make them afraid."*

With the men now seated in the front rows, Brandon commented, "The children were brainwashed into believing that those servants of Satan are gods, or some kind of superior alien beings. But the sons of Lucifer struck a bad deal with their infernal master, and will never achieve the status for which they sold their souls to attain. They're all in hell now."

Lying flat on his back, Rex faintly murmured, "Praise be to God."

The engines roared as the large plane began to taxi along the vacant dark air strip. Soon, in a sudden burst of power, it sped down the runway and, moments later, the lumbering aircraft left the ground, carrying its precious cargo skyward.

When the noise level was reduced, Alex said, "Hopefully, we put a dent in the rank and file of the New World Order."

Brandon responded, "They were only a fraction of the Illuminati hierarchical pyramid. I can assure you, there's plenty more quasi-humans to take their place."

Eric looked over at him from across the isle, and asked, "Are you suggesting that we should do an encore performance?"

Gazing out the side oval window, down at the receding city lights below, Alex fielded the question. "And why not? We're called to wield the sword of truth and shine the Light of Jesus Christ wherever there's darkness."

Tony asked, "So … where's the next dark rat hole to illuminate?"

The maligned author answered, "There's this place in Nevada, called Area 51. It's located in the remote desert, near Las Vegas – the pedophile capital of the world – not far from Pompoos Lake, just South of Groom Lake. It's run by the U.S. military, so *that* should tell you something. These same generational bloodlines have constructed six levels of underground laboratories where they house hundreds of children used for genetic engineering and cloning experimentation … with animals … and demons. They breed human-demon hybrids. The children are programmed with electroshock and trauma-based MK-Ultra to become Delta slaves, lethal saboteurs, government mind-controlled assassins. There exists other similar underground military facilities throughout the world. The scope and magnitude of evil in these Illuminati-controlled research facilities would make the Castle of Darkness seem like a boy scout camp."

The street-wise Bible scholar commented, "The only way to get rid of the Luciferian globalists is by exterminating every last one of them. They're like a cancer that must be destroyed clear down to its roots. Throughout the Old Testament Scriptures, the LORD God warned what would happen if the spawn of Satan were allowed to re-produce and populate the earth. Today, the entire world has became corrupted by them, like it was during the time of Noah. As in the case of King Saul who disobeyed God's command to totally wipe out the enemies of God, these pagan nations inbred with the Israelites to lead them into idolatry, child sacrifice, and other occult practices that God abhors. Since the time of the Flood, the human race has once again become corrupted with the spiritual genetics of demonic angels." He paused before reiterating, "The unfailing truth of God's Holy Word proclaims that the only way to effectively deal with them is to physi-cally destroy them."

"When it comes to upholdin' the truth of God's Word, real servants of the Lord don't negotiate *nuthin'*," mumbled Rex. "God's Word *is true* because He says it is. The lug head patriots think they're gonna' *infowar* 'em ta' death. Ha! What a disinformation joke. It's the Illuminati who told 'em that."

Alex agreed. "It's almost as humorous as the forty million Pro-fessing Christians in America who wouldn't think of opposing a gov-ernment that devours them and their children. The FEMA Clergy Response Team is more than 100,000 pastors in America who agreed not to speak out against government tyranny, and to tell their congregations to turn in their guns and not resist taking the human implant-able microchip, which is the Mark of the Beast of Revelation 13."

As the plane leveled off in the night sky, they began to serve the ready-made dinners to the children and issue them clothing and warm blankets. Eric was carrying an armful of blankets when he announced, "Maybe we should do it."

Distributing the meals, Brandon exhaled a tired breath of air. "Yes, perhaps *we should*. But that's *another* book. First, I've got to write *this* one."

"Hey Brandon," Rex called out, his devitalized voice partially muffled by the rumbling engines. "We gonna' be famous?"

The researcher turned around and flatly stated. "If we did, we'd soon all be dead. There's a wise old proverb: *Many who wear swords are afraid of goose-quills*. The book will be written in such a way as not to lead them back to any of you. I promise anonymity."

"It should be interesting," said Eric. "Sure to be a bestseller. Can't miss!"

Brandon forced a smile when replying, "Don't count on it. The Illuminati-controlled media will blacklist it; they collect and burn books exposing their clandestine activities and the evil deeds done by their people. And, they will not want a book in circulation that instructs the Remnant of True Christians in Scripturally righteous judgment. Besides, no publishing house will touch something with this much truth in it. That's especially true of the so-called Christian publishers, which are actually secular publishers controlled and owned by the satanic International Hierarchy. These are some of the creatures we just dispatched. Like most of my other works exposing the hidden truth, this one will circulate outside the mainstream; it will be an underground book. Only the most righteous will read it."

Adam was attending to the children when he spoke prophetically. "There are still those who love the truth. God will insure that it is read throughout the world. God's Word goes forth and will not come back void. Nothing can stop it. *Nothing*."

After all the children were well fed, clothed and bundled in warm blankets, Brandon resumed his seat, and gazing down at the heavenly cloudscape far below, pensively reflected, "The hope of the wicked is their portion here on earth. They believe they are *gods*, supernatural beings who will continue to live and reign forever. But, obviously, that is not true. They're expert at mind-control propaganda; they are masters of deceit. But their greatest weapon by far is *people's ignorance.* Their Plan depends on it."

Eric returned from comforting the children, and observed, "When people one day read your books, some of that ignorance will be dispelled."

The researcher replied, "As time goes on, there will be increasing confrontations between God's people and Satan's people. Meanwhile, all I hope to do is steer those who love the truth in the direction of *The* Truth – Jesus Christ and His Word, the 1611 King James Bible. Give *Him* the glory."

"Amen!" the others proclaimed. "All glory and honor be to the LORD God Almighty the Lord Jesus Christ!"

Throughout the flight, the men continued to assist the hurting children, and as the plane soared imperceptibly into the darkness of the now clear starry night sky, their minds were focused upon an uncertain future, keenly aware of the dangers that awaited them back in America. Returning to their former lives was an imminently perilous reality that, until now, had not commanded their full attention. Finally, Brandon spoke. "We go back to be persecuted by the wicked men from whom we fled."

As if on cue, Howard's voice came over the speakers. "If you look out your left window, gentlemen, you will see the northwest coast of Africa."

"*Africa?*" they all said at once.

The pilot, anticipating their surprise, added, "Yes, Africa. We're going home by a different route because *our home* is now located in *South America.*" The others exchanged glances, dumbfounded. "Sorry

I didn't tell you sooner, but I saw no need to risk an inadvertent security leak that would alert our pursuers. It would have ruined everything."

Alex paused from feeding one of the children, and broke out into a broad smile. "You son of a gun, Howard! You did it again!"

The elder continued. "I hope you men didn't really think I could ignore that most important detail. We have the Lord to thank for providing for our needs. Eric's God-given genius suggested the purchase of a 100,000 acre tract near the Amazon basin."

His partners looked askance. In stunned disbelief, Brandon repeated, "*One hundred thousand acres?*"

Eric further explained. "It's located near the border of Brazil and Bolivia. Very secluded. And it can only be accessed by air. There's a crude landing strip and thirty good-sized houses presently under construction as we speak – three hundred rooms in all. Before our U.S. departure, Howard's real estate contacts handled the purchase and hired the construction crews using some capital from the sell of his futures holdings. There's plenty of vacant land down there, and labor is cheap."

Adam quoted appropriate Scripture from Proverb 27:12: "*A prudent man foreseeth the evil, and hideth himself; but the simple pass on, and are punished.*"

Alex added, "*When righteous men do rejoice, there is great glory: but when the wicked rise, a man is hidden. When the wicked rise, men hide themselves: but when they perish, the righteous increase.* Proverb 28:12,28*"*

To not disturb the sleeping children, they all said in a lowered tone, "Praise God!"

"You'll love the place," continued Howard's broadcast. "Needless to say, you won't want to return home to your previous routine. It's a tropical paradise – food literally grows on trees. So there's no need for a grocery store. It has the greatest biodiversity of plant and bird life in the world. *That* should give you some idea of just how secluded and pristine this part of the Amazon is…. Oh, and it's the *perfect place* to raise children."

"A Garden of Eden," mused Eric, reminiscing of Tony's mountain enclave. Pausing, he halfheartedly added, "What a relief to know that we won't have to go to jail."

Brandon stated, "And no orphanages for the children! No hospital trauma centers! No foster homes and foster parents! No Big Brothers or Big Sisters! No Satanist-run pre-school child abuse centers! These are all part of the government organized crime network that keeps children within the satanic stronghold. They're not going back into the corrupt system that sent them to the Castle of Darkness. These children will be spared the institutions that are infiltrated and run by witches and Satanists." He then read Jeremiah 15:19: "*Therefore, thus saith the LORD, If thou return, then will I bring thee again, and thou shalt stand before me: and if thou take forth the precious from the vile, thou shalt be as my mouth: let them return unto thee, but return not thou unto them.*"

They were all silent for a long moment as the Word of God remained a lingering impression in their minds. Hearing the spoken Word had the effect of a soothing balm upon the children.

Brandon passed the Holy Book to Alex, who read aloud Psalm 68:5,6: "*A father of the fatherless, and a judge of the widows, is God in his holy habitation. God setteth the solitary in families: he bringeth out those which are bound with chains: but the rebellious dwell in a dry land.*"

Eric was next to receive the Word, and he read Mark 10:14: "*Suffer the little children to come unto me, and forbid them not: for of such is the kingdom of God.*"

Adam further prophesied of the children when quoting Isaiah 54:11-14: "*O thou afflicted, tossed with tempest, and not comforted, behold, I will lay thy stones with fair colors, and lay thy foundations with sapphires. And I will make thy windows of agates, and thy gates of carbuncles, and all thy borders of pleasant stones. And all thy children shall be taught of the LORD; and great shall be the peace of thy children. In righteousness shalt thou be established: thou shalt be far from oppression; for thou shalt not fear; and from terror; for it shall not come near thee."*

Rex was given the strength to declare from Psalm 9:9: *"The LORD also will be a refuge for the oppressed, a refuge in times of trouble."*

Finally, Tony recited Psalm 97:10: *"Ye that love the LORD, hate evil: he preserveth the souls of his saints; he delivereth them out of the hand of the wicked.* Except for the Word of God, there's no guarantees in this life. A true servant of the Lord Jesus Christ must be ready to die, without notice. The unsaved are the only ones who should fear death, since they're unprepared for eternity. We shouldn't be worried about leaving this place for a better deal somewhere else – an everlasting future with the living God. So why not go there in a blaze of glory to the honor of our Lord and Master, the Creator of the universe?" He looked back to gaze at the many rows of little children. "God will heal you," he said to them all, and truly believed in his heart that God *would* heal them. He knew there was no human doctor that could do for them what only God could accomplish. Taking up the Bible, he read to them from Psalm 121:5-8: *"The LORD is thy keeper: the LORD is thy shade upon thy right hand. The sun shall not smite thee by day, nor the moon by night. The LORD shall preserve thee from all evil: he shall preserve thy soul. The LORD shall preserve thy going out and thy coming in from this time forth, and even for evermore."* Emotionally moved, there was a tear in his eye when he said, "We – us seven – will be your family here on earth ... and in heaven, you belong to the family of God."

The children were asleep in their seats as the plane soared through the clear night sky, high above the deep ocean and over the lofty mountains, above the great masses of evil far below – up, *up*, into the infinite beyond, the abode of angels, and the Almighty God Who delivered them.

INTERNATIONAL PEDOPHILE RING
"TRIED" IN THE ARLON, BELGIUM COURTS

Excerpt from a commentary on a Belgium news report:

"Judge Jean-Marc Connerotte wept while testifying on March 4 [2004] describing death threats and high-level intrigue that obstructed his pursuit of the Dutroux's case."

From 1995 – 2004, Marc Dutroux, pedophile, procurer of children, kept starving sex slaves in his basement dungeon, and offered them for sale ($3500 @) for ritual sacrifice to international slave traders. Court proceedings for his multiple murders were indefinitely postponed by the Illuminati Hierarchy. Dutroux was an undergound supplier to the Castle of Darkness.

And ye shall chase your enemies, and they shall fall before you by the sword. And five of you shall chase an hundred, and an hundred of you shall put ten thousand to flight; and your enemies shall fall before you by the sword. — Leviticus 26:7,8

The LORD shall cause thine enemies that rise up against thee to be smitten before thy face: they shall come out against thee one way, and flee before thee seven ways. — Deuteronomy 28:7

And the LORD, he it is that doth go before thee; he will be with thee, he will not fail thee, neither forsake thee: fear not, neither be dismayed. — Deuteronomy 31:8

Let the saints be joyful in glory; let them sing aloud upon their beds. Let the high praises of God be in their mouth, and a twoedged sword in their hand; To execute vengeance upon the heathen, and punishments upon the people; To bind their kings with chains, and their nobles with fetters of iron; to execute upon them the judgment written: this honor have all his saints. Praise ye the LORD. — Psalm 149:5-9

When thou passest through the waters, I will be with thee; and through the rivers, they shall not overflow thee: when thou walkest through the fire, thou shalt not be burned; neither shall the flame kindle upon thee. — Isaiah 43:2

Hearken unto me, ye that know righteousness, the people in whose heart is my law; fear ye not the reproach of men, neither be ye afraid of their revilings.... I, even I, am he that comforteth you: who art thou, that thou shouldest be afraid of a man that shall die, and of the son of man which shall be made as grass; And forgettest the LORD thy maker, that hast stretched forth the heavens, and laid the foundations of the earth; and hast feared continually everyday because of the fury of the oppressor, as if he were ready to destroy? and where is the fury of the oppressor?

– Isaiah 51:7,12,13

Behold, they shall surely gather together, but not by me: whosoever shall gather together against thee shall fall for thy sake.... No weapon that is formed against thee shall prosper; and every tongue that shall rise against thee in judgment thou shalt condemn. This is the heritage of the servants of the LORD, and their righteousness is of me, saith the LORD.

– Isaiah 54:15,17

And I will make thee unto this people a fenced brasen wall: and they shall fight against thee, but they shall not prevail against thee: for I am with thee to save thee and to deliver thee, saith the LORD. And I will deliver thee out of the hand of the wicked, and I will redeem thee out of the hand of the terrible.

– Jeremiah 15:20,21

Thou whom I have taken from the ends of the earth, and called thee from the chief men thereof, and said unto thee, Thou art my servant; I have chosen thee, and not cast thee away. Fear thou not; for I am with thee: be not dismayed; for I am thy God: I will strengthen thee; yea, I will help thee; yea, I will uphold thee with the right hand of my righteousness. Behold, all they that were incensed against thee shall be ashamed and confounded: they shall be as nothing; and they that strive with thee shall perish. Thou shalt seek them, and shalt not find them, even them that contended with thee: they that war against thee shall be as nothing, and as a thing of nought. For I the LORD thy God will hold thy right hand, saying unto thee, Fear not; I will help thee. – Isaiah 41:9-13

What the Illuminati Globalists **FEAR** the most …

THE AUTHORIZED 1611 KING JAMES BIBLE IS THE ONLY WORD OF GOD.

There is one body, and one Spirit, even as ye are called in one hope of your calling; One Lord, one faith, one baptism, One God and Father of all … (Ephesians 4:4-6).

THERE IS ONLY ONE WORD OF GOD … JESUS CHRIST,

his name is called the Word of God (Revelation 19:13), *the way, the truth, and the life* (John 14:6), *the sword of the Spirit* (Ephesians 6:17), *quick, and powerful, and sharper than any twoedged sword* (Hebrews 4:12). *In the beginning was the Word, and the Word was with God, and the Word was God. The same was in the beginning with God. All things were made by him; and without him was not any thing made that was made. In him was life; and the life was the light of men. And the light shineth in darkness; and the darkness comprehended it not* (John 1:1-5).

Jesus Christ is God, One God, the *spoken* **Word of God**; His 1611 King James Bible is One Word, the *written* **Word of God**, Jesus Christ.

Sanctify them through thy truth: thy word is truth (John 17:17).

1611 King James
Bible

For I testify unto every man that heareth the words of the prophecy of this book, If any man shall add unto these things, God shall add unto him the plagues that are written in this book. And if any man shall take away from the words of the book of this prophecy, God shall take away his part out of the book of life, and out of the holy city, and from the things which are written in this book (Revelation 22:18,19).

BOOK ORDERING

The following books can be ordered online
from *bn.com* or *amazon.com*.

Any other websites are unapproved and unauthorized.
These titles can also be purchased direct from retail bookstores.

__ The Great Deception

__ The Coming of Wisdom (sequel to The Great Deception)

__ Fools Paradise: *The Spiritual Implications of Gambling*

__ Seven Who Dared

__ The Criminal Fraternity: *Servants of the Lie*

__ *When* Will the Illuminati Crash the Stock Market? *An Insider's Look at the Elite Satanic Luciferians Who Dictate the Rise and Fall of Global Economies*

__ Genesis 1:29 Diet:*Perfect Health without Doctors, Hospitals, or Pharmaceutical Drugs*

__ Fractal Trading: *Analyzing Financial Markets using Fractal Geometry and the Golden Ratio*

__ Everything is a Test: *How God Delivered Me from "Impossible" Situations*

Media Contacts: info@getperfectwisdom.com

CPSIA information can be obtained
at www.ICGtesting.com
Printed in the USA
BVHW072101270219
541369BV00001B/23/P

9 780984 127986